The
BUCKSKIN
Saint

A Novel by

Joseph Berube

CCB Publishing
British Columbia, Canada

The Buckskin Saint

Copyright ©2014 by Joseph Berube
ISBN-13   978-1-77143-191-0
First Edition

Library and Archives Canada Cataloguing in Publication
Berube, Joseph, 1951-, author
The buckskin saint / by Joseph Berube. -- First edition.
Issued in print and electronic formats.
ISBN 978-1-77143-190-3 (hbk.).--ISBN 978-1-77143-191-0 (pbk).--
ISBN 978-1-77143-192-7 (pdf)
Additional cataloguing data available from Library and Archives Canada

Cover artwork by Ginny Glass: www.wordsugardesigns.com
The artwork contained herein is in the Public Domain and is used without malice.

Disclaimer: This is a work of historical fiction. It is based on actual events and characters, but many of the motives and relationships in this novel are either products of the authors' imagination or are used fictitiously.

Extreme care has been taken by the author to ensure that all information presented in this book is accurate and up to date at the time of publishing. Neither the author nor the publisher can be held responsible for any errors or omissions. Additionally, neither is any liability assumed for damages resulting from the use of the information contained herein.

Publisher: CCB Publishing
             British Columbia, Canada
             www.ccbpublishing.com

Dedication and Acknowledgements

This book is dedicated to my father who was the reason for the work. I drew inspiration from his bravery. I also dedicate this book to my wife who helped me in the process.

+++++

I must acknowledge the help and support of the following people:

- First, my good friend, Teddy Kuzmeskus, whose encouragement and insights kept me going.
- To my editor, Caroline Tolley, whose efforts gave my main character his voice.
- To my publisher, Paul Rabinovitch, a man who helped me plot a course that allowed *The Buckskin Saint* to see the light of day.
- To my artist, Ginny Glass, whose dedication to get things right is evident for all to see.
- To my daughter, Heather Gates, who helped me get it right.
- Finally, to all the real men and women who endured those times that gave us the opportunities we enjoy today.

Preface

The Reason *The Buckskin Saint* was Written

The year 2008 was a rough one on the US economy and on my household economy as well. With my position gone our family struggled along with thousands of other men and women to make a go of things, and prospects weren't too bright. Insomnia from stress and worry visited me on many of those nights. Poring over articles recounting anecdotes from the 18th Century helped me to relax and fall asleep. I loved history with the local history of Colonial America my absolute favorite. The stories that were the most interesting I put in a personal journal for a purpose that wasn't known at the time.

In the spring of 2010 our family received the terrible news that my father had terminal lung cancer. This, added to the already diagnosed COPD, meant a tormented frightening death for him. Suddenly an epiphany happened for me. The journal that was compiled during those sleepless nights would be the foundation of a story I would create to read to my dad.

When I was young I had a huge fear of the dark and bedtime was an awful time for both me and my parents. Some nights Mom would read to me, but many nights it was Dad spinning tales from out of a book, recounting experiences of his, or making up tall tales. I could relax, feel safe, and fall asleep. Now it was my father's fear that needed tackling and the tool I would use would be my story. We would combat the fear together so Dad could relax and get the rest needed to fight his fight.

Parts of the book came easily while other parts had me stymied. It was during those blocked times that I would sit at my lap top and invariably the story went from my fingertips onto the screen. I decided I had a muse there doing the work with me, for him. Some nights fifteen to twenty pages appeared, other nights, only four or five. No matter, they were shared with Dad at his bedside that night. He often nodded off and when I stopped he would arouse and say something like, "I wasn't sleeping, I was in the story, I was there." He was letting me know the circle of our lives was unbroken.

My father lost his fight on Sept. 13th, 2011; two weeks after I finished the book. I like to think it was a help to him. I know it was to me.

Rachel Silverthorne warning settlers, Big Runaway

Queen Esther inciting the Indians to attack the settlers at Wyoming

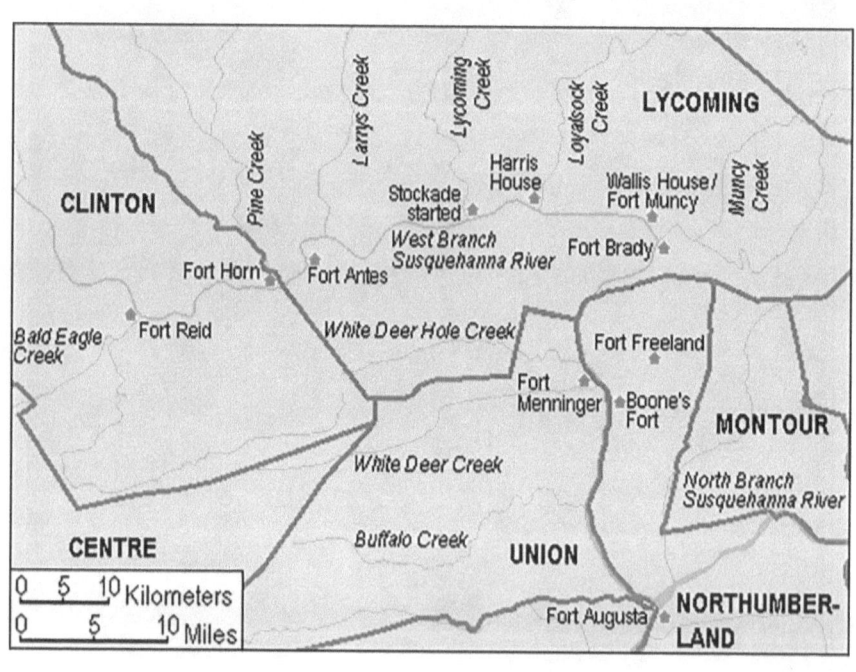

Big Runaway map showing locations of the frontier forts

Massacre at Wyoming, Alonzo Chappel, 1858

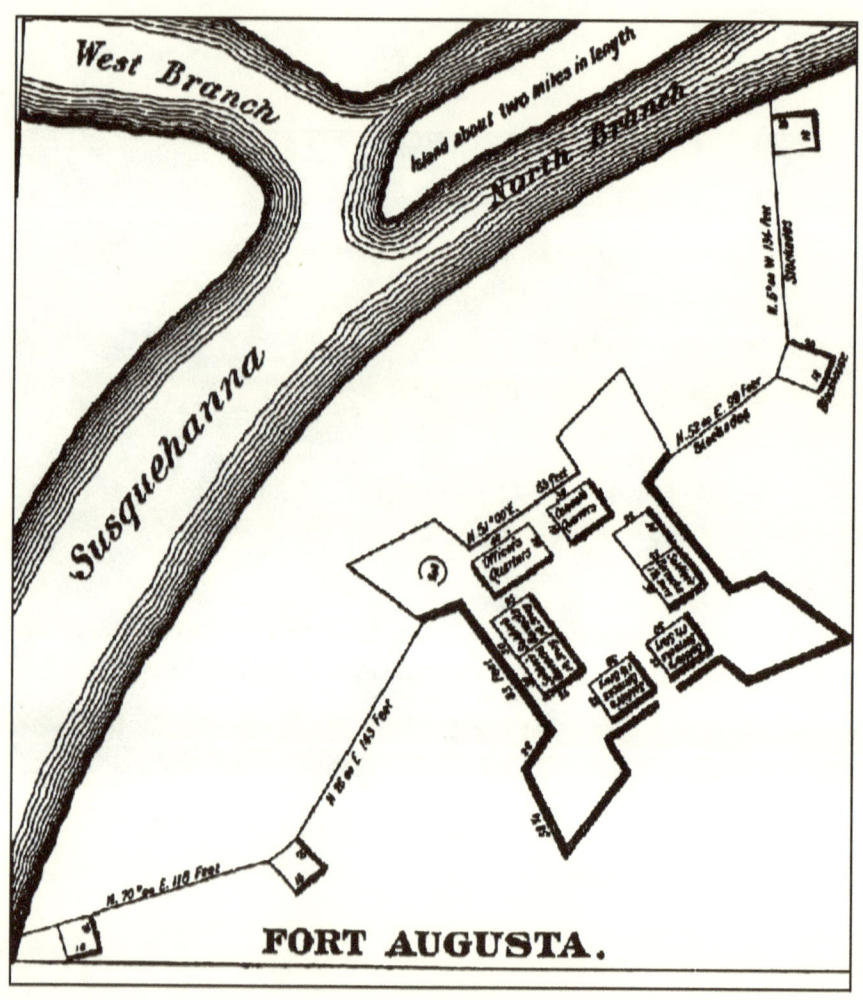

Fort Augusta, at the confluence of the
West Branch and North Branch of the Susquehanna River

Chapter 1

Henry St. Albans was up on deck for the second time since supper. The rolling of the British merchant ship, *Ligonier,* in the swells of the North Atlantic had caused another bout of seasickness in the fifteen-year-old.

"Ahoy, land lubber! Checking the ship's water level again I see," laughed a coxswain's mate as he passed the suffering boy.

How had he come to find himself aboard the *Ligonier* in the middle of the open sea? He was alone, frightened, and heading for the American Colonies. Only four weeks earlier he had arrived back at his home in London from Oak Hall School, a graduate of the school with Sandhurst Royal Military College awaiting him in the fall. His father had been so extremely proud of him. William St. Albans, Henry's father, was the fourth Baronet of Medford and a member of the House of Commons. Henry was the youngest of three sons by Sir William and his first wife, Lady Alice Pierce St. Albans. William, the first-born, had died while Henry was quite young and he had no memories of him. His beloved mother had passed away a little over a year later. The cause of death had been consumption, but his father maintained it was from a broken heart at the loss of her first-born child. Only brief memories of her remained for him. A lovely face with light brown curls framing it after the fashion of the time.

Henry left the railing and let out a heaving sigh. Sitting down on a coil of rope, his thoughts overtook him. *Father married only six months after mother died!*

William St. Albans had married the widow Eleanor Spencer only six months after Lady Alice's death. Lady Eleanor's late husband had died in service to the king fighting in some far off outpost of the empire. She had two young sons of her own so the person charged with Henry's upbringing for the next two years had been Mrs. Halsey, a governess with a reserved, almost cold nature.

Alfred was older and held his own against our step-mother, but why couldn't father see what this did to me? Henry thought.

As Alfred was already at a boarding school, his contact with his stepmother and stepbrothers was infrequent and of a short duration when it did occur. Henry had wished fervently back then that he could go with Alfred when he returned to boarding school.

Eventually, at the age of eight, Henry was sent off to Oak Hall School, a private preparatory school some twenty-five miles northeast of London. Oak Hall was one of the prestigious schools the sons of the privileged attended before Cambridge, Oxford, or in Henry's case, RMA at Sandhurst. As lot would have it Alfred, the oldest of the remaining sons, was now being groomed to assume his father's title and obligations when that time came, Henry would be groomed for service to king and country either as a member of the Foreign Service or as an officer in the Military Service.

The queasiness in his stomach was subsiding and the lad's memories raced ahead. The ugly rumors began to appear about the baronet during Henry's senior year at Oak Hall. Whispers and exchanged glances among his classmates whenever he entered a room had eventually been brought to a head.

"What did you say about my father, Higginbottom?"

"Higgie" knew that his closest friend at school had heard him cast an off-color remark about the baronet. A bare-knuckled battle royal ensued. Both combatants were summarily sent to the headmaster where the incident would be sorted out and justice would be administered.

"Two seniors fighting like two unruly new boys?" the headmaster was truly disgusted. "Well, I'm waiting for an answer, gentlemen."

Both boys stared at their feet. Finally Henry said, "I'd rather not say sir". The split lip he suffered made speaking both emotionally and physically painful.

"What about you, Higginbottom?" snapped the inquisitor who had started to lose what was left of his patience.

"Higgie" remained silent, scuffing his shoe on the headmaster's oak floor. A nasty mouse had appeared at his left eye, foretelling it would be blackened soon. Some blood was still coming from his nose.

"I see," muttered the dean, standing and coming around from behind his massive desk. "You leave me no choice. Both of you immediately lose your class positions."

2

This hurt both boys. Higginbottom had been class monitor; Henry had been advisor to the underclassmen.

"And, as Christmas holiday is approaching, both of you are to forgo your holiday and remain here to help get the school ready for spring term."

While his co-defendant slumped in emotional agony, the baronet's son shrugged. He would miss seeing his brother Alfred, but he knew his father would not be home, as his work would demand all his time. His stepmother had long since placed her flag on the St. Albans' home. Henry felt uncomfortable and unwanted when in her company.

A sudden blast of salt spray increased the amount of shivering Henry did at the thought. Startled back into the present, he made his way below decks.

By the end of his time at the preparatory, it was evident to everyone that Henry's father was on the verge of professional and financial ruin. Alfred had just completed his second year at Christ's College Cambridge and joined Henry at the Baronet's London apartments. Lady Eleanor and her offspring had fled the city the month before and were in seclusion at one of the country estates she possessed prior to her first husband's death.

The high court had made its ruling concerning the fourth Baronet of Medford. He was found guilty of financial impropriety and misuse of office. William St. Albans was ruined. The Crown would confiscate his estates and properties. Alfred would not be returning for his third year of college and Henry's college or military career could never begin. Indeed, as part of their father's reparation, as ordered by the high court, Alfred was to be apprenticed by one of the financial institutions that held most of his father's worthless promissory notes. Henry's fate was to be more severe. He was to enter into a condition of involuntary servitude and was to be sent to Philadelphia where an agreement of indenture-ship was to be concluded by the same counting house and one of its American clients. Because they were not blood relations, Lady Spencer's children were spared a similar fate. That and dubious backroom legal wrangling had kept them free. But, as for Henry, for the next seven years Master St. Albans would have a master.

Chapter 2

With all his holdings confiscated and his hereditary title in review before the House of Lords, William St. Albans, Fourth Baronet of Medford, retired to his rooms in London, removed one of a matched set of Wogdon dueling pistols from its rosewood case, and blew his brains all over the draperies. The scullery maid found his body late the next afternoon slumped in a sitting position to the side of his desk. Out of respect for the widow St. Albans, most of the sensational details were omitted from the constable's report.

Henry was already nearly a week at sea traveling in steerage aboard the ship *Ligonier* and never learned his father's fate. The *Ligonier* would take a month and a half to make its journey from Land's End to the port of Philadelphia. It was during that time Henry became convinced beyond any doubt by a never-ending bout of seasickness that a life at sea was not for him.

At the docks of Philadelphia, Henry was met by the bank's agents.

How unalike they seem. Henry mused to himself.

Mr. Finch, the older and more slovenly of the two, was barely five feet in height while Mr. Brown was easily a foot taller with not a hair out of place. These agents were charged with receiving the servant in question and inspecting him to insure that their client would get what he contacted for and expected. It was not impossible for a servant to have caught a disease while in steerage and be judged unfit to complete the agreement. In fact some contracts in the past were nullified due to the death of the servant during the voyage. It was soon determined that while Henry was a bit weakened by the journey, he was generally in good health and could fulfill his indenture-ship.

The agents knew the fate of Henry's father, having received word from a faster packet ship arriving several days before the *Ligonier*. After some debate, the agents chose not to tell him believing that such news, given to him in his weakened state, could endanger the successful completion of the contract. Arrangements were made for the trip to

Trenton where the master would inspect the goods for himself and, if satisfied, would sign the final agreement, pay the bank's agents 150 pounds sterling, and take charge of his new property.

"He doesn't appear to be twelve let alone fifteen and from the looks of his hands he hasn't seen an honest day's work in his life." Thomas McAdoo was a Scotsman who owned a farm some 20 miles to the north of Trenton. Henry was staring at an imposingly large man standing well over 6' tall with large calloused hands and a wild red beard that was only slightly darker than his fiery red hair.

"I do not like his color either, is he sick?" he inquired.

Both Mr. Brown and Mr. Finch, agents for Egger & Dobbs Ltd. that met Henry in Philadelphia, had several prior dealings with the large man now inspecting young Henry's teeth. As a soldier in His Majesty's Royal Highlander's Regiment, Thomas had distinguished himself on the field of battle, both in Europe and in the New World. As a result of 25 years of service to King and Country, Sergeant Major McAdoo was granted a half pension. Because of his scrupulous saving during his military career he was able to purchase goods and property in the colony of New Jersey where he settled with his wife, Constance, a plain woman of Puritan stock, and his two daughters Abigail and Katherine. The Scotsman retained the financial house of Egger & Dobbs on the advice of his regimental colonel; so that all the contracts of this newly landed gentry were executed properly and fairly. It was with his bankers he was now in negotiations.

That huge lout with the rough hands nearly tore my ear off! Henry thought bitterly. *My father would have had him whipped for such insolence!* Suddenly again aware of his present circumstances, he shut his eyes tightly and gritted his teeth.

"We have documentation confirming the young man's age. More importantly, Mr. St. Albans can read and write and is said to be competent with figures. If I may please refer to our contract, it was stipulated therein that he have these talents, not calloused hands." Mr. Finch, the elder of the two bankers, knew that he had to respond to each concern quickly or the whole contract might be in jeopardy.

"As for his pallor, he has spent six weeks at sea and the experience did not agree with him, nothing more or less," he added.

Henry St. Albans stood at 5 foot 3 inches and after his experience at sea weighed scarcely 100 pounds. His dark brown curly hair sat unruly on his head contrasting with his pale skin. This did make him appear to be sickly. He was dressed in a white blouse, a tan waistcoat with gray short breeches, and white stockings. In his hands he held a blue tri-corner hat.

"Still, a do na like the looks of 'im." Whenever McAdoo found himself on the losing end of an argument his Scotch accent became more pronounced.

Mr. Brown, who was the younger and more reserved of the two agents, now spoke up, "He is a prize for whom any number of our other clients would pay top price."

This was true. Many of the colonists did not know how to read or write and Mr. McAdoo was among that number. Nearly all of the schooling done in the colonies outside of New England or the largest cities was done in the home and no one in the McAdoo household knew the 3 R's. Until now, this farmer had to rely on the honesty of his bankers in all his business dealings and it pained him to pay a commission on even the simplest of matters. Having a servant whom he could trust to read him contracts and deeds would save him that expense. McAdoo was far from being a stupid man; he was just illiterate, as most people in his time were.

"A din na say a din na wan 'im," the Scotsman replied. "E'l af ta work with 'is ands too is all."

"That is understood," the elder agent responded, "Now let us go over the terms of the contract one last time before it is signed."

"I've 'ad a thought," McAdoo's blue eyes twinkled as he continued. "I want young 'enry 'ere to read the articles of the contract ta me." His accent was beginning to soften.

Both agents looked hard at one another. They had taken for granted that a senior boy from such a prestigious school as Oak Hall could read and write competently but neither had the foresight to test him.

"Agreed," said Brown finally and handed the parchment to Henry.

Henry took the contract from the banker and began to read: "The Indenture-ship of one Henry Pierce St. Albans, a freeborn subject of His Majesty King George III hereafter to be known in the Articles of Agreement as servant."

I am a servant. The reader said to himself. He then went on:

6

Articles of Agreement between Egger & Dobbs Ltd. London hereafter known as Principle of the First Part and Mr. Thomas Alistair McAdoo hereafter known as Principle of the Second Part

Article I Principle of the First Part shall provide or demonstrate proof of the servant's age and health to the satisfaction of the Principle of the Second Part.

Article II The servant shall be of sound mind and believe in The Lord our God and His Son, Jesus Christ

Article III The servant shall be able to read and write and have proficiency with figures.

Article IV Principle of the Second Part agrees to the period of indenture-ship to be of seven years duration during which time he shall feed, clothe and provide shelter for the servant. In exchange for such an obligation, the servant shall provide such labor as the Principle of the Second Part deems fit except for that which will cause permanent injury, disfigurement, or death to the servant.

Article V This contract shall be deemed fulfilled upon the death of the servant or Principle of the Second Part so long as such death not be the illegal deed of either.

Article VI The Principle of the Second Part, at the conclusion of the period of indenture-ship, shall provide a new set of clothing for the servant prior to his release.

Article VII The Principle of the First Part shall provide the servant written proof of the fulfillment of the agreement and his restoration as a freeborn subject of His Majesty King George III.

Article VIII The Principle of the Second Part shall pay the Principle of the First Part the sum of 150 lbs. sterling upon validation of the Agreement.

This Contract and Agreement dated the second day of September in the year of our Lord, 1772.

Henry looked up from the document that spelled out his life for the next seven years. He felt like he had the wind kicked out of him. The terms had been vague generalities before. Now he had read each item out loud and specifically. The exercise made him feel sick. Many poor unfortunate young men and women in Great Britain willingly entered into such arrangements in order to get a fresh start in the Colonies, but

Henry was the son of titled gentry and such a thought had never entered his mind. The bankers and Mr. McAdoo were smiling at him. The contract would be signed after some more minor haggling, money would change hands, and the new bondservant would begin his trip with his new master to the farm, which had been given the name Stony Brook, just outside of the town of Somerville in the King's Colony of New Jersey. This entire area around Stony Brook was blessed with a rich soil and an abundance of clear water. The limestone rocks found in the fields had leached nutrients into the ground and the resulting crops attested to that fact. First, the settlers had come to clear the land and farm. Then there came the merchants who started towns to provide both goods and services to the settlers. Towns were usually built where at least two foot paths or roads crossed or a river allowed for the best method of receiving goods from larger towns and cities.

Chapter 3

The trip to Henry's new home would be nearly uneventful with McAdoo. There followed a day of travel and a night spent at one of the many taverns located along the King's Highway between Trenton and their destination. These public houses, large and small, built of wood or stone provided meals and lodging for the traveler and a gathering spot for the local men. Henry, after eating a meal of potato soup and bread, bedded down in the stable with his master's horse. He had never slept in a stable before but the sounds coming from the livestock bedded there didn't bother him that much. He decided it was much better than the ship's quarters he had.

Early the next morning, after a breakfast of oatmeal and tea, the travelers set out again for McAdoo's farm arriving before noon at Stony Brook Farm. Henry had sat with his master at the table for breakfast that morning and something he said to Henry made the boy think that this gruff man he found himself calling "Sir," might just treat him fairly.

"I'll not stand for laziness from ya," McAdoo paused as if weighing what to say next, "But if you give me a day's work I'll deal square with ya. There's a new feel to the way people treat one another here. I think it's that folks need each other more in order to get by here."

The road was dry and unpaved. The wagon kicked up dust that lingered behind the rig for some distance as it made its way toward the farm. There were many fields that were cleared or in the process of being cleared, stretching out on either side of the roadway. But most of the land was forested.

I'm to spend the next part of my life living in a wilderness. Henry concluded.

Henry tried to size up the place he was to call home for the next seven years. There were times in his past when he would accompany his father on trips to visit farmers that tended the estates of Baronet. They were usually dilapidated affairs with scrawny looking animals and peopled by tenants dressed in rags who always seemed to be having trouble. Usually the trip involved much the same thing. Henry had his father's speech memorized:

"Bodkins, man! You are four months past due on your rent. Before the sheriff serves papers on you, as an act of Christian kindness I have come to you so things can be set right."

It was then that a tale of woe and catastrophe would told by the tenant. His father would listen impatiently for a few moments and then interrupt.

"Yes, yes man. I cannot let this type of thing happen. What if it got around that I was lax in such matters? Very soon all of you would be telling me tales of calamity that are beside the point. If your grandfather hadn't been a Man at Arms for my father in the Irish Campaign (or some such other affiliation) you would have been put off a month ago."

The Baronet would then pace about in an animated state until he would have an idea. It would go something like this. Marching up to the now shaking tenant with a large smile on his face he would clasp the man by the shoulder and begin.

"I will forgo the rent collection until the next harvest (or the lambing, etc.) In the meantime you have a son (or daughter) that is of age to enter service. He (or she) will be pressed as a stable boy (or maid) until the debt is satisfied as an act of good faith."

The Baronet would collect the rent plus gain the services of another laborer for the main grounds. He always saw to it that he came out ahead. That is until …

A tear appeared at the corner of Henry's eye.

This tract was different. The farmhouse and barn were tidy and the animals well cared for. The pulse that was pride of ownership set the drumbeat to this place.

Stony Brook was a typical large colonial farm with livestock – cattle, pigs, and chickens plus field crops - wheat from the old world and corn from the new. Mrs. McAdoo's garden had beans, cabbages, squash, carrots, turnips, and potatoes. The cabbage would be salted and stored in the root cellar along with the turnips, carrots, and potatoes for use in the winter months. There was an orchard with apple and pear trees loaded with ripe fruit. What couldn't be eaten or sold at market would be preserved and used during the winter.

Likewise wheat not sold at market would be ground into flour at Mr. Hall's mill and used in making the family's bread. Henry's master had loads of work needing to be done and Henry had arrived not a moment too soon.

"Go in the house and meet your Mistress, Henry. She will give you your work clothes to change into and then meet me in the barn."

Mrs. McAdoo was in the kitchen before the large stone hearth preparing the midday meal. She stood and turned round as Henry entered the room. Putting her hand to her mouth hiding a smile Mrs. McAdoo addressed the lad in a sweet voice.

"Welcome, I have your shirt, pants and boots arranged for you in your room but I'm afraid they might be bit big. Mr. McAdoo was hoping for a strapping boy closer to his own size. Don't worry, Abigail and I will take them in after supper."

She showed Henry to a storage room that had been partially converted into his sleeping quarters. A rope strung across the room with a large woolen blanket thrown over it afforded Henry his only privacy.

How far have I fallen? Henry thought as he remembered his room at home in London or even his dormitory at school. London and Oak Hall was a million miles away. He found himself dreaming of the times he studied Latin with his roommate, Higgie, as he changed into his work clothes.

Snapped back to the present by a sound from another room, Henry saw that the effect was complete as he stared down at himself with his ill-fitting work wear. The shirt hung down to below his knees and the waist on his pants needed to be taken in by six inches and needed hemming by as much. He could walk out of his boots. He shuffled out of the storeroom back into the kitchen where he was met by the three McAdoo women.

Three sets of eyes widen and three pairs of hands clasped over mouths in unison. Mrs. McAdoo turned away and her entire body shook with silent laughter. Abigail, the eldest girl sat in a chair, stomped her feet, threw back her head, and let out a burst of laughs which Henry was sure they could hear in the next county. Katherine, the youngest, let out a whoop and made straight for the barn to fetch her father. Having heard the ruckus from the barn, McAdoo was starting for the house when Katherine met him.

"Come quick, Pa." was all she could manage to say running back into the kitchen with her father in tow. The Master's eyes widened as he gazed upon his servant dressed in his new work clothes. Then his huge hands went to his waist and he threw back his head much in the style of Abigail and laughed even louder than she did. Henry's head lowered. He had never felt as humiliated as he did now.

McAdoo spoke first. "That's one fine laugh we've all had at your expense, Henry. Now we'll go about setting it right. Abigail, take one of our laying hens to the Silverthorne's. Oliver's youngest son, Evan is about Henry's size. Ask him if he would be willing to trade a set of Evan's work clothes for a fine laying hen and ask him if he could spare a pair boots he's grown out of too."

Abigail was off like a shot to the chicken coop and soon was on her way to the next farm over with a white hen tucked under arm. She returned a little over an hour later with two shirts, one blue and one red; two pairs of trousers, one pair brown and one pair tan; three pairs of socks and a pair of boots that appeared to be only slightly worn.

"Mr. Silverthorne thought that this would be fair trade for such a fine hen." Abigail exclaimed clearly proud of the bargain that she struck. "Evan's feet grew so fast this summer that he barely broke in these boots."

Henry returned to his room to try on his "new" outfit. He had been calmed by the words of Mr. McAdoo and was sure now he would be treated fairly by his master and his family. Everything fit, even the boots. He returned to the kitchen to the nodding approval of the McAdoo's.

"Oh, heavens," Mrs. McAdoo suddenly blurted, "With all that was going on we've not taken our noon meal."

She quickly went over to the hearth and satisfied that her stew was not spoiled, began to get the meal on the table. Abigail sliced bread from a loaf baked that morning, and Katherine poured freshly pressed cider into pewter mugs. When all was ready the mistress of the house called everyone to the table. Mr. McAdoo sat first and everyone else was then seated. Even though Henry was a servant, in this household he would take all his meals with the family at the table. Mrs. McAdoo insisted and her husband readily agreed. The large redheaded man seated at the head of the table bowed and prayed.

"Heavenly Father, we ask that You bless this meal we are about to partake in so that we have the strength to do the work You would have us do to glorify Thy Name." All of the grace up to this point had been pretty much standard for the McAdoo table, but now Thomas added a new line, "Bless Henry, a new face at our table. May he grow strong and wise in Thy ways and may the work not kill him in the meantime. All this we pray in your Son, Jesus Christ's blessed name. Amen."

The sisters threw sideward glances at one another and smiled. Henry swallowed hard.

Chapter 4

The food, while simple fare, tasted like a royal feast to Henry. He ate with a relish that was not lost on his master. "If you work with the same vigor with which you've just eaten your meal then I'll be satisfied." Thomas pronounced.

After finishing his meal, Henry followed McAdoo out to the barn. There he was handed a canvas bag with a leather strap attached to it. "Put on the pickers bag and follow me to the orchard. We have apples to pick."

There are times in the early fall, when the angle of the sun in the afternoon sky coats all it shines on with a golden hue. This glow and the crisp sweetness of the autumn air made a lasting impression on Henry as he walked to the orchard. He would forever after cherish time spent in the outdoors.

The remainder of the afternoon was spent climbing up and down ladders propped on trees, picking bags full of apples which were dumped into large baskets loaded on a wagon pulled by the horse. At around five o'clock the men led the horse and wagon back to the barn with eight large baskets full of apples. Two of the baskets were for personal use with the remainder to be sold at market on the next trip to town. McAdoo spoke to Henry as they unloaded the baskets into a shed located beside the barn.

"On a farm the animals must be tended to first. Abigail, Katherine, and I will show you how to feed and water the livestock. It must be done in the morning before we eat our breakfast and again in the early evening before we take supper. You will also be responsible for milking the two dairy cows and taking the milk to Mrs. McAdoo for her to make butter and the like. This is to be done twice a day after they have been fed and watered," McAdoo noticed the look of concern on Henry's face. "Don't worry lad, I'll show you how it's done."

In a matter of a week Henry learned this and much more. He helped cut and harvest the last of McAdoo's wheat crop. He helped his

Master clear and drag away trees from the south field. His use of the axe was becoming more proficient and he learned to use a horse and drag line to skid the trees to where they would be sawn later. He cut, hauled, hoed, threshed, and raked until the blisters broke and his hands bled. Each night he would fall into his bed after supper only to rise once more at six o'clock to start the process again. The mistress would put salve on his hands each night before he went to bed and give him a word or two of encouragement.

"The Mister told me he has never seen a faster learner," or, "The girls said that the livestock is well cared for and the hens are laying the most eggs they ever gathered."

The two main trips away from the farm were to Mr. Hall's mill at Bound Brook or to the Somerville market. McAdoo's first practical test of Henry's reading skills came at the mill some two weeks after his arrival at Stony Brook. Mr. Hall had a standard written contract, which he carefully duplicated for each of the farmers who used his mill.

Pastor Simmons, one of two or three people in the area who were literate, had drawn up the contract. It seemed sensible as Pastor Simmons was beyond suspicion and would favor neither miller nor farmer. Certain basic facts had to be agreed upon such as how many pecks of flour could be gotten from a bushel of grain. There were four pecks to a bushel. Mr. Hall maintained that he could grind three pecks of flour from a bushel of wheat and the contracts used this ratio. Mr. Hall's fee was one half peck of flour for each bushel of wheat he ground. That left two and a half pecks of flour for the farmer for his own use or as product he could market. Most farmers would consign any surplus flour back to Mr. Hall. Townspeople came to the mill to buy flour. Bakery shops from the nearby towns also bought their flour there. The miller also kept a journal of sorts with each farmer's mark and the amount of flour consigned and sold. Everything seemed on the up and up. And as most farmers had learned basic arithmetic everyone was satisfied. Henry read the contract and he could see nothing wrong with it. The Scotsman was satisfied and sent Henry out to the wagon to wait for him while he settled with the miller inside.

Mr. Hall had a bondservant, too. His name was Edmund Crane and he was in his fourth year of voluntary servitude. Barely eighteen, tall and extremely skinny, Crane bore the marks of beatings on his craggy face and bony arms.

"Does your master beat ya?" Crane asked Henry.

"Why would he do that? I've done nothing wrong," Henry replied.

"You don't need to be do'n nothin' wrong to get a tann'n 'round here," the older boy looked at his bare feet and kicked the dirt to pause before he continued, "I know a secret 'bout what Mr. Hall is do'n that'd get him run outta town. That redheaded man looks big'n mean. I'll bet he'd kill'em if he knew what he's 'do'n. Does your man feed ya enough?"

Henry pitied the boy standing by the wagon kicking the dirt. He didn't have the heart to tell him that he sat at the family table for his meals so he simply replied, "Yes."

Now Crane looked straight into the boy's eyes. "I git fed thin porridge most times. Once in a while I git some meat the dogs won't eat. I'm hungry all the time," Crane then took a deep breath as if he had made a momentous decision, "Mr. Hall is cheating the farmers. He tells them that he gets three pecks of flour for each bush'l a grain, but its three and a half pecks or better. The chaff ain't that much. I know 'cause I'm in there with 'em. He's skimm'n a half peck off each bush'l he grinds."

Henry sat dumbfounded in the wagon. It was a servant's word against his master and Edmund had good reason for trying to get back at the miller. Suddenly Mr. Hall came out on the porch and was screaming, "You lazy good for nothing! Get those sacks loaded in the wagon before I hide ya!"

Henry jumped down and helped Edmund load the sacks into the wagon. Then he climbed up beside Mr. McAdoo for the trip home.

Neither spoke for the first couple of miles of wagon ride home. The Scotsman noticed the pinched expression on Henry's face and believed his servant was wrestling with a question.

"You look in sore need of the privy, boy," he finally said.

"It's not that, Sir. I believe I know something that is of great importance, but I don't know if it's true. If it is true though, I know that it can't continue," he thought about what Edmund said his master might do to Mr. Hall and fell silent again.

"It sounds like you got a lot to think over. When I need to make a big decision I pray about it and sometimes I confide in another whom I trust." McAdoo then shrugged when Henry didn't reply and got back to the business of driving the wagon. The rest of the trip home was done in silence.

After supper and final chores were done Henry asked to be excused and went to his room. Mrs. McAdoo thought Henry was taken ill in that he barely looked at anyone at the table and hadn't said more than three words all night.

"I'll get a plaster for him," she suggested.

"The lad's troubled, not sick," McAdoo told his wife. "Something happened at the mill today that's weighin' on 'im."

In his room Henry thought about what he had found out at the mill. *I'll not get a good night's rest until I decide what I must do.* Henry said to himself. *Father taught us that we are duty bound by our position to right every scurrilous wrong we know.*

His decision made, Henry climbed into bed. The night passed slowly for him still. He adjusted his covers and fluffed up his feather pillow, but sleep wouldn't come. Until he shared his burden with someone there would be no peace for him.

Chapter 5

The next morning after chores and breakfast Henry, armed with an axe, was on his way to the South field when he met Katherine who was on her way to the kitchen with a basket of eggs she had collected. Katherine was almost twelve, had a young girl's stocky build. She also had dark brown hair and green eyes like her mother's. She loved stories and was known to tell a whopper from time to time, but Henry made the decision that he could trust her. Of the four members of the McAdoo family, he had found he was the most at ease around her.

"If I tell you something you must promise not to tell another living soul," he began. "Can I trust you to keep a promise?"

Katherine eyed the servant boy and replied, "If I make a promise to you, I will keep that promise."

"Well, do you promise?" Henry was becoming exasperated and turned toward the field.

"I promise." said a voice from behind him.

He turned back to Katherine, "When you bring water to your father and me in the field, then I will tell you," satisfied by her answer, Henry pivoted and walked to the field being cleared.

About an hour and a half later, Katherine came carrying the water bucket and dipper. She went to her father first. He had just felled a tree on the far side of the field and was preparing to burn out the stump. Then she crossed the field to Henry.

"Pa says he wants you to come and clear the branches off the trunk of that tree he just cut."

Henry took a drink of water from the bucket, "I'll tell you the secret quick then. Mr. Hall's bondservant told me that his master is cheating all the farmers."

"Pa will kill him! How?"

Henry was worried by Katherine's reaction, "I don't have time to go into that now. You must keep your promise to tell no one."

"I told you I keep my promises, Henry."

He left Katherine feeling somewhat better about sharing his secret with someone he trusted. Standing beside the fallen tree he began trimming off the branches.

McAdoo and Henry returned from the South field just before noon to wash and have their midday meal. Katherine ran out of house to meet them.

"Hello Kate, have you put the wash basin and towel by the door?"

"Yes, Pa." his youngest answered.

The farmer then went about cleaning his face and hands to pass his wife's inspection and so be deemed fit to sit at her table.

Katherine turned and stared intently at Henry, "You've not done me any favors by sharing your secret with me in so far as that went. There wasn't a minute's peace for me all day," she whispered. "I must call a family meeting to get it all out into the air."

Henry sympathized with her about having no peace and decided that a burden shared was still a burden. The weight of a heavy bundle could be shared, but this was a different type of weight.

"What's a family meeting?" Henry didn't like the sounds of this at all.

"It is a device of my mother's. My father's been known to lose his anger and sometimes he wants to do things before he thinks. One of the rules of the family meeting is that no one leaves the room until the meeting is officially adjourned. Another rule is that everyone gets to speak his peace. You aren't a member of the family, but you are one of the household and what you know concerns the family so I'm sure you'll be included."

Not feeling at all sure about this meeting he was about to attend, Henry went to the basin and washed the dirt and wood chips off his hands and face.

The meal was snare caught wild rabbit done on a spit, potatoes, turnip greens, homemade bread, and cow's milk. McAdoo attacked his meal with the zeal of a hardworking man. Henry ate a few bites of the rabbit and when the sliced bread was passed to him, lost his appetite completely.

"We'll have apple pie with our dinner tonight," happily announced Mrs. McAdoo while she began to clear the table. "Henry look, you've barely eaten a thing."

Katherine rose from the table and spoke, "As is my right as a member of this family I am calling a family meeting here and now. Henry has important information which pertains directly to the welfare of the family so I am asking you to allow him to tell us what he has learned."

Everyone looked at each other and then at Henry. He felt his knees go weak as Thomas McAdoo stared what he felt was like a bore hole through him.

"Well get on with it, there's work to be done," the big man seemed angry before Henry even started and the farmer's disposition made it even he even harder to begin.

Mrs. McAdoo and Abigail knew this could be a monumental event. Katherine had never called a family meeting before; that was usually done by either by the Mr. or Mrs.

Constance admired the way her youngest daughter called for the meeting. *She did it with the formality and the purpose of a barrister.* She thought.

Henry St. Albans, the bondservant, slowly rose to his feet to address the McAdoo family meeting. "What I am about to tell you was told to me by a fellow bondservant who may want vengeance for sore and ill treatment from his master, but I was persuaded that he truthfully spoke to me about the matter," he then began recounting his meeting yesterday with Edmund.

As he spoke McAdoo's face flushed and a previously unseen vein began to show on his neck. The farmer quickly rose from the table with a fixed sneer on his face. In a bound he was at the fireplace and had removed his long rifle from its place above the mantle. The long rifle was McAdoo's service issued weapon, commonly called a "Brown Bess" this firearm was accurate up to 150 yards and it could blow a hole the size of a fist in a man.

"Thomas McAdoo, you are to be still!" Henry had never heard his mistress speak in that tone or so loudly, and from the looks on the girls' faces, they had never heard their mother speak in such a manner, either. "You will not break the rules of this family's meetings. Especially rules you yourself have made." The truth was that Constance had made the rules, but she had let Thomas believe he had done so, "Katherine is youngest; she will have her say first." Katherine rose as Henry happily gave up the floor to her.

"I think this man has cheated a great many people and should be given over to the sheriff to stand trial for his crime," Katherine based her reasoning on better the sheriff to deal with a thief than the sheriff to deal with a murderous father.

As Katherine sat back down, Abigail stood and quietly said, "What of poor Edmund? What will become of him if the charges are proven true or even worse for him, false?"

Abigail sat as Mrs. McAdoo took the floor next, "Mr. McAdoo you have two bright daughters; where they get it from puzzles me. Katherine is right in that it is a matter for the sheriff and you need to bring this to his attention right away. He has the authority to have the miller grind a bushel of grain and witness the outcome for himself. As for Edmund, no matter the outcome he will need to leave the Hall household immediately."

Most of the anger had left the large man's face. He stood and faced Henry and his family, "I'll begin by saying I have two beautiful, smart girls. No I have three beautiful, smart women," All three McAdoo women blushed. "I also have a good man in Henry St. Albans. I'll see the sheriff yet today to handle this charge of thievery in the best possible manner. Hall will be made to give up his bondservant whether he is guilty or innocent. Henry's account of Edmund's treatment won't be allowed in a community of God-fearing men. Hall will have to sell the remainder of the boy's contract and possibly his mill as a stipulation of repayment if he is found guilty. As a sign to show these are my intentions, I return the rifle to its place above the mantle." McAdoo replaced the weapon with a theatrical flourish.

"And you'll be taking Katherine with you," said his wife. "We all know that you could kill Mr. Hall with your bare hands."

Henry was relieved that the meeting was over. Such a meeting never existed in the household where he was raised. The Baronet was the first and last authority. A smile crossed Henry's face. He had the respect of McAdoo.

Chapter 6

The sheriff of Somerset County was Ben Crisp. He could be found most days in his office in Somerville. Ben served as deputy for the previous sheriff and became the current High Sheriff by appointment of the Governor of the Colony of New Jersey after the previous High Sheriff had died. He had been the sheriff for only a few months, but as top deputy he was expert in the proper means of conducting an investigation.

"Now Thomas, are you willing to bring charges against miller Hall?" Crisp would act in an official capacity or he wouldn't act at all.

"Aye, why do you think I'm telling you this instead of wringing the scoundrel's neck like a chicken?" the farmer fumed with an angry impatience.

"In order for me to conduct an investigation, I'll need a written warrant listing the charges so they may be read aloud to the accused." The sheriff couldn't read, "Pastor Simmons is away visiting a sick parishioner and is not expected back at least another day and it will take longer to use the circuit judge's clerk."

Judges in the colony traveled to several towns in a circuit schedule. The judge was currently holding court in Princeton according to the court calendar.

Katherine tugged on her father's coat, "Send for Henry, Pa."

"The day's nearly done girl. We'll go home now, Ben. Henry and I'll come back after chores in the morn'n."

Henry once more lay in bed for quite a while before sleep found him that night. He wondered again if he had done the right thing by telling his master about the shady dealing miller. Finally he decided it was better to lose some sleep over it now than to spend the rest of his indenture-ship worrying because he hadn't.

At eight the following morning sheriff, farmer, and bondservant met in the sheriff's office. Henry was seated at a desk with parchment, quill pen, and ink well. "Take this down, boy," the sheriff began, "On this day, October 12th, 1772 I, Thomas McAdoo, accuser, do ..."

"Wait, Ben. There'll be more of us wanting justice than just me." Crisp looked at Thomas and coughed. "Well yes, I suppose you're right, McAdoo. Strike through "do"..."

"I didn't write it yet, Sir," replied Henry.

"Write this," the exasperated sheriff answered, "with others to be named at a later date, do charge Geoffrey Hall, the accused, a miller late of Bound Creek Mill with Theft by Deception. To wit the accused did knowingly and willingly withhold rightful goods of the accusers for his own benefit which is a crime against the Crown." Here the sheriff paused until the boy looked up.

"Read it back to me," Henry read back the warrant. "Good, finish with "Attested to and witnessed on this date." Make three lines. Write, behind the first line, "High Sheriff of Somerset County" Write behind the second line, "Accuser" and write behind the third line, "Witness" Now give me the pen and paper." Crisp was illiterate, but he could write his name which he did on the first line.

"Now make your mark there, Thomas," the sheriff handed the farmer the pen and the large man made his mark on the second line.

"Who will witness this?" asked Henry.

"You will," the sheriff handed the lad the pen and paper.

"But I'm a bondservant, Sir. Am I allowed?"

Sheriff Crisp smiled and began, "There was a case which caused a sensation in Philadelphia several years ago where a bondservant was the only eyewitness to a man who murdered his wife out in the streets with a knife. The woman's cries brought others who saw the man standing over the victim with the weapon in his hand, but the only one who actually saw the man kill his wife was the bondservant who was accompanying them. Her testimony sent the man to the gallows. If she was able to testify in a capital murder case in Pennsylvania, you will be able to witness a theft warrant in New Jersey."

With the warrant drawn, signed, and witnessed the trio set off for Hall's mill. Hall met them on the porch of the mill when they arrived.

"What's going on here?" was all Hall could think to ask.

"I have written charges of theft which have been made against you by your accuser, one Mr. Thomas McAdoo and as such, duly witnessed."

"I never stole a thing in my life," cried the miller. Ben Crisp put up his hand.

"That remains to be seen. As charges such as these represent a serious threat to the peace and sanctity of the Crown, I am hereby authorized to conduct a formal investigation once these charges have been read to you."

Henry stepped forward with the document and began to read. At first his voice quivered. He was a little frightened of the miller, but he was even more frightened that McAdoo might suddenly leap on Mr. Hall and strangle his life out of him. But as he read and saw that McAdoo was restraining himself, Henry's reading gained strength.

"It's a lie! You have no right ..."

"I have every right and duty," interrupted the sheriff. "Now take me to your mill works."

Some mills were powered by wind; others relied on oxen or other beasts of burden to move the heavy stone. The mill here used a waterwheel set in Bound Brook for its power. Mr. Hall led the way down a set of stairs into the millworks. Two large stones did the work of grinding the grain into flour. One laid flat on the floor while another stone, in the shape of a wheel, traveled around on top of the first stone. A sluice diverted water to another wheel made of wood located outside. This set the works in motion. The outside wheel or waterwheel was connected to the inside wheel or grinding wheel by a series of wooden gears and axles. On the floor near the works were five bushels of grain. Two were from a farmer named Hobbs, and three were from the McCorkles, Hall explained.

"Grind'em while I watch," instructed the sheriff.

Suddenly a flash of realization crossed the miller's face. "I'll kill him!" He screamed, and tried to rush out of the back of the mill to get his bondservant.

McAdoo was a big man but his years of military training had taught him how to move like a cat. He had Hall by the throat before he made three steps.

"If there's any killin ta be dun taday, I'll be do'n it! McAdoo hissed through clenched teeth.

"Giv'em air," commanded the sheriff to the farmer, "and you," he pointed at Henry, "Go fetch in the servant boy."

Henry found Edmund hiding behind the outhouse. "He'll kill me sure as I draw breath," whimpered Crane as he came out into the open.

"Not with the way my master has him, he won't," Henry chuckled. He approached the shaking miserable bondsman and said, "Your time suffering in this hell is over, Edmund. The miller is in the hands of the law and I expect that justice will be done."

Once back inside the sheriff asked Edmund if he knew how to work the mill. When he said that he did Crisp's instructions were to the point,

"Run it then." It became quite evident after the running of just two bushels of wheat that the miller had been stealing from his customers.

"In the name of the Crown, I place you, Geoffrey Hall, under arrest for the crime of theft. You will accompany me back to Somerville where you will be held to await trial." He then placed his prisoner in irons, "I don't think I'll have any trouble with him." Crisp told McAdoo and the two boys, "So if you want to get back home I fully understand."

"What's to become of me?" asked Edmund.

"Mrs. Hall is likely to wish you ill, so staying here isn't in the cards," Crisp reasoned. "Could he go home with you, Thomas?"

"This lad has done me and other farmers like me a kind service so if Henry here doesn't mind sharing his room, he can come with us."

Once back at Stony Brook the women quickly took over the care of Edmund. The work clothes originally intended for Henry were altered to fit young Crane and he had a nourishing meal under his belt in no time. Edmund was openly moved when he was shown his place at the table.

"No one has ever treated me with this much kindness since I was a small child. I was sent to a work house after Ma died when I was little," Crane's eyes filled with tears. The women were now crying too.

"Ah, now this is just too much," blurted out McAdoo as he turned away, hiding his much affected face.

Henry just smiled. He had a roommate again like back at the preparatory. Edmund was no Higgie, but what he lacked in formal training he made up for with practical knowledge and common sense.

A runner was sent to the McAdoo farm the following week to tell them that Hall's trial was to be the first Tuesday in November. Crane would be needed to testify against his former master. It was also learned that 30 other farmers had come forward and were now participants in the proceedings. No one liked being cheated and more than anything they wanted to see the dishonest miller get the justice he deserved.

Things got back into a routine at Stony Brook with Edmund pitching in. In addition to doing farming chores, it was quickly discovered that the new arrival was a skilled carpenter having learned the trade at the workhouse, which had been a furniture and carpentry shop. McAdoo had carpentry tools, but not an aptitude for the work. Mrs. McAdoo descended upon Edmund with a list of items to be repaired. A chair needs fixin' here, and a latch there; could he level the kitchen table? The shutters won't close properly and the roof leaks in the girl's room. Mr. McAdoo finally took his wife aside.

"Look, woman you can have him for a project or two a week. I need 'im with me'n Henry."

"What in the world did you two ever do before Edmund arrived?" Mrs. McAdoo wondered out loud as she walked away.

Chapter 7

The day of the trial arrived with McAdoo, Edmund, and Henry travelling to Somerville for the proceedings. Anyone who had seen Crane when he was working for his master would hardly recognize him now. He was dressed in church clothes that Mr. McAdoo had "out-grown," his hair had been neatly trimmed and combed, and most striking he had put on twelve pounds of muscle. Edmund Crane, it was discovered, was a nice-looking man. This fact was not lost on several of the women of the town and it certainly wasn't lost on McAdoo's six-teen-year-old daughter, Abigail. Abigail was tall and lithe with auburn hair and blue eyes. She was, in a word, beautiful. A skilled seamstress like her mother, she was a bit of a dreamer too. No one had a kinder heart than Abigail. Now that young heart beat just a little faster when she was in Edmund's company or even when she thought about him. Such was a young girl's tender love.

The trial was to be held in the town tavern, the usual place for tri-als. Each tavern had rooms for travelers and it became common prac-tice to hold rooms in reserve for the judge and his clerk while court was in session in the town. These rooms were referred to as the judge's chambers. Court was called to order by the bailiff at nine a.m. with his grace Bernard Knowles presiding.

"All present be upstanding," called the bailiff.

This first sentence in the bailiff's call to order is where we get the phrase "upstanding citizen" as it pertains to those thought to be lawful and obedient citizens of a community. The first case called was the Crown vs Geoffrey Hall. The charge of Theft by Deception was an-nounced and Mr. Hall was asked how he pled.

"Not guilty," Hall tersely responded.

"Are you represented by a barrister, Mr. Hall?"

"No, I am not," the defendant replied. Now, several lawyers also traveled the court circuit any one of which defendant Hall could have retained, but he chose not to hire one. Lawyers cost money.

"That is your right, Mr. Hall," Judge Knowles acknowledged. "Is the Crown ready to proceed?" he asked the prosecutor, a Mr. Terrence Land, Esq.

"Yes, your grace," Land replied, clearly bored. The prosecutor would not be noticed by trying mere theft cases in some small backwater town. He needed capital cases in Trenton or Camden in order to be noticed and considered for an appointment as a judge.

"Is the defendant ready to proceed?" the judge asked Mr. Hall.

"Yes, your grace," Hall answered.

The Crown would begin with a brief opening statement. Mr. Land rose from his chair and paced back and forth, "With the court's kind permission, the Crown shall prove beyond a reasonable doubt that Mr. Geoffrey Hall did knowingly and maliciously misappropriate the property of his clients for his own personal gain. A copy indicating the body of the charges is the Crown's exhibit #1. Land handed the Judge a copy of the charges in detail."

"Duly noted and accepted," replied Judge Knowles as he handed the paper to his clerk to be recorded as exhibit #1. The prosecutor then returned to his seat.

"Does the defendant wish to make an opening statement?" the judge asked the man in the dock.

Mr. Hall rose and began, "I don't know what half them words that stuffed poppin jay just said means."

"Objection!" shouted Land as he jumped up out of his chair.

"Yes, yes, sit down Terrence," the judge mildly admonished the prosecutor by using his given name. He turned back to Hall, "continue."

"Well, if it means I cheated or took something that wasn't mine then he's a damn liar!"

"Your grace, please, is this to be permitted?" the prosecutor said it with a sort of tired indignation, not even rising from his chair.

Judge Knowles frowned, "There is to be respect shown in this court by all parties. I will not tolerate intemperate, vile or profane language. Its usage demonstrates contempt for this court. I hereby fine the defendant the sum of one pound and caution him not to use profane language in this court again." With that Hall sat back down.

The prosecutor rose and began, "If it pleases the court, the Crown calls as its first witness, Edmund Crane."

Geoffrey Hall was quickly on his feet and addressing the judge, "Your grace, this man is in a condition of servitude. He should not be able to testify in this court."

Judge Knowles looked to Mr. Land who sat silently staring straight ahead. The judge was waiting on the prosecutor to cite a precedent. Otherwise he was inclined to rule in favor of the miller. It seemed class prejudices sometimes died hard. This lawyer, who was so cocksure of himself and the outcome of this case, had just been upstaged by a country bumpkin. Ben Crisp was present in his capacity as an officer of the court. He quickly made his way to where Mr. Land sat in an apparent stupor.

"Request a recess Land, we need to talk."

"Your grace, the Crown requests a fifteen minute recess."

"Counsel and defendant please approach," Knowles waved them both to come before him. "Mr. Land there has been an objection brought by the defendant that I must rule on. I'm not going to grant a recess."

"Then will you allow Mr. Crisp, who is an officer of the court, to address the bench?" Land was grasping at a straw. He had no idea what Crisp would say, but he also knew that without Crane's testimony to lay the foundation for the warrant, then all evidence obtained by the warrant and the testimony of other witnesses would be considered "fruits of the poisonous tree" and therefore inadmissible.

"This is highly irregular, but as he is a sworn officer of the court I will allow it."

"Your grace," the sheriff nervously began, "it seems to me there was a case in Philadelphia a few years back ..."

"Pennsylvania vs. Telford, capital murder case, 1767 spring docket, Court of Common Pleas case # 33...er...49," Land was shocked to his feet by the sudden revelation, "A fifteen year old female bondservant of the accused was allowed to testify as an eyewitness to the murder of her mistress."

Of course, Land thought, how could I have forgotten it? Land's one consuming interest was capital murder cases. He would study them in fine detail so he could cite them chapter and verse should he prosecute a murder. Those in attendance in the court began to loudly murmur and the bailiff had to call for quiet.

"This violates the sanctity of the court and I will not suffer any further outbursts," declared the judge. "Now is the sheriff or the prosecutor to address this court?"

"I will address the court, your grace," said Land, now firmly back in control.

Crisp, with an expression of relief on his face, returned to his spot at the rear of the tavern. The prosecutor had been held to the fire by one bumpkin and had been saved from it by another one. It was a humbling experience.

Judge Knowles had been aware of this particular case from Penn's colony and felt it had precedence in establishing the Crown's right to call this bondservant to testify, but he was not going to hear and prosecute the case, too. Land had to do his own work.

"I will now rule on the defendant's objection. Overruled, please call Edmund Crane to the witness chair." A cheer went up from those present to which the judge sternly warned he would have the bailiff clear the court unless order was maintained.

"Your grace, that happened in another colony. Why would you use something that happened there against me here?" the miller was trying his best to keep his emotions under control.

Penn's colony did have some unique methods regarding sentencing in its court system. One of these quirks was in sentencing the convicted to incarceration for a period of time in a penitentiary. There the "penitents" would toil, pray, and reflect on their crimes in order that they be rehabilitated to return to society as useful God-fearing souls. The Quakers had established such a prison just outside Philadelphia and named it Graterford.

Jails in New Jersey were used to hold prisoners prior to their trials, not for years of incarceration. Restitution, when applicable and possible was a type of sentence. Corporal punishments such as dunking, the stocks, and flogging were sometimes passed on the convicted. A more serious punishment of convicted felons was forfeiture of rights & property and banishment. Sometimes impressments, a type of forced servitude, would be the court's ruling. Finally, death was the ultimate sentence and only meted out for capital crimes such as treason or murder. The judge trying the case of the Crown vs Geoffrey Hall was very aware of the differences. He was even more aware of the likenesses.

"Both Pennsylvania and New Jersey are Crown Colonies of His Majesty George III and the Court of St. James," Knowles adjusted his powdered wig and continued, "as these are the foundational facts then it is both reasonable and prudent to hold that a case tried previously in Pennsylvania can and should be used as a precedent in this case, over-ruled."

Hall now wished he had hired a lawyer to confer with, but it was too late. The sheriff had gone to get Edmund and the young man was passing him on his way to the witness chair. Hall barely recognized his bondservant in his present condition and he was suddenly frightened of him. Not only of what he would say, but now what he might be capable of physically doing to him.

The clerk of the court now swore in the witness and the prosecutor began his direct examination, "Please tell the court your full name and occupation."

"My name is Edmund Lawrence Crane, carpenter, but for the past four years in bond service to Mr. Geoffrey Hall."

"Did you voluntarily indenture yourself to Mr. Hall?"

"Yes sir, I did, but I was promised decent treatment and what I got was…"

"Mr. Crane, did you as part of your duties, help Mr. Hall in his millworks?" Land had cut Edmund off. He wanted to stay on the facts pertaining directly to the case now before them, although he might come back to Crane's treatment at the hands of Hall later in the questioning.

"Yes, I did," answered the witness as he looked out at the courtroom.

"What specifically did you do regarding the operation of the mill, Mr. Crane?"

"I did every part of the work. I emptied the bushels of wheat grain onto the millstone. I went out and pulled the sluice over so that the water turned the wheels. I watched the grinding of the grain until the wheat germ and fruit was separated from the hull. Then I sifted the flour and bagged it into sacks."

"Now Mr. Crane, consider carefully my next question before answering. What was the yield on average of flour to bushels of wheat ground?"

"It was three and one half pecks of flour to one bushel of wheat ground. Sometimes it was a little more, sometimes a little less."

Land now addressed the judge, "No further questions of this witness at this time, your grace. But the Crown reserves the right to recall him at a later time."

"So noted and directed." Then the judge continued, "Does the defendant wish to cross examine this witness?"

Hall now rose and slowly approached the witness. Land had sat down and was ready to jot notes with a pen for a possible redirect.

Hall asked his first question, "Is wheat the only grain we grind at the mill, Edmund?"

"No, sometimes we ground rye and buckwheat and we also rolled oats and barley."

"Now Edmund, what is the yield of rye flour to bushels of grain?"

"It's about three pecks per bushel, sometimes a little more, sometimes a little less."

"And what about the yield of oats?"

"That's nearly one to one, there's very little waste."

"Now isn't it possible that when Pastor Simmons drew up the wheat sales contracts he mistakenly used the ratio for rye instead of the ratio for wheat?"

"Objection," Land was immediately on his feet. "The question calls for a conclusion that the witness is not qualified to make."

"Sustained," Judge Knowles quickly ruled. The damage had been done though. Sometimes the airing of a question was more important than having it answered. Even though the judge had ruled for Edmund not to answer the last question, it had introduced a doubt in the judge's mind. This defendant was no country bumpkin. Land began to wonder where this supposed illiterate had studied law.

"I am done with this boy, your grace," Hall's declaration had an ominous tone to it.

"Your grace, if I may redirect?" Land was on his feet approaching Edmund. "Mr. Crane, please refresh my memory. Did you say that you had been indentured to the defendant, Mr. Hall for four years?"

"Yes sir, four years and four months the beginning of last month."

"Now, in those four years and four months did he ever, to your knowledge, use any contract form other than the one Pastor Simmons had originally drawn up for him?"

"Your grace, this boy cannot read. How could he know what contract I used?"

"How could you, Mr. Hall?"

At this Judge Knowles stood and shot a fiery glance at the Crown's attorney. "You will limit who you address in open court to the witness or to the bench or so help me, your sleeping arrangements will be made at the jail tonight."

"I do humbly beg the court's pardon, your grace." the prosecutor seemed sincerely remorseful. "If I may, I would like to continue with my questioning of the witness."

"Yes, yes do go on."

"What about my objection?" asked Mr. Hall.

"Eh, well ... overruled," the jurist responded.

"I will repeat my question, Mr. Crane. To the best of your knowledge, did Mr. Hall ever use any contract other than the one Pastor Simmons had drawn up for him?"

"No sir, I do not believe he ever did."

"And so the contract remained exactly the same for that period of time."

"No sir, I did not say that."

Terrance Land had been looking at the seated defendant trying to discern any telling expressions on his face or from his posture. Now he wheeled around facing the witness and asked, "No? In what way were these contracts between the defendant and his clients altered?"

"In the numbers, you see the amount of grain brought in by the different farmers varied due to the type of a growing year we had and the size of their planting. Likewise in a bad growing year like that dry summer three years ago, the selling price would go up."

The prosecutor feigned a look of astonishment, "How could this be?"

"Oh, even the dumbest farmer knew how to figure," Crane blushed when he realized what he had said and a couple of farmers shifted uneasily in their seats at the remark.

"So the calculations within the contracts varied from farmer to farmer and year to year?"

"Yes, that's right."

"Was there any calculation, to your knowledge, that never changed in these contracts?"

"Your grace, this boy was never made privy to my business dealings so how could he testify to what was or wasn't a part of them?"

The judge had also realized now that the defendant before him might have had some formal training in the law, "The court has a question for the defendant as a clarification before it makes a ruling on his objection."

Hall's entire body moved as he sighed. He already knew the question that the jurist would ask. And there was, at this time in this court, no right against self-incrimination.

"Is the account of the witness with regards to the calculations and their alterations within the contract in question, accurate?"

Hall knew that if he answered falsely that there were over thirty other witnesses in court that would dispute his claim, he was trapped.

"Yes, your grace."

The judge now sat even more upright in his chair and made his ruling, "As the calculations in the body of the contract have been accurately described by the witness as agreed upon by both prosecution and defense it is therefore logical that he would have an accurate knowledge of other calculations contained within the contract. Defendant's objection is overruled."

"Was there any calculation in the body of the contract that never changed?" the prosecutor repeated the question to Edmund.

"Yes."

"And what was that calculation?"

"The yield of flour expected for each bushel of wheat," Land turned and smiled at Hall. "No further questions of this witness at this time, your grace."

Hall was on his feet and had uttered the phrase before he could catch himself, "Re-cross, your grace?"

It hit like a thunderclap on the other two legally trained men in the room. He was schooled in the law! If he was, he therefore was literate. Why would he perpetrate such a deception on his community? Why wasn't he practicing law, his given profession? Hall knew the game was up by the expressions on the judge and prosecutor's faces. It took every fiber of control not to panic now.

Hall took a step to try and gather himself as sweat appeared on his forehead, "Now Edmund how was it that you came to know the contents of the Simmons contracts?" asked the examiner.

"From you and the farmers talking about them in front of me and from you and Mrs. Hall talking between yourselves," answered Edmund.

At this, a large well-dressed woman of about thirty-five got up and made her way out of the tavern courtroom. Mrs. Hall also knew the jig was up. She had been squirreling away money at the outset of her marriage to Hall, nearly eight years now, and had close to one hundred pounds. She would drive her pony and cart, loaded with her belongings, to her sister's home in Trenton. The miller's wife had worked out a deal with the town's blacksmith to sell her pony and cart to him for fifteen pounds. The blacksmith's strapping son would accompany her to Trenton as a safeguard, then take possession of cart and pony and return to Somerville.

Hall saw her leave the room and the color drained from his face. He was just asking questions now to bide for time and try to think how to get himself out of this trap.

"How is it that you know about what you call, figuring?"

"I'd be a poor carpenter if I didn't know how to measure wood or where to drill holes and the like."

"Yes, I suppose you would," Geoffrey Hall was at his wit's end.

He just stood there for the next minute until the judge asked him, "Do you have any further questions for this witness?"

"No, I do not, your grace."

The judge then rose from his chair, "As my stomach is telling me it is approaching mid-day, I now declare this court is in recess until called back to order at two o'clock this afternoon."

With that everyone else rose until Judge Knowles had made his way out of the courtroom and to his room. On his way out, he paused by the bailiff and told him to have the sheriff meet him in his chambers. Sheriff Crisp knocked on the Judge's door a minute later.

"Enter!"

Crisp opened the door and went in, "You wanted me, you grace?" The sheriff saw that Mr. Land was also there.

The judge spoke first, "Ben, there is something more afoot here than just a trial for theft. Both Mr. Land and I are convinced that our Mr. Hall has been a practicing barrister in the past. On a hunch, and nothing more, we would like you to bring us all the fugitive fliers you have at your office."

Mr. Land added, "Please have Pastor Simmons and the judge's clerk, Jenkins join us. They'll be able help in our research."

"I'll fetch McAdoo's bondservant, Henry. He can read too," the sheriff suggested as he walked quickly to the door.

"Yes, do that!" both the judge and prosecutor shouted after him.

Ben Crisp found Thomas McAdoo and Henry doing what they had been doing since nine a.m., which was waiting in a front room of the tavern to be called as witnesses. When court was in session, the tavern owners could serve no food or drink. Thomas was thirsty and hungry. Henry was nervous. Being sequestered away from what was happening out in the main room had him anxious. Every once in a while the volume of the muffled voices would rise. Only a word out of perhaps ten was able to be understood and this led Henry's imagination into an undiscovered territory of worry.

"Henry, you are to go to the judge's chambers immediately. Thomas, come with me."

The farmer was ready to complain to the sheriff that he was hungry and thirsty but the sheriff's expression told him they were facing some serious business. The two men had gotten to the middle of the dirt street on their way to the sheriff's office when the deputy in charge of Hall's custody came staggering out of it holding is head.

"Hall's gone! And he stole your horse, Ben!"

Crisp ran around to the side of his office where he had tied his horse and sure enough, she was gone. Next, he ran into the jail and just as his deputy had said, Hall was gone, too.

"How?" was all the sheriff said when he returned to his deputy and Mr. McAdoo.

"He said he had to, you know, go to the outhouse and could I remove his leg irons as they wouldn't allow him to pull down his trousers far enough to go. I had just removed the irons when he struck me hard on the back of my head. When I regained my senses, he was gone."

"Clover was the best mare I ever owned," lamented Crisp. "Well, he's got a good start on us and he has one of the fastest horses in these parts. We had best collect the fugitive fliers and get back to the judge with them. I'll see about going after him later."

Chapter 8

As they carried the posters across the street to the tavern Henry asked Crisp about them. Ben looked at Henry and began to explain, "Some officers of the law, sometimes even ordinary citizens in the colonies, circulate these fliers or wanted posters when an especially evil criminal escapes justice. Not everyone does these fliers and those that do don't do it every time, but it's worth going through this two-foot stack of them just the same. First, we need to get the news about Hall's escape to the men waiting on the posters back at the tavern."

"This proves to me that the answer we are seeking just might lie in that stack of papers," Land remarked after Crisp told them of Hall's escape.

"No man would commit such a desperate act if he was facing only a charge of theft," added Judge Knowles. "Jenkins, notify all concerned that court will stand in recess until further notice and find that man Abbot, the town crier, It's time that he earns his tuppence." Jenkins, the court clerk, went off to fulfill the judge's orders.

The news of Hall's escape came to the town's attention as Abbot walked Somerville loudly revealing the sensational details. Meanwhile, the party of literates had moved to one of the larger rooms in the tavern were they all could work together sifting through the stack of fliers. Crisp and his predecessors kept the notices even though they couldn't read them. They had been useful reference materials for the court in the past. These notices seldom had drawn likenesses of the fugitives, but some contained accurate verbal descriptions and other details that could help in the accused's apprehension.

"Did you keep these papers in some type of order Crisp?" The judge asked the sheriff.

"Ask your man, Jenkins. He's had near exclusive use of them."

Jenkins, a fastidious law clerk, shook his head.

"Oh, well," sighed the judge, "divide the stack into five parts and let's be about this business."

The group began the labor of pouring over the bills. Meantime, McAdoo had reluctantly returned to his farm with Edmund. Before he left though, he instructed Henry to head for home before nightfall.

Cold chicken and joints of beef along with ale and cider were served to the men in the room while they worked. It was thirsty work.

"Here's one from New York." Land's outburst broke the silence, "Wanted for Murder and Assault - James Appleby - late of Harlem. Description ... No, wait. The date doesn't work out."

The research continued on for over an hour when Jenkins spoke up, "I think I might have something here." He then began to read out loud, "Cambridge, Massachusetts March 15th, 1758. Wanted for the crime of Capital - Murder and Theft- Jeffers Halstead - freeborn male - twenty-seven years of age - five foot nine inches - one hundred and forty pounds."

"That last part doesn't fit," offered Sheriff Crisp.

"Hush Ben, time has a habit of putting pounds on a man," Knowles advised, "Continue, Jenkins," the clerk cleared his throat and went on.

"Distinctive features – prominent scar on left hand running from little finger to thumb. The accused, the victim's attorney, is alleged to have committed the killing, after the victim discovered he was being swindled by the accused." Everyone in the room looked at one another.

"We've all seen that scar on Hall's hand. Hall just might be Halstead!" Crisp now loudly declared what had become obvious to everyone.

"Hall, or Halstead, fled New England and began to work a swindle here under the guise of an illiterate miller," Land reasoned. "He used our poor unsuspecting pastor here as a pawn in his scheme. I wonder how much Mrs. Hall knew of her husband's past."

This revelation was more than merely sensational. An accused killer had operated for ten years in their midst and no one suspected a thing. Judge Knowles faced his clerk and issued orders,

"Jenkins, write a fugitive warrant for Jeffers Halstead also known as Geoffrey Hall for criminal flight and the crime of theft. Note on the warrant that the fugitive is also wanted for capital murder by the authorities in Massachusetts. Include a current description of him. Make a copy to serve as a flier and send it by mounted messenger to the printer's in Princeton. Have the messenger instruct the printer to make 200 copies and post them to the proper authorities in the surrounding colonies. The printer should have a standing list to use for addresses."

Next, he spoke to the prosecutor, "I intend to call the court back in session tomorrow morning and try this scoundrel, Hall or whatever his name is, in absentia."

Then, Knowles turned to Sheriff Crisp, "Ben, send the boy home now with word that he, the boy named Crane, and his master will be present for testimony in court by nine a.m. tomorrow."

Finally, the judge spoke to the ashen-faced pastor, "Please be here too, Simmons. I'm sorry that this rascal has mixed you up in his underhanded dealings. But tomorrow should exonerate you completely, not that it is even necessary."

Crisp sent Henry on his way then returned to his office where he had asked his two deputies to wait for him.

Henry made for Stony Brook with all haste arriving there at dusk. He had his supper while he recounted to a rapt audience what transpired after Thomas and Edmund had left.

"I never liked that man at all," McAdoo pronounced to his household.

With all labor of the day being completed, the residents of Stony Brook made their way to the parlor. McAdoo was enjoying his pipe by the fire while his wife and Abigail, seated nearby, were knitting woolen sweaters for the boys. Katherine was playing with her rag doll, Betsy. Edmund and Henry were locked in a game of checkers. Suddenly, they heard the beat of horse's hooves at a gallop and then a man shouted aloud.

"Every able bodied man of the house! Sheriff Crisp has sent me to fetch you to the flourmill! He has Hall trapped inside!"

"Go saddle my horse, Henry!" Thomas shouted to his servant as he ran to his chest, which sat just inside the storeroom. From it he withdrew a powder horn, a leather pouch containing wadding, flints, and balls and two loaded military issue pistols, one of which he stuck in his belt. Next he ran back to the fireplace. As he was going past the stunned Crane, he handed him a pistol and matter-of-factly said, "Cock the hammer, aim it, and pull the trigger." The farmer grabbed his rifle from atop the mantle then strode toward the front door saying to Edmund simply, "follow me."

The men met out in front of the farm's porch. Henry had McAdoo's horse saddled and ready. The ex-sergeant major now barked out orders. "We'll ride two men to a horse. Henry, climb up behind me. Edmund get up behind Gill. We will ride at a trot. Gill, your horse has had a hard gallop and another with two men aboard would kill it." Gill nodded in agreement. "We'll get there in time, have no fear. Ben Crisp is a cautious man."

Henry was excited and terrified at once. The danger and suspense of what was about to happen had his mind racing as sweat showed on his forehead. *My blood seems to be boiling and I can't say why.* He thought.

Riding behind McAdoo, especially at a trot, was jolting him to a conclusion. *Caesar once said in his journal, "The die is cast." Well, the die certainly is cast for someone tonight.* He shivered and wiped his head. *What lies ahead is anyone's guess. That unknown is frightening for me.*

Chapter 9

Ben Crisp had also been known to be a man of hunches. When he returned to his office that afternoon he laid out a plan to recapture the fugitive, "Hall's a clever customer so we have to be just as clever in order to catch him. Think of it like a game of checkers; you have to figure out your opponent's next move."

"What's his next move?" Roberts asked. He was the deputy knocked witless by their ex-prisoner earlier in the day.

"It's not safe for him to be seen on a road around here because everyone knew he was standing trial and most folks would recognize Clover as my horse. So I think he'll get someplace outside of town and hide till its dark so he won't be so easy to recognize."

"Why wouldn't he just make a dash for parts where he's not known?" Gill asked. He was the deputy without the headache.

"Because he's a greedy man and that's his weakness."

"How's that?" both deputies asked the question at the same time.

"I'll bet you a month's wages that our man has a large stash of money hidden back at the flourmill. He won't leave until he's retrieved it."

"Sheriff, it's getting close to dark now."

"Then we had better get riding."

They arrived at the mill just after sunset. The place was in darkness except for a light that shown through a window of the millworks. Gill stayed with the horses while Crisp and Roberts quietly barred the back entrance and then crept to the lit window and peered in. There was Hall or Halstead on his knees removing a large sack from a hole that had been covered by one of scores of stones making up the floor of the millworks. The sack appeared to be very heavy. Hall had on a bandolier that had a brace of four pistols hanging from it. Outfitted with the holster rig, he looked like a highwayman or a pirate. Beside him lay a fifth pistol, cocked and ready. He was proving to be a truly dangerous man.

"Stand and hold!" Crisp shouted through the window.

The fugitive glanced up reaching for his pistol as he did so. He fired the readied pistol a second later, the ball passing through the window barely missing both men. A fragment of glass did manage to bury itself in Robert's left cheek. It simply was not his day. The sheriff seeing that his deputy was only slightly wounded clamped a handkerchief on his cheek and shouted down to the fugitive again.

"The back way is blocked. You're trapped Halstead, give yourself up!"

The light went out in the millworks.

"I'll never swing from a gallows. I've seen men who have and I'll fight you to the death before I'll suffer that end," a crazed voice screamed from inside.

"Gill, ride to McAdoo's. Fetch him and the boys quick before blood is spilled."

When the reinforcements arrived at the mill the siege had been going on for a little over two hours. The mill had been a stronghold against marauding Indians in earlier times. Windows only existed on the front of the building. Firing slits big enough for a rifle barrel but not big enough for a man were strategically located on all sides of the building. A small force could hold off a much larger force from inside if provisioned. But a force of one had small chance of doing so no matter how well supplied. Torches had been placed in the yard so if Halstead tried to make a break there would be light enough to see to use their firearms. Both Crisp and Roberts were careful not to stray into the torchlight so that Halstead could pick them off from the darkness of the mill. The posse now held their council of war.

"We thought about settin' fire to the place, but the whole danged thing is made of stone." offered Roberts.

McAdoo stroked his red beard looking over the situation with a soldier's perception. Finally, he spoke. "If we try to rush him tonight we could end up getting one or more of us killed before we got to him. I'm thinking a diversion in front with a two man attacking force at the rear just might do the trick. We'll go at dawn."

The sheriff came up with the diversion. They would set fire to a small hay wagon they found nearby and run it at the front door while it was ablaze making a terrible racket at the same time. If they stayed behind the wagon there was little chance of getting shot by Halstead.

While the group in front drew the fugitive's attention, McAdoo and Crane would scale the back of the building using the firing slits as handholds and footholds to gain the roof. Once on the roof they would remove a thatch portion and drop down inside hopefully to gain the advantage on Halstead and take him into custody.

"Look around for a branch bigger round than my thumb," instructed the ex-Sergeant Major.

Soon Henry was back, "Will this broomstick do?"

"Aye, handsomely," replied McAdoo.

"What do you want with a broomstick, Thomas?" asked one of the deputies.

McAdoo had broken the broomstick into three pieces by bending it on his knee and using his massive strength. "I intend to wedge these pieces of broomstick into the slits on the back wall and use'em like rungs in a ladder so Edmund and I can scale to the roof."

"Why not just use that ladder over there?" suggested Crisp.

"Why didn't you tell me you found a ladder?" the exasperated farmer asked the sheriff.

"Because we were looking for branches like you said."

With that last retort from the sheriff the big man threw up his hands and walked away muttering something about working beside daft fools.

Meanwhile the fugitive now known as Halstead had done an admirable job in barricading both front and back doors with furniture, stones, and heavy sacks of flour. He could detect some movement by members of the search party outside, but it was too dark to get a clear shot. The trapped man reasoned that he was the true victim in all this. The man he killed, Grey, had threatened to take him before the authorities, to have him disbarred and arrested, even after Halstead had promised to return all his money to him. Mindless rage had built up in him and the letter opener was beside his hand on Grey's desk. It had happened with such swiftness that he still sometimes believed it was a bad dream.

And the farmers here; what right did they have to complain? He ground their grains and sold their consignments for them the year round. Everyone was profiting! What right did they have to complain? That big red headed lummox, McAdoo, he was the worst of them. He was Halstead's accuser! Blind hatred again washed over the miller until he shook with hideous anger.

"I will kill that bastard before I leave this world," Halstead swore out loud. For now though he was trapped in this mill and had to wait until daylight before he could figure out his next move.

Dawn came and with it all the preparations of the posse were completed and in place. Sheriff Crisp was to fire his pistol as a signal to the two men in back. It also might bring Halstead to a window where Gill, the best shot of the posse, could possibly get a shot at him. Gill had been placed behind an oak tree some forty yards away directly in front of the mill. With him were the rifles of the sheriff and McAdoo as well as his own. Even if he couldn't get a clear shot at the fugitive he would pin him down so Halstead couldn't shoot the men behind the wagon.

Ben Crisp waved the torch at Gill to indicate the diversion was starting. Next he placed the torch on top of the mound of hay in the wagon, held his pistol into the air firing it, and yelled push to Henry and Roberts. Started alert by the pistol shot, the miller made his way to a window in time to see a blazing wagon come hurtling at the front porch. A rifle ball crashed through the window just missing the miller's head making him squat down. The wagon had almost reached the porch when Halstead fired one of his pistols at it. The ball hit the sideboard of the wagon tearing off a large splinter, which impaled the right arm of Roberts.

"He's the most unlucky man I know," muttered Crisp as Roberts fell to the ground. Another rifle ball whizzing past an inch from his ear kept Halstead at bay long enough for Henry and Crisp to pick up their wounded comrade and whisk him out of range of the besieged man's pistols. The wagon had crashed into the porch which was now also on fire.

The blithering dolts, that won't … Halstead was stopped mid thought by a sound coming from above him.

At the sheriff's signal, Thomas McAdoo and Edmund Crane, a pistol tucked in each of their belts, rushed to the back of the mill with the ladder. They climbed to the roof and began removing the thatch so they could enter the mill from above.

"Maybe they've wounded him," said Crane hopefully after hearing the three other gunshots.

"We'll soon see," McAdoo replied as he dropped himself through the hole made in the roof. The farmer landed in the bedroom of the millhouse. As he was straightening up a voice called out to him from the shadows of the room.

"Stand still, you son of a bitch." Halstead walked slowly out of the shadows toward McAdoo holding a cocked pistol in his hand. "You are the cause of my suffering. Behold farmer, the righteous hand of God!"

The loud explosion of a pistol discharge along with the weapon's smoke filled the room. When the air cleared a second or so later, Halstead lay on the floor, shot through the body, stone dead. McAdoo was near faint from the shock. A moment later a pistol dropped into the room through the hole in the roof. Crane was weeping loudly outside. The truth as to what just happened suddenly struck McAdoo square between the eyes.

That boy just saved my life, Thomas thought. And the additional realization, *that bondservant just killed his master.*

Chapter 10

At nine a.m. Judge Knowles, Prosecutor Land, Pastor Simmons, and several interested spectators were seated in the Somerville courtroom. Missing from the court were the sheriff, McAdoo, and the bondservants, Henry St. Albans and Edmund Crane Also missing was the defendant Hall or Halstead or whatever his name. The judge knew why the defendant was missing. He did not know why everyone else was missing, but he was determined to find out.

"Bailiff, I want you to send a runner out to the McAdoo farm. Find out why he isn't sitting in this courtroom along with the two bondservants in his charge."

The bailiff bowed to the bench then walked out of court to find a runner. The judge next turned to Jenkins, his clerk. "In the spirit of Christian Mercy," he glanced at Pastor Simmons, "I will give that sheriff and his deputies just a quarter hour more to be present in this courtroom or have a very good reason for their absence. Otherwise they will be spending time in jail as occupants."

The bailiff ran back into the courtroom. "They're coming down the street, your grace."

Five men, each leading a horse, slowly made their way down the street toward the courtroom. Seated on one of the animals was the wounded deputy, Roberts. Tied to another was a body. Every last one of them had a vacant stare on his face. It was apparent that there had been quite an ordeal experienced by them all.

Henry had never seen a dead body before. His father had spared him that due to his young age both for his brother and his mother. The violence of the fight with the blazing hay wagon, the reports of gunfire loud in his ears, the wounding of Roberts, and finally the witnessing of a man's life suddenly and terribly ended would leave a deep impression on him.

Henry thought about the finality of what had happened at daybreak. *It is something like a line that is crossed that can never be re-crossed,* he thought. It went beyond the simple emotions of fear or anger and even pain. It was a mind-numbing state of being. Generals and historians talked about the fog of war in the texts he had studied back at school. It seemed to Henry that every participant that morning was enveloped in a fog of their own.

Crisp felt like he had failed in his mission to bring back the fugitive for trial. He had underestimated the desperation of the man who now lay dead across the back of a horse. His miscalculation had also led to the wounding of a deputy and in putting his entire posse at risk. He would have a lot to reconcile and hoped Pastor Simmons could help him to see things in the right way once again.

It was Gill's first experience with anything like this. Even though older than Henry and Edmund, he was no less susceptible to the emotional results of what just occurred. Gill was having trouble shaking the images of combat. He had shot at another man, an act that could have resulted in his taking a life.

Roberts was in pain. They managed to remove the large splinter from his arm and staunch the bleeding back at the mill but during the ride back it started to bleed again. They dressed the wound as best they could but infection was the real threat to Roberts now. He might lose the arm or even his life.

McAdoo had many experiences in combat during his years with the Royal Highlanders. He had fought hand to hand with both the French and with Indians, but what stepped out of those shadows back at the mill was a crazed, raging animal. It was a sight he couldn't easily make go away.

Crane had killed a man. Nothing can prepare you for the gut wrenching remorse felt no matter the circumstances. The man he killed had been his master. Crane knew a few, not many, but a few would twist this fact into a bondservant rebelling against his master. He was sure the court would clear him of any guilt once the facts were presented, but the court of public opinion might be a different matter.

The courtroom cleared to view this spectacle coming toward them. Townspeople crowded up against the troop asking all kinds of questions. The posse silently kept staring straight ahead toward their goal and went on walking without a pause. When they arrived in front of the tavern Judge Knowles saw the condition they were in. Knowles ordered the tavern keeper to have food ready for them and to have brandy on hand.

"As court was never formally called to order," he told the prosecutor and the clerk, "it will remain in recess until these men have had a chance to recover. Only then will we hear their testimony." To a random man standing nearby the judge commanded, "Lead the horse with the body on it over to the undertakers. Have him prepare it for Christian burial. And fetch the barber."

The sheriff and his deputies were led to a small room where they were given food and drink. The barber, who also served as the town's surgeon, would look at Roberts' wound there, far from prying eyes. It was common for barbers to serve as surgeons at this time in history. Actually it was a tradition that dated back to medieval times in England. Anatomy classes were part of the curriculum in American barber colleges well into the twentieth century as homage to that fact. Indeed, the red and white striped barber's pole is a reference to it.

Likewise the townsman led the horse carrying Halstead's body over to the furniture store. Its owner also served as the town's undertaker. The wagon he used to deliver a table or a chest of drawers was also used to carry the departed to the burial grounds in a wooden casket he constructed.

McAdoo, Henry, and Edmund sat down at a table in the main room, which also happened to be the courtroom. The serving girl brought them a cut of ham, bread and butter, tankards of cider, and a bottle of brandy. McAdoo grabbed the brandy bottle and poured a shot of it into each of the mugs of cider. Then he took a big draw of it directly from the bottle. The boys had no appetite, but were parched from the ordeal. Henry took a drink of the fortified cider. It burned all the way down to his stomach. Edmund gulped down some cider then looked over at Henry with an expression of surprise. McAdoo had seen the same look on young soldiers faces many times before.

"You will need ta eat ta keep up your strength." Before they tasted food though, McAdoo quickly prayed, "God, give us all the strength we will need for this coming time and don't let this experience be lost on these boys."

As the boys quietly ate, the farmer thought about what he needed to say to them. It was a raw, stark experience had shaken him to realize that he needed to speak some words of encouragement to both of them. He knew what he said now would be of a lasting importance.

"It is a horrible thing to see a man killed. Still more horrible to be the one what done the killin'."

At this Edmund's eyes swelled with tears.

"Edmund, I saw that man's face. He was no longer a man. He was an animal that would have killed me sure if you hadn't done what you did."

The tall boy now bent his head to the table and covering it with his arms began to weep openly. Henry's eyes now filled recalling the sight at the mill. He placed his hand on the shoulder of his friend.

McAdoo continued, "I have killed in the past, too. It was my duty as a soldier. It didn't make it easier. It was still the taking of another man's life. I'm here to tell you, Edmund that you will never forget it or get over it. What you will do is deal with it as a necessary act you committed to save another man's life."

Edmund with a tear-streaked face looked up at the large man, "He was my master, Sir."

McAdoo looked back at Crane with kindness in his eyes and softly said, "He was a murderous thief son, with murderous intentions that you stopped just in time. There was no other way. We'll have you meet with the pastor. I'm sure there is scripture from the good book that will comfort and encourage you."

With those last words, Edmund sat back up, wiped his face with his sleeves, and began to eat again.

The words weren't lost on Henry either. He realized it was a terribly grim, but sometimes-necessary thing, to take another man's life in this wild country.

The barber arrived at the tavern and was shown into the room where Roberts was lying on a table. He removed the bandage and quickly saw that this man would not require his bloodletting services today.

"Get me a hot iron and some fresh bandages," he called to the tavern keeper and his serving girl. Next the surgeon withdrew a probe from his kit and began to inspect the wound for any additional splinters. This sent Roberts into a spasm of pain. He screamed and thrashed about on the table.

"Hold him!" he commanded Gill and Crisp. When he was satisfied there was no more wood in the wounded man's arm, he looked at the sheriff and deputy again and said, "This time, really hold him." The tavern keeper had just returned with the fireplace's poker, which he had heated, to a red-hot glow. The barber took the poker and rolled it across the wounded man's arm. Roberts let out a high-pitched shriek and then passed out. The surgeon next applied bandages to the seared wound.

The barber/surgeon had done three things right in the treating of his patient. He was entirely ignorant as to why they were the correct course of treatment though. Bacteria would not be discovered as the cause of infection for nearly a hundred years. By probing around for more splinters he made the wound bleed again effectively "washing" away infection causing germs. Next he seared the wound to stop the bleeding. What that did was kill any remaining bacteria left from his probe and tightly close the wound from any further threat of infection. Finally, bloodletting, which was a surgeon's first line of treatment at the time, might have further weakened an already weak man, and sent him into shock which might have killed him. The barber looked at sheriff Crisp.

"I think he'll live. Somerset County still owes me three shillings for the work no matter what."

Roberts would live and would carry with him a five-inch long scar on his right arm the remainder of his life as a reminder of this day. The barber returned to his shop.

Roberts remained unconscious on the table for some time during which Crisp and Gill had several tankards of ale, also on the County. When Roberts regained his senses, his two comrades had just toasted him with their third mug full of ale.

"Oh, my aching arm," he complained. Next he looked around the room. "Where's Hall's coin bag?"

The other two were shocked sober by the question. Both of them bolted outside to Crisp's mare where the money pouch was still securely strapped.

"Get the judge and his clerk," Crisp told Gill. "We'll meet in the small front room for an accounting."

Judge Knowles and the clerk, Jenkins, met with the three peace officers in the front room a short time later.

"Your grace, this is why Hall went back to the mill." Crisp dumped the bag of currency and coins onto a table. A quick tally was completed with over nine hundred pounds the final count.

"Jenkins, create a document which will be signed by the court stating that the deceased had in his possession, at the time of his death, nine hundred thirty seven pounds, four shillings, and a tuppence. Also record that a gold and ruby necklace and gold signet ring were found in the bag. Now prepare a special courier dispatch for the authorities in Middlesex County, Massachusetts. Include this ring with the note telling them what has transpired here. I seem to remember a gold signet ring missing from Halstead's victim being listed on the fugitive warrant. Further I want it recorded that Sheriff Ben Crisp is ordered to impound this money pending an official court of inquiry which will be held four days hence."

Judge Knowles approached McAdoo and the boys. "Take them home, Thomas. A court of inquiry will be called in four days after Roberts is back on his feet. I'll need all of you back here then. Meantime, you have a farm to attend to and women who are worried about you."

The journey home was a solemn quiet one. Constance and her daughters met the three in the front yard. Elation of their return unscathed was soon tempered by the news that Edmund had been forced to kill the fugitive. When Abigail learned that Edmund acted in order to save her father's life, the love she felt for the young man deepened. All shared a sense of gratitude for Crane's quick action.

It was hard for Henry to reconcile with himself that tomorrow morning he would be again doing his work as though nothing had happened. Something had happened and tired as he was his mind kept on going over the events of this horrible day until he finally fell into a fitful sleep. Even then there was no relief. The nightmare's climax made him gasp and sit bolt-upright in his bed. His brow was wet with perspiration and his mouth was dry.

Getting out of bed he heard Edmund saying, "I can't sleep either."

"I have to get some water for my parched mouth," Henry croaked and headed for the well.

Chapter 11

The next day McAdoo and Henry went hunting. Edmund was not able to bring himself to join them and stayed behind to work on another of Mrs. McAdoo's carpentry projects. Thomas had been working with Henry on his marksmanship using the long rifle. After a few weeks he found that the boy had a talent for using the weapon.

It was late in the morning as the two were just clearing a small rise when Henry spotted a large buck some sixty yards in the distance. "Over to your right, Sir." Henry whispered to his master.

"Here, boy," McAdoo handed Henry his flintlock. "You saw 'im, you take 'im."

Henry took the firearm and carefully repeated what he was taught by the farmer. He knelt bringing the weapon up to his shoulder. Next he rested the barrel of the rifle against the trunk of a tree to help steady his aim. Once he was in a stable position, he cocked the hammer of the rifle and looked down range to find his target again. The deer had moved a short way further to the two hunter's right. Now with his quarry found, Henry placed the front sight, called the blade, just behind the front shoulder of the animal, and then he centered it and leveled in the rear "U" sight. He took a deep breath letting it halfway out. With his right index finger he slowly squeezed the trigger.

"Ker-Wham!" The report of the shot echoed through the shallow valley. At the sound of the gun, the buck bounced off through a thicket.

"I'm afraid I missed him, Sir."

"Reach in your pocket; get your potato and eat it," replied the farmer. "You hit him square."

The boy was puzzled. "If the ball was true, then how could he run?"

"I've known a deer to run a hundred yards shot through the heart," replied the master. "First, we'll eat our tubers, and then we'll find his trail."

A little over five minutes later both stood at the spot of the impact. It was evident for two reasons. A deer normally doesn't disturb the leaves, twigs, and moss as it walks in the forest. It leaves a small distinct hoof print in the ground. Here the ground was torn up. Leaves and small branches were scattered about from the violence. And the most important evidence of the hit was the blood left behind on the leaves and the ground.

"Now we follow the blood trail to the deer," explained the experienced hunter to the novice.

"Why didn't we follow right away?"

"Well, Henry I was pretty sure it was fatal wound, but I wasn't positive. From what I see here this deer will have gone a short way and then lay down. If we had gone after him and he wasn't hit as hard as he was then we would have pushed him to drag himself on. It would have taken a better part of the day to find him, if at all. And the meat of an animal that is hotly pursued always tastes worse than if it had been left to bed down and die."

The trail led into a thicket were after only a little time the buck was found lying next to a fallen log some forty yards from where Henry had shot him. Mature male whitetail can weigh upwards of 200 lbs. this one was a little smaller, but only a little. Henry was admiring the large eight-point rack when he was snapped back to reality by his master's voice.

"It's a fine buck, but we have no time to be gawking at him. Here Henry, hold his hind legs apart and I'll show you how to dress 'im."

McAdoo took the eight-inch knife he always carried on his belt and made a cut from just below the deer's rib cage to his rear end careful not to cut into the intestines or anus. Next, he turned the animal on his side and spilled its insides out on the ground.

"Henry, take off your coat and roll up your sleeves."

The newly minted hunter obeyed the experienced hunter's instruction. The chill of the late autumn air stung the skin of Henry's forearms. *What a buck*, Henry excitedly observed as he helped ready the deer for gutting. *I was with my father many times when he took deer on his property and I don't remember any that was this size.* "Now reach up into the buck's chest and pull out his lungs and windpipe." Henry slowly obeyed. He felt the sticky warm organs of the fallen buck and he quickly began to remove them. "Grab the windpipe and yank, boy." McAdoo commanded. With a firm pull Henry now had his first deer fully dressed.

"You only nicked his heart, but shot him through both lungs, a good swift kill,"

McAdoo observed this with a little sense of pride at Henry's accomplishment. *He's a smart boy and learns quickly,* he noted. McAdoo now handed Henry a towel from out of a large pouch he was carrying.

"There's a creek just down there. Wash off your arms and dry them good. And get your coat back on before you catch your death."

Henry did as he was told and when he returned a short time later he saw that McAdoo had been busy. The red-bearded hunter had cut down a thin sapling and now had a pole about seven feet long. Next he produced two three-foot pieces of rope from his pouch. He tied the deer's front feet together then he tied its back feet. "Help me slip this pole through the animal's feet and we'll be whistling the whole way home."

Chapter 12

The hunter's success was greeted by Edmund and the women with clanging pots and whistling. The girls told Henry that his buck was even bigger than the one their father had gotten last fall. Mrs. McAdoo suggested Henry hang the trophy antlers in his room. Edmund admired the whitetail and congratulated Henry's on his success. He had seemed less troubled to Henry than he had been that morning. The deer was skinned and prepared for butchering right after the noon meal. Lots of wood and clean water were needed. Thomas, Edmund, and Henry produced stacks of hardwood and applewood to burn in the smokehouse and for the kettle fire. The women produced a large copper kettle, which was scrubbed until it shined. Buckets of water were carried from the well for the kettle and for the tubs of salted brine needed to cure the meat. A large fresh venison roast was slowly being cooked on the spit of the fireplace, which would be the centerpiece of supper. The rest of the animal would be cut into roast portions or strips of meat and hung in the smokehouse to cure. Some of the meat would be rubbed with salt to help in the preserving process. Two pigs would also be killed and butchered with hams wrapped in muslin cloth and soaked in salt brine later to join the venison in the smokehouse. Lard would be rendered from the pig's fat in the large kettle along with cooking the livers and hearts for pickling. The smaller cuts of meat would be ground into sausage using spices and the pig's small intestines as the casing. The sausages would be smoked, too. Cuts of the back and sides of the pigs would be rubbed with salt and put in the smokehouse to become fatback and bacon.

The butchering was hard work thought Henry, but it was fun too. The girls apparently felt the same way because they were singing as they tended the kettle, giving the cooked cracklings to the men as treats and warning them they were hot. McAdoo was laughing and humming as he butchered while a ring of pipe smoke surrounded his head. Mrs. McAdoo was using the grinder spilling the ground meat into a large mixing bowl that had the spices in it. She would run into the kitchen every so often to check on the roast, turning and basting it when needed. The sausage mixture would pass again through the grinder with a casing affixed for the sausage links. The girls helped their mother with this process. Edmund and Henry's job was to keep the fires burning properly at the smokehouse and the kettle and to help McAdoo as needed. Everyone was busy and enjoying their work. The livestock still needed tending, this wasn't ignored. The evening meal was relished as the spit roast was tender and succulent. It wasn't until late in the evening that the work was done to the mistress of the house's satisfaction. Henry fell into his cot at last exhausted, but happy. He had never had such an experience before. As he lay there considering the day's events, Henry couldn't help feeling a fondness for this family, and an odd sort of kinship. He never remembered doing one thing like this back in England and he felt a pang of sadness about it.

Pig's skins as well as the deer hide would be taken to the tanner's at Somerville when they went in for the court's inquiry. The hide of the pig could be fashioned into sturdy work gloves and pouches. Deerskin could be made into soft supple leather gloves and mittens or to make a type of shoe called a moccasin. Indeed the Indians made shirts, pants and even dresses out of deer hide. Very little went to waste if you expected to feed and keep your household comfortable over what could be a long, snowy, cold winter.

Chapter 13

The time for the court of inquiry had come. An interesting development had occurred while Henry was out hunting, too. Mrs. Hall, upon hearing of the tragic death of her beloved husband at the hands of his wretched bondservant, had returned. She claimed the body and had it decently interred and was living back at the mill. She had also heard of the nine hundred thirty seven pounds that was recovered from her late husband and was there to see she got what was coming to her. To counsel her in that endeavor she had retained the services of one Bertram Barlowe, Esq. of Trenton. If there were a prize for courtroom dandies then Barlowe would have been awarded first place. He was tall and wore a powdered wig, which only Judge Knowles saw fit to wear in his court up until now. Barlowe had a pronounced nose that he carried quite high except when looking down on someone he was examining. He was dressed in the latest colonial higher-class fashion and would have been described by the late Mr. Hall as a poppin' jay.

Court was called into session at nine a.m. with all the requested parties present. Prosecutor Land rose from his chair and began, "If it pleases your grace, the Crown at this time seeks an "et Terminus" ruling regarding its charges brought against Mr. Geoffrey Hall also formerly known as Jeffers Halstead."

Both prosecutor and judge were looking directly at Mrs. Hall when the last of Land's request was uttered. Both saw the shock that registered on the widow's face and so concluded she had no idea about her husband's former life. The formality of the court would now be played out.

"What is the reason for the Crown's motion?" asked the judge.

He knew the reason. Even the town idiot knew the reason. Judge Knowles had to ask the question in order that it became part of the court record so that the real reason for court today could be "brought into the light of day."

"Your grace, it has come to the Crown's attention that the defendant, Mr. Hall is deceased."

"The Crown's motion is hereby granted. Court will be in recess for one half hour to be reconvened at ten a.m." Knowles bent forward and softly requested his clerk meet him in chambers right away. "Jenkins, post an official court letter to the authorities in Middlesex County, Massachusetts informing them of the demise of their fugitive, Halstead. Ask them to see if the estate of his victim wishes to seek redress from this court. Now go and get me the sheriff."

Crisp entered the judge's room a few minutes later.

"Ben, I want you to be especially prepared to assist the bailiff if I order the courtroom cleared. The way the day's developments could unfold might lead to violence by some present in court."

At ten the bailiff strung the floor with his staff and pronounced, "All yea, all yea! All those present in this King's court for the Colony of New Jersey who has business before this court, bid you now come forward. You will be heard."

Land again addressed the bench. "If it pleases your grace, as it has been made a matter of record regarding the death of one Geoffrey Hall, the Crown now requests a formal inquiry into the nature of this death."

Such an inquiry was conducted to arrive at four possible conclusions, Land had told the members of the posse. The homicide would be declared criminal, justified, accidental, or unable to be determined.

What could follow an inquiry was charges (criminal), vindication (justified), civil suit (accidental), or further inquiry (indeterminate). The inquisitor, Land, would call witnesses who had direct knowledge as to the circumstances leading to the death, which was under scrutiny. In addition, the judge could examine the witnesses for clarification, and finally a qualified representative of any party of interest could examine witnesses called by Land. The realization of what was happening landed like a weight on Henry's chest. *I could be tried for murder*, he thought.

The "macaroni" now stood. "If it pleases your grace, my name is Bertram Barlowe, counsel for the widow of the decedent, Hall. I have with me credentials attesting to my qualifications."

"Approach the bench," said Knowles gruffly to the here-to-for stranger. When the jurist had finished examining what Barlowe had produced he continued, "I will tolerate no theatrics in the King's court.

You will be on a very short leash. Step back."

Land called as his first witness, Deputy Alfred Roberts. After the bailiff swore him in Land told the fidgety deputy to relax and then began by asking him his name and occupation. Now Land truly began, "Deputy Roberts, what were you doing the night of the thirteenth of November?"

"We were after Mr. Hall, who whacked me on the head and stole our sheriff's horse."

Land stifled a smile as the courtroom broke into low laughter. The judge called for order.

"And did you find Mr. Hall?"

"We sure did. He went back to his mill and that's where we caught up with 'im." Land paused only for a second and then continued, "What did you do next?"

"Well, me 'n the sheriff left Gill with the horses, 'an snuck up to a window we saw was lit up and looked in."

"What did you see through the window?"

"Mr. Hall was wearing a highwayman's pistol rig 'and pullin' a big bag of money outta a hole in the floor."

"Your grace please, as the contents of the bag has not yet been established. I must object," Barlowe had risen to his feet and made his first objection.

"Well, that's what was in it ya fancy pants!" Roberts blurted out before the judge could render his ruling.

Judge Knowles was livid and amused at the same time, "I will maintain order and decorum in this court. Deputy Roberts you will confine yourself solely to answering questions. Another such intemperate display and you won't be sweeping out the jail; you will be living in it. As to the objection, it is sustained."

Land went on with his questioning unruffled, "Now tell the court what happened."

"Ben, he yells for Hall to "Stand and hold" and that miserable skunk shoots one of his pistols at us! I got nicked on the cheek," Roberts pointed to a small scar just under his right eye.

Land paused, waiting for another objection from the widow's lawyer, and when it didn't come, said simply, "go on."

"Ben yells ta Gill to ride and fetch McAdoo and the bondsmen, then me 'n Ben got some oil soaked torches from out our packs and lit 'em.

"Why did you do that?"

"Ben said the only way out for Hall was through the front and if we stuck enough torches in the yard then we would get a good look at Hall if he made a break for it."

"Did he make a "break" for it?"

"No, Ben figured that if he didn't run then he'd get himself hold up inside tighter than a tick on a coonhound," laughter came again from the courtroom.

"Did Gill return?"

"Yep, and he had McAdoo and the boys with him. McAdoo had been some general or somethin' in the King's army so he figures up a plan to get Hall. Sheriff Crisp is plenty smart, too. He finds a wagon full 'a hay and tells Thomas we'll light it and have a run at the front porch while he and Edmund sneaks down through the roof and surprises Hall. We waited for it to get light out and then commenced."

Still no objection, Land thought, *what is Barlowe up to?* "Continue."

"Sheriff Crisp puts Gill behind a tree so he could shoot at the cur."

"Objection, your grace," Barlowe was picking lint from his silk vest and didn't even bother to stand.

"Sustained, the witness will refrain from using vulgar references for the deceased. Al, stay with the facts."

"Well, Ben fires the hay wagon and shoots his pistol to let Thomas know that things were happenin'. Me, Henry, and Ben starts pushin' the wagon towards the porch and makin' a commotion at the same time. Then Mr. Hall shoots at us and I get hit again!" Roberts raised his right shirtsleeve to reveal the angry red wound on his forearm.

"After that I don't remember much."

"Objection, your grace," this time the widow's lawyer stood. "The witness could not possibly know who shot him from his vantage point."

Land now rose, "I would cite the reasonable man's exception Crown vs. Driscoll 1768 Colony of New Jersey which states that if, from a logical perspective, no one else could have performed an act then it may be presumed a fact and therefore admissible as testimony."

"Your grace, I could give you several scenarios …"

61

"And none of them would stand the test of logic," the judge had interrupted Mrs. Hall's barrister abruptly. "Motion is overruled."

This was a court of inquiry where wider latitude in testimony was allowed. If it had been a capital murder trial, for example, the judge would have been less inclined to overrule the motion.

"I have finished with this witness for the moment, your grace," Land said to the court.

"If it pleases your grace, I should like to examine this witness," Barlowe had not sat back down.

"You may do so, Mr. Barlowe," responded Knowles.

The widow's counsel slowly walked toward the seated witness, "Why were you, deputy Gill and sheriff Crisp at Hall's Mill on the night in question?"

Roberts' answer was forthright, "Because Ben 'ah, Sheriff Crisp is a good sheriff. He figured out that a man like Mr. Hall does what he does for only one reason. Greed. That means he's not runnin' until he gets his loot. So we go there and Ben was right."

"So you went to the mill expecting to find the deceased with a large amount of money?"

"We went to the mill to catch Mr. Hall," Roberts corrected the attorney.

"Let's move on. When you shouted to Mr. Hall through the window did you announce yourselves as peace officers?"

"No, not exactly," said Roberts, now a little unsure.

"Well, then exactly what was said, Mr. Roberts?"

"Ben shouted "Stand and hold" to Mr. Hall."

"Stand and hold? Like what some highwayman might say to his victim?"

Roberts was now completely befuddled.

"I have no further questions for this witness, your grace," and with that, Barlowe triumphantly walked to his chair.

Land was up and out of his seat in an instant, "With your grace's permission I should like to examine this witness further."

"Granted," the judge replied.

"Deputy Roberts, you stated that Mr. Hall, I believe the term you used was whacked you on the head."

"Yes sir, he made me see stars."

"You were quite angry at Mr. Hall for doing that to you weren't you?"

"Well, I wasn't exactly happy with him."

"Did you want to kill Mr. Hall for doing that to you?"

"No sir, of course not."

"Did any of the three of you talk of killing Mr. Hall while you were pursuing him to his mill?"

"No sir, I don't think that we thought about that at all. None of us wanted to kill Mr. Hall. We wanted to catch him."

"The Crown has nothing further, your grace."

When Barlowe didn't stand, Judge Knowles began his own examination, "Deputy Roberts, the court should like to know why you and the others were pursuing Mr. Hall in the first place."

"Like I said, your lordship, he knocked me out and stole Ben's mare."

The judge, somewhat amused at his promotion to the peerage, sought further clarification, "Ah ha, let's try it this way. What were you doing just before Mr. Hall incapacitated you?"

"Taking off his leg irons so he could use the privy."

The exasperated judge went on summoning his little remaining patience, "And why was he in leg irons?"

"So he couldn't get away?" answered the deputy, again unsure.

"God grant me strength to suffer fools like this!" the judge exploded. "Strike that last utterance," he commanded his clerk.

"Deputy Roberts, was Mr. Hall in your custody?"

"Yes"

"And why was Mr. Hall in your custody?"

"'Cause he was standing trial for stealing. Gosh, your lordship, everybody knows that."

"Step down!" Judge Knowles face was a vivid red and his face twitched as he roared. "This inquiry is in recess for an hour. Jenkins, summon Land and that idiot's boss to my chambers now!"

A short while later in chambers Judge Knowles exploded, "I am going to control this inquiry or there will be hell to pay. In my nearly twenty years on the bench, I have never come so close to committing a physical assault on a witness as I did just now. You two are here to assure me that this will not occur again," Land and Crisp looked at each other and then at Knowles who was staring fire at them.

"Crisp, you are next on the Crown's list of witnesses. Reassure me that you are somewhat smarter than that dunce, Roberts."

"I'm not makin' any excuses for my deputy, you grace, but this might be the second time he was ever on the witness seat."

"I'm taking that into account. It's the reason he wasn't found in contempt for his last outburst. Mr. Land, I'm counting on you to move this inquiry forward. I won't tolerate a repeat of this morning."

"I fully understand your grace," The prosecutor said.

"Good, good, then leave me. Jenkins! Go get that peacock, Barlowe for me."

As Land reached the room's threshold he turned to the judge and remarked, "Roberts was just answering truthfully, your grace."

"Get out!"

Chapter 14

Bertram Barlowe always tried to make an entrance. He did so now into the judge's chambers.

"Mr. Barlowe, as you represent an interested party in this inquiry, this court has seen fit to grant you a certain amount of latitude in your examination. However, this court will not tolerate unsubstantiated claims that impugn the reputation of an officer of this court. If Land doesn't see fit to yank you back by objection, I will."

"Your grace, my only purpose here is to best represent the interests of the deceased's widow, nothing more," the barrister responded in a somewhat condescending tone.

"I have my hand on your leash," warned the judge.

The inquiry resumed one hour later. The inquisitor began by calling Sheriff Crisp to the witness seat. After standard preliminary questions were asked and answered, Land requested, "Tell us, sheriff about the night in question."

Crisp corroborated Robert's testimony and added, "We knocked in the front door when we heard the gunshot. Gill and I went upstairs. Young Henry stayed with Roberts tending to his wound. When we got up there, Thomas McAdoo was bent over Mr. Hall and I heard Crane call down from the roof asking if he was dead."

"Who was dead?" Land asked as a point of clarification.

"Mr. Hall, sir," Crisp answered.

"Go on."

"McAdoo answers that he was deader than a stone and Crane commences to cryin'. I'm still about collectin' my thoughts when McAdoo says ta me…"

"Objection. What the witness is about to say is hearsay testimony, your grace." Barlowe was correct and not correct. While it is indeed hearsay and not allowed in criminal trials it is however permissible testimony in civil cases and inquiries such as this.

"Overruled, you may continue, sheriff."

"Ah, McAdoo says ta me, "That man would have killed me, certain if Edmund hadn't shot first.""

"What happened next?" asked Land.

"We got Crane down off the roof, carried the dead man downstairs, tied him to a horse, fetched the moneybag from downstairs in the mill and tied it to Clover, my horse, got Roberts up on his horse, and then we came back."

"If it pleases your grace, just a question or two of this witness, if I may," Barlowe slowly stood as he spoke.

"Go on," was the bench's brief reply.

"Sheriff Crisp, you testified that when you entered the upstairs room Mr. Hall was already dead."

"Yes, he was," Crisp verified.

"Now let me take you back to the day you arrested Mr. Hall. Who was with you when you made the arrest?"

"McAdoo was there and his bondsman, the St. Albans boy, Henry."

"Did Hall need to be restrained at the time of his arrest?"

"Yes, you see Hall had ..."

"Your yes will do nicely," Barlowe quickly put in. "Now, sheriff who did the restraining?"

"Thomas."

"You mean Mr. McAdoo?"

"Yes."

"Did Mr. McAdoo happen to say anything to Mr. Hall while he was restraining him?"

"That is hearsay, your grace."

"What's good for the goose is good for the gander, Mr. Land, over-ruled," Knowles stated.

"Please tell this inquiry what Mr. McAdoo said to Mr. Hall while he was restraining him?"

Ben Crisp squirmed a bit in his seat and then declared, "Thomas said that if there was ta be any killin' done on this day, then he would be the one doin' the killin'.""

"Nothing further of this man, your grace," said Bertram Barlow with a smirk on his face.

"This court of inquiry is in recess until two o'clock this afternoon."

With that, judge Knowles retired to his chambers. Land went over to the room where Henry, Gill, Edmund, and McAdoo were sequestered away from the proceedings, waiting.

"Gill, you're next on the witness list to be called, but something has happened at the inquiry that compels me to call Thomas before you."

Gill seemed relieved. He also was a new deputy and was agonizing over being called to the stand.

"Sure, I'll go next," McAdoo affirmed. "I've got a few things ta say about that murderous cur."

"Thomas, it might not be easy to bring in facts about Hall's former life."

"Why not, you called him Halstead back at the start. I know 'cause Ben told me so."

After he testified, Ben raced back to the witness room and quickly brought everyone up to date about the inquiry. Land would have to have a talk with the sheriff about this. Such an act in a criminal trial could result in a mistrial.

"That was done so I could judge Mrs. Hall's reaction and frankly, Barlowe let me get away with it. You were Hall's accuser and had made murderous utterances concerning Hall that other people heard."

"What if I did?" said McAdoo. "He had been cheating me and plenty others like me outta what was rightfully ours. I was very angry at him."

Land was suddenly glad that the large man beside him wasn't angry with him.

"We need to lessen the impact of the last witness's testimony. I will do that if you just answer my questions truthfully and remember to keep your temper while in the witness seat."

"I'm a very even-tempered man."

With the last remark, Henry and Edmund stared wide-eyed at each other and tried not to laugh.

Barlowe was in council with his client, the widow Hall during the mid-day recess.

"We're making points, but I'm not sure if there will be enough of them to sway the judge to our way of thinking," Barlowe told Mrs. Hall.

"You're bein' paid a good deal of money to see to it that I get that money those buffoons took off my dead husband. And I want to see

McAdoo and that Crane whelp swing for killin' my dear Geoffrey."
Claudia Hall was not mincing any words. How sincere Mrs. Hall was
about anything but the money her counsel still hadn't ascertained.

"One goal might lead us to the other," Barlowe reasoned. "I must
get to that red-bearded giant when I get him on the stand. If I can make
him lose control, and then break that bondservant, I believe the ruling
could go our way."

"See that you do it then," commanded his client.

Chapter 15

The court of inquiry reconvened promptly at two o'clock in the afternoon. Terrence Land called Thomas McAdoo to the stand after informing the court and interested parties of the change in the witness list. McAdoo was duly sworn in and after the initial questioning, Land began examining the farmer in earnest.

"Could you please tell this inquiry what transpired at your farm on the evening of this past thirteenth of November?"

"At about an hour after sunset deputy John Gill rode into my yard making a ruckus. When I went out onto the porch, John called to me that Sheriff Crisp had Hall trapped at the mill and needed our help to capture him. Me and the boys got what we needed and rode back with the deputy to the mill."

"How did you find things when you arrived, Mr. McAdoo?"

"Well, the yard was lit by torches and Roberts was cut on the face. Ben told us how Hall had fired at them with a pistol. I quickly saw that while he couldn't get out, we couldn't get in without a few of us getting killed, so we came up with a plan to capture Hall without any blood being spilled."

McAdoo then described the plan in detail up to the point of dropping down through the roof.

"What occurred next, Mr. McAdoo?"

"As I was righting myself from the jump, I saw Hall come out of the shadows into the sun."

"Was Mr. Hall holding anything?"

"He had a cocked pistol aimed at my mid-section and he had a mad look on his face."

"Objection, witness is not qualified to make such an observation." The widow's counsel was attempting to earn his fee.

"About the weapon or the man's facial expression?" deadpanned Land.

"Counselors to the bench!" the two men approached the judge.

"Both of you continue to try the court's patience. Land, that last remark has cost you a pound for contempt. More fines in open court are awaiting either of you if you are not mindful of the weight this seat commands."

Both men returned to their places, one of them a bit poorer for his wit.

"Describe the look on Mr. Hall's face for the court," Land instructed.

"It is a face that I shall never forget. His eyes were wide and filled with hate. His nose was flared, and spit was dripping from one side of his mouth. He was breathing heavily."

"Did Mr. Hall say anything to you?"

"Yes, he told me to be still," Thomas's face tensed and he looked off into the distance. "Then he accused me of being the cause of his troubles."

"Did he say anything else to you, Mr. McAdoo?"

The farmer sat up straight in the witness chair and focused on the inquisitor, "What he said was quite strange. He said, "Behold farmer, the righteous Hand of God!""

The thought of the dead man's last words had a deep effect on McAdoo. It also had an impact on all in attendance. Terrance Land allowed a moment to pass before his asked his next question, "What happened next?"

Chapter 16

McAdoo stroked his red beard and cleared his throat. It was clear that remembering the details of the event was hard on the big man.

"A gunshot; it was loud and the smoke blocked my vision. I thought for a moment that Hall had fired his pistol, but I saw him lying on the floor when the smoke cleared. Then I imagined that Hall's pistol had misfired and injured him, but when Edmund's piece fell through the roof I knew the lad had shot him. I went over to the downed man to check him and saw he was gone. There were noises coming from downstairs then the sheriff and Gill arrived in the room."

"Mr. McAdoo, you mentioned that Edmund Crane was with you when you scaled the wall onto the roof and that he had shot through the hole in the roof you had just passed through. Could you tell what he was doing at this time?"

"He was up there bawling like a young calf. Then he asked me if the miller was dead and I told him that he was. He started fussin' even louder."

Land wrapped up his questioning of McAdoo by having him describe what the posse did at the scene and on the journey back to Somerville. He was puzzled by the lack of objections by Barlowe. He was about to discover why.

Bertram Barlowe, Esq. slowly rose from his chair and addressed the court, "By your kind consent, your grace, I should like to examine this witness. Further, depending on the direction of examination, I request some latitude in the examination."

Knowles glanced quickly at Crisp as an alert then stared directly at the questioner.

"It is granted, Sir. But remember I will pull you back so fast you will be dizzy from the experience if you cross my line."

Barlowe smiled slyly and began his inquiry of the witness, "Mr. McAdoo, what was your profession before you became master of Stony Brook?"

"I have twenty-five years in his majesty's Royal Highlander's regiment, the last eight years spent at the rank of sergeant major." Said the red bearded man with great pride in his years in service for king and country.

"Now in those years of service, did you happen to see any fighting?"

"I should hope to tell you I did, both here and on the continent."

"And in these engagements, were there ever any close quarters fighting?"

"Indeed, sir. Once there was this Huron who raced towards me with a stone war club," McAdoo leaned forward and continued, "I had just fired my rifle and knew I hadn't time to reload. The savage knew it, too. He ran headlong into my bayonet and swung his club as his dying act. That warrior knocked my tam o'shanter clear off my head giving me quite a head wound."

"Did you happen to see the expression on the Indian's face?"

The ex-sergeant major looked to the floor and with a voice suddenly subdued replied, "I see that red man often in my dreams."

"Yes, my good man, but can you tell us of the man's expression?"

"Up until he was mortally wounded his eyes were wide and he had a hideous smile on his lips."

"Would you say that was the expression of a man locked in combat or a man locked in madness?"

"Objection, your grace," Land wasn't about to let this pass. "While Mr. McAdoo might be an expert as to the former, Mr. Barlowe, by his earlier objection, knows he is not expert on the latter."

"The question is withdrawn," replied Barlow before the judge had time to make his ruling. "Mr. McAdoo, would you say that the profession of soldiering is a profession of violence?"

"I would say that soldiering is a profession of duty, honor, discipline, and service sir."

"But by its very nature going to war is an act of violence is it not?"

"Yes it is," the farmer admitted.

"The rank of sergeant major is quite an achievement for a man beginning as a conscript, isn't it Mr. McAdoo?"

The trap was being set, both Land and Knowles knew it, but neither could stop it until a legal line was crossed. *Keep your temper.* Land thought.

Knowles also knew where this could head. He was bound by his own sense of duty to rule on Hall's death by what was presented in the proceeding in spite of any personal thoughts about the matter. This barrister Barlowe knew his craft and was plowing ahead to introduce evidence that might lead to a wrongful death ruling with even a conspiracy thrown in.

"Isn't it true that your promotions up the ranks were due to your performance on the field of battle?"

"Most times it was because of what I done in battle, but near as often it was due a thinning of our ranks."

"Would you please explain?"

"For instance, when McClellan, our first sergeant, got killed at Poitiers the captain called me into his tent and says, "Allen's had it. You're the new first sergeant.""

"So in battle, whether you did the killing or someone above you was killed; that was how you were promoted."

"Yes, I guess it was," McAdoo had never looked at his rise in rank in that way before and it unnerved him a bit.

"So it was the violence of battle that accounted for your advancement in your career." At this point the Trenton lawyer turned away from the witness and faced the judge, "Violence addressed your needs; got you what you wanted."

The judge eyed both bailiff and sheriff sensing the need to be ready. They both took up positions nearer the witness chair.

Land wanted to break in and diffuse the situation somehow, but he still had no grounds. He stood and shouted, "What does the sergeant major's resume have to do with this inquiry?"

"It goes to the state of mind of this witness which has a great deal to do with this inquiry," the widow's counsel quickly retorted.

"Overruled," the bench responded ignoring his earlier admonition.

"Hall did you a great wrong, didn't he Mr. McAdoo?"

"Aye, and thirty others like me." The big man was confused and agitated; he gripped the arms of the witness seat tightly.

Barlowe faced the witness and pointed his finger at him, "Violence got you what you wanted in the past, why not now? You are a violent man aren't you Mr. McAdoo?"

"Only when provoked!"

The red bearded giant was on his feet and nearly had his examiner by the time the bailiff and sheriff got to him. Land motioned for the farmer to sit back down before any further damage was done. McAdoo, realizing he had been played for a fool, slumped back into his seat.

"No further questions, you grace," Barlowe paraded triumphantly back to his chair.

"With your grace's kind permission, I should like to ask the witness an additional question or two," Land had to rehabilitate this witness in the eyes of the court. A great deal of the final outcome could be weighed on his success.

"Proceed."

"When did you become a pensioner, Mr. McAdoo?"

"It was seven years ago, last month," the farmer answered.

"And in those seven years, until this current trouble, have you ever threatened to kill another man?"

"No, sir."

"Have you even struck another man in anger?"

"No, sir."

"Mr. McAdoo, in the past seven years have you even raised your voice to another man?" the big man's face reddened.

"I'm not proud of it. I have a bit of a temper," everyone in attendance unconsciously nodded in agreement to this admission.

"I'm like one of our Navy's assault rockets. I flare up, fly off, and explode, but after the explosion I'm over it. I confess I've raised my voice a time or two. Like when I told the Nolan boy to head for home when I caught him makin' improper advances toward my Abigail two Sunday's ago. He tried to hold her hand while walking home from the church meeting."

Land couldn't help but smile, "Please tell the court why you chose to become a farmer."

"It was the one thing I could do to give life, like when a calf is born or a new planting of grain is growing in the field. I wanted to be about giving life after twenty-five years of taking it."

"One last question, if you please. How old were you when you were brevetted into the Royal Highlanders?"

"I had just turned fifteen. I was big for my age."

You're big for any age. The inquisitor thought. "Your grace, I'm finished with this witness."

Edmund Crane was the next witness on the list. Henry and deputy Gill could still be called, but Land was hoping to end the inquiry with the young man currently on the stand. After initial questioning, Land asked,

"Mr. Crane, you are currently in a condition called voluntary indenture-ship are you not?"

"Yes, er, I don't know. My master, Mr. Hall is dead."

"Legally, until this court makes its ruling, all contracts are in force," Judge Knowles explained to the witness. The questioning continued.

"How long had you been indentured to Mr. Hall?"

"Four years and four months, on a seven year contract."

"Did Mr. Hall ever hit you?"

"Yes, sir nearly every day and I got the worst beatings if I didn't do what he thought I ought to be doin'."

It seemed like Land was doing Barlowe's job for him by introducing Crane's mistreatment at the hands of Hall. But by bringing it out first, Land hoped to control its portrayal and lessen its impact.

"What were you given to eat in a typical day?"

"Mornings I'd get a bowl of thin oatmeal or barley gruel. At noon a soup made from potato peelings or other table leavin's. For supper a mealy bit a meat or sometimes nothin' at all if he was mad at me."

"How were you clothed?"

"It was mostly from Mr. Hall's old things, but I was a good deal taller and thinner than my master so they didn't fit too good."

"Didn't Mrs. Hall alter the clothes to fit you?"

Claudia Hall sat bolt upright in her chair at the mention of her name.

"Mrs. Hall didn't want anything to do with me. She called out Mr. Hall for having me in the first place saying I was a waste of good money."

"Now let us talk about the morning of the fourteenth," Land brought the witness through the details leading him up to the point where McAdoo had dropped through the roof. "After Mr. McAdoo entered the bedroom, what happened next?"

"I was gettin' ready to jump when I saw a glint off the pistol Mr. Hall was aiming at Mr. McAdoo."

"Objection!" Barlowe was up, "The witness had no idea where the pistol was pointed."

Knowles was tired of this peacock parading in his court.

"As a prior witness, who is expert in such matters, has already testified to that fact, I will allow it. Go on, Mr. Crane."

"I jumped back and pulled out the pistol from my belt. As Mr. Hall came forward into the light he was swearing at Mr. McAdoo. I saw then that his pistol was cocked so I cocked mine. My master was shouting and when he raised his arm I aimed at him and pulled the trigger. Oh my God, I killed my master!"

Reliving the event brought back the flood of memories and Edmund broke down into a quiet sobbing.

"Mr. Crane, can you continue?" asked the judge.

"Yes, your grace. I will be fine."

Land went back to be seated and Barlowe asked the court's permission to be allowed to examine Crane which was allowed reluctantly.

"When you were Mr. Hall's servant, he beat you and half-starved you."

"Yes sir, I've already said that he was hard on me."

"And you toiled long hours for this man, didn't you?"

"From early morning until into the night sometimes."

"What all did you do for Mr. Hall?"

"I loaded and unloaded the wagons that came to the mill. I swept the store and kept the place tidy for doing business. I also ran the grinding most of the time, and kept the gears and pulleys of the works in good repair."

"As a result of this treatment you deeply resented, even hated Mr. Hall, isn't that correct?"

"Yes, I hated him," as Crane said it, it was almost a relief.

"Hated him enough to want him dead? To kill him? Here was your opportunity. You could just shoot him and be done with it!"

"For the love of God, objection, your grace! This is merely a blatant badgering of this witness, not an examination."

"Sustained, you know better Mr. Barlowe. That last bit of histrionics will cost you a pound for contempt."

Worth it, thought Barlowe as he saw Crane glowering at him. *I didn't break him, Land did that. I did something better.* "I'm done with this witness, your grace."

"Call your next witness, Mr. Land," the bench instructed.

"The crown is satisfied with the evidence presented in this inquiry and wishes to call no further witnesses."

Now here is where a court's inquiry differs from a criminal or civil trial. There is no other side per say so no list of witnesses from any of the interested parties can be called. There are no closing arguments as there aren't recognized sides in arriving at the truth in this type of session.

Judge Knowles now addressed the assemblage, "As the hour is getting late, I will take all evidence gathered in this inquiry under advisement and will render the court's decision tomorrow morning. Court is to be reconvened at nine a.m."

And with an, "All rise!" by the bailiff, the judge was swiftly off to his chambers closely followed by his clerk. Those present at the inquiry made their way outside. No one felt sure about the decision and it weighed heavily on a number of them.

"It sounds to me like Crane murdered his master," a shopkeeper opined. He had a bondsman himself and didn't want him getting any ideas.

"From the way the miller was treat 'n 'em, I don't blame the boy for killin 'em," offered up a farmer. "I'd a liked to have had a chance at him myself."

"The judge will rule on whether Edmond's action in taking Mr. Hall's life was with malice, was reckless, or was justified," all those in the discussion turned around and faced the last speaker, it was Henry. "As he acted to save the life of my master, Thomas McAdoo, I am confident in the court's ruling regarding Edmund."

With that Henry strode past the gawkers and joined Edmund and the McAdoo family.

Chapter 17

The widow Hall and her lawyer were supping together at the tavern.

"Well sir, what do think the old fart will do tomorrow?"

Barlowe chewed thoughtfully on his beef roast and replied, "He gave no real indication one way or the other, but I believe my performance today in court just might induce him to bring in a ruling of wrongful death. Not so much from how I started with the deputy and the sheriff; it was how I ended with the farmer and that servant boy."

Barlowe was full of himself and the widow told him as much and then added. "I saw the way that Crane filth looked at you. He would have shot you with the pistol he used on my dear Geoffrey if he had it in his hand. You seem to have earned the contingency fee we agreed on."

The legal "macaroni" nodded and both continued their meal in silence.

It was a quiet evening meal at Stony Brook as well. Finally Mrs. McAdoo could stand it no more and demanded the men tell her about the inquiry. Her husband looked at her and answered in a subdued tone.

"I don't think either Edmund or I did too well on the stand today. Thank God Henry was spared that experience. I lost my temper after I was warned against it and I witnessed that crafty lawyer twisting round a lifesaving act into a merciless act of revenge by Edmund."

Henry thought about what his master said. *Barlowe wouldn't have had such an easy time with me on the stand. Edmund and Mr. McAdoo both had been terribly abused by the miller while I did not. I should have been the one to go up on the roof instead of Edmund.*

A drawn look appeared on the boy's face as he carried on his thoughts. *If I had been the one up on the roof then it would have been up to me to shoot Hall. I don't know if I could have done it.*

Edmund put down his fork and his eyes seemed to blaze as he recalled the eternity he spent on the witness stand that afternoon.

"It was so painful to speak of that morning in court and then when that man started on about how I hated my master and wanted to see him dead I realized, heaven help me, that it was true. I didn't want to be the one to kill him though. I had to do what I did to keep my master from killing you, sir. That being the truth still doesn't give me much comfort," Crane glanced at his benefactor and then off into the distance. "I did want to kill that lawyer today, though."

Land was having a tankard of ale in the tavern when Jenkins passed returning from having delivered the judge his meal along with a bottle of dry sack.

"Any news?" the attorney asked the judge's clerk.

"I brought him all the transcripts from the proceedings along with several volumes of law he requested. He tells me then he wants a joint of mutton and some bread and cheese, then he says, "Fetch me a bottle of old dry as I won't be sleeping much tonight." I did as he wished and he kicks me out without another word!"

Land considered what the clerk had told him and said to no one in particular, "I won't be getting much sleep tonight either."

The next morning the courtroom was packed. Everyone wanted to be there to hear the judgment. Henry, McAdoo and Crane were in the front row along with the McAdoo females. Constance and her daughters would not miss this ruling as it could have life altering consequences for them all. The sheriff and deputy Gill were present as was Mrs. Hall and her counsel. Jenkins prepared to record the session while the bailiff called the court to order. All stood as Judge Knowles entered and then took his seat with the assemblage upon the bailiff of the court's instruction.

Knowles took a sip of water and began, "I have read all the transcripts and reviewed case law at my disposal that pertains to this inquiry. It has been a long and convoluted set of facts and arguments that I have had to go through to arrive at the truth of the matter. A strong argument was made about the men that apprehended and ultimately took the life of the decedent. Nearly all seemed to have had a motive for seeking revenge from the deceased and they all appeared on the surface to have acted in a conspiratorial manner to the end the life of the man in question, Hall. The facts remain however, that this group was legally appointed acting within the bounds of the law in order to apprehend a fugitive from justice. There was no negligent death and likewise no accidental death in this instance and the court has heard sufficient testimony to rule on whether the death was wrongful or justified. The overwhelming weight of evidence leads me to the conclusion..." Everyone leaned forward in their seats. "That while the outcome was far from desirable, it was nonetheless justified. Edmund Crane is exonerated as are all other parties involved in the death of Jeffers Halstead alias Geoffrey Hall."

It was like air was let out of Mrs. Hall. She made an audible exhaling sound and stared angrily at the lawyer setting next to her.

Knowles continued with his ruling, "I am prepared to probate the estate of the executrix, Geoffrey Hall heretofore known to be Jeffers Halstead, at this time."

At this pronouncement both Barlowe and the widow Hall sat up alertly.

"The court has received word by special dispatch last evening that has confirmed the identity of Geoffrey Hall as that of Jeffers Halstead, a fugitive from justice and accused by Middlesex County in Massachusetts of the crimes of capital murder and theft. The claim on Mr. Halstead by the estate of his late victim is for a sum of six hundred seventy two pounds which I will order be taken from the impounded assets of Jeffers Halstead and transferred to the estate of Frederick Timmons through the estate's agents. Now I will deal with the swindling of the farmers here in Somerset County. Since the criminal charges have been dropped by necessity the court has introduced a civil lien against the estate of Jeffers Halstead."

"Can he do that?" Mrs. Hall blurted to her lawyer.

"He can and he has," Barlowe dryly replied.

After a sharp look in the direction of the widow, Knowles went on, "The court hereby awards to the collective group the deeded property of the estate to include the house and mill works and the surrounding pasture. Additionally the sum of five pounds shall be paid to each party of the group. The Halstead estate shall pay all court costs which amount to forty-eight pounds, four shillings and a tuppence."

"That only leaves sixty two pounds!" Claudia Hall cried out in open court.

"That leaves sixty one pounds." corrected the judge "I fine you

Mrs. Hall, one pound for contempt of court."

The sullen widow looked to her counsel who could only impotently shrug.

Judge Knowles adjusted his wig and continued, "Now, as to the contract of Indenture-ship that existed between the decedent and Edmund Crane. This contract was solely between those parties named in the contract and upon the death of either party, the contract is null and void."

Crane looked at McAdoo and whispered, "Am I Free?"

"Aye ya are, my boy," the Scotsman smiled.

Crane started shouting "I'm Free" right in court.

"Bailiff, get that free man out of here," the judge ordered wryly. Waiting until his instruction was accomplished, the jurist finished, "Finally certain other valuables were found in the possession of Mr. Halstead at the time of his death. To wit a gold signet ring found to be the ring of Mr. Halstead's victim, Timmons. And a gold necklace with ruby stones which looks to be of considerable value."

"It was his mother's necklace," as Claudia Hall spoke, she seemed stripped of all the hardness she had previously displayed. "He showed it to me once right after we were first married. Geoffrey loved his mother very much though she died while he was quite young. I guess he loved the memory of her. He spoke of her often and with reverence. That was the one thing he had that was hers and he would never part with it."

Judge Knowles was moved by the lady's revelation, "It proves once again that there are no totally evil men. Mrs. Hall, that article is allotted to you along with the balance of the estate's assets. This court is adjourned."

The judge was out of the room before the bailiff could call the court to rise.

Chapter 18

It was over. The biggest event in Somerset County's history up to that time was over. But it wasn't completely over yet. A meeting of the thirty-one farmers was called for that Sunday after church meeting. In addition to the landowners, Pastor Simmons and Edmund Crane were asked to attend. Henry had stayed because Edmund had asked his master's permission. Henry also was present because of his talent in reading the written word. Pastor Simmons made that request of his red bearded parishioner. The young bondsman was excited to be part of the meeting. It felt like a coming of age and also he felt the further sense of belonging in the community, not just at the farmstead. Simmons now offered a prayer before the meeting began.

Thomas McAdoo then stood and began the meeting, "All of us are here today because the judge made us owners of Bound Brook mill. First off do any of you know how to run a mill?"

A farmer named Price stood and spoke, "There's a few of us that could learn the trade quick, but that's not the problem. Not a man here has the time to do the job."

Now the pastor rose and addressed the group, "My friends, the answer is setting here today among us. Edmund Crane is well versed in operation of the mill and could continue to manage its operation for your group."

Price picked up on the idea, "We could pay him a fair wage from the profits we make and everyone makes out fine, much better than before."

"You need to set up a compact first and then there needs to be an employment contract for Edmund," Henry stated.

"Seems we have a solicitor among us and didn't know it," Boomed McAdoo and the men exploded into laughter.

"Henry's right," said Simmons, "I'll help you with the compact and the contract and Henry will help me."

The group appointed officers and details on Edmund's contract were drawn.

"What shall we name our business?" someone asked.

Finally the name, The Somerville Grain Cooperative, was approved. One of the items the newly freed mill manager insisted on in his contract was that when the grinding season was over and the mill became a retail operation that he be allowed to ply his trade as a carpenter if he could find a replacement to mind the store. Now everyone highly suspected a "replacement" in such a situation meant a wife. No other partner would be truer to Edmund's trust or work harder at the task. Tongues would be wagging.

Pastor Simmons asked to speak to Henry and Thomas privately after the meeting about an idea he had concerning the children of his congregation.

"I've prayed about this since Henry entered your home, Thomas and now I'm asking you to let your man teach a school class on Sunday. He is competent in both the written word and with figures. And he has a better than average knowledge of the scriptures."

"I don't know Pastor; he's needed at home and with Edmund at the mill now it will fall back to Henry to help me keep the farm running as it should," the farmer looked sheepishly at the ground as he spoke.

"And what a sinner you appear to be, Thomas McAdoo," the clergyman was sorely affected by McAdoo's reaction and let him know it with his loud pronouncement.

"First, Edmund Crane wasn't your bondsman to begin with and I'm sure that the amount of work you had him do more than paid for his room and board. More importantly Sunday is a day of rest meant for peaceful reflection and meditation on the Word of God and, until now, I believe I was among the few of my parish that would truly do so. You reaffirm my fear. Henry has a skill that can benefit the entire community and you are a selfish man if you don't allow him to use his talent."

"Why can't you do it, pastor?" McAdoo sheepishly asked.

"I can and will but I need your man's help. I'm stretched thin with all my duties as the shepherd of my flock and a venture of this type hadn't a chance of success until now. With Henry starting the young ones and teaching them the basic elements of reading, writing, and arithmetic it allows me to take the more advanced pupils and continue developing those skills until there would be many among us that have the blessings of literacy."

Henry's master was thunderstruck. There was no man on earth the big Scotsman feared, but he did have a healthy fear of God. This was God's man here on earth condemning him as a sinner and he was quite uneasy about it.

"What if Henry doesn't want do it?" asked the chastened man.

"I want to do it," Henry replied before he realized he had spoken.

"Good, then its settled," said the minister. "Henry, I have ten copies of a book called "The New England Reader." I also have a chalk board which will be mounted to the wall for next week."

"We'll need slates, too," again Henry spoke before he could catch himself.

"And you'll have them for your class, Henry," the pastor smiled at the young man. Then he fixed his smile on McAdoo.

Henry was beaming. *I'll be back in a classroom even if it is only one day a week and this time I'll be at the rostrum,* he thought.

The ride back to Stony Brook was a quiet one until the big man broke the silence by saying, "It'll be a good thing we'll be doing for the community, Henry."

Then he winked and smiled at the boy. It seemed that McAdoo had warmed to the idea after he had time to reflect on it.

"This is just the opportunity Katherine needs to learn the written word and be able to calculate figures so she can take on those duties at Stony Brook when my indenture-ship is over," Henry looked at Katherine's father expecting his agreement.

I don't believe Kate or any other girl needs teach 'n other than at the knee of their mother. Teach the boys who'll be their husband's someday," the huge man shifted in his seat and spurred his horse on with a crack of the reins.

Henry was surprised at his master's parochial attitude. He knew McAdoo's younger daughter had a natural ability and an inborn determination that would let her excel in the classroom.

Henry had to say something, "Kate would be a natural in the classroom. She could thrive there and still learn the duties of the home from Mrs. McAdoo. Letting it up to the man she might marry someday is not the best plan in my estimation."

McAdoo squared around and faced Henry, "Abigail is my first

born. Shouldn't you be worried for her and her prospects?"
The rest of the trip was completed in silence.

Chapter 19

Edmund Crane was now the manager of the Somerville Grain Co-operative and had a growing carpentry business on the side. He was young and handsome, in a word, a catch. Many eligible women in the area had designs on him. Edmund on the other hand had come to know and love McAdoo's daughter, Abigail and the feeling was mutual. The big obstacle to Edmund's way of thinking was the intimidating red haired Scotsman father of hers that reminded him of the giant from the Bible, Goliath. He knew without any doubt he was no David. True, he had saved the man's life, but this was his eldest daughter. Sweat formed on his forehead when he thought about it.

Henry tried to encourage his friend with little effect. It seemed hopeless until the bondservant came up with a plan. He shared his idea with Edmund and saw the glimmer of hope rise in the young miller's eyes. This would be a way, maybe the only way, to discover if McAdoo would consent to the union. For now he would have to be content with the few moments he had Sundays with his Abigail. This was his only opportunity to see her since he had moved from Stony Brook to the mill. The protective father had hawk's eyes when it came to the moths attracted to his auburn haired flame of a daughter, Abigail.

Mrs. McAdoo knew of the young couple's feelings for one another and she approved. She occupied her husband's attention after the service so Edmund and Abigail could have a few private moments together.

"Thomas, I've left my shawl back at my seat in church. Please go and fetch it for me."

"I'll send Henry," her husband said.

"Henry is teaching now and Katherine is with him, you go," Constance was craftily steering her husband clear of his daughter and her suitor.

The first Sunday of the new Sunday school had arrived. Henry had eight students in his class including his master's youngest daughter,

Katherine. Constance had used her wifely persuasion to convince McAdoo that "his" idea of sending their youngest to class was an excellent idea.

The New England Readers that each student had told stories from the Bible in such a way that those first learning to read and write could, with instruction, follow along. Henry knew that the more basic elements of the alphabet needed to be taught before the readers could be used so the time-honored process of learning the letters began. Henry discovered a joy in leading these children through the 26 shapes and their sounds. The lesson began.

"A" is for Adam whose sin stained us all," read Henry as he wrote the letter "A" on the chalkboard. "Now I want you to make the letter "A" on your slates."

As he looked over his class Henry happily realized that it was a typical class with one big exception, among the classes shining faces there was the face of Katherine beaming back at him. In Great Britain, boys and girls were separated for their education. Without knowing it, Henry was part of an innovation in education that would eventually take over and become a common reality.

Edmund and Abigail did have their private moment together, thanks to Constance's quick thinking.

"You promise you will ask Father for my hand this Christmas, Edmund?" Abigail was growing more beautiful in Edmund's eyes each time he saw her.

"Henry and I have come up with a way to ask for your father's blessing which will hopefully win him over."

"Here comes father," with Abigail's warning both stepped back to a respectable distance.

"Ah, Edmund, How goes it, boy? Me and the Missus want you to come to supper this evening," McAdoo boomed the invitation as he placed the shawl around his wife's shoulders.

"Yes, thank you for your kindness, sir," Edmund was supremely pleased.

"Please, call me Thomas. You're the manager of a good business and have another trade to boot. And Edmund, you're a free man."

The big man's warmth encouraged the sweethearts and his wife as well.

Sunday school was finally over and the pupils filed out of the class.

"How was it, Kate?" her father asked her.

"I like it very much, Pa. And Henry is a good teacher," said Kate as she bounded into the wagon beside her mother and sister. Henry stood at the church doorway discussing the day's lesson with Pastor Simmons.

"The class went quite well, I thought. The mix of boys and girls caused no disturbance, but the boys from the town seem to look down on Caleb and Katherine.

Six of the pupils were sons of town merchants and felt themselves superior to the farmers' children. In terms of a pecking order, it seems those that deem themselves the biggest and strongest always seem to exert themselves in the beginning. But even though Caleb is shy, I believe he'll hold his own against the others. And as for Kate, none of them would stand a tinker's dam of a chance if she gets her back up."

"How did they treat you, Henry?" Pastor Simmons worried that one or two of the bigger boys might try to bully the bondservant because of his situation.

"I was a senior boy at a prep school in England. I know a thing or two about pecking orders so I simply employed what I knew along with what I observed my instructors do in keeping control of a class."

"That's splendid, Henry. Keep up the good work," the good pastor couldn't have been more pleased. It seemed his goal of a congregation having many literate among its rolls was beginning to become a reality.

Chapter 20

The Sunday supper was a chicken potpie, which Constance prepared Saturday evening. It was allowed to stew very slowly all day Sunday over a low fire. Cider and milk, bread and butter with apple butter and farmer's cheese completed the menu. Labor was to be avoided on Sunday unless it was essential. That meant the animals needed to be cared for and fed. Very little else was allowed. Meals had to be crafted ahead of time to avoid Sunday toil. It was a delicious meal, which everyone enjoyed. The table talk complimented the meal in that it was also enjoyable to all.

"I believe you've outdone yourself my wife, so far as Sunday suppers go," the head of the house observed as he had just finished a second helping of potpie and had consumed half a loaf of bread with apple butter.

"Edmund, follow me out to the porch so I can take my pipe in peace."

Once outside the two men sat and reflected on what had recently happened and what might happen in the near future.

"Henry tells me that the two of you nearly have the mill house's porch rebuilt."

McAdoo had lent Henry to Edmund for a few afternoons to rebuild the porch that was burnt when they had stormed the mill several weeks before.

"The porch just needs a few more shingles and it will be better than new. Henry's a quick learner as well as a teacher. He could be a good carpenter if he put an effort to it."

McAdoo stroked his beard and took a puff on his pipe, "I think that laddie could do just about anything he wants in this world. To tell you the truth Edmund, I've grown fond of the boy. He reminds me of some of the best conscripts under my care when I was with my regiment."

Both men saw the shadow they knew was Henry's returning from the barn. The bondservant had done a last check on the livestock for the evening and had put out his lantern using the house's light as his guide back.

"He's my closest friend in the world, Thomas."

McAdoo shifted in his seat, "That brings me to what I wanted to talk to you about. Your wife should be the closest person to you in the world and I think you need to make plans to take one."

Edmund's heart soared. *He knows*. He thought.

"How wonderful!" Constance whispered. She and Abigail were both eavesdropping at a nearby window. "Your father's a wise man," Constance said as she hugged her daughter.

The Scotsman leaned toward the miller and continued, "The general store's owner, John Lawrence has a daughter, and I believe Mary is her name. She seems the type that could step in and help you with the store's runnin' as she already helps her pa with his."

Edmund was crestfallen and silent.

"You father's a dunderhead," Constance told her daughter as the girl wheeled around and ran toward the girl's room holding her hand over her mouth.

Henry had just come up on the porch and saw that neither man was talking.

"With your permission sir, I will help Edmund finish the porch tomorrow afternoon after chores."

"Yes, yes fine Henry. You do that."

The master of Stony Brook was puzzled by the silence his suggestion received. Later, after Edmund had gone and everyone was in bed, Constance turned to her husband and said; "I knew I wasn't marrying a scholar when I married you, Thomas McAdoo, but I thought you were smarter than that." And so having said her peace turned her back on him pulling the covers about her head.

The following afternoon after the last clapboard shingle was nailed into place Edmund and Henry were having a mug of warmed spiced cider that the daughter of the tavern owner had sent over for Edmund.

"I'm worried, Henry. Abigail's father is trying to fix me up with one of the townspeople's daughters. And all the attention that I'm getting from everyone with them sending me my meals and this lumber and nails for the porch is well, making me nervous."

Henry took a sip of the remarkably good beverage and advised his friend, "I'd like to tell you it was all from Christian charity, but we both know the treatment you are getting is all about a gaggle of marrying age women and their attempts to appeal to you. If this is a sample of what you are getting, I'd keep'em guessing." Henry liked the cider.

"This is serious, Henry. Abigail knows that I love her, but all this attention from others is sure to alarm and dishearten her," Edmund took another swig of his beverage, "And Thomas doesn't even suspect our true feelings. Henry, that large man scares me."

"Have faith, Edmund. Our plan is sure to work and besides the mistress is for your union and that is truly the one you need to get your blessing from. By the way, how are your projects coming along?"

"I've finished with three of them and have two more to go."

Chapter 21

Back at Stony Brook every spare minute the women had they spent on their Christmas gifts for Thomas, Henry and each other. This year Abigail was also making a special gift for her Edmund; for that was the way she had come to think of him. Christmas gifts were nearly always utilitarian. There was little frivolity in colonial New Jersey. Winter was cold and the best gifts addressed that fact. A typically clothed colonial farmer of the time wore a layering of clothes. First, the person working outside wore long undergarments and two pairs of woolen socks, plus a woolen shirt with heavy woolen or canvas trousers. A knit sweater under what would later become known as a "barn" coat was the outerwear. The barn coat was usually made of a tough canvas that was treated with mink oil, which gave it some water repellency. Leather boots, likewise treated with mink oil, heavy woolen or pigskin gloves and a variety of hats and caps completed the outfit. Scarves were optional as many felt they got in the way while they were working. Thomas favored a wool tam 'o shanter. Henry wore a knit wool cap called a watch cap named for another famous Scottish regiment, the Black Watch. Women spent less time outdoors so an extra petticoat plus a wool shawl was fine, but Katherine was a tomboy so when it got quite cold she borrowed Henry's duds and worked outside like a man.

Kate was physically strong like her father, and was nearly as strong willed. She was an animal "granny" and loved to care for the livestock. Often she would brush the horse or fuss over one of the new calves like a pet. She liked Henry, too. Kate saw how smart the bondsman was and knew that it would take someone of his wit to keep up with her later in life. He was a good worker and didn't have ugly ways like those town boys did. And Caleb, poor Caleb, he wasn't even a little bit smart in her estimation. He was a big strong boy, but was too timid and never said more than a word when she tried to speak to him. Caleb would have to find a backbone when it came to the teasing and taunting by those mean boys from town. Several times she was tempted to step up to those dullards and put them straight. The mess she would get into when her mother found out about it made her reconsider her action.

The youngest McAdoo girl was developing "first love" feelings concerning her Sunday school teacher. Thomas suspected what was going on and would shoo Kate back to the house when he caught her "mooning" over his servant. Henry was not really sure why McAdoo was chasing off Kate. Her help made the work go faster and in the New Jersey winter the less time spent outdoors, the better.

But for as astute as McAdoo was about his youngest, he was completed in the dark about Abigail's feelings for Edmund. His wife knew of the plan concocted by Henry and Edmund, but she was still tempted on more than one occasion to open her husband's eyes about the situation. Abigail and her mother managed the household as was the order of the time. Kate reluctantly helped with those duties when her father chased her in.

Finally Henry had to know why Thomas was acting that way toward Kate, "Sir, please tell me why you're so gruff with Kate? She's like having another hired hand in getting the work done and hasn't done anything wrong that I can see."

"We can get along fine out here without her. I don't want her to come down with the gripe because she's working out in this cold. Besides, she needs to be a helping with the household duties as they have grown due the time of the year." Thomas knew his reason was weak at best. Kate was hale and hearty. Henry's stare told of his disbelief.

Chapter 22

It happened the Sunday before Christmas. James Benson and Aubrey Knox, the two oldest boys in Henry's class chose this time to test their teacher. Both had been teasing Caleb unendingly and now prepared to show their dominance over their instructor.

"You know you're nothin' more than a bondservant so you are, Henry," James was going to pick the verbal stones and Aubrey was going to throw them.

"My Pa says that's like you was property. So I don't think I'm going to listen to you anymore."

This was a preliminary test by the town boys and St. Albans knew the direction it would take depended on quick thinking with an unflinching reply, "I'm a bondsman, that's true, but here and now I'm your instructor. I won't tolerate any mutiny or mischief in this class while it is being conducted. It's your choice Aubrey, stay, listen, and learn or leave. I can find another pupil to fill your spot without any trouble."

"My pa wouldn't like it if you kicked me out. He might even have you flogged,"

Aubrey was up out of his seat and coming toward Henry.

"Why wait for a flogging? Let's beat him now," James chimed. Both boys were coming at Henry and each were half a head bigger than their teacher.

I'm in for it now, Thought Henry as he stepped away from the chalkboard.

Suddenly both antagonists were lifted off the floor as if by magic. The magic was the farm boy, Caleb, "I'm here to learn! No one is taking that away from me. I've put up with your teasing, but when you try this I'll stop you. I'll stop you hard!"

Both boys were shaken violently by the scruff of their necks and then shoved to opposite sides of the room.

Henry knew that Caleb had a breaking point, everyone did. He was glad to learn that it was a kind, brave heart that beat in that lad's chest. Caleb could tolerate the mistreatment of himself. The mistreatment of others was the boundary line James and Aubrey had crossed. They paid for their error. It was up to Henry to see they didn't pay more.

The mutineers shook themselves back to their senses and stared at their surprise opponent. Both of the farm boy's hands curled into fists as he glared at each of the offenders.

"Return to your seats or leave this class," Henry demanded as he regained his composure.

The three boys returned to their seats. Class then resumed as though nothing had happened.

Katherine understood now that she had misjudged Caleb. He was big, strong, and suddenly quite comely, like a knight errant, which her father spoke of as the warrior poets in his beloved Scotland's past. Kate's affection was now focused on her schoolmate.

Henry asked for Caleb to remain after he dismissed the class. He wasn't sure exactly what to say to his pupil. Caleb took care of that.

"I'm so sorry for what happened, Mr. St. Albans. I just got so angry with those two ruffians. The way they were threatening you was all I could stand."

Henry's hand went to his chin. He was suffering from a state of bemusement. While he was grateful for what happened; he couldn't afford any further outbursts from anyone in the class. Also, it was the first time anyone had called him "Mr. St. Albans."

"I'm grateful that no one got hurt in the melee. I want you to seek the aid of Pastor Simmons concerning your angry outburst, though."

Caleb nodded his agreement then quickly ran off in the direction of his father's rig.

Kate couldn't wait to tell her family about the way Caleb stood up for Henry. "He'd have given both of those two bullies a good whipping too if Henry hadn't broken it up."

"Fighting in church, I never heard of such a thing!" Constance cast a critical glance about.

"Now Mrs. McAdoo," her husband said, "there were no fisticuffs so it was more of a physical reasoning young Caleb did."

After a moment of letting what McAdoo said sink in, everyone burst into laughter.

Chapter 23

Christmas was a snowy Thursday. Edmund was invited to celebrate the Savior's birth at Stony Brook and he happily accepted. Mrs. McAdoo had knitted socks and sweaters for the three men. Abigail sewed some fine flannel shirts and Katherine made them all beautiful handkerchiefs. The women made aprons, sleeping kerchiefs, and work dresses for each other. They had done an admirable job. Henry had been given the deer hide from the whitetail he had killed and had the tanner's wife make soft deerskin gloves for everyone. For her work the tanner's wife received half of the buck's tenderloin and the balance of what was left of the hide. Thomas had stockings filled with oranges (a great delicacy of the time) hard rock candy, maple sugar candy, and peppermint sticks all presented to every participant. He had store bought dresses for each of his girls and a large ham that he gave to Edmund. Everyone laughed at that. The big man, to Henry's mind, was a visage of Father Christmas. Now the master of Stony Brook Farm looked at his servant.

"Henry, you will find your gift lying on your bed. Go and get it."

St. Albans entered and crossed the storeroom and pulled back his privacy blanket. There lying on his cot was a long rifle, powder horn, and a leather pouch containing wadding, flint, and lead musket balls. It was a Pennsylvania long rifle made in Lancaster, Pa. and it was a fine example of master gunsmith's Isaac Haines' skill in creating a weapon that was also a work of art. Haines used curly maple wood for the stock and a "swamped" .45 caliber barrel. The barrel had been "browned" by capping the tang end and muzzle end with wax and then burying it in cow manure for three months. This process allowed the acids in the feces to oxidize the iron's "white" state into the desired finish. It was actually a type of controlled rusting that would protect the barrel when coated by gun oil. The flintlock mechanism was treated the same way. The butt plate, stock plate, rear sight, front blade, trigger plate, and lugs were made of brass and either drilled and screwed into the stock or into the barrel. The barrel ram was made of black walnut and was attached beneath the barrel end of the stock by the lugs. The stock plate looked of an arabesque nature. Likewise, ornate carvings in the stock added to the effect. It was the most beautiful rifle he had ever seen. Henry was overcome by his emotions. The boy sat on his bed with his hands over his face for some time before he could return to the party. He walked into the great room of the house with the rifle before him to the applause of the others.

"This weapon is a tool Henry, like a hammer, saw, or an axe," explained his master. "With it you put game on our table and defend this farm against enemies, both four legged and two legged."

Crane and the women were admiring the piece.

"It's called a Pennsylvania rifle," McAdoo continued, "the rifle was made by a Dutchman over in Lancaster County who put some special work on it to make it one of a kind. I got it in a trade with Lawrence at the general store and it was some haggle. It cost five dozen eggs and a side of bacon."

Plus a marriage discussion about shopkeeper's daughter with me. Thought Crane.

"Thomas McAdoo, telling the cost of a gift is impolite," chided his wife.

Everyone laughed as the big man's face turned red and he began a fit of coughing.

Edmund asked Henry to help him bring in the gifts he had brought for the occasion. They had been left out on the porch until the right moment. Edmund had used nearly all his spare time; sometimes working by lantern light into the wee hours of the morning to get everything finished. First, he presented Mrs. McAdoo with two wooden bowls. Among the tools in the mills shop was a foot-powered lathe. With this tool Edmund was able to turn out two remarkably beautiful walnut bowls. Polished to a glass smooth finish and preserved with limn seed oil. The bowls became an immediate treasure. Next he presented Mr. McAdoo with a pipe he had fashioned out of a cherry burl. Edmund had to gouge and drill the burl very carefully so as not to split it. He had fashioned a mouthpiece out of walnut and had "broken in" the pipe by firing the bowl. The Scotsman was overjoyed.

"Now my tobacco will always have a taste of cherry to it," he happily exclaimed.

The pipe was to be a truly prized possession.

Now it was Katherine's turn. The gift was a doll's cradle made from American chestnut, polished and preserved as her mother's bowls had been. Kate ran and got her doll; it fit perfectly. She hugged and kissed the carpenter on his cheek. Even though her days of playing with dolls were numbered, Katherine cherished the gift just the same.

Henry got two gifts from his friend. Edmund had mounted the antlers from Henry's buck on a handsome walnut plaque.

"I wondered where they had gotten to, Edmund," Henry joked.

Next Edmund handed Henry two round pegs.

"What are these for?" the puzzled boy asked his friend.

"I've brought my drill and mallet with me, and with the master's permission, I intend to place these two pegs on the mantle directly under his rifle so you can rest yours there, too."

McAdoo nodded his assent. Henry hugged his friend as he got up to perform the task. In short order there were two rifles mounted above the fireplace, ready at a moment's notice.

Abigail was beginning to think she had been forgotten and began to pout. Edmund and Henry made one last trip to the porch returning a short time later with what was Edmund's most beautiful creation. It was a dowry box or "hope chest." Made of heart wood birch, it almost blazed as its depth and luster of its graining became apparent. Edmund had used banker's box corners in the making of the chest. It involved painstaking filing and repetitive fitting, but the result was nothing short of perfection. On the top Edmund had inlaid the named "Abigail" in walnut and inside there was a fragrant cedar bottom. Cedar was a rare wood with the effect of repelling moths while providing a pleasant smell. Everyone was momentarily overcome with the beauty of the box. Abigail then rushed to her love and kissed him square on the lips. McAdoo's eyes were suddenly opened, but before he could utter a word of protest his wife spoke.

"Tell all present my age when you took me to marry."

McAdoo looked at his wife, but he knew he was beaten. "Tha' was …" he started.

"Tell them," Constance repeated.

With head now down the farmer simply said, "Sixteen."

"Abigail will be seventeen in May. We will have a June wedding."

Thomas McAdoo stood alone on his porch late Christmas evening long after Edmund had said good night to his fiancée, her family, and his best friend. The women had retired. He was going over in his mind all that had just taken place when Henry joined him.

"It's late, Henry. We've got a full day ahead of us so you'll be needin' your rest."

"Yes sir, I know," replied the boy. "With all you need to think about I hate to even ask, but the season has me thinking about my father. Would you consider sending word about me to him? I don't want him to worry."

"Consider it done."

The bankers hadn't told their client about Henry's father' death at their meeting, either.

"I have one more favor to ask you, sir," Henry had stammered.

"Go on, lad."

"That rifle is so beautiful it should be given a girl's name. With your permission, I should like to name it Kate.

"Kate it is."

Chapter 24

The winter of 1772 gave way to the spring of 1773. During that time Henry had learned of his father's death. A note was sent by packet ship through McAdoo's financial firm with only the sparest of details concerning William St. Albans' passing. It stated the date of his death but very little else. While the details of the way his father died were still unknown to Henry, the news nevertheless laid him low. It didn't seem real. It was Henry's secret hope that his father would someday soon come for him and everything might be set right and back to normal. *It was the foolish dream of a foolish boy.* He scolded himself for ever dreaming such a dream. Even though the McAdoo's were kind and fair to him, the small part of the boy left in him yearned for his own loving father.

It was with a great deal of patience and insight that his master and the McAdoo family were able to pull him out of the doldrums and back into life. Henry threw himself into the work around the farm and it helped ease his suffering. Thomas saw to it that he spent more time with Henry practicing with the rifle the boy had gotten at Christmas. The practice paid off and soon the lad was crack shot.

"I wish my Father could see me and what I can do with this rifle," as soon as Henry said what he was thinking an air of sadness swept over him.

"He sees and is most assuredly proud of his son's skill," a knowing glance and the slightest of smiles was Henry's reply to his master's assertion.

With his talent with the long-rifle, Henry soon became Stony Brook's primary hunter. He studied the habits of his quarry as best he could and began to have greater success with his hunting. Still, he knew there was much more he could be taught.

One evening, after the first thaw, there was a commotion in the chicken coop. Henry hopped to the mantle and grabbed his rifle before Thomas had gotten out of his chair. He went to the porch, raised his weapon and fired. When Kate brought out a lantern, she and the men went to the coop to find out what the commotion was about. There lying dead in the yard was a gray fox with a dead chicken still in its mouth.

"How did you see in this light to kill that fox?" wondered McAdoo aloud.

"I just shot at what didn't look like a chicken," was Henry's answer.

Henry took to wearing the fox's gray tail on his belt like he heard the natives sometimes did. The news of his exploit soon was all over the county with several embellishments added.

"I heard that coop was some two hundred yards from that porch," someone would say.

"I heard he shot that fox in a howling rain storm," someone else would add.

The truth was that it was a clear night and the coop was about fifty yards from the house. Still, to shoot a varmint, even in a moonlit night, under those conditions was an accomplishment.

The spring of 1773 was a milestone for Henry in another way. It was the first time he saw an Indian. Now Henry had seen the gentrified red man on many occasions during his trips to town but this native was different. He accompanied a trapper named LeClerc into Somerville with a large string of furs and pelts. LeClerc lived among the Indians in an area called the Poconos where he trapped beaver, fox, mink, weasel, and martin. He liked to trade with Lawrence and a rumor had it that there was a widow in town he liked to visit too. His partner was a Delaware of the turtle clan. Henry found out later that you can tell a Delaware by the distinctive tattoos on their face and arms. His name was Spotted Wolf and he looked to be in his mid-twenties. Spotted Wolf was dressed in a dark cotton shirt which he wore open, a deer skin loincloth worn Indian fashion with buckskin leggings. On his feet he wore a pair of beaded moccasins. Around his neck was a bear claw necklace and in his long hair were two red tail hawk feathers worn down and to the side. Over his right shoulder he wore a wide leather belt with a scabbard in which was an antlered-handled knife. Also on the belt down his back was a quiver of arrows. In his left hand he carried a bow made from alder wood. He made an immediate impression on Henry. Thomas was just finishing his business with Lawrence when the trappers walked in. Spotted Wolf immediately saw the fox tail hanging from Henry's belt.

With a smile he said in near perfect English, "Boys wear fox tails on their brag belts, men wear scalps."

The farmer was turning toward the native when LeClerc stepped between them.

"Dis man, he say tings before he tinks sometimes. He means no harm."

"Tell him that some of my friends' hair has ended up on those belts so he'd better stay clear of me and mine."

The antagonist merely smiled.

On the trip back to the farm, Henry was the most animated Thomas had ever seen him, "I could never have imagined a savage would look like that. The drawings I saw back at school in England didn't do him justice. He was magnificent! The trapper looked to be an odd sort, though. He was dressed in skins, not at all like a Frenchman."

"The trapper, LeClerc, has spent so much time living among the heathens that he's adopted most of their ways. But he's not alone in turning his back on our way of life. Some do it to escape the law or perhaps an unhappy family. Others have spent so much time in the wild that returning to the civil world has been made impossible for them. Now as for his partner, he is only one type of many natives that I have seen." McAdoo shifted around in his seat seeing he had Henry's undivided attention, "There is a nation of Indians called the Mohawks who shave all but a center strip on their heads. It looks like a horse's cropped mane. Some of the Lenape clans paint themselves blue before going to war. They believe that blue is their god's favorite color because the sky is blue. And some warriors of the Algonquin nation dress up in wolf heads to make themselves look fiercer. In all, I know one thing about Indians for certain; Indians are a nasty business to fight."

After McAdoo finished telling Henry about the native tribes he had seen firsthand, he finished by saying, "There's land stretching who knows how far in all directions. I'll guess that there are more of these people that I haven't seen than what I saw."

Henry sat back in his seat and thought about the events of the day. *How many different tribes of Indians will I see in my time?* He wondered.

Chapter 25

Back at the farm final preparations were being made for the upcoming wedding.

"Did the material finally come in for Abigail's dress?" Mrs. McAdoo wanted to know having met the men out in the yard before they had a chance to pull up the wagon.

"Yes, dear wife. I have it here," replied her husband.

"Well give it to me," and with that she ran back into the house calling for her daughters to join her.

"Hitch the horse to the plow, Henry. We will try to get the rest of the West acres done today." Thomas then turned and went off to the side of the shed, leaving Henry to his task.

Both her mother and her sister were in lather about details for the nuptials, so Katherine took this moment to seek out Henry. She found him just ready to plow.

"Kate, will you pick rocks for me? The plowing will go much faster if you do."

Kate agreed and soon both were busy readying the field for planting.

"How are you doing with your reading lesson?" asked Henry when they reached the end of a furrow and he needed to turn the plow around to go back the other way. The class had progressed nicely and without incident since the failed insurrection back in December.

"I have it memorized. But I need to ask you a question," Kate replied using her most serious tone of voice. Henry stopped the horse and gave her his full attention.

"The Silverthorne's just sold their farm and pulled up stakes heading west into the frontier. Now Caleb says his pa is thinking of doing the same thing. What's to stop my pa from all at once thinking about doing the same thing? With my sister getting married to Edmund and with his position as important as it is here I'm sure they wouldn't pull up stakes based on a whim of my Father. Henry, I might never see her again!" Tears filled the green eyes of Kate at the thought and they started to shine like stars.

Henry's eyes filled too as he thought of his brother across the ocean toiling in some counting house alone in the world. Even though he was alone here he didn't feel alone. The thought of Alfred all alone brought him to the point of tears.

"Here now Henry, I really don't think Pa would really do such a thing. I am bent on worrying needlessly at times," Katherine' kindness toward him made it worse. She didn't understand what the bondsman was going through. Henry found the strength to compose him and reassured her.

"Your father has made a good life for his family here at Stony Brook. His roots are sunk deep in this soil. He will never willingly move. After a career spent serving his king all over the empire he has exhausted any of the wanderlust he might have had at one time."

After smiles made for convincing each other were exchanged, both returned to working the field until they were called in for the evening meal.

Chapter 26

The wedding of Edmund Crane and Abigail McAdoo was held on the third Sunday in June at the church in Somerville with Pastor Simmons officiating. The wedding dress was made of finely carded muslin with a silk bow and sash. The white of the gown made Abigail's auburn hair standout in contrast dramatically. All the men wore their Sunday best with Thomas sporting a green silk ascot. Henry stood by Edmund's side fulfilling his duties as best man.

"This is a marvelous gathering for Abigail's big day, Edmund," Henry whispered to the nervous groom.

"I play a little part in all this, Henry," Edmund whispered in reply. This got both young men to chuckling then coughing behind closed hands.

Henry gazed out again at the scene and thought, *I've seen more pageantry and splendor at other occasions back in England, but none of them compare in purpose or match for me the feelings of joy at being here.* It was a profound realization.

Thomas escorted his eldest daughter through the parishioners to the church's alter where Rev. Simmons waited with the groom and best man. Katherine, the Maid of Honor, had preceded her sister down the aisle in a lovely pale blue dress that matched the bouquet of flowers she held. Now she would stand by her sister, as she became Mrs. Edmund Crane. Many folks in attendance remarked at what a lovely young woman Katherine had grown to become. Mrs. McAdoo sat in the left front pew wiping her eyes with a lace kerchief and smiling at the same time. Several young unmarried men and women felt a brief pang of jealousy toward the bride and groom, but this quickly passed as they saw how much in love the two where. As a part of the service, each member of Henry's Sunday school class read a verse from the Bible. Everyone did well and Henry's pleasure was displayed plainly on his face. After the service everyone retired to a long series of tables set out in the grove at the side of the church. On these tables were a cornucopia of meats, chesses, breads, and other mouth-watering food. Everyone was made welcome and the feasting continued until the evening. Henry was munching on a sour pickle when he saw off in the distance a glow above the trees. Suddenly Thomas saw it and was on his feet.

"That's my farm!" he shouted.

A short time later Henry and the McAdoos stood in the yard at the farm. A bizarre scene greeted them. The barn had been burned to the ground but all the animals in the barn had been removed first. They were milling around the yard and nearby pasture, all except for a white goat that was tied to the porch's stair railing. Fashioned on the goat was a bloody red tail hawk feather.

"What does this mean, Thomas?" asked his wife.

"I don't know what it means, but I'm going to find out."

The next morning as the men tended the livestock and began clearing the remains of the barn, they were visited by sheriff Crisp and a character the locals called "Injun Willie."

"After he looks it over, Willie says he can tell you more about the message," the sheriff explained. Willie was the product of an unhappy tryst between a Shawnee squaw and one of the white settlers who no longer called the area his home. Willie's mother couldn't return to her people without suffering unbearable shame so she found work as a scullery maid at the tavern. As soon as Willie was able, he helped his mother with her daily chores. Some of the unthinking patrons thought getting the half-breed child drunk was great sport, so Willie developed a taste for alcohol at an early age and became the town drunk. As he was half Shawnee, his mother's people tolerated him, especially after her death, which happened while he was in his early teens. The drunk would come to Somerville and tie one on and then crawl back to his tribe to sober up. He dressed like the settlers except for a shell necklace, a felt hat with a turkey feather stuck in it, and moccasins. Willie was about twenty years old but he looked twice his age.

"Spotted Wolf is your enemy," Willie began. "Not a family blood feud by the looks of it or he would have burned the house. You are his declared enemy and he is yours. His blood is on the Hawk's feather. He'll use the same knife that caused him to bleed to take your scalp. Spotted Wolf must think your red scalp will look fine on his brag belt," Willie said the last while admiring the enormous man's hair.

Thomas set his chin at the news. At least the savage didn't seem to want the scalps of his wife or daughters.

"Have you seen Spotted Wolf, Willie?" asked McAdoo.

"Spotted Wolf left town with the Frenchman. They've gone back to the Poconos. He bragged to anyone who would listen he'd come back when the time was right."

Many colonists misjudged the intellect of the native people. When it came to the craft of torture they had no equal and it wasn't always the physical method of torture. Spotted Wolf knew that McAdoo would now perform his chores with a pistol in his belt and that Henry would always have "Kate" propped against a nearby tree.

Chapter 27

Spring turned to summer at Stony Brook. In the fields and in the garden, crops were growing and so it was likewise with McAdoo's bondservant. Henry's physical and mental disposition responded well to the work on the farm. The work in the Sunday school class helped him in fashioning patience and a kind of delight that comes when knowledge is given to another. Because of his literate talents, he not only was helping McAdoo with the correspondence of his business, but he also found time to work on similar duties for the Grain Cooperative and Crane's carpentry business. As Henry's duties grew, so did Henry.

"Henry, I swear I let these pants down just last week, and you've outgrown all your shirts," Constance McAdoo let out a mock sigh of resignation then continued, "Do you know you've outgrown the boots you had gotten just since this past Christmas?"

Mrs. McAdoo's feigned exasperation made her husband smile. The farm life with its hard work and good food had seen the young man grow broad at the shoulders and nearly four inches taller than when he first arrived almost a year ago. Katherine was sprouting up too but the stocky tomboy was giving way to a slender girl whose form was more akin to her older sister's. "My fingers will be worked to the bone sewing for you three."

Kate had begun doing more of the sewing since her sister had become Edmund's wife, but Mrs. McAdoo now did the lion's share. Soon she would receive word that would have her knitting and sewing even more. The Crane's would bring their first child into the world the following spring.

The new barn was taking shape and both men worked on it when not doing the chores. Edmund would come join them on some of the afternoons, which helped the project along. The new barn was slightly bigger than the old one and included a room for Henry in one rear corner. A small fireplace with a mantle in the room would be his rifle's new spot.

"We'll have the last of the trusses in place today and can begin on the roof by tomorrow if the weather holds," the pleased master of Stony Brook said to his assistants.

The timbers for the trusses had been cut and hewn and would be lifted into place using Thomas' horse pulling on attached ropes through a block and tackle. This arrangement was mounted on temporary scaffolding. As each piece was set into place large wooden pins were driven through drilled holes in a mortise and tenon fashion. Slowly and painstakingly the trusses took shape. The weather had cooperated for the most part by raining in the evenings so that the crops got what they needed, but hardly in the afternoons when the building occurred.

"When do you move into your new quarters?" Edmund asked his friend.

"Very soon; when the roof is on then I'll be in," Henry cheerfully replied. "The master and I can finish the chimney afterward. Before the cold nights come."

Having a room to call his own, instead of a curtained section of the home's storeroom, was the best thing to come out of the loss of the old barn to Henry's way of thinking and the extra work didn't trouble him one bit. His place wouldn't be much bigger, but it would have a door, a small table and chair, and a window from which he could look out onto a grassy pasture and the tended fields beyond. At night he could count the stars from his bed until he fell asleep.

The start of September saw the barn finished and the chimney mortared and pointed. Henry happily retired to his room in the evenings and read by the glow of the fireplace. The grain harvesting had begun in August with early crops of wheat and rye so Henry saw less of his good friend Edmund and on top of that everyone was missing Abigail badly. It was on just such an evening in late September when Katherine ran into the barn calling for him.

"What's wrong Kate?"

"We need you in the house right now!" and with that, Kate turned on her heels and ran back. Henry grabbed the rifle and rushed into the kitchen. There sat the McAdoo's and the Crane's around the table.

"Are ya goin' huntin', lad?" Thomas quipped and everyone burst into laughter.

A red-faced Henry set aside "Kate" and joined them at the table.

"We've got something to tell you," Abigail started,

"And something to ask you," Edmund added.

Everyone looked happy and excited. Edmund stood and hooked his thumbs under his armpits. He looked like the yard rooster. "Abigail and I are expecting."

Henry was bewildered, "Expecting what?"

"A baby you silly!" answered Mrs. Crane. "If the baby is a girl then we'll name her after Edmund's mother, Sarah. But if it is a boy, we would like to name it after you."

Henry went from bewildered to the apex of joy in a heartbeat, "Yes, you have my permission and my very best wishes." He hugged both husband and wife and laughed until tears came to his eyes.

Chapter 28

That fall the people around Somerville held a harvest festival to commemorate a good crop. This was a custom they had brought with them from Britain and it could be traced all the way back to pre-Christian times. Pies were judged, cattle and fowl were sold, and contests were held. Thomas, unbeknownst to his servant, had entered Henry in the rifle marksmanship contest. John Gill had won this event the last three years running and the big Scot thought the deputy needed a little competition.

"I don't know sir. I might get too nervous and embarrass both you and myself."

"You've a talent, boy and the side of beef top prize is nothin' ta turn up your nose at."

The contest began with ten riflemen, who had put up a one-pound entry fee, each shooting at their targets beginning at fifty yards. Henry found out the targets were wooden boards about eight inches wide by two feet high. If he hit his target from that distance the target was then moved back another twenty-five yards where he shot at it again and so on. If he missed, he was out. There was one more rub. The bad luck of splitting a target meant aiming at the widest part of the target, not both pieces. The targets were made from soft pine so that hardly ever happened but there had been a time or two when it did.

The contestants and a large crowd gathered at a field on the edge of town that was dubbed "The Long Acre" It was only about eighty yards wide but some five hundred yards long. All ten contestants hit their targets at fifty yards and likewise at seventy-five and at one hundred yards. There were three misses at one hundred twenty-five yards and Henry's was called a miss too.

"Let me see Henry's target," asked Gill. If he were to win for the fourth time, it would be on the square. "See here? Look at the shape of that hole, its oval. Henry nearly put his shot through the same hole as his one hundred yard shot!"

The crowd applauded the shot and the honesty of the competitor. There were four misses at one hundred-fifty yards leaving only three competitors remaining. A miss at one hundred seventy-five yards left only Henry and Gill. Both hit their target at two hundred yards, but Henry split his in two.

"Tough luck, Henry." muttered Gill.

The distance was now two hundred and twenty-five yards and Henry's target was nearly three inches narrower than Gill's. Both men shot. Both men hit. At two hundred fifty yards the targets appeared to be dots out in the distance. Both men shot. Only Henry hit. The crowd erupted in applause.

"Henry, would you be willing to try one more shot?" asked his vanquished rival.

"Sure John, I'll try."

"Take his target out to three hundred yards." Gill told the target runner. When it was done, Gill looked at Henry and said, "Alright boy, show me somethin'."

Henry sighted his target and, allowing for distance and windage, squeezed off the shot. A whoop and jumping about by the target runner revealed to all that the bondsman had hit his mark. When his target was brought back they saw the grouping of Henry's shots was five and one half inches, including the splitter round, by six inches.

"Best shot in the county, maybe all of New Jersey!" McAdoo crowed.

The beef would taste good that winter. Gill wasn't too unhappy. Second prize was a large ham and Gill loved ham.

Chapter 29

During this particular winter and spring events occurred that would shape Henry St. Alban's life and the direction it would take. Henry was spending a great deal of time in the woods hunting and learning as much of its ways as he could on his own. So too was his work on the farm a learning process for Henry. Remembering his visits with his father to Medford's overseers he was now keenly aware of just how much his Father and frankly, the overseers, were ignorant of what went into supporting and sustaining the business of crops and livestock. It made him wonder how his Father's estate was able to do as well as it did.

The Sunday school classes were progressing nicely. In fact, he had handed off his first class of students to the pastor and had begun a second one. *I'll miss having Kate and Caleb in the class each Sunday. In truth, I'll miss them all.*

Ten new smiling faces sat before the blackboard and this new class seemed as eager to learn as the last. This time the number of students from town and from the farm was more evenly split. He looked at it as a testament to the newly perceived value of education by the entire community. The lessons were the same but the new students brought a fresh feeling to the task. Henry noticed something else which made him grin. No student was bigger than Henry this time. He had continued to grow and was now a powerful youth of seventeen. He never quite reached the height of six feet, but he got awfully close. And he weighed in at a respectable one hundred and sixty five pounds.

Caleb had also continued to grow and now there were two huge men in Somerville. Caleb was taking on the proportions of Kate's father although he was a thinner version of Scotsman.

As Miss McAdoo sat in the pastor's class she had a revelation. Watching Caleb during the lesson, she knew in her heart that he would be her husband one day. Now her task was getting him to know it. Caleb was coming into his own with regards to his social skills. He might never be the most talkative one in the room, but now he put together a sentence or so when engaged in conversation. This allowed for some pride and a sense that he was making a real contribution for Henry.

At the beginning of April Edmund and Abigail Crane welcomed their first child, Sarah Elizabeth Crane into their home. She was all pink and a quite plump, healthy baby.

"Where's her hair?" Edmund's question got his wife and mother-in-law bursting out in a fit of laughter.

When they regained a bit of composure, Constance explained, "Now Edmund, many fair-skinned babies are born without any hair. She'll grow hers in and probably have red tresses like her mother did."

Convinced by the women that time was the answer to his question, Edmund held his daughter in his arms and the age old bond that was between a father and his newborn started to form.

Spring also brought the French trapper; LeClerc and his partner Spotted Wolf back to Somerville. Ben Crisp met up with the two in Lawrence's store.

"A warrant is being completed by the court clerk and once I have it you will be taken into custody for arson."

Why this wasn't done at the time of the crime was a misstep he would forever regret, "Meantime I'm watching you, Spotted Wolf. If you step one foot out of line I'll be after you and you won't be likin' that one little bit."

"Sheriff," opined LeClerc, "we have heard of Mr. McAdoo's misfortune and we are both very sorry for him. As for these charges, je impossible. We were falling down drunk at the tavern when this unfortunate thing happened. "

Crisp studied the trapper and the brave. He had heard from a few folks that the Frenchman was in the tavern around the time the barn was set on fire, but no one vouched for the Indian.

"You'll be seeing me again real soon," with that parting promise the sheriff left them to their business.

Henry saw Spotted Wolf on a trip into town later that day. The Delaware had just come out of the tavern where he was apparently drinking.

"Boy with the fox tail! You have gotten bigger and wiser in the ways of the forest so they tell me. You are called, "Tucka Hakem" by the Shawnee. That means sure shot. Say, where is that red bear they call McAdoo? Tell him I will be seeing him soon."

McAdoo's first meeting with Spotted Wolf was in Lawrence's store and when the huge man started for him a fear had fermented in the Delaware. Fear in the heart of an ill-intentioned man festers quickly to hatred. As unreasonable as it was to a reasonable person, so it was rational in the mind of Spotted Wolf; a deep hatred, a blood oath, death for McAdoo.

Henry reached around behind him in the wagon and pulled out his rifle, "Kate." Laying it across his lap he told the brave, "Then you'll be seeing us both."

The Indian took out a red tail hawk feather from his hair as he walked toward Henry. Next he removed his knife from its place on his belt and then cut the palm of his hand letting his blood drip onto the feather. Handing the feather to Henry he said simply, "Yes, I will."

Chapter 30

Spotted Wolf was not expected to ever return by anyone in Somerville in spite of Injun Willie's quoting the Delaware as promising just that. Now it was clear to Ben Crisp that he meant carry on this honor feud contrived in his unbalanced mind with McAdoo. Crisp came out to Stony Brook after supper to plan a way to head off the impending danger. They choose Henry's new room out in the barn for the meeting so as not to upset Mrs. McAdoo or Katherine by how the conversation might go.

"I understand Spotted Wolf will be trying to collect a feather off you, too," the sheriff said to Henry.

"As well as my scalp," replied Henry. The level of danger he found himself in was beginning to register with Henry and made him ill at ease. Not just for McAdoo and him, but now also for anyone near to them.

"I don't like waiting for this fiend to try something," railed the farmer. "I want to go and break him in two."

The sheriff shook his head. It had to be done according to law. His sacred pledge to uphold the law permitted him no other way.

"We're not going to be waiting for him," Ben Crisp walked out toward the barn's front doors with Thomas and Henry following. "We are here to figure out how to end this before any of us are hurt or killed. I have deputies watching his every move in town with instructions to follow him should he head this way. They are to fire a warning shot when within hearing distance to alert us."

Thomas was looking back at the farmhouse when he saw a form rush the door. A second later there was a scream and the candles that were burning in the house went out.

"He's got my wife and my Kate!" McAdoo screamed as he bolted toward the home. Neither man's efforts to hold him back delayed him for more than a second as the big man made his mad rush. The Scotsman had gotten nearly to the porch when the first arrow hit him in the chest. He smashed through the door as the second one hit him. Ben and Henry were in the yard now running to the big man's aid. They heard the scalping cry of the Delaware as they approached the porch and the anguished moan and cry of the Indian's victim. It froze them both for and instant. In that instant another arrow flew striking the sheriff in his shoulder. Henry threw down his rifle as Ben slumped forward. He pulled his hunting knife as he rushed inside and met Spotted Wolf just inside the threshold before the Indian could release another arrow. The fight that ensued was vicious. By the light of the hearth fire, both men embraced in what appeared to be a death hold while each looked to strike the other with their knives. The brave's experience and cunning soon overcame the youth's strength and Henry was lying on his back with a wound in his side.

"Now Fox Tail, I take your scalp for my belt!"

Spotted Wolf was just about to raise his cry when a pistol shot from behind him struck him in his arm. His knife flew out of his hand and his cry was a cry of pain. Kate had run to the storeroom as Spotted Wolf attacked her mother. This is what both her father and mother had instructed her to do in case of an attack. What she did next she did on her own. Her parents had told her to barricade herself in and go into the root cellar. Instead, Kate broke open her father's chest and took out his two pistols. She knew these weapons were always ready and she meant to use them on her mother's attacker.

Katherine had just reentered the room when she saw the native get the best of Henry. Cocking the first weapon the girl fired breaking the intruder's right arm. As she discarded the first pistol and was bringing the second to bear the Delaware was in full flight. Her shot struck the doorway as Spotted Wolf rushed out. Katherine gathered herself. She then relit a candle, brought it up to eye level, and slowly turned witnessing the carnage.

What Kate saw made her drop to her knees and weep uncontrollably. Her mother was lying on her back behind the table dead from a gaping wound in her neck. Her father was lying on his side and quivering as he entered his death throes. Two arrows were in his chest and his thick red hair had a large patch torn away clear to the skull. Henry's moan snapped her back to attention. She needed to stop his bleeding or he might die too. Kate found the blanket her mother had been knitting for the baby and packed it around the young man's side.

The pain of being ministered to snapped Henry out of a state of semi-consciousness. There was movement on the porch. Kate recovered Henry's knife and shaking in fear and anger prepared to meet the attacker at the doorway when the sheriff staggered in. The arrow in his shoulder had just missed his lungs and hadn't hit a major blood vessel. The shock of the wound had temporarily knocked the lawman senseless but now he was up. Because the arrow was released from such a short distance it had tremendous penetrating power and protruded out the wounded man's back until just the fletching on its shaft was all that could be seen from the front.

Ben dropped into a chair by the table and leaned forward, "Grab the arrow girl and pull it out my back."

Kate hesitantly grasped the arrow with both hands below the point, placed her right knee in the small of Crisp's back and heaved with all her might. The arrow came through clean, but the pain of the extraction sent the sheriff down to the floor as he lost his senses once again.

The pack on Henry's side had stemmed the flow of blood. Again, by some miracle, no organ was pierced and his gut was intact. Henry's rib directed the course of Spotted Wolf's blade away from being a fatal strike. Both men were wounded and weakened, but with care and barring infection or pneumonia, would survive.

"Don't go outside until its light," cautioned Crisp after he came around. "The cur might still be out there."

Henry didn't think so, "He's a bloodthirsty cur, but he's also a coward. He's gone."

The fact was with a broken arm and a bleeding wound the attacker no longer liked his odds. If things weren't heavily in his favor his courage would fail him. Spotted Wolf might not have been a complete coward, however he wasn't brave either. He would flee back to his mountains and heal. There would be a next time though, he knew. Henry's fate was tied to his own. Spotted Wolf was determined that "Fox Tail's" hair would join "Red Bear's" on his brag belt.

Chapter 31

Kate began both of the wounded men's first treatments. Neither man seemed to be bleeding badly now. After washing both wounds on the sheriff, the girl applied a pack of pitch salve and tied it into place using one of Henry's shirts she had been repairing. Henry's wound required "stitching." She washed the wound and then with a needle and thread began to close it. The pain was monumental, but Henry gritted his teeth and took it in silence. Next she applied another salve pack using a strip torn from a bed sheet to bind it securely. Katherine disregarded the sheriff's warning and carrying a lantern in one hand and a reloaded pistol in the other and made her way to the barn in the dark where she hitched up the horse to the wagon. She then drove the wagon to the porch and slowly, carefully loaded both men into it. She would take them to Somerville and get help.

Kate couldn't spend another minute in that house with her dead parents lying there. She wasn't sure she could ever return there again. The violence of what happened to Henry had somewhat fogged his memory about the details of the fight and its grisly outcome. He did know one thing; his master and mistress had died at the hands of his enemy.

The trip in was a painful experience for both men as the wagon's movements on the rutted road jarred them. The rough treatment fortunately didn't reopen either man's injury. The cries for help from the girl when they reached the town roused men from the tavern and nearby homes.

"My Ma and Pa are dead!" she cried in anguish as she fell into the arms of Deputy Gill.

"Why didn't you follow that Indian?" Crisp demanded of his deputy as he was helped into the sheriff's office.

"Roberts did, Ben."

The realization of what probably had happened to the unluckiest man in the world now occurred to Crisp. Spotted Wolf had doubled back on the deputy and had disposed of him in the quietest way possible, with an arrow.

He was truly the unluckiest man I ever knew. The sheriff sadly thought.

LeClerc was among the number who had come out of the tavern.

"Know this, Frenchman!" Gill spit through clenched teeth, "while you had no hand in the murderous acts that took place tonight, you brought the vermin here that did. Tell him when you see him that he will be shot on sight. And you, you son of a French whore, are no longer welcome here. Get out while you can."

The crowd that was forming needed very little more reason to turn into a lynch mob. Crisp was out of action and Gill couldn't stop them in his stead. The Frenchman had figured out as much on his own. He quickly got over to his horse and pack mule and had them loaded and ready to go in short order. Then, with a fixed smile on his face, LeClerc climbed his mount and was gone.

Help arrived at Stony Brook the following morning too late to save its master and mistress. A runner had been sent to the mill with word of the horrible tragedy. Abigail collapsed at the news of the death of her parents. It was only with Edmund's gentle comforting and the reminder of the needs of her baby girl that she was able to recover her senses. A large party of townspeople and those from the neighboring farms got the farmhouse cleaned and fixed up. No one had found the body of deputy Roberts, and it was thought that it had been carried off by some large scavenger. Human remains were unearthed by a farmer's plow nearly a hundred years later. It was thought that they belonged to a soldier who had been part of a nearby battle from the War for Independence. They couldn't quite figure out why this soldier had been killed by an arrow instead of a musket ball as an arrowhead was only object recovered from the body.

McAdoo and wife were prepared for their burial. Both were laid to rest side by side under the great oak that provided shade for the farm's yard. Abigail and Katherine wept inconsolably as a bagpiper played his skirl. Both Edmund and Henry tried to remain composed, but large tears flowed down their cheeks as Pastor Simmons spoke of the lives of this couple and of how this terrible act had led to the orphaning of their children and of never seeing their infant granddaughter grow to womanhood.

Terrence Land had prepared a will for Thomas several years before and now that will would be recorded with the circuit court and probated. Additionally the financial house of Egger and Dobbs would send a representative, as they were McAdoo's financial firm. All financial information would be transferred to his heirs once they were known. Attorney Land would read the prepared document and its contents would be recorded by the court's clerk and certified. It was no surprise that Thomas had named his wife as primary beneficiary or that should she precede him in death that the co-beneficiaries would be their daughters. The Egger & Dobbs agent, Mr. Brown, released actuarial and fiduciary papers to the girls who looked at him in confusion. Mr. Brown smiled and reassured them that from a financial standpoint, nothing would change and his firm intended to care for their monetary interests as it had for their father's. Some banking houses had no desire to have female clients as they often proved to be too "impulsive."

Edmund Crane would have been the new master of Stony Brook except that he did not want it. He would accept his father-in-law's interest in the grain mill, but he wanted nothing else. Thomas it seems, over the course of the year and a half since the Cooperative was started, had bought the interests of a good many farmers who wanted only a cash reward for their part in the grain mill scandal. Edmund now owned over eighty percent of the mill and would own it entirely in another year or two.

Katherine was now the sole mistress of Stony Brook. There were a great many unscrupulous men about who would take such a fourteen-year-old girl as consort and, without lifting a finger, become master of a sizable estate. Henry thought of Katherine like a sister. He would do all he could do for her once he learned his own fate.

"Now, we will address the matter of the indenture-ship contract currently in force between Thomas McAdoo and the firm of Egger & Dobbs, ltd of London," Land read the last in a dry monotone. He looked up over his reading glasses at Mr. Brown. "I see that the agent for Eggers & Dobbs is present. Are you ready to execute the pertinent articles of the contract Mr. Brown?"

"Yes we are," the banking agent responded. He then began to read from an official-looking document. "As to Article V, it is agreed that the indenture-ship of one Henry Pierce St. Albans is fulfilled as a result of the death of Thomas McAdoo, Mr. St. Albans having contributed in no way to the death of Thomas McAdoo. Further we petition the estate of Thomas McAdoo for the sum of three pounds for a new set of clothing as agreed to in Article VI. Finally, we have here the release document for Henry Pierce St. Albans as stipulated in Article VII of the contract. Let all men know by this record that Mr. St. Albans is a freeman and a loyal subject of King George III."

"Mr. St Albans, do you have anything to say?" asked the barrister.

"Yes sir, I do," began the newly made freeman. "Mr. and Mrs. McAdoo were the kindest master and mistress one could ever hope to have. Because of my affection for them I would like to enter into a new agreement with the present mistress of Stony Brook." Everyone perked up to hear this unusual marriage proposal only to be disappointed at what was said next.

"I offer my services as a hired worker for a period of two years. During this time, Edmund being her closest male relative can look out for his sister-in-law's best personal interests. And because Kate, err Miss McAdoo is literate, she can quickly learn what she will need to know about her properties."

Judge Knowles who was present and sitting en banc for the proceeding now spoke, "The estate of Thomas McAdoo is duly probated as recorded. All provisions and revisions having been accepted by this court, we are in adjournment."

Chapter 32

Spring gave way to summer and there was much to be done at Stony Brook. Caleb was sent by his father to help Henry with the duties at the farm. Henry's former student was the second of four boys in the Green family. At eighteen he had finally stopped growing and was a good hand over six feet in height. He weighed over two hundred pounds with broad shoulders and massive arms. Katherine had set her bonnet for this young man and his presence at Stony Brook seemed natural and right to her. Often Caleb's younger sister, Lucy would accompany Caleb. She was a year younger than Kate and loved helping with the household all the while chattering about this and that for what seemed like the entire time. Lucy was tiny for her age in contrast to her brothers who were all strapping youths. Edmund and Abigail with baby Sarah visited whenever possible and the farm continued to flourish nearly as well as when the red haired Scotsman and his wife were at its helm. Henry found less time for his forays into the woods as the fall harvest began consuming most of his waking hours.

On one of his trips into Somerville Henry visited the tavern. There in a darkened corner sat Willie in a slouched stupor on a stool.

"Willie, get awake. I've a proposal for you," Henry shook the slumbering drunk.

"Do you have some whiskey for me Sure Shot?"

"No, I am talking about something far better."

"A tankard of ale then, perhaps?" Willie guessed.

"Money, Willie, but you'll have to earn it."

"Henry was now earning a pound, two shillings per month and would share in his boon with the half- breed if he agreed to two conditions. First, as he was somewhat famous to the local Shawnee for his prowess with the rifle, he wanted to see if he could meet with the clan's warriors to learn all he could of their ways. Second, Willie would have to curtail his drinking.

"What good is money if you can't buy whiskey with it?" Willie wanted to know.

"I'll show you Willie, if you'll agree."

The following Sunday after school Willie was hanging around the church yard when Henry came out.

"You are welcome at my clan's fires if you want to come."

Henry had been hoping for this opportunity and had brought his woods man's clothing just in case. He explained to Kate that he would be going with Willie and then asked Caleb and Lucy to get her home. After changing out of his good clothes, Henry grabbed his rifle and gear and followed Willie into the forest. When he was sober, Willie moved through the woods like a bobcat. He was quiet and he was quick. Henry had to put forth his best effort to keep up. Willie made it look effortless. Henry was just about played out by the time they reached the village. As Henry caught his breath, Willie disappeared into a nearby lodge and reappeared a short time later with a Shawnee brave. Eastern Woodland Indian lodges were quite often similar to the log cabins the settler's built. The biggest difference was at the standing height Indians began to interweave saplings the way they weaved vines into baskets. This was continued in a constricting manner until a large round hole was left in the middle. It was in the middle of the lodge that they built their fires and the hole in the roof allowed for the smoke to escape. Skins were placed over the intertwined branches to keep out rain and wind.

Willie made the introductions. "Tunka Hakem, this is Odhamen. His name means "Two Hawks," explained Willie.

Two Hawks grasped Henry on the inside of his elbow and the gesture was returned as it was a form of greeting Willie had previously told him about. The brave was several inches shorter than his student and about twenty pounds lighter, but his grip had strength in it.

"You are welcome Sure Shot," said Two Hawks in English. "Willie has told me you wish to know more about our ways and I have agreed to show you."

The next two hours were spent in an explanation of the Shawnee's beliefs and how they thought of themselves as a part of the natural order of things. Two Hawks spoke frankly about his people's view of the white settlers.

"You seek to fight nature and conquer it. We are surprised that the Manitou hasn't struck you all down."

The discussion covered things Henry wanted to learn.

"Spotted Wolf wasn't nearly as strong as I am and yet he was able to overpower me very quickly." Henry rubbed the scar on his side as he spoke.

"He used your own strength against you. I will show you the right way to fight and how to defeat your enemy. You will need to understand our ways before you can hope to fight Spotted Wolf as an equal."

"Why did you agree to help me if I hope to kill Spotted Wolf?" Henry wanted to know.

"He will seek you to reclaim his feather which is his manhood. Spotted Wolf's pride is the cause of this feud and he is seen as a madman for this. He will not come to the Shawnee, as we will not help him anymore. The Frenchman will tell him that any white man will shoot him if he returns here. No, Spotted Wolf will seek you again, but he will let seasons pass before he does so."

Henry then told Two Hawks and Willie about the way whites would handle the attempted return of Spotted Wolf.

"Seasons may pass, many seasons in fact, and it will make no difference. Spotted Wolf will be shot on sight."

"That will not stop him from trying. He is like a snake that will slither from his den and strike you when you don't look for it."

Henry remembered reading of how assassins throughout history managed to evade traps and ambushes set for them and kill their target. How much more cunning this savage was. It put everyone he loved in jeopardy. Henry had a decision to make.

On the trip back to Somerville Willie was in good spirits until Henry asked him the name the Shawnee gave him.

After moment he answered his friend, "I am called "Poona Huck." It means Little Dog."

Chapter 33

Nearly every Sunday afternoon for the next year Henry spent with Willie and Two Hawks acquiring the skills he would need when he clashed with Spotted Wolf again. He learned how to travel in the woods silently and why the Indians moved in that fashion. While it obviously was to avoid detection by animals hunted or by an enemy, its real reason was to respect what they considered their home.

"The white man moves about like a wounded bear making noise that is ignorant and disrespectful," Two Hawks explained. "We know better."

Henry also learned that the red man believed that all living things had a spirit that needed respect less they offend Manitou.

"When you make a kill Sure Shot, honor the animal by thanking it and telling it that its death was not in vain."

Henry learned how to track by observing signs that were not at first apparent to him. A stick lying askew or hair left in a tree trunk's bark now became clues for staying on track. He learned to judge the age of a track by its appearance and even the moisture of the ground in which the track was made. Sure Shot learned how to use the sun and shadows in making an approach on quarry. He learned how to make his approach down wind.

"Remember, the turkey will see you, the deer will hear you, and the bear will smell you. It is their nature."

Henry learned how to throw and use the tomahawk and how to use the knife to attack and to defend. He learned the art of wrestling with the arm and leg throws and how to use his balance to throw his opponent off his. His stamina improved to the point where he could run with his companions without becoming winded.

The time spent with Henry also was having a positive effect on Willie. The process started when Henry found Willie drunk on a Sunday. After dunking his head in a rainwater barrel several times he ran him the entire way to the Shawnee village. Two Hawks then took the miscreant and placed him in a sweat lodge. It was not the first time this therapy was used on Willie. The brave then began Henry's training for the day. After a half hour of running and wrestling, they checked on the backslider. The alcohol was mostly sweated out of him and he was more than ready to leave the lodge. He hadn't escaped earlier because a stout squaw with a canoe paddle stood guard outside. Now he wanted water, which he drank with enthusiasm. Willie looked up, smiled at Henry, and then passed out.

"We'll have him on his feet by morning," Two Hawks assured his pupil as class resumed.

Willie's drunken episodes became fewer and fewer as the weeks passed until one Sunday as they were on their way back to Somerville, Willie told Henry he stopped drinking.

"I've found something more important for me to do," Willie announced.

"Well, tell me what it is," asked Henry.

"I'll show you soon," replied his friend.

Chapter 34

The end of the second year of Henry's contract saw Edmund now the sole proprietor of the mill at Bound Brook. Abigail was expecting their second child and baby Sarah, sporting bright red curling locks, was toddling everywhere. Caleb and Katherine were betrothed and would be married that summer. At nineteen and seventeen respectively they would be the youngest couple in the region to manage such an estate. Ben Crisp had hired and trained a deputy to replace Roberts and John Gill had made his intentions known to Mr. Lawrence concerning his daughter and was courting her with her father's consent. Henry was now just as at home in the wilderness as he was at Stony Brook or in town. He knew he had arrived at a crossroads and needed to determine what he would do next. Pastor Simmons had given Henry still another option when he spoke to him after school that Sunday.

"Henry, I have watched you mature and grow strong in the word of God these past few years and I couldn't be more pleased. I've taken the liberty to write Yale's theology department about you and they have reserved a spot in this fall's class for you."

Henry was surprised and grateful to the minister, but he explained that he felt no "calling" from God to enter into seminary.

"Please understand Pastor that I need to get my own house in order before I can think of doing any shepherding in God's house."

Simmons was disappointed but not surprised. He had hoped that with Henry's departure to New England the whole nasty affair between him and Spotted Wolf might be put to an end. What he didn't realize was that such a vendetta could no more be stopped than the spinning of the earth. Henry only had two options. He could return to Britain and try to win his older brother's freedom or he could strike out after his nemesis and bring about a showdown. He knew that by staying he was endangering the people he had come to love as family and ultimately he knew that Spotted Wolf might exact a revenge on them if he returned to England. In the end the only thing that he could do was to strike out west and face this berserk warrior who haunted his dreams.

Henry met with the Crane's and the newly engaged couple at Stony Brook that evening. He told them of his intention to leave and asked them to pray for him and keep him in their thoughts as he would pray and think about them every day.

"We want you to stay and we'll face this thing together," Edmund told him.

Henry glanced at the group around him, "That would be foolhardy and selfish on my part. This poison is meant for me and none of you will share in it."

Once they saw that there would be no persuading him to stay, Abigail and Kate withdrew and returned with a shirt, tunic and pants all made from buckskin.

"We knew in our hearts that this was the decision you would make and there could be no changing your mind so we were determined that you would be dressed for the journey," said Kate.

Abigail also produced a red cap that would later be called "le bonnet rouge" during the French Revolution.

She placed it on his head saying, "Keep your hair safely tucked under this cap till we meet again."

Caleb had a wide belt made for Henry. On the left side was the gray fox tail and on the right was located his ammunition pouch and a knife scabbard. In the scabbard was the antler- handled knife Spotted Wolf left behind when Kate shot him.

"Make sure you give this back to the wretch, Henry," Caleb told him.

Edmund then took Henry out on the porch. There tied to a post were two horses.

"Clover," Henry cried as he recognized the sheriff's mare.

"Ben thought you might need to cover some ground so he wanted you to have her."

"Tell him thanks for me, but I'll cover the ground on foot."

The training Henry had for tracking and stalking would need to be done quietly. A horse made too much noise.

Henry was to spend his last night at Stony Brook in the "bachelor's quarters" he shared with Caleb in the barn. Caleb, don't waste too much time out in this barn. Marry that girl in the house and be happy."

"That is my intention, exactly, Henry," His roommate laughed.

The next morning Henry left Stony Brook unsure if he would ever be able to return to the second place he thought of as home. He met with Ben Crisp in town at the tavern.

"I don't like the idea of you goin into that crazy snake's den after him," Ben told his friend. Ben had lost several close friends to this maniac and he didn't want to lose another.

Just then Willie entered the bar room. Gone were the trappings of the white man; he was dressed as a Shawnee brave from the turkey feathers in his hair to the moccasins on his feet.

"I have been reborn into my clan," Willie proudly said. "They now call me Tunka Hakem Wicum, Sure Shot's Strong Arm."

Willie extended his right arm toward Henry. In his right hand was a pair of moccasins. These moccasins differed from the low cut loafer types of today. Each had leggings incorporated into them. They were held securely in place by rawhide straps tied just above the calf. "They are for a warrior's feet. My people want you to have them. I am to go with you until the Manitou tells me differently."

After a mug of cider, Henry and Willie made final preparations for their journey west. Both of their packs contained dried venison jerky and hard biscuits called tack. Also an extra shirt and socks for when the weather turned, a bedroll, a razor with strap and mirror, a canteen, plus a Bible that rounded out Henry's kit. They needed to travel light.

"I've sent word west by smoke and drums that Fox Tail is coming and he carries Spotted Wolf's feather in his hair."

"Good Willie, he won't risk traveling east now that he knows I'm coming to him."

Henry still couldn't come to grips with the circumstances, as he was able to bring them to mind, and how they led to the tragic loss of his master, Thomas McAdoo. In spite of the situation of Henry's servitude, Thomas had become more like a father instead of a master. It felt like losing his actual father all over again. It was as if a deep wound that was slowly healing had been ripped wide open again in an instant. But now Henry's sadness had given way to anger and resolve.

As they began the journey west, Henry asked his companion about his full English name.

"My mother named me for my white father, William Miles." Then he added, "But I don't feel like a William Miles today."

Chapter 35

The two made their way due west until they made camp close to a Lenape encampment. The Shawnees and Lenapes were usually cordial toward each other so Willie thought it would be all right. Just the same, he went to see the village elder to get formal permission. He returned a while later with a puzzled smile on his face.

"You are known in their village, Sure Shot. Before we leave tomorrow, the Lenape chief wants to meet you."

At dawn the following day Henry and Willie broke camp and made their way to the Lenape village. Waiting to meet them was the Lenape chief, Black Rabbit. After the formal introductions were completed, the chief addressed Henry.

"I have heard that you can kill a squirrel from two hundred paces with your spirit rifle, Sure Shot."

Henry blushed, "I have made such a shot, great chief. Why do you call my rifle a spirit rifle?"

Black Rabbit simply replied, "You have given your rifle a name. If that is so then a spirit needs be in it."

Smart man Henry thought.

Black Rabbit continued, "I have a great mission for you. If you do it you will have the love of the Lenape people. There lives in these woods an evil spirit in the form of a panther that has come to plague our people. He has made the game of the forest disappear and the Lenape children's bellies are empty. Two nights ago he entered our village and killed one of our dogs. That is how I know he is a spirit. No mere cat would challenge a dog. It is against their nature. Last night your messenger comes to our village. We knew then that you must have been sent by the Manitou to rid us of this evil. Our bravest warriors go to challenge this creature but none have gotten close enough to kill it. With your spirit rifle though, you can kill this beast."

"I will try to help your people," Henry told the chief. "Show me the sign the animal has left."

After pouring over the tracks left in the village by the cougar, Henry whispered to Willie, "This is a large cat."

Black Rabbit took the pair to the edge of a cliff.

"He makes his home down there," the Lenape explained. "But it is so cleverly hidden and he crosses so much rock in getting to it that we haven't been able to find his den even with our best efforts."

Rather than trying to track over solid rock or trail a cat that possessed senses nearly a hundred times better than his, Henry figured the best way to deal with the predator was to wait on the cliff for it to return to its den. He sent Willie up a butternut tree to act as his spotter and got some branches around him to act as a blind while hunkering down to wait.

The most predictable thing about big cats is that they're unpredictable. It was getting close to sunset and there had been no trace of the panther.

"We need to get a fire going if we're staying here tonight," Willie cautioned his companion as he shinnied down the tree. "The best place for us to camp is at the base of this cliff with the rocks to our back. We'll make a fire about forty feet away from the cliff and bed down between the fire and the rocks. Hurry, we need to get enough wood to keep the fire going all night."

The night was cool, but not cold and Henry didn't understand why Willie made such a big fire or why he insisted on keeping it going like that so he asked him,

"Seems like a big fire for a night like this, doesn't it?"

"This cat hunts at night which isn't right. It has no fear of its enemy the dog, also not right. I just hope it still fears fire."

At that moment out in the distance, a panther screamed. The scream of a panther isn't something Henry would soon forget. It was easy to believe that this one was possessed by a demon by its unnerving call. Henry was startled into alertness. Both now watched out through the light of the fire for any sign of the cat. Suddenly a set of bright red eyes appeared on the other side of the blaze. That was all either of them could see. The cat screamed again sending cold shivers up and down their spines. Henry was unsure of his shot because each time he tried to sight in Kate, the heat from the fire distorted his aim. Willie was having no better luck with his bow. The big cat paced back and forth on the other side of the fire looking for an opening to rush through. Both men fed the fire and the night was spent in a desperate standoff. Luckily the wood supply lasted and just before dawn the cat seemed to realize that the hunter's aim would soon be true. With one last scream, the mountain lion ran off into the woods.

"I don't care if I ever spend a night like that again," Willie assured his cohort.

"Let's pack our kits and look for the cat's sign," Henry realized just how dangerous this predator was for the local people, both native and settler, and this doubled his determination to get it. The tracks showed that the cat was heading for the Lenape village. Both hunters followed as quickly as they could but the scream of the cat and the cries from the people told them they were too late. As they ran into the middle of the lodges they saw to their horror that the cat's victim this time was a child. Henry's rifle was up in an instant but he couldn't get a clean shot fearing he might hit the papoose. The babe fortunately was in a wooden framed carrier the natives used for their infants. The infant was still crying as the mountain lion carried it off at a run.

"We must push this animal as hard as we can so it won't have the time to stop and feed on the child," Willie shouted as he and Henry chased it on foot.

Normally the big cat could easily outdistance his pursuers, but the pack slowed it down considerably. For once the panther acted like a normal cat and quickly climbed a tree. It placed the howling infant in a crotch of the tree and began screaming at its tormenters. This was the opening Henry was hoping to get. He quickly brought Kate and fired just as the cat leaped to the attack. The ball hit the puma in the shoulder sending it off its target slightly but still knocking Henry to the ground.

Willie's arrow flew true a second later and the cat lay dead at his feet. Henry regained his senses and went over to where his friend was standing. The dead beast amazed both men. It was an enormous male. The cries of the child in the fork of the tree refocused both men's attention and they soon retrieved the baby.

When they returned to the encampment; the crying baby's mother met them. She quickly removed her child from his carrier for inspection. There wasn't one scratch on him. She dropped to Henry's feet sobbing.

"Tell her you got the cat," Henry told Willie

"We both got him, Sure Shot," Willie told his partner.

The panther was skinned and its hide was stretched over a drying board where it would be preserved in the Indian way.

Hunters were dispatched and soon brought back a deer, which would be roasted for the feast in the two men's honor. With the spirit cat gone, the other animals had returned and peace and balance was once again in the Lenape's home. Willie explained to his English friend that both of them would be remembered in stories told around the Lenape fires for generations. Black Rabbit said that the child they saved would be given the English name "Willie Henry" as well as his native name. That way the child, as he grew and became a man, would be a constant reminder to his people of the two heroes and their deed.

The next day, provisioned as best they could be by the natives, Henry and Willie set out again heading toward the river named for the Delaware.

Chapter 36

Once the two travelers reached the river, they followed it northward till they came to a place run by a Dutchman named Dingmans. He ran a ferry across the river at one of its slower moving stretches. Two teams of horses pulled the big raft back and forth across the Delaware by long thick ropes tied to either end of the craft. After paying the fee for passage, the two travelers settled onto the barge waiting for is launch. Also on the barge was a Delaware chief named Bald Eagle. He saw the young white man with the foxtail on his belt and approached him.

"Tuckahoe, Fox Tail, I see you are traveling west to meet your destiny. That is good."

Willie knew this chief and didn't trust him. He replied in the native's tongue,

"We are traveling into the frontier to seek our fortunes. Do you know where they might lie?"

The chief crossed his arms as a sign of sincerity and replied, "Across this water and into the land of the Minnisink; that is where you will find it." He then knelt by Henry and said in a low voice, "I have seen the bright red hair on his belt. It tells of his bravery. Now he waits for you."

Henry was shaking with rage as he remembered how Spotted Wolf took McAdoo's scalp, but somehow he kept himself from showing it too much.

"And I seek him," was Henry's simple reply.

The trip to the western shore having been completed, the sojourners headed further north till they came to the settlement of Milford. There they stopped at a tavern to catch up on any news of importance. The bartender was expounding on the exploits of a local hermit, "I hear he's killed at least forty of 'em with the one he got last week."

"Pardon me, sir. What are you talking about?" Henry asked.

"Why I'm talkin' about that crazy man, Tom Quick. He's killed around forty Indians so far and says he won't quit till he gets to one hundred!"

"What makes him do such a thing?" Willie wanted to know.

"Well, it seems he and his father was crossing the Delaware after it had frozen over. A band of Indians ambushed them and wounded his father with a musket ball. Tom Senior begged for his boy to get away as he was done for. Tom listened to his pa and lit out. He heard the scalping of 'ole Tom and vowed that all Indians were his enemies and he would avenge his pa one hundredfold. That boy practically lived with the Indians up to that point so he knows their ways. He took to living out in the woods and visiting his ma and his married sister every once in a while. And he took to killing the red man. He isn't too particular about women or children either. He keeps score on a coup stick. A big notch cut for a brave, a medium size notch for a squaw, and a nick for a child. He's been doin' it for over ten years now."

For just a moment, when McAdoo had been killed, Henry felt a similar flash of hatred for the native people. He was quick to realize the wicked act of an individual shouldn't be held against an entire race. He felt a level of sympathy for Tom Quick, but also was strongly opposed to the man's wanton acts of revenge.

"Why hasn't anyone tried to stop him?" Henry wanted to know.

"Most folks around here feel it's his right to do what he's doin'. Besides, if anyone tried to stop him they might not come back," with that, the bartender left the two to serve other customers.

"I feel like Willie Miles today," Willie confided to his friend.

"Spotted Wolf wouldn't spend time in these woods constantly lookin' over his shoulder for a man crazier than he is. We need to head west to find him," Henry said.

It was decided that they would pick up what items they needed in Milford and then head west to get some distance away from the land where the mad hermit exacted his revenge for the killing of his father many years before.

Willie's wish to be considered white and not native in Milford wasn't lost on Henry. How would Quick react to meeting Willie? Neither man knew. Neither man wanted to find out.

Chapter 37

Both men saw their quest from a different perspective. Henry wanted to end the blood feud between him and Spotted Wolf. He also wanted to retrieve the last bit of his former master still above ground and give it a proper burial. Willie had claimed his companion as a true brother. He had been the first to treat Willie with respect and now Sure Shot's Strong Arm meant to be just that. He would give his life for the man who had returned it to him.

They struck out toward the area referred to as Sho Hola but before they had gotten very far from Milford a strange scene began to play out before them. A thin spry man dressed in native garb but wearing a coonskin cap was running along a footpath not more than forty yards in front of them. He appeared to be unarmed. It had to be Quick. About fifty yards behind him were three Minnisink warriors armed with rifles intent on chasing the solitary man toward his obvious doom. One of the natives stopped and shot at their prey. The musket ball kicked out a shower of bark off a tree to the target's right as he ran by. Henry and Willie noticed that the man being chased was laughing!

"He is mad," Willie pronounced.

Henry knew it was wiser to move off, but the bizarreness had both he and Willie mesmerized.

A little farther along the man in the coonskin cap suddenly stopped and reached into the hollow of an oak tree. He pulled out an oilcloth bundle and quickly removed two rifles from it. Placing one of the firearms against the oak, he brought the other up to bear just as his tormentors stopped short. The hermit's musket ball found the first native before either could begin to aim their pieces. Quickly discarding the discharged rifle he had the second on his shoulder just as the remaining brave with a loaded piece fired his weapon. The shot went about an inch high knocking off the coonskin cap as it did so. A cruel smile appeared on the ambusher's face as he killed his second victim. The warrior who had fired the first shot ran past his two dead comrades with a

tomahawk in hand crying his battle cry. The hermit produced a tomahawk and a knife and did likewise. The battle was violent and terrible.
The adversaries each had great skill in the use of their weapons but the
one with the coonskin cap soon caught his enemy's tomahawk blow
with his own and finished him with a knife thrust to his chest. He then
calmly sat down and brought out a pine stick from its place on his belt
where it had been stuck. Tom Quick had just finished his third notch
when Henry and Willie carefully approached him.

"That makes forty five of 'em I've sent off to see my pappy," Without looking at them, Tom Quick demanded, "Who be you two?"

"I'm Henry St. Albans and this is my friend, Willie Miles."

Quick returned to the oak tree where he cleaned and reloaded the
two rifles. Then he wrapped them again in the oilcloth and returned
them to the hollow of the tree.

"I'll wager your friend's got some squaw for a mammy if he
doesn't, Henry?"

Both men took a step back and placed a hand on a weapon.

"Relax boys," Tom laughed, "his pappy's blood is what counts with
me."

Quick pointed toward the three dead braves. "That trick only works
when there's no more than three of 'em. Otherwise I takes 'em to the
cliff."

Both men shook their heads in wonder. Henry asked, "What about
their bodies? You can't just leave them here."

"Their family knew what they were up to. They'll be along directly
to collect their carcasses. If not, the critters around here will make fast
work of them." Quick took the time now to look Henry and Willie over
more closely, "What brings you to these woods?" the hermit wanted to
know.

"I have a blood feud to settle with an Indian named Spotted Wolf."
Henry explained.

"Ne-Tuk-He-Do, eh?" Quick used his native name, "I've a standing
invite for him to come see me. Now I know he's got some unfinished
business to settle with you first. Say, I'm going to my ma's for supper
tonight. Why don't the two of you come along? She's a good cook and
you can tell me more about this feather you are a carryin'."

Mrs. Quick's home was a tidy affair with a working gristmill attached. Tom was right about his mother's cooking. Spring gobbler with canned potatoes and a sausage stuffing had both Henry and Willie paying their compliments to the mistress of the house. After the meal, while Mrs. Quick was cleaning up, Henry told Tom about Spotted Wolf's vendetta. Tom exhaled some pipe smoke and made a simple but correct comment.

"It's you or him in this scrap."

"Let me ask you something that is puzzling me," Henry started, "Why haven't any of the tribes in the area tried to kill your mother or sister?"

"They tried once early on," the hermit replied, "but killing a Quick these days is no easy thing to do. I set up a snare on a path near the house back then and sure enough soon there was a brave in face paint hanging from his ankles. I led him back to his village and sent him to my pa in front of his family telling them I would burn their whole village if anyone tried that again."

Henry and Willie stared at each other. Quick was mad with a blood-lust and both had goose bumps when Quick told the gruesome tale much as one would tell of a trip to town.

"So long as I don't stay the night, no Indian will attack this home. They've come to think me possessed by spirits and the death of my mother or sister at their hands would give me big medicine to use against them. I'm leaving now, but Ma says you two are welcome to stay the night if you wish. My brother, Kurt is expected back from town anytime now."

The scourge of the Delaware was gone for only a few minutes when his younger brother returned home. Kurt told his two guests that Tom had more than a dozen places where he would camp for the night, and never for more than one night each time. He also told them about the many times his family pleaded with Tom to forget his quest only to get the same answer. "My pa's hair and his silver shirt cuff buttons are in some Minnisink's bag and I mean to have 'em so he can rest."

"It's strange a warrior hasn't caught him in all these years," Willie wondered out loud.

"He has been caught a couple of times," Kurt replied. "One time a brave had him dead to rights near the cliffs north of here. Tom thought fast and asked the Indian if he wanted a crack at Tom Quick."

"Take me to him," said the warrior cocking his rifle.

So Tom leads him to the cliffs, points down and says, "He's right there."

The red man rushes to the edge, looks around, and asks Tom, "Where?"

As Tom shoves him off the cliff he says, "Here."

Chapter 38

The two guests bid Kurt and Mrs. Quick a fond farewell early the next morning. Henry was sure that he wouldn't meet anyone as strange as Tom Quick again. He was thankful for the use of the outbuilding where Willie and he had spent the night. In spite of the assurances that no local native dared to try anything, Henry slept that night with his rifle even closer to him than normal. The two began heading for the wooded country known as the Sho Hola. This was a hunting ground used by the Delawares, Muncees, Tunkhannocks, and Iroquois. They soon came upon a small party of Tunkhannocks. Willie knew they were a hunting party because they wore no face paint. He knew they were Tunkhannock because of the way most of them wore their hair in a single braid to the left side. Willie asked them about Spotted Wolf, and was shocked to hear that he was no longer in the Poconos. They explained that Bald Eagle had sent for Spotted Wolf and several more of his best warriors to accompany him north to a place called Tioga where a large council of nations was being called. A Mohawk war chief named Two Sticks, but known to the whites as Joseph Brant had gotten the nations to cooperate. Brant could speak all six Iroquois dialects and was fluent in the Delaware and Shawnee tongues.

Educated at what would later become Dartmouth College, he was a favorite of the British and a hero of his people.

"Only a war chief/sachem with big medicine could get all the nations to come to him," Willie told Henry after the hunting party had gone on their way.

It was 1776 and the American Revolution was visible in New England and the colony of New Jersey. William Johnson, the brother-in-law of Joseph Brant, was Britain's vice governor for Indian affairs in New York and wanted a powerful ally in place so Great Britain could start a second front on the western frontier, if desired. Brant agreed to hold a council to prepare the natives to be that ally.

With their quest now taking on a twist, the two wayfarers traveled to Tobyhanna, a trading post in the middle of the Poconos. There Henry and Willie would calculate the next moves to be made. Henry wanted to charge ahead to Tioga and end the matter. The burden of the quest and the unexpected changes that surprised them at each turn were weighting more and more on him. Willie knew on the other hand that blood feuds sometimes took years, even decades. Henry needed to carefully consider each move much like in a game of chess. The final move in this contest wasn't turning a king on its side; it was putting a man in the ground.

It was at Tobyhanna where the two young men met up with some Yankees from Connecticut who were traveling to the Wyoming Valley to settle in that colony's Westmoreland County. Willie convinced Henry that offering to scout for them until they reached their destination was in everyone's best interest. The Yankees readily accepted, and the next leg of the journey began. The settler's destination was a stockaded town on the north branch of the Susquehanna River named Forty-Fort.

Both woodsmen noticed signs that they were being watched. A grouse would explode out of cover a distance away or a squirrel would begin scolding without apparent provocation. No incidents occurred otherwise and they reached the settlement of Forty- Fort that evening.

The colonists from Connecticut and Pennsylvania both claimed the wide fertile Wyoming Valley as their own and as a result a half-hearted separate conflict now raged in the area. When the boys from New Jersey heard about this extra little complication they wasted no time in making plans to strike out further west into the land of the Lenape-Hanne and the Susquehannocks.

The next day, freshly provisioned, they started out for the village known as French Margaret's Town. The niece of a mixed breed named Lady Montour started this trading village some twenty years before. Both Lady Montour and French Margaret acted as interpreters for Pennsylvania's Executive Council in that council's dealings with the Iroquois. This gave both women great status among the Indians and the colonial government, too. Indeed, Pennsylvania granted a tract of land at the confluence of the west branch of the Susquehanna River and Lycoming Creek to French Margaret for services rendered and that is where she built her town.

As they sat on a bench outside the mercantile a settler named Peter

Smith stepped on the porch to go inside and with Smith was a familiar face, Evan Silverthorne.

"If that just doesn't beat St. Peter playing his harp!" exclaimed Henry as he hugged his friend. "Henry, and is this Willie from Somerville?"

Willie had been transformed from a lost soul into strong capable frontiersman since Evan last saw him. Evan couldn't believe his good fortune in meeting up with his old friends.

"We have a farm up on the Loyalsock River about a half day from here. Peter here owns a neighboring homestead. Evan quickly introduced Smith to his old friends.

"We travel in groups when going for supplies anymore as the natives around here have been convinced by the Tories from up north that we mean them harm. It's been through the diligence of Samuel Brady and Robert Covenhoven that we have thwarted several Indian attacks."

Chapter 39

Brady and Covenhoven were gaining reputations as skilled Indian fighters and the area had settled into a tense standoff. The natives who wanted nothing to do with war would warn settlers who they traded with. Those settlers would send a runner or mounted messenger to the militia and either Brady or Covenhoven would rush out to repulse the raiders. Indians were beginning to send out raiding parties to kill or kidnap white settlers. To encourage this heinous act the British were paying four pounds for a white scalp. Ransomed hostages demanded even more. Other kidnap victims such as Simon Girty turned renegade and raided along with the Indians. The wanton raiding of villages wasn't done exclusively by the natives either. Certain "militias" were formed for the express purpose of attacking Indian settlements and they weren't particular if they were peaceful or not.

One infamous example was the militia raid on an Oneida village by Captain Jack Wilson. This village was located in a place called Old Town, which was across the Juniata River from a white settlement. Wilson and his men entered the village and after determining that most of the braves were absent, and using a stolen pig as a pretext they slaughtered those that remained and fired the encampment. Yellow Beeches Creek Massacre was one of the most brutal killings perpetrated by whites against native people up until that time. The men of the village were off on a hunting foray and returned with their arms full of game to what remained of their home. Afterward some headed north to Tioga to join Brant and the English, but most stayed with their chief, Cuttenugenaga who was better known by his English name, John Logan. Logan led what remained of his people into the Ohio country were his exploits continued to add to his reputation.

One of the acts he is best remembered for was a moving speech given before the signing of a treaty with the United States many years later. It is known as Logan's Lament. A once famous, but now forgotten, passage of his speech is a haunting prediction as well as a personal sorrow. "Who is left to weep for Logan? No one."

Evan told Henry and Willie that Brady's father was a captain in the Continental Army and was serving with Washington in New Jersey. Samuel and his brother James also served in Washington's army, but were released to return and care for their mother in their father's absence.

Covenhoven was part of a group of settlers called the "Fair Play Men." This group of settlers came about due to an error in the Treaty of Fort Stanwix some ten years earlier. The treaty laid out the western boundary for the expansion of white settlers in Pennsylvania. That boundary was to be Tiadaghton Creek. The problem with that was there was no Tiadaghton Creek. The natives declared that the border was really Lycoming Creek. The "Fair Play" men said it was Pine Creek some twenty miles to the west. Curiously, the Executive Council of Pennsylvania sided with the Indians so all claims to land west of Lycoming Creek weren't recognized by the government. The "squatters" had a simple solution to that problem. They established their own form of government.

Three "select men" were chosen by the landowners and sat in on mostly judicial disputes that occurred from time to time. The most unusual rule was also the most important one. A landowner had to be present on their land. Absentee landowners couldn't provide for a common defense if attacked by raiding parties. The only exception to this rule was if you were serving in the army as several volunteered to do. Otherwise if you were gone for more than a couple of weeks you were banished. They actually loaded the offender and his belongings on a raft and floated it down the river toward Fort Augusta.

It seemed like a fair system to Henry and Willie and they made a joke about it. Evan told them that it was no joke and that family's lives depended on the steadfastness of their neighbors. "It's a tried and true reality out here on the frontier," Evan assured them.

Thomas said that very same thing to me the day I met him. Henry remembered.

Chapter 40

Evan wanted to know what had happened back in New Jersey after his family left. Henry told him about the death of his master and mistress.

"A terrible thing it is," Evan remarked. "My Pa will be saddened by hearin' it. This feud with that Delaware sounds like the worst business."

"It's a business I mean to put behind me just as soon as I can. Evan, how are your sisters Sarah and Rachel?" Sarah was just a baby when the Silverthorne's moved west, but Rachel was around Katherine's age.

"Sarah's near four and is into just about everything. Rachel is still the best rider in the family and bosses me around something awful. You two have to come back with me. My family wouldn't forgive me if I didn't bring you back."

So Henry and Willie agreed to postpone their mission in favor of going back to the Loyalsock with Smith and Evan. They got a rousing welcome from the Silverthorne's when they arrived.

Mr. & Mrs. Silverthorne had moved into this region because both of them grew uncomfortable with the trappings of civilization. Both had a frontier spirit that made them get up and go when things got too complicated. This had been the third move west for them in the last ten years.

Henry Thought that Rachel was about the most beautiful creature he had ever seen. She was barely five feet tall, but carried herself with assurance. She had long chestnut colored hair and large expressive brown eyes. Henry found himself lost in those eyes, and lost for words as well. If it wasn't for ending the feud with Spotted Wolf Henry was tempted to have asked Mr. Silverthorne's permission to court her.

The Silverthorne's offered Henry and Willie the use of their barn if they wanted to stay the night.

"If it means getting some more of those biscuits with honey in the morning then I'm all for it," Willie pronounced.

Henry mumbled something no one understood, but it was interpreted as his agreement.

"What was wrong with you?" Willie asked his friend later after they bedded down for the night in the barn.

"I don't know what you mean," Henry, now with his ability to speak restored, replied to his sidekick.

"Yes you do," chided his friend.

It was several hours after sun down when the call of a jay woke both men up.

Jays don't call at night both thought. Both armed themselves in a moment and raced out the front of the barn.

"I'm making for that bunch of trees over there," Henry pointed. "Come around the other side of the barn and circle around about a hundred yards out and I'll meet you in the middle."

Both men left their long-range weapons with their bedrolls and armed themselves with tomahawk and knife. Henry raced for the stand of trees while Willie slipped around in the other direction. He had just made it to the trees when he heard the sounds of a pitched battle off in the direction Willie had taken. Henry ran directly toward the sound to help his friend. In the moonlight he could make out two braves attacking Willie, so he ran straight into the melee striking one of the attackers with his tomahawk. A third brave stepped out from behind a nearby tree and joined in with his knife. With one of their number wounded, the three intruders took the first opportunity to make off into the woods.

"It would be foolhardy to chase them at night especially if there are still more of them out there," said Willie. "Besides, I don't think I can run."

Henry realized at once that his friend had been wounded. Half carrying and half dragging his friend to the farm house, Henry's pounding on the farmhouse door brought lit candles and help. Willie was laid on the table and his wound was inspected. It was a long nasty gash on his left leg. During the course of the contest Willie had redirected a knife thrust meant for his chest and the leg wound was the result.

The cut was cauterized and bound in short order. Henry's traveling companion was going to be laid up for at least a few days.

"He'll stay right here," Mrs. Silverthorne declared. "He saved our home from being sacked and burned and my men from being killed.

He's to stay in our own bed, Mr. Silverthorne, till he's well enough to leave it."

Mr. Silverthorne nodded his assent.

Willie asked to speak to Henry in private once everything had settled back down. "Sure Shot, I got a good look at the three of them. This family might be in real big trouble. I'm sure they are Smoke Warriors from the Mohawk nation," Willie went on to tell his friend about this particular class of warrior. "They are trained for one purpose and that is war. They don't hunt for a village. They don't marry. They take women from other tribes and rape them to satisfy themselves. When there is peace they are used as assassins and kidnappers by their chiefs. The only way to stop them is to kill them or wound one so that he can no longer function as one of them. Your tomahawk blow to that brave's shoulder probably has sealed his fate, but he will face it with a smile on his face."

Henry was trying to make sense of what Willie had just told him. Finally all he could think to ask was, "Why do they call them Smoke Warriors?"

"Because," Willie glanced out the window and finished, "these warriors are as hard to grasp as smoke."

Henry helped the Silverthorne men with chores the next morning. It felt good doing the tasks he had been taught by Thomas McAdoo once again. Rachel brought them the water bucket at mid-morning and Henry was god-smacked by her countenance again.

"The Henry St. Albans I remember was a chatterbox," Rachel teased.

Henry's mind flashed on what Willie had told him last night and he found his voice, "Rachel, I need to meet with Sam Brady today if possible. I mean to follow those three from last night and with Willie on his back, Brady or someone like him who knows these woods can be a big help to me."

"Sam and James are working their father's homestead and caring for their mother. It's by Wolf Run, maybe an hour by foot south. Just follow the creek here and you'll come to it."

After lunch Henry went in to see Willie and told him of his plan. Willie was starting on a fever that sometimes is the aftermath of a wound like he suffered.

"I can't seem to get warm, Sure Shot."

Mrs. Silverthorne applied a cold compress to Willie's head and put another blanket on him.

"I could use that sweat lodge right now, Henry."

Just as he was about to leave, Willie, in an apparent delirium, shouted to his friend, "Watch out for the wolf. He will appear from out of the smoke."

The journey to the Brady farm took an hour just like Rachel said and out toiling in the fields were the two Brady men. Samuel was in his mid- twenties, tall and muscular and James, several years his junior, thinner and shorter and with bright red hair and freckles. The hair, Henry thought about how much it was like McAdoo's. He would take a liking to this fellow immediately.

"I've heard some stories about these Mohawks," Samuel began after Henry had told about what had occurred last night. "You're right in trying to take the fight to them and I'm going to join you. You need to be aware about undertakings like these, though. They usually turn out in a way that no one could have expected."

Brady's words were like those of a prophet. Samuel would go, so would a hired hand named Barker who had experience as a tracker. James would stay behind and look after his parent's interests at the farm.

Before the group had departed James approached Henry and asked, "Did you see Rachel before you left? Did she tell you anything to say to me?"

Aha! Henry thought. *One of Rachel's conquests. I wonder how many more there are?*

"I am to convey to you her best regards," Henry made up.

A smile spread from ear to ear on the young man's face, "That sounds just like her, too," James said wistfully.

Chapter 41

The three made it back to the Silverthorne farm and picked up on the tracks left by the three attackers when they fled.

"They have a big start on us," Barker remarked. "Even with a wounded man they will make it to "Prayer Rocks" and beyond before we can close on them."

"The wounded man won't slow them down. He is probably with his ancestors as we speak. And I don't think they are running, at least not to get clean away." Samuel paced back and forth, "It seems too coincidental to me that on the night Henry and Willie arrive that this attack takes place. The retreat seems odd too. There were still two of them and they could have continued the attack expecting success unless…" Samuel's voice trailed off as he continued his pacing.

"Unless what?" Henry asked.

"Unless the purpose was to surprise you, kidnap you, and take you away for ransom."

"Spotted Wolf!" The revelation had come to Henry like a bolt from the blue,

"He couldn't or wouldn't come himself so he sends minions to do his dirty work. They can't kill me because I carry his feather. He has to do that himself or he would be disgraced. They meant to carry me off to him."

"And I mean to take the fight to them," Brady was moving and then abruptly stopped. "If I know anything about these types, it's that they'll head to water to regroup afterward trying to lay out an ambush for anyone on their trail. Instead we will lay our own ambush. By going directly up stream for about two miles to where the Great Shamokin Path runs we can get ahead of them. Then we wait. I know they'll be coming along this path eventually and we'll already be there set to ambush them."

"What if they are watching us now?" Henry wondered.

"That's what I'm counting on. What are some things you carry or wear that let's someone recognize you from a distance?"

"I guess it would be my rifle and my cap. Those are the two things that people seemed to know I have even before I get to a place."

"You are going to swap rifles and hats with Evan; and to make it look good, shirts. Evan, Oliver, and Barker are going to set out following the Mohawk tracks making a big show about it and not getting very far. We are going to slip away and go up stream. After about a half hour, Evan will take off the cap to show them that he isn't you."

"What if they attack them out of anger?"

"I don't say there isn't some danger to the ruse, but if they are who Willie says they are, then they won't let their anger jeopardize the chance to bring you back to Spotted Wolf and their master, Two Sticks."

Henry and Evan went into the farmhouse and a short time later the diversion began. While the three decoys made a loud demonstration for the benefit of any lurking smoke warriors, Samuel and Henry quietly slipped out the back way and soon reached the creek bed. They used the embankment of the stream as cover and soon came to the spot where the stream and the path came closest.

"Now we conceal ourselves and wait." Samuel said in a low tone.

It is the squirrels and blue jays that call out a warning when danger is approaching telling you need to be on the alert. They calm down in about ten minutes or so if you keep still and quiet. That same alert system works again when other threats venture into the area. Soon the squirrels were acting agitated again. Up the path came the two Mohawks making for the creek for a drink and plot their next attempt.

Smoke warriors wore no special adornments except for two beaded leather gauntlets that were worn on the forearms. Necklaces and breastplates made noise and smoke warriors' eschewed noise. The first brave suddenly began to move even more cautiously than he had before. He notched an arrow in his bow and slowly moved in a crouch. The second brave stopped but didn't adopt his companion's stance.

They haven't found us. Henry realized. *They're hunting for food.*

A feral pig suddenly broke from its cover. It was the ancestral offspring of a domestic sow that had gotten loose decades before. The pig ran. The smoke warrior's arrow found its mark just as Henry and Samuel sprang their ambush. Samuel's target fell were he stood, but Henry's shot, which was a second after Samuel's, missed as his adversary threw himself to the ground at the sound of the first rifle's report. No battle cry. These warriors lived and fought in silence. The brave was up and on a dead run toward Henry. Henry with tomahawk and knife at the ready prepared to meet the onslaught. Samuel was hurriedly trying to reload his weapon. The native leaped much as the mountain lion did when it came at Henry from the tree. This time Henry fell backward bringing up his feet and propelled the Mohawk over him just as Two Hawks had shown him. The thrown man and Henry were both up and facing each other in an instant. They circled each other looking for an opening each might exploit. Samuel had in the meantime reloaded his rifle but couldn't fire as each combatant dashed and feigned at one another.

Use his strength against him. Two Hawks' words were with the student. Henry took a step back and the brave saw this as an opening, perhaps a sign of fear. The Mohawk lunged swinging his hatchet down at his victim as he did so. Henry's step back was followed quickly by a side step so that he was able to deflect the strike with his tomahawk and strike with his knife as the attacker passed by. The blade found entry between the third and fourth rib of the Indian. It was a kill strike and both the victor and the vanquished knew it.

As he lay on the forest floor the Indian looked Henry in the eyes. There was no fear there nor was there hatred. He tried to sing his death song but as blood began trickling from his mouth, he found it was impossible. Henry bent down to the dying man to sing a song the Shawnee taught him. The warrior smiled and grasped Henry by the elbow in an expression of thanks and then was gone. Samuel stood over the two until it was over.

"If I live to be a hundred, I'll never understand the red man," Samuel muttered.

"Help me take these gauntlets off of them, Samuel. We'll send them back to Spotted Wolf to show him their failure. That piggy needs to be dressed out too. It'll make a fine meal for us tonight."

Henry was fine until after the two of them got back to the Silverthorne homestead. Past midnight, lying on his bedroll, Henry was dreaming of the afternoon's fight. In his dream his adversary lunges forward like he did before except as he leaps he transforms into a wolf that runs on as Henry misses with his strike.

The wolf laughs as he heads off saying, "The wolf will have the fox yet."

Suddenly Henry is looking down into the face of the dying warrior who changes into Thomas McAdoo. The Scotsman's red hair is missing. Looking with widened eyes at his man McAdoo utters, "Taking a human life is taking a thing that cannot be repaid. It is a personal cost which you must somehow bear."

Henry sat bolt upright on the floor of the barn. His heart was nearly pounding out of his chest as he quickly glanced around while coming to his senses. His forehead was beaded with cold sweat that he wiped away and then, putting his hands to his face, he broke down. Still shy of eighteen, he had the terrible realization that he killed a man.

Sure Shot checked on Willie after chores and breakfast the next morning.

"Sounds like I missed some battle," Willie remarked. "I'm beginning to feel like an old woman stuck here as I am."

"Those biscuits with honey are plenty good, huh Willie? I bet they make up for it."

Henry's sidekick chuckled and nodded.

"Mrs. Silverthorne has cured your fever and another couple of days will find you mended well enough for us to travel. We need to get away from here so we cause no harm to befall our friends," Henry then told Willie about his dream.

"You have truly been visited by messenger spirits who have given you your path to follow. There must be a shaman in French Margaret's town who can fully explain the dream to you. Wrap the leather wrist pieces in white wampum. That will show that they were defeated honorably in battle."

"What happened to the third smoke warrior?" Sure Shot wondered out loud.

"His wrist pieces have already been delivered," Willie assured him.

Chapter 42

It was a fact that the council held in Tioga had produced mixed results for Joseph Brant. Four of the six nations of the Iroquois people had sided with the Mohawk chief. The Oneida and the Tuscarora chose to go their own way. Likewise only certain clans of the Delaware pledged loyalty to the British. Some natives could still move between the loyalists and the rebels with little difficulty. Likewise some colonists could do the same thing. Battle lines on the frontier were sometimes fuzzy.

Barker had returned to the Brady farm to rejoin James working the land. Samuel agreed to accompany Henry to French Margaret's town to send off the legacy of the smoke warriors. French Margaret had passed away nearly a decade before and her son, Peter Quebec, was now proprietor of the trading post. He carried on his mother's business and her prohibition of alcohol.

Henry asked the Seneca half-breed, "Where can I get wampum? I need to send a warrior's talisman back to his chief."

"Did he die a good death?" Quebec wanted to know.

"Both died in battle," Samuel broke in.

"I would also like to know if there is a seer here," Henry finished.

"You will find both items you seek in the lodge at the end of town," Margaret's son said. "It is the home of old Lacomus."

The outside of Lacomus' lodge was covered with amulets and totems denoting its resident as a shaman and oracle. A young boy stood at the lodge's entrance so that if Lacomus ever needed anything all he need do was to call out and it would be fetched and brought to him. The doorman also announced anyone wanting an audience with the shaman. The boy made the old man aware of the two whites seeking admittance.

"Send in the one who carries his enemy's knife," the old man said in a raspy voice.

Henry was stunned by the utterance in English and also by its divining nature. Inside sat an old man wrapped in a blanket by a small fire. The weather was far from cold, but the old man was shivering.

From a leather pouch the shaman withdrew a small amount of powder and sprinkled it into the fire, which made the powder sparkle and give off a red tinged cloud of smoke.

"Come and sit at my right side. The spirits speak to me in my left ear. The Delawares and Iroquois call you Fox Tail. The Shawnee and Lenapes call you The Sure Shot. You will be given yet another name by your white brothers. It will be your spirit name and all will come to call you by it."

"I need to get these back to the chief who sent them," Henry showed the shaman the gauntlets."

"Leave them with me. They will find their way back to their sender," Lacomus set the gauntlets down at his left side.

"I have need for you to explain the meaning of a dream I had last night," and then Henry described his dream to the shaman.

"I see a pack of wolves chasing a fox through the forest. No matter what the fox does he cannot trick them because the wolf is also the spirit trickster. The fox is finally trapped, but he is no longer a fox. He is Kii-Ree, the eagle, and he flies out of the pack's reach. You will find the meaning of your dead chief's words only from the words of your holy men."

Henry left the dead braves belongings with the oracle knowing they would reach Spotted Wolf. The meeting left him with more questions about his dream now than he had before. Rejoining Samuel, they made their way back to Silverthorne's farm where Evan joined them for the trip back to the Brady's. It was starting to get on toward dusk when the two old friends began their return trip to the Loyalsock homestead. Henry was hungry not having anything to eat since breakfast, but rather than taking the evening meal with Samuel and his family, he decided to push on back with Evan opting to chew on some jerky from his pouch to quell his hunger. Halfway back in the moonlit night they chanced upon a solitary brave coming in the other direction. Both saw the native at the same time. Rather than hunker down the brave raised his arm in a greeting.

"This could be a trap. Evan I want you behind me and slightly to my right. If you hear any call I want you off this path and running back to the Brady's as fast as you can run."

"I'd …"

"Evan, we don't have time to argue. They'll kidnap me, but they'll kill you. My only chance is you getting help to rescue me before they get me to Tioga."

Not a minute later a jay call echoed through the forest.

"Run!"

Evan did as he was told. The Fox Tail broke to his left running down into a shallow gully and began to run due west toward an Indian village named Otstuagy. (Today named Montoursville after its founder, Lady Montour. Lady Montour was the aunt of French Margaret and was a Christian. Likewise were nearly all of the residents of her village.)

The Fox Tail had nearly two miles to cover to reach the village and an unknown number of pursuers. If both he and Evan had tried to make it back to Brady's, both would have probably been captured and Evan's life would have been forfeit. He took some consolation in that when they broke up it caused some hesitation for his would-be captors. He needed to cover ground now and again his conditioning and the knowledge he gained from his time with Two Hawks served him well. He could hear his adversaries as they came on much as a wolf pack would pursue its prey. He was racing up the side of a mountain now. The rocks and undergrowth were having an effect on his progress not to mention the grade of the slope itself. His muscles were on fire and he was becoming winded. The "wolf pack" seemed to be closing on him. He saw the summit ahead in the moonlight and used every ounce of his strength to reach it. He was about thirty yards in the lead at the top where the other side simply dropped off. In his mind he heard the cry of the eagle, *Kii-Ree!* He leapt into space.

About forty feet down branches of the pines that grew below began to break his fall. He reached out trying to gain a hold on one of them and nearly had his arms ripped off, but it slowed him some more. Now Kate, which was strapped to his back, did its part in slowing him down by catching in some of the smaller limbs. He tried again to grasp onto the tree. This time he caught and held on. He was on a lower branch of the tree, battered and bruised, but alive and still free. Below him it was pitch black and the sound of water could be heard. Should he try to crawl down and continue his race or should he hold up here in the tree until daylight? His physical condition dictated his course; he was spent.

There would be no easy way to track him and he needed rest.

They probably think I fell to my death, Henry thought as he rubbed a battered shoulder. *I nearly did.*

The morning would be a bit of an equalizer for Henry. In the light of day his skill with Kate would make any group of kidnappers wary. If he had reasonable field of sight he might even be able to reload and dispatch two of them before they would be on him. Trying to slip up on him quietly would be suicide for them. Henry knew every trick they could use and they knew he did. They could press the issue, but with a poor outcome. The young man sitting on his perch that night recalled the words of Lacomus. Sleep came in fits. *I need to get into my Bible as soon as I can.* Henry decided.

Morning broke in the east and with it a peace surrounded the young man. He quickly saw that there was a ledge directly below the tree he was in. The ledge dropped away at an angle toward the river below. The west branch of the Susquehanna River was about four hundred yards wide and about three feet deep at this point. There was a current but a strong man could ford it here without too much of a problem. The real problem was one of exposing himself to capture once out in the openness of the water. Henry was sticking to the tree for now. His shoulder throbbed with pain and might be dislocated. His right shin felt liked it was scraped to the bone. His face was bruised and swollen and one of his teeth was loose. His hands, although hardened by work, were friction burned and sore. He did an inspection of his gear and found he hadn't lost anything except his cap and soon located that lying on the ledge below.

Kate looked in proper working order after his inspection. It was light out now and Henry felt a compulsion to get out of the tree. After a pain-filled effort, he reached the base of the tree and tried his legs on solid ground. They held him and he could walk, even run if he had to again. Picking up his cap and placing it on his head showed him that his left arm could be brought up to his chest but no more without crippling pain. He could hide or run; fighting wasn't possible. By propping Kate in the bough of a tree he might get one of them. He couldn't reload the rifle without use of both arms so that would be a foolish or desperate act. Fording the river started looking more attractive. Still there was not one telltale giveaway that those trying to kidnap him were nearby. He would stay put for now hoping that Evan had reached Samuel and that they were tracking him. One hour passed and then two hours. Finally at mid-morning Henry heard the animals reacting to a human presence. He hunkered down on the ledge trying to become as small a visible object as possible. Minutes went by then, after perhaps a half hour, a voice called out his name. It was Brady and young Silverthorne was with him.

Once the rescue party saw Henry's condition it was decided that a trip to the Indian village across the river was the best choice. There was a river ford was about a mile upstream and the trio was in the hut of Lady Montour's son, Andrew Croc an hour later. Croc welcomed them and served them sassafras tea and corn meal cakes. He sent for the town's healer who used homeopathic remedies with better results than most traditional medical treatments of the time. After a general inspection of injuries, she brought forth a liniment made from the bark of a certain birch tree that also had the strong odor of mint. She rubbed the concoction on Henry's shin and hands then put some on a stick and motioned for Henry to rub it around his loose tooth. The pain was lessened substantially by the salve. A derivative from an acid in the bark would become the active ingredient in aspirin a century and a half later. Next she motioned for Henry to lie on his back with both arms extended out at a ninety-degree angle from his body. Stooping over him, she stuck the liniment stick between his teeth, dropped to the floor in a sitting position with both legs extended straight under his left armpit. She leaned forward grabbing his arm with both hands then leaned back and pulled with all her might. Henry bit through the stick as an audible pop could be heard. Both parties to the treatment rose from the floor and to almost everyone's surprise, Henry had his shoulder restored to working order. It was sore, but it worked.

"I should like to pay the healer for her services," Henry told Croc.

Croc related his offer to the girl in one of the native dialects both he and the healer understood. She looked at the Fox Tail and told Croc her fee.

Andrew Croc asked Henry to take a walk with him as he explained what the girl wanted, "Before I tell you her price I think it is necessary to tell you about our healer."

Croc began, as they started walking the length of the town, "Her name is New Moon or A-Far-Ata in her own tongue. She was stolen away by an Iroquois war party from her people about four years ago. Her own people, the Juniata, always considered her born under a special sign and so she was taught to heal and to minister to the sick from an early age. This worked to her advantage when she healed a chief of a fever on the way back north to Tioga after her capture. That warrior just happened to be married to my niece, Esther. She took New Moon into her home and thought to marry her to one of her sons, but none of them wanted her at their fires. I think they feared her because she was touched by the Manitou. Esther visited me about three years back on a trading trip and brought New Moon with her hoping to sell her to someone. An old Shaman, who would use her previous knowledge and taught her his ways, bought her. The Shaman died last year and she has been waiting since then for you."

"What do you mean, 'waiting for me'?" Henry wanted to know.

"I wouldn't have given it another thought except that she told me about you six months ago," Croc replied. "She said that she had a dream that was so vivid that she knew it came from the Manitou. In it she met a stranger that had received wounds to the head, his arm, and leg. The wounds weren't received in battle with an enemy, but were of a spirit nature. The place of the wounds on the man revealed the message. The head indicated the man to be experienced in the ways of the forest with knowledge of how to survive there. The arm and hands showed him to be willing to use his talents to help another. The leg indicated a journey that he will make to fulfill a debt. "Clad like my people, but not of my people," were her exact words to me. This is important too, "He will offer; I will not need to ask. Fox Tail, she wants you to return her to her people."

Henry was absorbing Andrew's explanation of the payment. Samuel's words about how reaching a goal or plan was usually met with unexpected twists came to mind when New Moon sidled up to him. What she said next surprised Henry. Not the content so much as the fact it was in broken English.

"Take where two rivers meet, go to where two rivers meet again."

Henry looked at Croc with a puzzled expression.

"She's talking about Clark's Ferry, I think," Lady Montour's son offered.

Chapter 43

Three experienced frontiersmen on their guard presented a formidable obstacle for any kidnap attempt. They went as a group from Otstuagy to the Silverthorne homestead. New Moon easily kept up with them so she wouldn't be a problem. The problem was paying the debt. It would take them into a part of the frontier they hadn't counted on traveling through inhabited by those who might take exception to the visit. The traveling band reached the Silverthorne place where they exchanged Evan's company for Willie's, who by now was busting at the seams to get back out into the outdoors.

Willie didn't like the sounds of Henry's repayment and let him know it,

"This is bad. We could end up on some brave's brag belt. The Susquehannocks are fearsome and we are walking into their fires."

"Willie, this is a debt only I need to pay. You know I will miss you, but…"

Willie stopped his friend, "Our path is one path, Sure Shot."

The company made its way to Wolf Run where Samuel rejoined his family. Samuel suggested they go to Wallis' stockade and spend the night there. The Wallis house was built of stone and was nearly impregnable. It was a large affair with heavy shutters and gun slits. If they said Samuel sent them, they would be welcomed. The Wallis' did indeed welcome them and fed them too. The night was spent relatively carefree within the secure confines of the stone house. The next morning found Henry, Willie, and New Moon ready to travel to the Susquehanna River. They would trade for a canoe at the first opportunity and travel by water until they reached the confluence of the Susquehanna and Juniata Rivers. They made a deal for the canoe soon after coming to the river. It was an old second canoe used by a white trapper to haul furs down river to the trading post at Watson's Town. An old canoe but water-tight and serviceable. Now the three were floating downstream to their first destination, Fort Augusta. Several times all three passengers in the canoe caught a glimpse of braves making their way along the river's edge. They seemed to be following them from the outpost.

"Why don't they try to overtake us by canoe?" Henry asked.

"The outcome would be in doubt. I don't think there are more than three maybe four warriors tracking us. If they sent any more into this land the Susquehannocks would attack them. The reason New Moon's people are this far south is because they are protected here by the Susquehannocks."

They reached Fort Augusta before nightfall and hadn't seen sign of their followers for the last three miles.

"I doubt if they will follow us any further south, Sure Shot. They risk pushing the local people too far. I think they will wait for our return."

Henry considered his friend's words, "How long will they wait?"

"They will stay and wait until we return or until they are sent for by their chief."

The Indian village of Saponi was located about a half mile from the fort. New Moon asked if they might stop there before going on to Augusta, "I send word - my people."

She made her benefactors understand the reason for her request. The village was a Shawnee village with elements of Lenape and a few Susquehannocks present. Willie understood Shawnee and Lenape while New Moon understood the Iroquoian tongue of the Susquehannocks so everyone in Saponi was asked about the Juniata's.

"The last remnant of your clan lives with my people near the place run by the white man called Clark," said a Susquehannock brave. "The Seneca and Mohawk dogs have killed or carried off the rest."

"You have dogs just north of here, big brother," New Moon told him.

The warrior smiled and touched her arm. With a yell, he and four other braves went to their paint pots to ready their faces to meet the Manitou. Then they grabbed their weapons and headed north out of the village seeking their enemies.

"You have seen the actions of true warriors and they will no doubt find what they seek; whether it is a Mohawk scalp or a place at the fire of their ancestors," pronounced Sure Shot's Strong Arm.

With the war party between them and their pursuers, it was with a sense of relief that the three travelers made their way to the fort. The fort's commandant, Colonel Samuel Hunter, received them cordially, got them food, and a place to bed down for the night. The colonel was new to his post just having been sent there by Pennsylvania's Executive Council and was anxious for any intelligence as to hostile actions taking place upriver.

"Walter Butler and the Mohawk, Brant have stirred up the Indians at Tioga and now they head down the Wyalusing and Sheshequin Trails to loot, burn, kidnap, and kill settlers in the Susquehanna Valley," Henry told the colonel.

Hunter would include this information in his next dispatch to the council. The commandant was not a combat officer nor did he ever serve as a staff officer. He received his commission from the colony because of his ability to organize and his talent for reporting crucial facts back to them. He was a prolific letter writer and a tireless advocate for materials for his command. He also seemed to be a miracle worker in stretching the meager amount of supplies sent to him. The colony also did some puzzling things pertaining to ordinance. They had seen fit to send two five pound artillery pieces to arm the fort, but had sent no cannonballs to use. This restricted the guns use to a short-range sprayer of nails and scraps of metal that was also in short supply. Fort Augusta was currently being defended by militia who hadn't received pay or personal supplies in over a month. Medicine was in short supply and food staples were low. The council's response to Augusta was always the same. They needed to supply the Pennsylvania Units in Washington's army, but they would see what could be done. Militias normally served twelve-month enlistments. Then the towns and counties the militiamen came from would recruit and send replacements that would serve the next year. Word of the depravation the current unit was suffering made replacing them nearly impossible. Finally John Harris, Jr., whose father Pennsylvania's eventual state capital would be named after, sent the council 1,500 pounds for the express purpose of outfitting Ft. Augusta "Lest our Western Frontier becomes Lancaster." Henry, Willie and New Moon arrived shortly after the first supplies from Harris' donation got to Augusta.

With both their bodies and their spirits reinvigorated the former bondsman, town drunk, and Indian slave began the final leg of the river journey.

"Keep a sharp lookout just the same, Sure Shot," said Willie. "It would be a shame to be shot this close to the trail's end."

Not more than an hour later a drum announced their movements on the river. It was mid-afternoon when they rounded the bend on the river and spotted the ferry up ahead. This was the business of Duncan Clark.

Chapter 44

"We've got her here. Now we need to find her folks," Henry said to no one in particular.

Clark told them that New Moon's people were camped about eight miles further downstream in a place the Susquehannocks called Enola. The last part of the journey had to be covered on foot as the river was very shallow this time of year and its rocks treacherous to canoes unless, of course, you knew the river. New Moon entered Enola only to find nineteen members of her clan there.

"We are but a remnant of a people that once hunted our River from its birth to its end," New Moon eloquently told her travel companions through an interpreter they found in the village. "There is a legend of a very tall stone; taller than four warriors each standing on one another's shoulders, but no wider than a man. It was the most sacred totem of the Juniatas put there by the Manitou himself. One day the Great Spirit hid the Standing Stone from our people. We searched for it for many days, but to no avail. Finally the Manitou came to our highest holy man in a dream and told him that we would find the stone again one day and on that day the greatness of our people would be restored."

"It's a sad thing to witness the end of a people. The Great Spirit can do anything, but only He can restore the Juniata now," Willie's words rang true and not just for the Juniatas. The Iroquois numbered about twenty thousand, down from an estimated forty five thousand a century before. European diseases and encroachments plus intertribal wars accounted for the decline. In truth, the kidnapping of the other tribes helped fortify their current population because a kidnap victim sometimes took the place of a dead family member or was married into the tribe as Queen Esther tried to do with New Moon.

Henry wondered about all these things and the next day made a point to look in the Scriptures to try and make some sense about what the old oracle, Lacomus told him about his dream and of the words spoken by Willie regarding the Juniata. The words of St. Paul in his letter to the Romans spoke to him as he read in chapter twelve verses eighteen and nineteen: *If it is possible, as far as it depends on you, live at peace with everyone. Do not take revenge, but leave room for God's wrath. For it is written, It is Mine to avenge; I will repay." says the Lord.* Then Henry read in Proverbs chapter twenty-one verse ten: *The wicked man craves evil; his neighbor gets no mercy from him.*

I can't figure it out. I need to leave it in His hands. Henry thought.

When Henry got with Willie after his morning devotions he told him of their next move, "We're heading back up the river to find the Dutchman, Covenhoven. He's cast his lot with a group of settlers that are beholden to no government and I like the sounds of that. They base their lives on the tenants of fair play and that sounds good to me, too."

Willie considered his friend's plan and offered this observation and caution,

"To reach these men we must go back through a country of the Iroquois. We will need to be ready to fight. I have been prudent with my money and will buy a rifle from Clark. The journey we are on will continue to take us on paths we don't immediately understand."

Henry nodded, "I've placed my mission in my God's hands. If it is to be finished it will be in His time. I believe getting you a rifle is a prudent move, if he has a decent one. I will try to buy a pistol from the ferryman, too."

Chapter 45

The next three days were spent with the people of Enola. New Moon was especially sorry to see them leave as she felt affection for both of them. She told them keep their caps on tight and would pray that she would see them again one day. On the day of their departure the eldest brave of her clan gave Henry a small ceremonial tomahawk. Through the interpreter he asked that the two men take it to a place called The Grand Island and bury it there. The Grand Island was a sacred spot in the middle of the Susquehanna just outside the town of Lock Haven. It was a place of peace where no one could wear face paint for that would displease the Manitou. It was a custom among all the Indian nations to "bury the hatchet" which not only symbolized the end of a blood feud, but was also an act of penitence to the Great Spirit. The Grand Island was about four miles west and downstream from Pine Creek which was the western boundary recognized by the Fair Play Men.

At Clark's Ferry Willie was able to purchase a rifle for twenty pounds, an outrageous amount, but the weapon was of a good quality so the grousing was held to a minimum. Henry got his pistol for a good deal less. Clark had heard of his exploits in overcoming two raiding bands of Mohawk warriors sent to kidnap him so he was sort of honored to be selling him the gun. He would brag about it to anyone who would listen for years to come.

They crossed to the east bank of the river where it was less likely they would run into hostiles. In fact a militia group came across them about twenty-five miles south of Fort Augusta. They camped that night with the group.

"I'll keep first watch and wake you when the moon reaches its highest point."

With that Henry made his way outside the light of the campfire and took up a position where he could keep watch. It was some time after midnight when he heard the slightest rustle off about fifty yards away.

Henry worked his way around the tree he was using for cover ending up on the side closest to the sleeping company and Willie and began to silently crawl toward the sound. There it was again about thirty yards to his left. He adjusted his course to intercept the unknown intruder before it reached the campfire. Ten yards, now five, knife in hand Sure Shot leaped on the back of the crawling form. The sounds of the struggle alerted the camp and in a matter of seconds several men came to Henry's aid. They had taken a smoke warrior prisoner. None of the others of his raiding party showed themselves instead seeking a better opportunity later.

"Tuckahoe, Fox Tail. Two Sticks and Spotted Wolf send their greetings," the captured assassin greeted his captor in perfect English. "Both are anxious to greet you in person. Your story grows into legend at our fires. Such a fine scalp would be big medicine for our cause."

"You speak my tongue well," Henry admitted to his prisoner.

"Thank you, the renegade Girty is a good teacher."

"I thought Simon Girty was in the Ohio country," Willie broke in.

"Who says that he isn't?" The Mohawk replied.

"Hog tie him."

Henry was specific as to how this prisoner was to be restrained. First his hands and feet would be securely bound together and then a second rope run behind the man would in effect shackle bind him. Finally the second rope would be tied to a tree. After this was done, Willie inspected the job making sure the intruder could not undo his ropes. When he was sure the job was done properly, he took Henry aside.

"Sure Shot, we need to be doubly alert now. The Susquehannock war party failed. Now this cur's littermates will try to free him or kill him to save him from disgrace."

"I want to find out the fate of the Saponi braves," he went to the captive and asked him about the war party. The smoke warrior slowly raised his head wearing a sinister smile.

"They died like warriors. I wear one of their scalps."

"All killed?"

"All."

"And you lost no one?"

"I said they died like warriors, not women. Three of my brothers sit at their father's fires now," the Mohawk replied sullenly.

167

The reality hit Henry, "So, Two Sticks sent a war party, not a mere raiding party."

"I have many brothers in these woods tonight," the captive smirked.

With a forty-man company of militia even a war party would be hesitant to attack, especially now that the whole camp was alerted. Henry knew two things. First, the real danger would be from ambush once they moved out in the morning and two, Willie would be dead and he would be a prisoner if they hadn't come upon the militia when they did. He needed to talk with the captain of the company before first light.

It would be his first meeting with Robert Covenhoven, whose exploits later during the Big Runaway made him famous along the frontier. Covenhoven's last name would later be changed to the more English sounding Crownover making for some confusion in attributing later deeds to the same man.

"I'm Captain Covenhoven. I've been told you have some information from our captive that may prove critical to our well-being come first light."

"It's a pleasure meeting you, Captain. Yes, the brave gave us some items to consider," Henry replied. He was immediately struck by the captain's youth, barely older than himself.

"The Mohawk told me that he's part of a large body of braves. It would seem that the British have convinced their native allies to extend themselves farther than they have ever done before. Because of their boldness, I believe that they will try an attack us when we break camp in the morning."

"I agree with your thinking. They will not have the advantage of choosing the ground they will fight on however. We have been moving toward Fort Augusta. If they have been shadowing us they know that. Your sudden presence made a night attack worth taking a chance to them. Having failed they will surely come at us now, but we will not walk into the trap. We're going to fall back to some high ground we covered yesterday and let them come to us. It's important to quietly break camp and begin moving back before first light. We can use the war chief's confidence against them. As the largest war parties seldom number more than two dozen men, I'm fairly sure he didn't place any braves at our rear and has them all flanking and in front of us. If we time our retreat correctly, they will be flanking where we were, not where we are. The high ground we will be making for is less than a half mile away."

Henry and Willie were both impressed with the strategy of Coven-hoven. Henry decided that strategy and planning like this came with experience which surely also came at a price. Once they made it to the high ground half the company would become loaders for the other half. This would allow for a more continuous firing pattern in their defensive position. Even if the plan were discovered before completed it would still thwart the impact of the attack. The rangers of this company were well trained in orderly retreat while under attack as well as the method of counterattack to take the fight to their enemy.

Chapter 46

About an hour before daybreak, the first elements of the militia began to move back using utmost care in remaining as quiet as possible. Over half of the company was retracing its steps from yesterday when the first jay call was heard. The final dozen militiamen were moving out when the Mohawks discovered the maneuver.

"The die is cast! Full retreat!" shouted their captain.

The second wave of retreating men had among them Henry and Willie. With the spoken command all second line of the militia stopped and formed a firing line, but unlike British troops, these rangers used trees and rocks for cover.

This is my first true battle with formed lines and strategies employed, thought Henry. *Now it's not one man's strength and skill against another, it's a leader's tactics and the courage of his troops that will win the day.* A minute later, the crashing sound of the escaping troopers was heard. Then as the first light of day was cast on the scene, the last part of the company ran through the firing line closely followed by the silent smoke warriors. At a distance of no more than twenty yards after the last of the fleeing man made it past, the line opened up on the Indians.

The horrific sound of the skirmish line firing at once along with the smoke that accompanied such a discharge created confusion among the attackers. The second line with emptied rifles now began running toward their destination. The actual causalities caused by the counterattack were surprisingly light. Two Mohawks were killed outright and two more suffered wounds.

If the war party's leader was decent tactician, the lesson of the initial skirmish wouldn't be lost on him, Henry Thought. *They will chase, but not headlong into another line of fire.*

And sure enough, another two hundred yards further on, the first line of rangers was waiting in a firing line. The third group of militia had run past them and would set up two hundred yards further on. Now came the second line with Henry and Willie among them. They would run on to the furthest group and would reload and wait there with them. The sound of the second engagement took longer in coming and wasn't as simultaneous in its discharge.

The Mohawks were attacking in a manner that would undoubtedly lead to militia casualties. Some of Covenhoven's men wanted to turn and rush to their brothers in arms' rescue, but their captain knew better.

"They will be along soon enough and we will be in a better position to help them here," he said.

The sounds of the battle continued and then about ten minutes after the last shot was heard, five soldiers came through at a run.

"They've killed Taylor, Mason, and Jones," the out of breath sergeant told his captain. "I don't know about the others."

There were still four men out there. Three minutes later two militiamen hurried in helping a wounded man.

"Fellows is lost! I saw him kill one of them with his bare hands, then..."

The militia's' ranks were thinned, but so were their adversaries'. Still the Mohawks would come on. There was no doubt of that.

"Box formation! Five to the front, four on the other sides! Take cover! You doing the loading keep a loaded rifle in your partner's hands!" Captain Covenhoven drew his sword as he barked his commands.

"Make your rounds count! Steady, here they come!"

The attackers numbered some twenty braves; most with firearms of their own. They darted from tree to rock trying to close the distance to where their musket accuracy would improve. A rifleman fired at a brave just as he ducked behind a rock sending up a spray of stone but missing his target. Three seconds later Henry shot the same Indian as he tried to improve his position. Willie handed him his loaded rifle and began reloading Kate. A musket ball whizzed overhead. Suddenly musket fire erupted on all four sides.

Their captain shouted encouragement, "I still think they are concentrated at our front! They are trying to shake us into making a mistake!"

In a pitched fight, one of a soldier's greatest fears is to be surrounded by his enemy with all avenues of escape cut off. It was a psychological weapon the Mohawks now put into use.

"Steady men, they don't dare rush us as we would quickly win the day!"

With the rangers in their present formation no Mohawk warrior made an overt move.

Willie shared his thoughts with Henry, "Sure Shot, they are closing. I can feel it even if I can't see it. Watch and use all your senses."

A bush was moved three feet closer than before. Henry picked the center of the small clump and fired. A Mohawk stood then collapsed.

"Watch for any movement!" he yelled as he took back Kate from Willie.

A smoke warrior emerged from hiding not more than five feet from the woodsmen. Wielding a war club, he struck down one of the soldiers before Covenhoven ran him through. Now seven braves rose with tomahawks and clubs attacking the front from a distance of less than twenty yards. Three were killed outright and a fourth gravely wounded but three smoke warriors were within the defense and wreaking havoc. Two militiamen were hacked down and fell out of the fight dying. Covenhoven slashed one of the three and was clubbed a glancing blow to the head which dropped him senseless to the ground. Nine braves emerged from the other three sides and attacked. As they were a bit farther back a volley of rifle shot cut all but three down before they reached the formation. Henry and Willie, armed with tomahawk and knife, went on the attack, as the militiamen also took to the hand-to-hand fighting. The captive brave was freed by one of his compatriots and joined the melee.

The woodsmen, even with triple the number of the Indians, did not have the skills in close combat that the Mohawks did so the contest was in question. Indeed, if not for Henry and Willie's prowess in this type of fighting the Mohawks would likely have carried the day. Finally, it was down to Henry and the once captive Mohawk, the other attackers being either killed or incapacitated.

"I have failed Fox Tail, but I will take you with me to the fire of my ancestors where we will both receive great honor."

"Lay down your knife. No one here doubts that you are a great warrior. You will be traded back to your tribe," Henry was pleading with a man who, as a Smoke Warrior, was already dead in the eyes of his tribe.

"I have no tribe here in this land anymore; only a place with those who came before me. Please know it gives me no pleasure in killing you."

"Stand back Henry while I dispatch this dog," Covenhoven had regained his faculties and although bleeding from his head wound was threatening to run the Mohawk through.

"No, Captain. I'm the one who took him prisoner, so I'm the one who must set him free."

A knife fight among equal combatants has the disturbing appearance of some grotesque dance. Each will rush and feign in an effort to expose his opponent to a strike, which may or may not be fatal, but is usually debilitating. Then it is simply a matter of time until the wounded one, either in desperation or sapped of strength, makes another mistake and contest is brutally ended. Sometimes both receive wounds and then both fight on till the one suffering the most is overpowered. It is a savage spectacle and one that if witnessed will never be forgotten.

"What is your name, Mohawk?" Henry asked. "I will help you sing your death song."

"I am called James Haverford. I took the place of my brother who was called Grey Feather at my family's fires when I was seven summers old so I am also called Grey Feather."

The remaining militiamen closely scrutinized the brave. Under the black hair and painted face stared a pair of blue eyes. "You're a white man," Captain Covenhoven roared in exasperation. "Stop this foolishness!"

"I am no more a white man than you are a horse," the renegade replied. "I told Fox Tail my name so he will know me in the next life."

Chapter 47

Before the two men could begin the lethal contest, Willie, who had wearied of the spectacle he was witnessing, took the butt end of his rifle and slammed Grey Feather hard on the back of his head.

"This Mohawk and the two that are still alive will be worth taking back to the fort," said Henry's Strong Arm matter-of-factly. "There has been enough shedding of blood today."

Willie always chose being practical over a show of pride. The company commander assessed the situation. He had lost ten men killed and six more were seriously wounded or litter cases. Ten more were walking wounded, able to travel, but no longer able to fight. Out of his company of rangers nearly three quarters of their number were casualties. He needed to get back to Fort Augusta without delay.

"We need to make up litters for our wounded. Bind a prisoner to the front of three of them and make sure their feet are bound together to allow them to walk but not run." When this was done, the battle-scarred procession started making its way back to the fort. There was no time to deal with the dead. Recovery parties would be sent back for their bodies. Of the twelve able-bodied men remaining, nine were pressed into litter bearing service. The remaining three walked along with the litters carried by the prisoners; that left Covenhoven and Willie on point and Henry bringing up the rear.

The renegade known as Grey Feather was nearly mad with anger. He focused his anger at Willie, "You denied me a death with honor, you Shawnee squaw." He spat out his words like they were a poison at Willie Miles.

"Who knows what type of death you will have? The day has shown me a Mohawk warrior with blue eyes. Who knows what else might lie ahead," Willie replied.

The half-breed crossed over to take right point thus allowing the captain to fall back and check on his wounded. After two hours travel one of the more severely wounded men died and a little over an hour later another ranger lost his final fight. The second man was on the litter being carried by the renegade Mohawk. As they were undoing his bindings, Grey Feather snatched a knife and broke completely free racing away from the party. Two shots rang out, both narrowly missing him as he ran on like a panther. Covenhoven, Willie and Henry raced toward the sounds of the rifle reports to find the captive gone.

"He has no weapons except a small knife so he's no real threat," one of the enlisted men offered.

"On the contrary, his escape makes the danger to this expedition even greater," Covenhoven replied. "We must reach Augusta as soon as possible."

With the four men, including the guard of the escaped prisoner, now freed from litter bearing duty the band was able to protect the front and flanks with two men each while Henry covered the retreat. More than once, Henry thought he heard the sounds made by one or more unseen followers. Finally, in late afternoon Fort Augusta was seen in the distance from the Great Shamokin Trail. This trail edged close to the eastern bank of the Susquehanna River some miles south of the fort. The path was taken because it afforded the easiest and fastest route back, far outweighing any increased danger that might be waiting for them on it. About two miles from the fort they came upon a hunting party of Susquehannocks using the path to get to their hunting grounds. When they saw the Mohawk captives in war paint they began whooping and jumping about in an agitated manner. The leader of the hunting party tried to trade with Covenhoven for the two. Covenhoven knew that giving over the braves would only lead to a torturous death for them both so he told the trader that he must take them first to his chief at the fort and they could ask him for the Mohawks later. This seemed to ease what might otherwise have been a heated confrontation. Mohawks covered in war paint south of where the two rivers become one, was bad medicine. A council of the Susquehannock tribes would be called and the chance of these braves going on the warpath and further complicating matters was becoming a real possibility.

Grey Feather had raced into the woods toward the closest undergrowth. The first rifle ball hit several inches to the left making its distinctive whizzing sound as it crashed through the thin branches. The second round missed by several feet. As fast as his legs would carry

175

him, the renegade made his way back to the scene of this morning's battle. There he rearmed himself with bow, tomahawk, and scalping knife. Firearms were still scarce at the fort so the troop carried as many back as was feasible along with powder horns, wadding, and lead. The rest they smashed against the trunks of trees rendering them unusable. He took a minute to ask the Manitou to take every dead man lying there to his spiritual home fire. Then he retraced his path until he was only a hundred yards behind the rear guard.

What luck! The smoke warrior thought. *It's the Fox Tail!*

He would try to separate his quarry from the rest by slowing him down. Haverford began to deliberately make just enough noise to alert Henry hoping that the sound would make him pause to ascertain the threat. Then he would attack and carry off the Fox Tail back to his great chief, Two Sticks. It was working, but not in the way he expected it would. He heard Fox Tail make a perfect turkey call and then drop down out of sight.

He is a worthy foe. Grey Feather said under his breath.

It was then that the hunting party of Susquehannocks made their appearance.

"He must have a guardian spirit watching over him," the smoke warrior muttered.

The heightened attention of such a group of braves would not permit him to carry out his plan. The renegade silently edged away from the militia. He would cross to the western bank of the river and travel north meeting up with the British irregulars and Seneca braves he knew were ranging there. Failure was death to the mindset of this type of brave. He would keep the kidnapping he was charged to accomplish as his sole reason for drawing a breath. Only another mission given to him by his sachem, Two Sticks, would change his goal. Before diving into the water, Grey Feather turned and gave a loud jay call. Both Henry and Willie recognized it. So did the hunting party. With a chorus of whoops they ran off in the direction of Saponi.

"Press on men. We need to reach Augusta quickly," Covenhoven ordered.

"Captain, Willie and I are going to check the area where we heard that call."

"Be careful, boys. No telling what type of hornet's nest you might be getting yourselves into."

"We intend to hold onto our hair, sir."

So the party separated with the larger group on making its final leg to the fort and the two frontiersmen heading toward the bank of the river. Cautiously both men reached the eastern shore just in time to witness the lone swimmer reach the western bank. Grey Feather turned to look back across the river he just swam across and saw Sure Shot and his Strong Arm watching him. Silently the renegade raised his arm and then was gone into the thicket.

"I'm pretty sure we will meet with that one again, Willie. It will be a fool's trip to follow now though, so let's get back to Augusta. What surprises me is that the hunting party didn't chase after Grey Feather too. They knew that Mohawk call better than we did."

"It would have not suited the Manitou if they joined their elder's council fires without the spirit paint on their faces."

"War paint, Willie?"

"War paint, Sure Shot."

Chapter 48

Covenhoven had briefed Col. Hunter, seen to the welfare of his men, and the incarceration of the prisoners before Henry and Willie got to the compound. They met in front of the powder magazine near the soldier's barracks.

"Col. Hunter requests the pleasure of our company tonight as he dines. It would be appropriate to wear your dress duds and to wash and shave."

The two outdoorsmen blinked and stared at one another. Finally Henry sheepishly said to Covenhoven, "We do smell a might gamey, Robert. Also I'm afraid that the last several months we spent in the wild have left us bereft of proper dinner attire."

"You can draw clothing from our stores. There are scout uniforms that will fit you and as that is the purpose of the Colonel's request you will go correctly attired."

"I will not agree to any enlistment, captain. There are some areas of my life that prevent me from performing the duties of a scout."

"There are scouts and then there are scouts, my friends," Covenhoven cryptically replied.

Both men found cotton shirts, woolen trousers and short coats worn by the men who had served as scouts in the militia.

"I feel like a stuffed shirt in this get up," Willie remarked as he looked down over the brass buttons on his coat. Henry had just started dressing after having spent some time in a tub of hot soap and water.

"I hear that's how you get the grippe," Willie warned his friend.

Henry combed his hair and had it back in the style of the time. Then he placed a tri-corner hat of blue with gold trim on his head.

"Gosh Sure Shot, I barely know ya."

Henry look at his reflection in a hand held mirror and suddenly memories crashed about him. In the mirror he saw the image of his father.

"What's wrong my friend?"

"It's nothing really, my good fellow. Hurry or we'll be late for our appointment."

Henry heard his father's voice and phrasing causing him another moment's pause.

It seems quite odd, but somehow comforting. He thought.

Colonel Hunter was a short husky man with a deep voice and a rutty face. He had been a schoolmaster so Hunter warmed to Henry when he was told of the lad's time as a reading instructor.

"That's most admirable, well done, sir."

This was the word of approval from the fort's commander. After an austere meal of salt pork, bread and butter and sassafras tea the colonel laid out his offer.

"I need eyes and ears on the frontier. Unlike a regular scout, which is the eyes of a militia class you would be free to range about going to the scene of events or even anticipating them and doing something about it. The only thing I will require from you is a written report done weekly telling me what you have uncovered so that I may properly plan and make use of your intelligence for my correspondence to the Executive Council. A runner will be at Fort Horn each Friday to bring your report back to me."

"We have been told that there are three forts in that area. I will indicate in my dispatch which fort will be used for the next meeting and we should also vary the day and time of the meeting. We will be undone by habitual practices," Henry suggested.

"That's an excellent idea, Mr. St. Albans. We can work out a code that can be hidden in the report to show day, time, and place. I shall now commission you at the rank and pay of lieutenant of scouts. Your companion will be enlisted at the rank of chief scout drawing a sergeant's pay. Even though you will be listed as scouts, you will really be the first formal rangers attached to Ft. Augusta. Please accompany me to my office where we can sign the documents I have previously taken the liberty to have drawn up."

"You were mighty confident," Henry mused.

After dinner Covenhoven accompanied the newly minted scouts back to the barracks, "I'm leaving for Fort Horn tomorrow. You see my active commission has expired and I'm anxious to get back to my land there."

The news was a bit of a surprise for both of his companions.

"We'd be honored to travel with you," both scouts spoke the same words at once.

After the laughter subsided, on a more serious note, Covenhoven explained.

"There have been some brazen attacks committed against white settlers up and down the valleys north of here. It isn't always the native's idea either. Loyalists and Tories are traveling with the raiding parties guiding their actions and whipping them up to commit savage acts. I explained to Col. Hunter that you have drawn the special attention of the Mohawk named Brant. He seems to think that will make you an even more valuable asset. Oh, and speaking of assets, no one here has drawn any type of pay for over two months," after a pause, laughter exploded from all three of them.

Chapter 49

Dawn the next morning saw the three on their way to Fort Horn. It really was not a fort in the sense that Augusta was a fort. Augusta had twelve-foot high palisades built over ten-foot entrenchments. It also had triangulated bastions or redoubts of earth and timber at each of its four corners. The design of these towers allowed for crossfire protection of every foot of the palisades. There was a barracks, a powder magazine, and a well within the main breastworks. A perimeter stockade built around the inner works provided for a first line of defense. It was a British fort built to stem the rise of their French rivals and had been named after King George III's mother. Now it was one of America's main frontier garrisons that at one time offered comfort and shelter for those very same British. Augusta had the capacity for two hundred men and sixteen cannon, but with men and artillery pieces desperately needed by Washington's army it was currently manned by less than sixty militia and two field pieces. Offensive forays left Augusta undermanned, a secret that was well kept until Hartley's action in the fall of 1778 and Sullivan's March the following year eliminated the threat.

Fort Horn was a horse of a different color. It was estimated to enclose only about a quarter acre. The fort had a simple ten-foot high timber stockade where nearby settlers could flee in case of attack. In addition to gun slits, Fort Horn had crude ramparts built on all sides to permit defenders to fire over the walls. Most forts had only the gun slits; wagons were used instead of ramparts. These frontier sanctuaries gave protection for livestock and people in case of raiders and had in fact been modeled after the strong houses built by both the English and Scottish landowners along their common border some centuries before.

Raiding by a few Indians was one thing, but a coordinated attack orchestrated by the British military was quite another. No fort in the entire Susquehanna watershed outside of Augusta could hope to repel such an action. Even Wallis' stone house would be in peril, as it had no water source within its confines. It was up to the settlers to provide for their common defense and that would be done by the active pursuit and punishment of these antagonized natives by the militia when possible, or by the settlers themselves. This fort was destination of Henry, Willie, and the Dutchman, Covenhoven.

Coincidently, Covenhoven's enlistment expired on June 30th, 1776. The three arrived at Fort Horn on July 2nd.

"There seems to be a selectman's tribunal in session. Look at all the people. Fellows, something big is in the wind."

The three made their way to the gathering. Some two dozen settlers were present and everyone was trying to talk at once. The setting for the meeting was outside under a large elm tree as it was one of the hottest summers in memory. A slight breeze and the shade of the tree provided some relief. Bratton Caldwell, John Walker, and James Brandon were the elected officials trying to keep order in what was quickly becoming a mob scene.

"What's the trouble?" Covenhoven asked one of the farmers present.

"Everyone wants to say his peace about how fed up we are with other folks telling us what to do and how to live."

Finally Walker could stand it no more, and drawing out his pistol, fired it into the air. The loud report of the weapon stunned everyone into silence.

"Who in the blazes can write?" he shouted.

Henry raised his hand.

"Good, this man here will take paper and pen in hand and will record each man's opinion of what needs be in the document."

"What document?" Henry asked.

"Why, our Letter of Freedom, of course. Now line up in some order so we can begin."

Henry was led to a spot under the tree where he was seated on an armchair. Next he was given a lap secretary, which was a portable writing table that had an inclined writing surface and a compartment underneath in which he found papers and quills to be sharpened for pens. On top of the instrument there was an inkwell. Francis Clark, one of the three Clarks to sign the document started.

"I say we need to declare ourselves free from anyone who don't defend us."

Adam Carson was next, "Well I say we need abide with what they come up with at that Congress in Philadelphia."

"That bunch of fancies don't have no rights over us!" shouted Clark.

"Your boy's fightin' in their army, Francis." Carson reminded him.

"Every Fair Play Man has a right to say what they want included," Covenhoven said so everyone could hear. "Now let's get back to the business at hand without any more of this."

Henry had listened to each man's heartfelt opinion by mid-afternoon. The selectmen would arrive at a first draft the next day and present it to the full gathering. Revisions would be made and when the paper contained what a consensus thought it should say they would sign it and send it off to the Congress in Philadelphia to show them what freedom-loving people were willing to do.

A reporter by the name of Scully wrote an article over a century later in which he purports to include the words of this declaration. The original and its copy have been lost so this is open to speculation. The original was buried in a lead box within Fort Horn. The copy was lost when the two runners, which were sent to the Congress in Philadelphia, had the document confiscated after being captured by Indians and Tories shortly after starting their journey. With this caveat, here is The Pine Creek Declaration of Independence drawn up and approved beneath the Tiadaghton Elm near Fort Horn:

July 4th, 1776

Resolved - That whomsoever directly or indirectly in any way form or manner had invaded the free exercise of the Fair Play Men's rights, as has been attempted by all the branches of the government of Great Britain, is our enemy and an enemy to this country and the liberty of all mankind.

Resolved - That we the committee and members of the association of Fair Play Men, assembled his day on ground we hold by virtue of being free men entitled to reside where we choose, do hereby dissolve any political bonds which may have here fore connected us with the Old Country, or its Provinces in America, and finally absolve ourselves of all allegiances to the Crown family of Great Britain, abandoning all practical connection with a nation that has persistently trampled on our rights and liberties as Americans and inhumanely shed the innocent blood of Americans, and in the case of ourselves, denied their right to protect us.

Resolved - We hereby declare ourselves what we have long felt ourselves to be, a free and independent body of citizens, but ready at all times to assist our brothers who shed their blood at Lexington, and are and intend to be, a self-governing people under God's Rule, the American Congress, and the Fair Play Association, to the furtherance of which independence we hereby pledge our mutual cooperation, our lives, our possessions, and our honor as Fair Play Men.

Among the twenty-five signers was Robert Covenhoven. Some of the signatories were indeed literate including two of the three selectmen. Most had merely learned how to sign their names much as Henry's former master had done. Two hired men, Patrick Gilfillan, and Michael Quigley, volunteered to take a copy of the document to Philadelphia, but were captured later the same day and held by loyalists. They both escaped two days later and arrived in Philadelphia on July 10th. The messengers were dumbfounded to find out that the Second Continental Congress had likewise ratified their Declaration of Independence on the very same day.

Chapter 50

Meantime, Henry and Willie made a trip to the Grand Island to fulfill a promise made to the Juniata elder. The legend of Grand Island was that the Great Spirit had placed the original man on this island and sternly warned him that this place should never see bloodshed lest he return and destroy all Creation. For as long as any native could remember going back to the oldest stories told round the council fires, it was one of the sacred truths. It was a tale that reminded Henry of Adam and the Garden of Eden. Grand Island was about a mile and a half long and nearly a half-mile wide at its widest part. It was plunk in mid-stream of the West Branch of the Susquehanna River several miles below where Pine Creek emptied into it. In the middle of the island stood a stone altar where smoke offerings were made to the Manitou much as incense offerings are made to ancestors of Japan's Shinto religion.

A Miami from the Ohio country had made a pilgrimage to the island. He was asking healing spirits to intercede for a son who had taken a fever. A Mingo shaman had left a medicine bag near the shrine. Henry and Willie selected a spot a short distance away to bury the Juniata's wooden relic, which was done with a prayer of supplication recited for that people by the Strong Arm. Upon turning both saw Grey Feather standing about ten yards away with his arms crossed. He was grinning at them.

"Tuckahoe, Fox Tail and Little Dog, my enemies. As you are on a pilgrimage and here on sacred ground I cannot attempt to complete my chief's order. Here on this island my enemies become my friends. Come, I would speak with you and smoke a pipe with you as a symbol of my faithfulness to the Manitou's command."

The scouts were struck by their foe's sincere manner and soon all were seated with a pipe full of tobacco passing between the three of them.

"Why do you continue this farce, James? By your own admission you are not an Indian," Henry was trying his best to understand this man.

"I will tell you a story, Fox Tail. It is true and I'm sure that Willie already knows it. A long time ago the six tribes of our nation were known as the Haudenosaunee, "the people of the long house." We had many enemies and among the greatest of them were the Algonquin people. They called us the Iroqu, which means rattlesnake in their tongue. The French recorded it as Iroquois and in the end that is what we became to be called by all. The Algonquin are nearly all gone, but we still walk the land. I am still the person I have become no matter what I may be called by others. It is too late to change that and I wouldn't want to in any case."

Willie drew on the pipe and exhaled, "You have a claim in both worlds as do I, but I move freely between the two while you do not try."

"Your claim is both in your life as you have lived it and in your blood, but do you feel you really at peace in either world?" Grey Feather's words made the half-breed uneasily consider what was spoken about him. "I will tell you both something now as my friends. The "Old Father" across the big water has asked for more help in punishing his children here. I have been summoned back to my chief, Captain Brant, to help him to do so. I must forget my mission concerning you for now, who knows, perhaps forever. Brant has been to England, having received gifts from George III himself! He fights now in New York and summons all to him by the Hunter' Moon so you see I must go and prepare."

"This is July, the Hunter's Moon is in November ..." Henry began.

"I have been called to a new purpose more to my liking, Fox Tail. That is all that is to be said about it," the renegade smiled. "I have said my prayer to the Great Spirit and he has smiled on me."

"This is hallowed ground according to all tribal beliefs so I will ask my God for help and guidance while I am here, too," Henry told Willie and Grey Feather.

"I go now," said the renegade. "I hope our next meeting will be again as friends."

The Smoke warrior set out without making another audible sound and was soon out of sight. Henry went off to a large oak tree standing nearby, dropped to his knees and began to pray. Willie stayed near the alter offering up smoke and chanting a prayer for wellbeing that his mother had taught him. Later, as they were returning to Fort Horn, Sure Shot remarked to his friend,

"I have the information for my first dispatch to Colonel Hunter." Then he continued, "A small quiet voice came to me while I was praying and said, "You are right where I want you to be. Now, protect my flock."

Chapter 51

Both scouts became well known to the settlers in the area and throughout the summer and into fall their patrols seemed to keep any raiding parties at bay. Then in early October word was received from a friendly Oneida trading at Fort Horn that a large party of Delawares and Muncees had joined together to raid up and down Pine Creek and as far east as the Loyalsock What was surprising was that this was being done with the tacit approval of Queen Esther, who was the one and the same former owner of New Moon.

St. Albans' young face had a worn and worried expression.

"There will be English leading these raids and with the bounty paid for white scalps by the British provincial government, the blood-letting will be horrific if we don't warn the people and get some help. Willie, we can't wait for the next runner. I need you to take the dispatch to Col. Hunter immediately. Go by canoe. It is the safest way and you'll arrive quicker than on foot. I will tell you the words of the letter so you can still tell them at Augusta even if the letter is lost."

After making sure his partner had the message committed to memory, Willie shoved off using Covenhoven's own canoe.

The Dutchman began issuing orders, "No man is to work his farm without a loaded rifle within his reach. No man is to work alone but in groups of three or more. Livestock and horses should be gathered and rope foundered so that they can be moved at a moment's notice. Children should be sent on to the nearest fort. Henry, take a mount and ride east to warn those near Fort Hepburn then on to the Wallis' stronghold."

Selectman Walker let the scout borrow his mount, a large piebald stallion that could run all day according to his owner. He was soon off at slow gallop saving his ride should the occasion call for a sprint later. He rode first to the home of Jacob Steinmuller warning all there of the danger and relating the orders given him by the militia captain. Next, on to a small settlement located near present day Linden, where he repeated the message. Now onto French Margaret's Town spreading the warning.

It was outside of Otstuagy that a musket ball came whizzing out of a thicket just missing rider and horse. Henry laid his heels into the steed's haunches and took off at a full gallop toward the Brady's.

I hope I live to reach them. Henry thought as he crouched forward in the saddle to present a smaller target to his attackers. They were coming out of the woods now on both of his flanks, an almost perfect ambush.

If I can reach Wolf Run without them pulling me from the saddle I have a better than even chance. His mind was racing faster than his horse. It was then that everything went black. Henry awoke a short while later to find himself tied to his mount. The group of raiders appeared to be eight in number, evenly split between the tattooed Delaware and the long hair worn in double braids of the Muncee. Henry had been clubbed off his horse by one of the ambushers and had been hurriedly thrown back on it and bound in place. His captors were taking the Shamokin Path northwest to where it intersected with the Sheshequin Path then north to the Indian settlement of Sheshequin (present day Ulster) and then on to Tioga. That night as they camped, an argument broke out between the raiders as to what to do with Fox Tail. The Delawares wanted to take the prisoner back to Bald Eagle and Spotted Wolf to satisfy the now long-standing blood feud. The Muncees argued that as they had clubbed him off the horse, they needed to take him back to their ruler, Queen Esther. Esther had become supreme ruler of this tribe after the death of her husband, Eghobund the Muncee chief. She had the right to decide his fate. Henry watched in anxious amusement as the disagreement became more heated hoping to find an opening for escape. A brave stepped forward who appeared to be the leader of the Muncee party. He crossed his arms and closed his eyes then opened his arms and lifted them upwards to heaven. This quieted his men and had a similar effect on the Delawares. After another minute or so he opened his eyes and spoke, signing as well so the Delawares fully understood.

"We will let the Great Spirit decide what is to be done with this prisoner. It will be the trial of the two fires. Pick your man."

The trial of the two fires was relatively simple in its concept. Two wrestlers would fight between two large fires that were built behind each of them. The object was to throw your opponent into the fire. The loser seldom died but often was burned and scarred leaving a humiliating reminder for all to see forever. The Delawares had a huge muscular brave as their champion. The Muncees had a tall thinner warrior picked. Soon two large fires roared at the backs of the wrestlers causing a whooping and even betting among the audience. Both men stood to each other's side about a foot and a half apart facing each other. Next both placed their right foot against the side of the other's right foot. Now both men grasped the hand of the other like he was shaking hands. They were not shaking hands. Both were charged with not moving their anchor leg and not releasing their grip until one of them was literally thrown into the fire. The winners would get Henry, the losers would get Walker's stallion. Henry watched the contest as it unfolded. Neither man had a clear advantage over the other as they pushed, pulled, and strained. Finally, after several minutes, the Delaware pressed an advantage he sensed and had his opponent reeling backwards. It was only with the greatest effort and strength that the wiry Muncee was able to regain his balance and continue. After another ten minutes or so the Delaware pressed again. This time the Muncee seemed to be waiting for it and let what was resistance become a pulling throw taking the Delaware past him and forward into the fire. A scream pierced the night as the defeated brave rolled around on the hot coals escaping quickly but not before an angry red mark appeared on both his right leg and arm.

"It is done. Apply grease to the loser's wounds. We separate in the morning."

In the morning the Delawares went back south to where the Sheshequin Path connected with the Great Shamokin Path while the Muncees kept going north towards Queen Esther's Town. The raiders that were retracing their route encountered Samuel Brady and six other settlers at the place were the two paths converge. After a short fight that saw two natives killed and the other two take to the hills, Brady reclaimed the piebald horse and suspected the worst for its rider.

"This will just about kill Evan," Samuel shared with his brother.

"It won't do Rachel any good either," James replied.

Evan had been off on a hunt when the alarm was sounded. Gunfire near Wolf Run had alerted the Brady's and finding Henry's rifle, Kate lying in a thicket near the site of the kidnapping told the story.

"We need to finish the job of alerting everyone to the present danger and we need to get word back to Willie Miles at Fort Horn telling him of his friend's fate."

Meanwhile Willie had delivered his message to Colonel Hunter at Fort Augusta. Hunter had fired off a special dispatch to the Executive Council for more militia and supplies citing the present heightened danger as evidence they were sorely needed. As to sending relief to Fort Horn or anywhere else, Hunter was reluctant to act. After waiting for two days and receiving no word, Willie struck out back to Fort Horn again by canoe. Paddling alone against a current, even a slow current as was the case with the river this time of year, was slow going compared to paddling with the current. It took Willie nearly two days to reach Fort Horn even though the trip to Augusta had taken less than a day.

The news that he had to deal with when he returned shook him to his very foundation. Sure Shot was the first person, the only person, who saw him as more than a drunken half-breed and now he was gone. Sure Shot's Strong Arm started out for the Grand Island to ask the Manitou for guidance. After several days of fasting and praying Willie had a vision come to him in a dream as he fell into a trance. He witnessed a large whitetail with huge antlers running through a gully. On either side of the small ravine there stood warriors shooting arrows at the buck. The buck used his antlers to block some of the arrows while he dodged the others until he reached the end of the ditch. With a leap the deer cleared one last hurdle and bounded off into the forest.

Willie shook himself awake and shouted out loud, "He is alive! I have seen his spirit guide, Oskanu-tu, the great stag! I will seek him among his enemies. They have no power over him!"

Chapter 52

Henry was led through the Indian village of Sheshequin where women and children threw small stones at him and hit him with sticks all the while calling him derisive names. This was a shaming ritual not meant to hurt him but only to belittle and ridicule him.

It made Henry recall the English rhyme, Sticks and stones may break my bones, but names will never hurt me. *I guess they want to try it all on me.* He thought.

The antagonists were having great fun until the braves of the raiding party drove them away. He was then led to a post where he was tied up by the neck much as you would tie up a dog. An old toothless squaw eventually brought him a bowl of gruel and a gourd of water. The meal was a nourishing but nearly tasteless combination of chestnuts and corn crushed and cooked in water until it had the consistency of pea soup. He took a drink of water. It was as sweet as sugar. The women of the village had been tapping the maple trees that were abundant in the forest. The sap that they gathered they boiled, but not to the level of the maple syrup we know, but to a type of "simple syrup" that is made by heating water and sugar. The old woman motioned that he should pour the sweet water over the porridge. That was much better. The old woman smiled. Henry smiled back and held up the bowl as a sign that he liked the meal and was grateful to her. After the meal was finished and the old woman was gone Henry had a visitor.

"I am called Clear Lake," the brave said in halting English. "If you speak French, I am better."

"I never mastered French even though I had three years of it in school," the captive replied.

"Then we talk in English. I come to say you are something Queen Esther has and will hand over to the Mohawk sachem, but not maybe."

Henry wasn't clear on what he was told and the look on his face spurred his visitor to go on.

"Queen Esther a proud leader. She not do everything she is told.

She might just kill you herself, but not maybe."

This didn't help Henry's outlook at all.

"She knows the white man's Great Spirit so she kills sometimes not maybe."

He is trying to tell me she is a Christian or at least holds to some Christian ways. Henry realized. *I might be able to reason with her.*

The next day at dawn the band set out for their destination, Queen Esther's Town. For nearly two miles before entering the town itself, Henry was struck by the huge fields of growing corn that seemed to stretch to the horizon. Once in the village he saw a town complete with streets and over seventy neatly constructed log cabins that had stone fireplaces.

This could be any of a dozen large towns back in New Jersey. Henry thought. Queen Esther was seated on a high back chair on the front porch of her home. A small, thin, neat woman in her early fifties, Esther dressed in a cotton dress with a woolen short coat. She was adorned in large hoop earrings and a gold and emerald brooch given to her by her grandmother, Lady Montour. Around her neck she wore a necklace made of fresh water pearls and small colorful shells. The queen motioned for the leader of the raiders to come forward. The brave approached and then went down on one knee while he addressed his queen.

Esther leaned forward displaying facial expressions that betrayed her interest as she alternately smiled and frowned as the warrior completed his tale. Leaning back and audibly exhaling she motioned for her subject to return to his post by the prisoner and addressed the captive directly.

"I can do many things with you, Fox Tail. For instance, I can scalp you and send your hair to the British for a reward. I can give you over to my Mohawk brothers as Two Sticks wants. He will give you to Spotted Wolf who will scalp you and wear your hair on his brag belt. Maybe I'll just keep you as a slave or as a replacement for one of our squaws' dead husbands. Or I could try to send you on to Fort Niagara for ransom, but you would never make it there. So what is it that I am to do with you?"

The queen scratched her chin as though deep in thought until a smile came over her face. "I have just decided to kill you by burning you at the stake."

Henry was led to the center of the town where a charred pole stood like a silent witness to the brutality that had been committed there many times before. Henry was tied to the post and stacks of wood were piled around him. It wasn't so much that he would be burned to death, as he would be roasted alive. Queen Esther herself would apply the torch that would spell Henry's end. As she approached the pile and was about to apply the fire she heard Henry reciting the 23rd Psalm.

"The Lord is my shepherd, I shall not want... though I walk through the valley of the shadow of death; I will fear no evil for Thou art with me."

"What? Are you a Christian? Hallelujah! I have better idea," Queen Esther danced with joy upon her discovery. "You will run the gauntlet."

Chapter 53

There were several types of these running contests. Some consisted of two rows of women equipped with switches who would strike the unlucky runner as he fled down their length. A harsher trip was made down a line of young men not yet exposed to battle. These boys, in an eagerness to become tested warriors, would be given slightly thicker sticks to beat their victim. Sometimes these youngsters would continue until the object of their ardor was beaten to death, but the victim was usually spared his life. Finally there was the warrior's gauntlet. The braves observed a sick code that allowed for only one brave to step forward initiating the ordeal, but once the victim was off his feet everyone would join in. While everyone survived the first, and most survived the second, none had ever survived the third.

"It is to be the warrior's run. You will be allowed your knife as a sign of my Christian charity. What is your full Christian name?"

"I am Henry Pierce St. Albans a free man and a Christian."

"Men are known by deeds and bravery. If you survive, you will become a mighty warrior of the Muncee and will come or go at your own will. The Muncee will be your people and will go to war for you. Likewise, if the Muncee are at war then you are at war. But as no one has ever survived this contest," Esther cruelly added, "you will be just another dead white man."

The ordeal was to begin in a swale that ran for almost two miles toward a region called the Chemung. The village of Chemung lay a few miles further on. True to her word, Henry was given his knife and told to start his run. As he started out he noticed large rocks placed randomly in the gully by receding glaciers thousands of years before. Behind any of these stones could lurk an adversary waiting to bash his skull in. It wasn't long before he faced his first test. The first brave came out from behind his hiding place just as Henry was running by. As the club was brought down, Henry used the hilt of his antler-handled knife to partially catch the blow and divert it to the side. The force of the redirected strike brought the attacker with it and as he passed Henry, the knife was brought back in a slashing motion opening a wound on the Muncee's side. The shock of the cut caused the wounded man to drop his club and fall to a knee grasping his side. Henry used the opportunity to arm himself with the club and continued the course not wasting time delivering a coup de 'tat blow on the disabled foe. A second test await-ed the scout fifty yards on. It was the largest man Henry had ever seen. The club he carried looked to be made from the trunk of a tree and its business end from a boulder. He was easily half a head taller than McAdoo and some twenty pounds heavier, all muscle.

"Goliath!" Henry muttered as he beheld the behemoth. The way to the finish was behind the giant and it now seemed like a goal impossi-ble to accomplish. *Remember what David did.* He thought. *Pick up some smooth stones. I don't have a sling... maybe I can use my belt.*

The immense foe slowly started for Henry raising his huge club as he came on. The leather belt was a poor substitute for the chord and hide sling that the anointed boy king of Israel used to bring down his Goliath, but it was all he had. Using the pouch as the stone's receptor, Henry swung his belt over his head then let loose the end without the buckle. The stone shot out like a rocket clearing the gully and smashing through some tree branches as it fell back to earth. The big Indian was startled by the exhibition. He stopped and smiled. Boys used slings to bring down birds for food among the Muncee. A hearty cackle was heard up one side of the ditch; rousing laughter from everyone at the gully followed. The Muncees were getting a very entertaining gauntlet run today.

Henry reloaded his belt sling and after saying a quick prayer for de-liverance swung and released the second stone. The missile flew and struck the giant warrior in the most vulnerable of locations. Now the tower of a man doubled over as razor sharp spasms of pain racked his center. He passed out and fell forward in a heap. Raucous laughter ex-ploded from both sides of the swale. Putting on his belt and saying a prayer of thanks, Henry now walked cautiously on. No other warrior came to challenge him. Up a short way he saw the women of the town lining his course with switches in their hands. They were laughing so hard that they barely hit him as he ran through to the end of the course. Laughing with her hands on her hips at the end of the run was Queen

Esther.

"Tall Oak's squaw says to thank you. She has borne him six children and that is enough! Ha! Ha! Hee! Hee! Come, we will feast the making of a new Muncee!"

Chapter 54

The feast was a happy celebration. No lives had been lost in the warrior's run for the first time anyone could remember. The brave with the wound to his side had it packed with mud and moss in the Indian way and joined in enthusiastically welcoming the newest member of the clan. Tall Oak was walking very gingerly, but he too raised an open hand, palm forward and shouted, "Tuckahoe" to his newest brother.

Andrew Eghobund, Queen Esther's son, gave Henry a red strip of wampum. Standing up from the table he said, once in the Iroquoian tongue and then in perfect English. "Henry Pierce St. Albans, Fox Tail, the Sure Shot; all names of one man who today is born to the Muncee: after today I think the right name for him is the Sure Shot!"

Laughter erupted on all sides as he continued, "Let every man, woman, and child know that this beaded strip of wampum I have given him says that he is Muncee. His friends are our friends and his enemies are our enemies. He is welcome at our council fires and is free to come and go as he wishes. Tomorrow he will be bathed in the water that is our mother (the Susquehanna) and his hair will be braided in the Muncee way."

The water was cold and clear the following morning. Henry was pushed under the water four times to signify the elements of the world, Earth, Wind, Water, and Fire. It also signified the four directions of the world, North, South, East, and West. After returning to the bank of the river, Sure Shot's hair was slightly greased and then braided in the Muncee fashion. The le bonnet rouge cap, which Henry had stuck in his belt during his mad ride was produced and placed again on his head.

Queen Esther embraced him and gave him a bear claw necklace that had been her late husband's. "It has big medicine, you know," she confided to him.

Henry made plans to leave the following day.

"May your journey be safe and may you come back to your people soon."

This was the Queen's farewell, to which she quickly added, "We Muncee want to laugh that way again!"

Three braves accompanied Henry as far south as the Shamokin Path before turning back. It was only a few miles due east now to the Silverthorne's homestead and Henry longed to see Mr. and Mrs. Silverthorne and most especially Evan and Rachel. He had quite a tale to tell them.

Arriving at the farmhouse at around suppertime he found everyone gathered washing up for the meal. Evan saw him first and let out a "Huzzah!" Rachel turned and her eyes grew big then filled with tears as she ran to her dear friend. Her parents hugged him each in turn and then sat him down to join them in a fine venison roast Evan's hunting had provided.

"From the looks of your hair Henry I swear you've gone native," remarked Oliver as they took their dessert and coffee.

"You are looking at a full-fledged Muncee brave," Henry informed them.

He then went on to recount his tale in detail becoming quite red-faced as he got to the part about Tall Oak and the slingshot.

"That's a story to rival the likes of Dan'l Boone," Evan suggested.

"The good thing about it is that through me we will have an ally against the British and their Mohawk and Seneca minions. And at the worst it will keep the Muncee neutral and out of the fight."

Chapter 55

Henry wanted to get back to his duties as scout for the West Branch area so the next morning he collected his rifle and his borrowed mount then started out for Pine Creek. He stopped in at the trading post at French Margaret's Town to see Peter Quebec to see if he had heard any news.

"Much news and some about you, Muncee brave. There is a big split now in the Iroquois nations. The Mohawks and Senecas have thrown in with the English, but the Oneidas and their "little brothers" the Muncees and the Tuscaroras have decided to stay out of the fight. The Cayuga's and the Onondagas are split."

"What of the raids by the Delawares?" Henry wanted to know.

"Chief Bald Eagle has lost some of the respect of Joseph Brant, and is now more closely allied with the Seneca Chief, Old Smoke and the younger war chief who is known as Cornplanter. The Seneca have no presence here, as this is the land of the Oneida and the Mohawk. The Seneca are known as the "Guardians of the Western Gate" and make the Niagara their home."

"If the British have a say then we must forget the traditional hunting grounds. What of Willie, my Strong Arm?"

Quebec took a draw on the corncob pipe he was smoking and began, "Your friend has traveled north to Tioga and on to the place called Salamanca which is the home of Cornplanter. Willie has seen your spirit guide, the great stag, and knows that you are alive. He goes there to find you."

"My dear God, his life isn't worth a tinker's dam there."

Henry, obviously shaken, rose to his feet, but a hand on his arm by the post's proprietor made him pause.

"You going there will be certainly fatal for you and probably for him. There are Shawnee there who will be proud to call him a brother because of his deeds in helping the Lenape. He will have better medicine there alone. If you feel you must go, return to your Muncee brothers. Take them with you to Tioga and wait for him there."

Henry considered Quebec's temperate advice deciding it was in everyone's best interest. Running rashly into Tioga would likely seal his fate and the fate of his friend, Willie.

"Would you send word to Covenhoven for me? Tell him that until Willie and I return, he'll have to do our jobs. I'll return as soon as possible, God willing, with Miles. I will square things with you on my return."

The shopkeeper, Quebec, nodded his assent and watched as Henry headed off toward the land of the Muncee.

Chapter 56

Willie had headed north the morning after his dream. He knew that Sure Shot was alive because his friend's spirit had shown him. What the stag didn't tell him was where Henry traveled or when the ordeal he witnessed in the dream would happen. He had to find him, but how? He concluded that Tioga would be the best starting point. The Indian town seemed to be at the crossroads of all native travel to the north and west or to the south and east. He followed the Shamokin Path east until it intersected with the Towanda Path taking him north to the Lenape settlement of Towanda and then onto Tioga. At Towanda he found a Lenape brave who, along with his wife, were also going to Tioga and joined them.

Tioga was a large Indian town that stood at the crossroads of the traditional Six Nations homelands and their hunting grounds to the south and west. As the Iroquois became allied with other tribes and conquered enemies the range of their travels also expanded. There was also an element of the British present in town in the form of a small detachment of Butler's Rangers, a loyalist company of soldiers under the command of Major John Butler. At present these men had not formally been brevetted into the British Provincial Army, but they still performed service for the Crown in the form of leadership and guidance of Indian raiding parties. They were a reliable escort for kidnap victims and parolees taken to Fort Niagara. And finally they provided a scouting service for the British much as Henry and Willie were doing for the Americans.

The place made Willie nervous and he was anxious to see if anyone had word about his partner. As he was walking through the streets he came upon the renegade, Haverford.

"Tuckahoe, Grey Feather. Have you met with your great chief yet?"

The man being addressed turned and faced Willie. "Tuckahoe, Strong Arm. I am still waiting for him. He is needed at a place called Long Island now but he will be here soon enough. Come with me; let us get some English beef at the tavern."

It seemed to Willie that this Mohawk wanted to go to a more private place before speaking further. Once in the drinking house, the two found an empty table off in a far corner. Here they could talk more freely.

Grey Feather began, "Bald Eagle and his minion, Spotted Wolf, sit at the council fires of the Seneca now. This doesn't mean that a Mohawk here won't collect your hair though. We have been raiding in the Walawanna and south as far as Old Town taking plunder, captives, and scalps. The Mohawk are restless in waiting for Two Sticks and will follow the English plans until he returns. You would make a sweet diversion and most likely would be tortured in public before being put to death."

Willie knew that the English and the Indian tortured for different reasons. The white man tortured to obtain information from a prisoner or as an object lesson for mutinous subjects. Even so, some whites liked doing it. The Indians tortured for their entertainment and revenge. Their forms of torture were among the most grotesque ever conceived.

"Why are you telling me this?" the Shawnee was confused.

As a Mohawk, Grey Feather would be within his rights to capture or kill him as his chief wished. Yet here he was cautioning Willie lest he be captured and killed.

The smoke warrior smiled, "There is no great honor in adding your scalp to my belt. Now Fox Tail is a man of legend among the people. He is the only one ever to survive the warrior's run and has become a brother to the Muncee. The Great Creator has instilled in him the biggest medicine. He is a man that is worthy of my attention. The Sure Shot will come for you and I will wait for him."

"For a coup or for a kill?"

The renegade's answer would guide what he did next, "I don't know, Little Dog. I expect that I will be shown when the time is at hand. You will stay in my lodge as my guest. No one will dare challenge you when you're with me or my brothers."

Tioga had a cross section of tribes and nations within its limits. It was a town of the Cayuga but Oneidas, Mohawks, Senecas, Delawares, Mingos and Shawnee lived there. Muncee visited often, as did Tunkhannock, Lenape, and Onondaga.

"Wait, you said my friend is a brother of the Muncee? He survived the warrior's run?" Willie's spirit dream was making sense.

"I see you do not know what has happened to Sure Shot after he was taken by his enemies. Let me to tell you about it."

Chapter 57

Henry made his way to Queen Esther's town the following day. He was welcomed as any brave who would sit at the tribe's council fires. Esther invited him into her cabin. She was seated on her chair beside her hearth, with a fire roaring in her fireplace

"Sure Shot, you are a warrior of the Muncee. Along with this rank and its status you have obligations you must fulfill for your people. You are a skilled hunter and therefore must provide game for our pots and spits. You are a skilled fighter and therefore must defend your people with your rifle and tomahawk. You are a man and therefore must take a wife to tend your fires and give you children which is the future of your people."

The speech of the Muncee queen gave Henry no surprise until the last sentence. The wife and family part caught Henry completely off guard. He was twenty years of age, soon to be twenty-one. Most native men would have married by this time and started on a family. His thoughts turned immediately to Rachel. She was the woman who had his heart and that would never change.

"I respect the wise words of the leader of the Muncee whom I have come look upon as my Indian mother."

To this statement Queen Esther's surprised look quickly turned to a wide smile. Then she laughed out loud and slapped her knee. Henry returned her smile and thought to himself, *What have I done?*

Indian society was Patriarchal when it came to treaties and alliances between tribes and nations, but it was Matriarchal when it came to intratribal affairs. The linage of a family was traced through the mother so if a brave married a maiden from another village he lived now with her in that village and sat at her family's fires. By declaring Esther as his mother Henry gave her the authority to select a bride for him. He could reject her choice, but he better have good reason for doing so. New Moon was offered to both Andrew and Eli, her sons. Both said that they feared her because she had communion with the spirits. This was considered a legitimate rejection as New Moon was known as a shaman/healer and no man should fear his wife. Esther hoped to have a maiden promised to Henry before he left the next day.

A tribal council was called for that evening. The sole matter discussed was how many braves would accompany Sure Shot to Tioga. Too many might be considered a threat to the Cayuga or as disrespect. The one thing that Henry's proclamation did in his favor was gave him the prestige of being a son of the Muncee leader. This fact would count for something. Finally it was decided, after some vigorous debate, that four warriors would journey with him as brothers in his quest and another four warriors would accompany him as a son of Queen Esther. Eight braves were selected in total for the journey to Tioga. Tall Oak and Little Tree, the combatant Henry wounded, were among the number. Afterward, when he had Andrew alone, Henry asked his new brother for advice.

"What am I to do, Andrew? I have given my heart to a maiden back along the Loyalsock."

"Marry them both!" was Andrew's short answer. "Or find a legitimate reason for not marrying anyone."

"Would a blood feud be a reason?" Sure Shot wondered.

"It might delay the marriage until the feud is settled, but it's not a reason to stop a betrothal."

"Delay might be my only out," murmured Henry

"Tell me the reason for the feud. While we are not Mohawks, we still have those among us who kill or kidnap for my Mother."

"Just as Spotted Wolf wants my scalp for himself, I must retrieve something only I can retrieve. No, the Muncee must not stray too far from home. Not in my time, but in my Creator's time I will be given the chance. Likewise, I will tell the queen the reason for the blood feud so that she will not feel that her son has held back anything from her."

Andrew considered Henry's words and thought them to be wise, "Our mother will appreciate knowing what there is to know about her son from that son."

Chapter 58

The following morning as the band was preparing to leave; Queen Esther approached her new son leading a young maiden by the hand. She flung the young girl into Henry's arms in the tradition of the Muncee.

"Here is our wife, Sure Shot. Her name is Kaiwana Sausee or Snow Goose. Take her to tend your fires and give you sons."

In Henry's arms was one of the most beautiful young maidens Henry had ever seen. Snow Goose had seen fifteen summers. Both her hair and eyes were raven black and her skin was light brown and flawless. She was nearly as tall as Henry and was thin, but not too thin. Rachel suddenly entered his mind snapping him out of his immediate infatuation and to his senses.

"Blessed am I to have a mother who presents such a maiden for her son's lodge. This is a good thing. But her son has a black cloud over him. A blood feud exists' at present, between Spotted Wolf of the Delaware people and I. Until this is settled, I cannot take Kaiwana Sausee to wife."

Queen Esther's eyes narrowed and she rubbed her chin as she thought, "My son is right. No marriage can be consummated while such a dark shadow exists. I will tell you this as the truth. Spotted Wolf has become an enemy of the Muncee and I charge my warriors to seek out the sworn enemy of my son and kill him."

"My mother, allow me the honor of ending my enemy's life. I seek an honor reckoning with this coward that can only be done by my own hand."

"Very well, I will permit your revenge. Know that Snow Goose is your wife and will tend the fires of your lodge until you have completed your trial. You are charged with ending this feud quickly so you may return to become head of your house."

That did not turn out the way I hoped it would. I'm still married. Thought Henry.

As the group began its march to Tioga, Tall Oak ran up beside him

"You are not only the son of my leader, Sure Shot. You are now truly my brother. Snow Goose is my little sister."

Now Henry felt that the situation that couldn't get any worse suddenly got worse. Tall Oak's defeat at his hands could have been done only with divine intervention. Something he was quite sure wouldn't happen again. *It explains her height.* Henry thought.

All the matters Henry needed to attend to except one had to be put aside. He needed to find Willie Miles and, if he was still alive, rescue him.

Chapter 59

Henry had spent a great deal of effort in learning the Iroquoian tongue and the dialect of the Muncee. For now though, he used sign, which he had learned early on. He signed that they would camp outside Tioga that night and enter into the town in the morning.

The nine travelers made camp once the fires of Tioga could be seen in the distance. Little Tree took the first watch and Henry felt quite safe with his Indian mother's men. Sometime later Little Tree returned and another brave took his place.

"Two "Watchers," Little Tree signed to Henry, "Nothing odd."

At dawn they walked into the town of Tioga. They were met at the town's limits by Crooked Nose, the Cayuga chief, and his small entourage.

"The Seneca and Delaware here want to take your hair, Fox Tail. The Mohawks are of two thoughts about your hair and we Cayuga just want you to leave before war erupts."

"Is the man known as my Strong Arm in Tioga?" Henry wanted to know.

"He is here and a guest in Grey Feather's house."

"Send for him."

Henry was in no mood to play games or worry about protocol. The Cayuga chief sent for the renegade's guest. The messenger returned in a few minutes and whispered into his chief's ear. Crooked Nose nodded and addressed the white man.

"Grey Feather has invited all of you to be his guests at his lodge."

Henry noticed the Cayuga was shaking slightly when he spoke of the invitation. Henry signed for two braves to wait there and when the party turned a corner, he stationed two more braves to wait there.

Finally they arrived at Grey Feathers' cabin. The host was standing out in his front yard waiting for them.

"You are all welcome as my guests. Please come in and make yourselves comfortable."

209

"Where is Willie?" Henry demanded to know.

"He is inside waiting for you."

"Send him out!"

"You are in no position to make such demands of me. I will ignore your impoliteness, though. Please, come in."

"I beg your pardon for any rudeness on my part, but as your guest, I must insist on having Willie join us out here."

Prior to entering Tioga, Henry had come up with a sign that meant, "Prepare to fight." He would touch his nose with his hand, and then touch his knife. This he did now. The four Muncee braves separated slightly and everyone's senses were on high alert.

"Very well, Fox Tail, out here."

Four Mohawk smoke warriors appeared at the front door of the house. They brandished clubs and tomahawks.

"Your friend awaits you within. If you can free him he is yours."

Grey Feather raised his arms then dropped them. With the sign, the Mohawks rushed Henry and the Muncee braves. Tomahawks flashed and clubs rained down as the battle was joined. Grey Feather was a master of hand-to-hand fighting, but Henry had learned at the feet of a master, Two Hawks, and had learned to fight in this style with remarkable effect. It was a terrible battle with high casualties. Three Mohawks and a like number of Muncee lay either dead or mortally wounded around the front of the lodge.

Tall Oak had broken his foe's back and was approaching the last contest. Grey Feather and Henry each sported a number of cuts and now were locked in a tight embrace with knives each inches from the other's throats. The giant swung his huge right arm in a backhand motion like an enormous bear striking the Mohawk square in the head and knocking him several feet through the air. He had then grasped the throat of the stunned smoke warrior intent on snuffing out Grey Feather's life when Henry shouted,

"Enau! No!"

Tall Oak lessened his grip on his unconscious renegade. Shock marked the giant's face. Henry quickly signed for him to check the house and stood over his foe as he slowly regained his senses.

"I've saved your life for one reason. If you have killed Willie then as God is my judge, I'll cut your throat and let you die like a cow."

His senses having returned for the most part, Grey Feather hoarsely replied, "He was bait to get you here, but I have protected him from my own brethren who had sought his hair."

"Why?"

"It is a matter of hospitality. I took him into my lodge and, hostage or not, he was first my guest."

Henry found the native etiquette strange and yet logical. The Indian sense of honor actually reminded Henry of European chivalry from the past. The native giant returned to the yard with the hostage freed from his bonds. Willie looked none the worse for wear.

"I feel like I was wearing out my welcome," Willie quipped.

This made both his captor and liberator smile.

"We must work quickly now," Henry ordered. "We have a hostage of our own but I don't think this will discourage an attack." He signed to his future brother-in-law, "If he tries to escape, break his neck."

The giant's sinister smile unsettled everyone. Retracing their steps, they collected their lookouts and left the town of Tioga.

Chapter 60

The loss of three men was an enormous blow to the Muncee who were, at present, surviving only marginally due in part to their leader's blood alliance with the Oneida. By half dragging half carrying their hostage they managed a respectable pace back to Queen Esther's Town. Queen Esther met them and took the news stoically.

"I should like to kill this snake myself, but I will leave that for my sons to do."

Henry paused and then carefully replied, "Mother, you are wise and caring toward my brothers and me. It would be a great honor to draw lots to see who ends this wretch's miserable life, but I wonder if we would be better served by counting coup and sparing his life for ransom?"

The Muncee leader scratched her chin and thought out loud, "I wonder who would pay a ransom for a warrior of this kind? A smoke warrior is better off dead than disgraced."

"While this is normally the case, he is a white renegade versed in many languages and adept at the art of war. Mother, the circumstances might be better suited to an exchange of captives rather than goods or money."

Henry had found out about a warrior on his trip north to Tioga Queen Esther wanted back more than she wished for anything else. It involved a political feud between her late husband and Joseph Brant. It seemed that Eghobund had taken the part of a rival chief, Segoyewatha, over Two Sticks, due in part to his wife's being a cousin of the chief. As Brant rose in power he had manipulated a type of house arrest of his rival who was also known as Chief Red Jacket. If Brant would release Red Jacket to the Senecas then she would release Grey Feather to him and he could do what he liked with him. It involved a complicated web of honor and one-upmanship.

"I will consider what you have suggested, my son."

A runner was charged with taking the forearm bands from the hostage and delivering the offer to Two Sticks.

The next day the runner returned. The sachem Two Sticks known also as Brant was absent from Western New York and was taking part in the Battle of Long Island as a Loyalist officer.

In fact, he heroically distinguished himself in the action at Jamaica Pass. In his stead, a white loyalist officer who was put in command of the Mohawk warriors by Joseph Brant himself. This white man acted on the offer. It is not known if this Tory was ignorant of the extreme hatred Brant had for Red Jacket or if Grey Feather being a white man made the difference, but whatever the case, he agreed to the exchange. Brant's personal enemy would be sent to Handsome Lake, half-brother of Cornplanter, in Salamanca and Grey Feather would return to Chemung to face his fate. The renegade had lost his gauntlets and most likely would be put to death as he was already dead to his clan. But some factors worked in his favor. He was valuable as an interpreter and was inherently trusted far more than native linguists by the British. If he had very good luck there was a small chance he would survive. On the day of his release he met with Henry and Willie in Queen Esther's presence.

"I am no longer Grey Feather as that man has died in disgrace. I start on a journey to my fate as Grey Ghost. If I am to live again it must be far away from here. The land of the Sauk-Fox or the Mandan might be far enough; I don't know. My brothers will now be my assassins." He faced Willie and Henry saying pointedly, "It would have better for me if you had killed me on the burning stake."

Both Willie and Henry felt sudden compassion for their enemy. Taking a native warrior's honor was much worse than taking his life. Queen Esther was delighted.

"My white son is truly wise. This is a slow lingering death for my enemy plus an important ally has been freed that I could not have freed by force; and all without lifting a finger. It is a great day for Queen Esther of the Muncee!" With a cackle she addressed her captive, "You will be dead before you reach Chemung, Mohawk."

Grey Ghost bowed his head, "It will be a relief," he spoke softly.

Henry interrupted, "Willie and I will see that his man gets to Chemung."

"You will not!" Queen Esther had crossed her arms to signify how strongly she was against her son's offer. "The Muncee have lost too many braves on the path to Chemung and will lose no more. You will not go!"

"But I must go, Mother. It is a matter of honor."

The Muncee leader's face grew dark and her face contorted into a scowl, "What honor? It is surely not his honor as he has none. Is it my honor? No, it is more to my dishonor and the dishonor of the Muncee. If you insist on going it will not be as my son. Think about the maiden who tends your fires and everything else this rash act will cost you."

Willie bowed in deference to the angry woman and slowly began to speak as his idea was taking shape for him, "Mighty queen, perhaps the people this dog should have mentioned are the Cherokee and the Nanticoke to our south. The Susquehannocks are a strong nation that separates the Iroquois from these tribes. If he is released on the path to Chemung who can guarantee that he will continue on it or take instead the Shamokin Path south?"

The Muncee leader spit on the ground indicating that these would be her final words on the matter.

"I will not send one of my braves on this fool's trip, but I will not stand in the way of any warrior joining you as that is the right of any man. Go ask them and live or die with the answer."

Esther glared at her captive and then at her newly disinherited son and his friend, wrapped her blanket closely around her, and returned to her cabin.

The two scouts walked to the burning stake where Henry gave his warrior's call. Soon an assembly of about 25 braves stood around them.

Henry signed and spoke the words of the Muncee he was familiar with to the group. The intentions of Henry and Willie concerning the captive were soon put to the group.

A brave answered him by asking, "What does our leader say?"

"She says that you are men and make your own decisions."

"Then she is not behind it or she would be here speaking."

The men all dispersed except for one. They knew Esther's wrath when one chose to go against her.

"I will go with my brother so my sister will still have a husband."

"Tall Oak, your queen has disinherited me for disobedience. I'm no longer master of the lodge your sister tends."

214

Huge hands clasped Henry's shoulders in friendship, "I have more to say about whom my sister's husband will be than even Esther. She leads our people, but I lead my family. That is my lodge to give to you, not hers."

Willie clasped both men on the back and said, "We leave before first light tomorrow."

The next morning found the foursome outside the small village of Walawanna just to the west of Queen Esther's town and on the trail to Chemung. The trail led out of the village to both the Finger Lakes to the north and south to the land of the Susquehannocks and eventually to the Carolinas and the land of the Cherokee.

Willie stopped and asked the ransomed brave, "Which way? Do we go North or South?

The man once known as Grey Feather, the renegade Haverford now tossed a tuft of grass in the air. "I will go whichever way the wind blows. My life is likely forfeit so do I go quietly north or do I fight and strike out for a distant land to the south?"

The grass blew to the Southeast which told the men their answer and their demeanor. They would fight. They started on their way and met no one until they were about two miles north of the place called the Wyalusing Rocks. It was said that an old Indian Shaman once lived there and the place was held to have an aura of a spiritual nature much like the caves and shelters of English hermits centuries before. Another name for the place was Prayer Rocks.

Chapter 61

The four sojourners camped on the large rock cliff outcropping. It was a couple of hours after dark when three Mohawks walked boldly before their fire. The leader of this band raised his hand in a sign of peace and addressed them.

"Tuckahoe, I am one who is named Brown Dog and I have come to bury my brother, Grey Feather. For even while it appears that he walks among us; his spirit has died and only his form remains."

Three hands went for weapons, but the renegade motioned for them to stay their action. Grey Feather answered slowly and deliberately for himself, "It is true that I am dead in your eyes. I am now Grey Ghost and must live with that shame, but I intend to stay on this earth and will not give up my life without a fight. My three warrior companions are well versed in war and will also fight. You know it makes more sense to banish me than try to kill me."

Brown Dog pondered his former brother's words for quite some time before he answered him, "We have been sent to bury our brother and that we must do, but perhaps we can do this thing without shedding his blood."

Henry looked at Willie who was broadly smiling having understood what the smoke warrior meant. He quickly explained the matter to him.

"What Brown Dog is suggesting amounts to a ritual death and burial. The hair of a Mohawk warrior is the symbol of his strength and prowess, his life. Brown Dog means to shave the hair of Haverford and bury it. From that time forward he is dead and no one can ever mention his name again."

"That sounds like a great solution, Willie."

"It's not that simple. All the Mohawks present must agree and anyone who might have a grudge against him could oppose it and then it will be a fight."

Brown Dog huddled with the other two Mohawks and an animated conversation ensued. Finally Brown Dog returned and told them of their decision.

"It has been decided that we will take his hair, but even though the other two wanted to take scalp with his hair, they have agreed to the mark of shame so that all who see him will know."

The mark of shame was either removing an ear or part of the nose.

"I'll fight before I let them mutilate that man," Henry shouted.

The renegade smiled and said, "I've got two ears so I guess I can do without one of them. It is agreed."

At dawn the following morning a grave was dug and Brown Dog stood over the man whom he would soon "kill." He would cut the hair to stubble with his scalping knife but did not take actual scalp. Then, with the straight razor offered by Henry, he removed the remaining hair. The hair was placed in the grave along with the gauntlets of the "fallen" brave which Brown Dog now carried. The three Mohawks raised their arms heavenward and with bowed heads sang a death song for the one they had lost. Suddenly Brown Dog took the razor and slashed off a piece of Haverford's left ear. He took the piece of flesh and put it in his totem bag while Willie hurried to apply moss to the wound.

Willie whispered to Henry, "He didn't take the whole ear; only a small bit of it."

The smoke warriors gathered up their weapons and melted back into the forest. Once the bleeding was stopped, the four prepared to break camp. Tall Oak spoke with the group indicating his desire to return to his village because the deadly threat no longer existed.

"I do not know what it is that I face when I return. I only know that I am a Muncee and the head of my family. I can stand any humiliation from my Queen, but I fear what she might do to my own if I don't return soon."

Now three in number, they struck out for the Silverthorne farm. Henry's curiosity became too much for him on the way and he blurted out his question,

"Why not the entire ear, James?"

"I believe it was because I was taken into Brown Dog's family to replace a younger brother who had died of the white sickness. I was more than a brother warrior to him, I was his brother. When he was accepted into the Najemhei, the warriors who are smoke, he trained me and saw to it that I was prepared to join him when I came of age. He has lost his brother again and his sadness is full upon him."

"Why send him to be your executioner?" Henry asked.

"Our chiefs are constantly testing our loyalty and what we call our "center." Brown dog had two fellow warriors accompany him who had no special regard for him. If he failed his mission, it would mean his death."

"How did he convince them to let you live?" Henry was enthralled.

James laughed then said, "Ritual deaths are very real to the Mohawks. Also I'm sure he told them that he would return their gauntlets with mine if they disagreed with him."

Chapter 62

Native thought had it that a completely bald man was old, a shaman, or a fool so a large piece of cloth was tied to the bald man's head until his hair grew back in. At the town of Otstonwakin a beaver hat was bought to replace the cloth head covering. Haverford also got a shirt and coat plus a pair of trousers so that he now looked like a settler showing no outward signs of his native upbringing.

"That hat covers your ear and soon your hair will do the same job, and shucks, who is to know how you got that anyways," offered Willie.

"I will always know. That is the real point in any case," James replied.

"Do you still intend to journey beyond the reach of the Iroquois?" asked Henry.

"After my "burial" by my brother, they no longer consider me among the living so I have no fear of them. They can no longer even utter my name out loud as that would be disrespectful. Only a body remains behind, a solid form that contains no spirit of my true self."

Henry couldn't believe his ears. "You mean to tell me that after all Willie and I have done for you that you mean to give up? To go sit under a tree somewhere and waste away?"

The bald man removed his hat and faced his questioner, "Your help is appreciated, but I never really needed it. I believe everything that is to be done will be done with or without the interference of man. The life I have known since I was seven has been torn from me. I must be reborn another person to get my spirit back. I heard talk back at the trading post of some white men who have made it their life's work to save the spirits of Indians who they call their brothers."

Henry knew something of these German settlers that were known as Moravians. "I don't think what the Moravians do is what you think they do. Still, if you still want to see them after we report back and things have settled down a bit, we will see to it that you speak with a leader of that order at one of their mission villages."

It was now just a short walk to the farm of Henry and Willie's old friends. The trio stood on the front porch of the Silverthorne home just as Margaret, the youngest of the Silverthorne children, came busting through the door.

"Pa, them scouts from Augusta are here," she shouted as she rushed past them toward the chicken coop.

Oliver Silverthorne was soon on his porch welcoming his old friends and their companion, "Come in boys. The missus will whip you up some ham and eggs and lots of hot coffee."

The travelers attacked the meal as if they hadn't had a good one for days, which they hadn't had. After they had eaten their fill, all three listened as Oliver caught them up on the latest news.

"All the towns have to submit updated lists of grown men to the state's Executive Council. From these lists men will be conscripted into the militia and from the militia, to the Continental Army. Some have already volunteered to serve under General Washington. Evan will join Captain Brady's company in a few weeks somewhere to the east. I'm going to be shorthanded around here and with even me and the missus plus the two girls doin' all they can, I don't see how we can keep it all goin'."

Henry scratched his head in thought and finally spoke, "Willie and I need to get back to Augusta and make our report to Colonel Hunter or I would stay and help. As things are going now just north of here the Tories, with help from the Iroquois, are going to begin a set to of warring and killing. They're going to be pushing as far south into this land as they can go. We have had a chance to talk with our companion seated here with us who up to a couple of days ago sat at the British councils and heard the plans."

"Is he a loyalist?" Mr. Silverthorne wanted to know.

"Worse," chuckled Willie. "He's a renegade."

"What?!!" Oliver Silverthorne looked bewildered and involuntarily pushed his chair back from the table.

"James was, until very recently, one of the most feared warriors ever to walk the Great Shamokin Path, but that life has forever been closed to him," Henry assured his host. The young scout quickly related Haverford's story and the difficult circumstances he now found himself mired in.

Silverthorne eyed the hairless man up and down. "Well, he seems to know white man's manners as well as those of savages. He fooled me sure enough"

Haverford's face suddenly flushed, "I was taken away at the age of seven. The mother of my birth was a good woman who had taught me manners, but the mother who raised me to a man also taught me truth, fairness, and honor. The white man's idea of what is savage and what is civilized is as bent as an old man's back."

"That may be so boy, but if you want to live in the white man's world you'd better rein in your Indian ways."

Haverford's demeanor suddenly softened, "Your words have wisdom in them, Mr. Silverthorne. I have much to learn."

The verbal exchange was a little unsettling for Henry. *I need to get this fellow away from here as quickly as possible*, he thought. "Could you spare some jerky, Oliver? We mean to see Sam Brady and then start out for Fort Horn yet today."

"Of course, boys, I expect you'd be anxious to be on your way."

"Yes, please give our best regards to Evan and Rachel for us. Tell them we hope to see them soon."

"I'll be sure to do that, Henry," Oliver winked at Henry.

Their meager stores having been replenished, the three crossed Loyalsock Creek and then Wolf Run coming to the Brady homestead by mid-morning. John Brady's sons were gathering firewood for the home from a woodpile at the edge of a field they had cleared the previous spring. Both let out a shout as they recognized the figures coming toward them. Quickly the third member of the visiting party was introduced and this time his story was told before any misunderstandings could take place.

Samuel smiled and extended his hand to the newcomer, "You are welcome, James. Come warm yourselves at our hearth."

Samuel's younger brother slapped the new acquaintance on the back and chuckled, "I'm partial to your given name as I happen to share it with you. Hot mulled cider sounds like the best refreshment. I'll have Mother prepare some for us."

As the five men enjoyed their drinks by the Brady fireside it became apparent to Henry that both of the Bradys and Haverford seemed to hit it off. And when the subject of their hired man, Barker being mustered into Brady's company the month before came up, an idea came to him.

"Maybe you could use Haverford here for chores at least until we report to Augusta and then return."

"I know nothing of farming so how can be of help here?" asked the former renegade. "My only skill is making war."

Samuel smiled and said, "Until the spring planting, all the chores you will need to know can be shown to you in less than an hour. And your fighting experience might serve us well in defending our place."

"You have made me feel welcome so I would like to help here if I can," the last part was spoken as Haverford looked directly at Henry.

"I can't think of a better purpose for you at least till we get back this way again. I know if you give your word to do something then you'd as soon die as not do it."

"You have the one thing of value that is mine to give. I pledge that I will defend this place and help in its upkeep," said the Brady's newest hired man.

"So that there is no confusion with two James in the household, I propose that you call Haverford here "Grey" when you want him."

Henry's suggestion was greeted by smiles on all sides. After a quick lunch of soup and bread with apple butter, the two scouts started west for Fort Horn and Grey Haverford went with the Brady boys to finish bringing in firewood.

Chapter 63

Revolution on the Frontier began in earnest on the 23rd of December; two days before the Christmas of 1777. A settler who had been out alone checking on a trap line along Pine Creek was tomahawked, scalped and left to bleed to death. On New Year's Day, a farmer who had been out hunting a cow that had wandered off was slain north of Grand Island the same way. Reports of warring parties coming down from Tioga and Fort Niagara were forcing settlers to band together for their own protection.

Colonel Hunter fired off several missives from Fort Augusta about these attacks to President Wharton of Pennsylvania's Executive Committee and in a rare moment of decisiveness, sent Colonel Antes, and three classes (squads) of militia to help defend Fort Horn. Antes, whom Hunter referred to as an experienced ranger in his letters to Wharton, quickly assembled the thirty-six man force and struck out northeast to engage the threat.

Henry, Willie, and Covenhoven served as scouts on this expedition. Ranging ahead of the main body by about a mile they would be able to prevent a surprise attack against the main body and gather any knowledge of the presence of any enemy at the same time.

Two days out the scouts came upon a war party of about twenty braves who had with them eight prisoners. Two of the captives were women and three were young children. Two of the three male prisoners had been wounded and one could only continue with the aid of the unhurt man and one of the women. Willie saw them first and his turkey call alerted the other two scouts who joined up with him a short time later. After the situation was inspected by all three, Covenhoven came up with their plan of attack.

"Willie, get back to Colonel Antes and make him aware of what is going on. Henry, you and I are going to try to flank them without giving ourselves away. If we can get in close enough before the main force attacks maybe we can save some of the captives."

Willie took off toward the main group in the silent run natives and some frontiersmen were able to perform. Meanwhile, Robert and Henry began to quietly approach the war party.

It was quite apparent that the more severely wounded man was slowing down the retreat and that this would not be allowed to occur any longer. As the woman who was helping the poor unfortunate begged for his life, a Seneca warrior struck with his tomahawk. The defenseless man that was struck shrieked loudly then shuddered and died in a matter of seconds. Other members of the war party, their blood lust heightened, were drawn to the execution. The two scouts took this opportunity to close on the group and then to attack.

Henry aimed Kate at the executioner and shot him dead before he could scalp his victim. Covenhoven dropped a second brave with his long rifle and then drew a pistol as Henry threw his war axe downing a third. The war party was sent into a panic. European heroic ideals of a smaller force attacking a larger one didn't register with them. Indians were pragmatists. They assumed that they were being engaged by a large body of militia and so fled leaving behind their captives and their spoils. By the time they figured out that they weren't being chased and regrouped to counter attack, the main force of militia had caught up to the scouts and the newly freed prisoners. As the Senecas charged screaming out their war cry, a line of fifteen riflemen fired on command to be relieved by a second line of fifteen. Now the war party was in total disarray with an "every man for himself attitude."

Militiamen bragged later that the few savages that got away didn't stop running till they got to Tioga.

After everything had settled down and the captives had been seen to, the woman who had been helping the wounded man asked to see Henry.

"I want to thank you for the kindness you did for me and my poor husband, Isaac. My name is Jennie Lyle and two of the children here are mine. I don't fool myself that Isaac was ever goin' to make it for he was hurt awful, but you spared me and my babies from seein' him scalped before our eyes and for that I'm forever grateful."

Henry didn't feel like he had done anything except for being a second or so late from sparing a wife and children the execution of a husband and father.

Jennie continued, "My Isaac is a hero to me. He shoulda' give out long before he did, but somehow he knew if he stuck it out that help would catch up. And for just the two of you to take on so many of these raiders is the stuff of what poets write about. What are your names? I want to be able to tell my grandchildren the names of the men who made their lives possible."

Henry's embarrassment made him turn from the widow. Covenhoven told her, "I'm Robert Covenhoven and he is Henry St. Albans."

"This is truly an amazing day and you are both amazing men. St. Albans is properly named for he is a saint to me and mine."

Covenhoven smiled and mused, "Henry has been many things in his life, but I don't think "Saint," has ever been one of them."

When the story was told to the troop later as they were returning to Fort Horn it was readily agreed that Saint was much less of a mouthful than St. Albans and less stuffy, too.

From then on, Henry would be known as the Saint. It is interesting to note that in the tales of that day handed down by the Lyle family's descendants; Covenhoven's name was "anglicized" to Crownover. Additionally, the native languages had no word that corresponded with "Saint" so they used the closest approximation, "Shaman". A shaman possessed supernatural power and strength in the native's beliefs. By being given this recognition, Henry's spirit was held to be able to change outcomes and the paths of those around him. In some ways Henry's "spirit warrior" now outstripped his human exploits to the native way of thinking.

Chapter 64

As winter gave way to spring the attacks became bolder and more frequent. A large party of raiders crossed Bald Eagle Mountain and burned several homesteads carrying off plunder. Lieutenant Moses Van Campen, with a detachment of rangers from Colonel Cookson Long's battalion pursued them overtaking them near Pfout's spring. After a "sharp engagement," Van Campen reclaimed most of the stolen goods, which were returned to the settlers in the Buffalo Valley.

On May sixteenth, three farmers out planting corn were attacked, scalped, and killed near the mouth of Bald Eagle Creek. Several days later, what was probably the same war party took a family of three as prisoners and on the twentieth, a dozen more captives were carried off. Now the raids continued unabated even with settlers banding together for a common defense. Three families numbering sixteen souls gathered together at a fortified house several miles to the north of the Silverthorne homestead on the Loyalsock A raiding party of approximately twenty-five Seneca and Delaware braves under Loyalist command attacked the house burning it to the ground, killing at least three of the defenders, and carrying off the remainder to Tioga. A quick reaction by Samuel Brady along with a number of other militia locals could not overtake the raiding party before it reached Prayer Rocks and pursuit became too risky.

It was becoming apparent to many in and out of the government and military that the meager number of militia could not cover such vast area with hope of any sort of success. But still no major moves were made to better protect the populace.

At the end of May, Andrew Armstrong along with his wife, small son, and a servant girl named Nancy Bunday were surprised by raiding party at their cabin near the big spring just outside the small settlement of Linden. Mrs. Armstrong was in the bedroom when the natives broke in. She managed to crawl under the bed pulling some garments over her. The war party thought they had captured the family intact assum-

ing the servant to be Armstrong's wife, so the bedroom received a cur-
sory glance. They had another reason for haste as a lookout's call sig-
naled rangers close by and approaching the cabin.

Owing to this, they fled without even taking time to fire the home.
Twenty minutes later Covenhoven, Miles, and the Saint, as Henry was
now known, entered the Armstrong's abode. Mrs. Armstrong quickly
explained what had happened and the frontiersmen were after them at a
run. About two hundred yards into the forest, the rangers came upon the
terrible sight of the scalped corpse of Armstrong. Still further along the
escape route they found the maidservant, her throat cut and also
scalped. The causalities slowed down the pursuit and sent a clear signal
to the rangers. *Press us hard and the child will be next.* It was a horror
beyond the horrors of war for Henry. *We got the message, but too late
to save Armstrong and the girl*, he thought. *What are we to tell Mrs.
Armstrong? That our aggressiveness caused the death of her husband?*
The Saint buried his head in his hands.

The would-be rescuers held a hasty meeting.

"A brave is trailing the main body and is reporting our progress to
them," Willie's assessment of the situation made perfect sense. "If the
child is to have a chance, we must break off now and hope it will stay
their knives."

Covenhoven spit on the ground and asked, "Is there no way we can
out flank them to gain the advantage?"

Willie responded to the suggestion, "I believe the spy has his eyes
on us now and the only thing that will save the lad's life is to retrace
our steps."

It was a bitter admission The Saint had to make, but Willie's logic
was uncontestable.

"Mrs. Armstrong's worst fears have come to pass. The death of her
husband is terrible enough but her son's unknown fate will be a fate
worse than death to her."

Over a decade later an Indian knocked on Mrs. Armstrong's cabin
door. He told the widow he was one of the raiders who attacked her
family and had carried off her young son. With him was a native youth
looking to be in his early teens that, upon closer inspection, proved to
be white. Mrs. Armstrong would never be sure if the young man before
her was truly her boy as he was just four when kidnapped. The boy on-

ly stayed with her for a week when it was mutually understood that his life would be better spent among his adopted people rather with her. Mrs. Armstrong shed no tears at the lad's departure for she had buried the hope of regaining her son along with the body of her husband years before.

Less than a week later as Long's rangers were preparing to leave Fort Horn, a man ran into the fort soaking wet and naked except for his shirt. His name was John Hamilton and he was the sole survivor of a party of four men who had started out from Fort Horn that morning to get a flat boat which they would use to get their families and property down the river. Foresight on the part of the men had them bring their wives and children to Fort Horn before proceeding to Fort Antes for the barge. Hamilton and a man named Donaldson took a canoe and scouted ahead of the other men who were poling their craft slowly up stream.

At a point just north of where Pine Creek pours into the Susquehanna, the men in the canoe pulled onto the north bank of the river to wait for the barge to catch up to them. As the two men began securing the craft several rifle shots erupted from the woods nearby.

Donaldson grabbed his rifle and shouted, "Come on!" to Hamilton. He fired his rifle and was trying to reload when Hamilton noticed the angry red stain on his friend's back. Donaldson continued to try to re-load his piece as though he hadn't been shot, but now his body was be-traying him and couldn't do what he struggled to finish. A second vol-ley exploded ending Donaldson's effort and raining lead balls about Hamilton.

Knowing from the start that escape was his only choice, Hamilton swam under the canoe and broke it free from its lashings. Allowing the current from the creek to push him out swiftly from the shore Hamilton kept the canoe between him and his attackers until he managed to beach it on the other bank. Several rounds crashed through the birch sides of the craft narrowly missing him. Once on the other side his wool clothing was so heavy from the soaking that he could barely move. He stripped off everything except his shirt and ran the two miles back to Fort Horn.

The Saint along with Willie and four other militiamen snatched their rifles and hurried to the boats tied up nearby. As they paddled across the river they beheld the last acts of the massacre of the other two men who had set out with Hamilton that morning. Fleming and McMichaels, the men from the flatboat, had hired a boy to help them pole upstream. Now that young lad was making a run for his life with ten raiders in hot pursuit.

"He's smart to run with the current. We'll be able to put in below and stage our own attack. Make for the bank about three hundred yards below."

As Henry shouted his order and everyone now put their backs into it he hoped the boy had enough left in him to make those three hundred yards. The pursuers were at first solely intent on the boy, but soon they had three canoes with armed men making for them to consider. With a yelp from their leader the attack was turned to a hasty retreat as the raiding party made for Augenbaugh's ravine and north. The rescue party came ashore to find the boy out of wind and shaken, but unharmed. Fred Baskins was the hireling's name. His father had a farm south of Antes' Fort and he had been there by chance and agreed to help the men with the barge knowing they would return to Antes that day.

"I value my life at more than a dollar," Baskins said after he regained his breath.

"Never mind that," the Saint replied. "Tell us what happened."

"Well, we decided to start for the north bank when we heard firing off in the distance upriver. It took us a while, but we got in and started to head toward the commotion. We only got a few hundred yards when we were ambushed. Both the men went down right away and I started running back to the boat, but for the life of me I didn't know what I would do if I reached it."

Sometimes the Lord takes care of those who don't know how to take care of themselves, thought Henry. The rescue party recovered the three bodies. Donaldson had been scalped, but the other two had been spared that abuse due to the quick nature of the events surrounding the second ambush. Willie took the boy back to Fort Horn in one of the canoes while the rest of the men set out to complete the dead men's mission. Remarkably the raiders had left the cache of goods staged by the men alone. Perhaps they originally thought to ambush them there and saw a better opportunity when Hamilton's canoe came in a short distance away.

"It's no damn good for the people around here anymore!" one of the

229

militiamen cursed as they loaded the barge. "We can't be everywhere and the savages watch us and attack when we leave an area."

The remark gave the Saint an idea. Back at Fort Horn he proposed his plan to Covenhoven and then to Cookson Long.

"It's a dangerous plan that could blow up in your faces," Long told Covenhoven and the Saint.

"I don't say there isn't danger involved in a plan like this but I can't think of another way to stem the boldness of these raids," Henry reasoned. "If you can think of another way I'll listen."

Long stared into space for what seemed to be an eternity to the scouts. Finally he said, "I'll take it on myself to authorize this venture. I'm tired of being a colonel anyway."

Covenhoven thought he meant he would get a promotion; the Saint knew he meant he would be court-martialed.

Chapter 65

Three days later a force of three squads numbering about thirty men made its way from Fort Horn to an area called the Pine Bottoms about eight miles to the north of the fort. A small enclave of German farmers had hold up in a large barn that was equipped with firing slits and stood some distance away from the surrounding woods. The barn's occupants, in all numbering ten adult men all with wives and children had sent a runner who miraculously made it to the fort the day before. A small raiding party would hesitate to attack such a structure, but a larger force certainly would assemble and attack. Time was critical and the plan The Saint came up with seemed suited for such a rescue. The rescue party made it to the barn without encountering any hostiles, but every ranger knew they were there just out of sight. The men wanted to stay and fight so when the plan was explained to them they readily agreed. Soon the relief party made its way south taking the women and children out of harm's way. What the raiders didn't realize was that some of the "militia" was actually women and some of the older children in disguise. In all half the rescue forces remained behind to mount what would be a most surprising defense.

Miles, Van Campen, and The Saint doubled back as soon as a good distance had been put between the rescued and the barn. They came back upon the barn as the attack was starting to get underway. The Indians believed that only ten men remained behind and if they attacked from several sides at once they would quickly discover the defense's weakness and quickly exploit them. Covenhoven had remained behind in the barn to direct a coordinated defense. Twelve militia riflemen with farmers and the remaining rangers to serve as loaders stood ready as the attack commenced from three of the four sides. The order was given to man the appropriate sides and to hold fire until that command was uttered.

The warriors closed to about fifty yards and Covenhoven yelled, "Fire!" Twelve rifles erupted at once doing merciless damage.

"Look!" yelled Henry pointing to the fourth side. At least a dozen other raiders had waited until the battle commenced and were making for that as yet untested side. A few of these appeared to be Tories.

"The first attack was a ploy; this is the real attack," Van Campen cried.

It seemed like the second wave of raiders would reach their objective when a volley from inside the barn cut most of them down. Covenhoven had spotted them just in time to move his line of militia and order them to fire. Now more braves and Tories poured out of the woods. The order was given to fire at will and the riflemen and loaders worked in that unique concert that comes about when one is fighting for one's life. The Saint had noticed smoke coming off a ways to his left and made for it with Willie and Moses at his heels. Willie instinctively ran out at a diagonal angle to make for a type of small firing line with Moses doing likewise in the opposite direction. In the distance they saw Iroquois lighting pitch-tipped arrows.

All three knew they meant to fire the barn. Henry knew they were outnumbered better than two to one. *We need to make every shot count*, he thought.

The ranger firing line of three knelt and touched off their first volley. The result was that it took the braves attention away from the barn and placed it squarely on the more immediate threat that had killed three of their brothers. Four attackers remained at the fire, two still armed with lit arrows. These they fired at the rangers as they came on.

Van Campen was a crack shot, but better still he could reload a long rifle like nobody else. His second shot came thirty seconds later and hit a charging brave in the mid-section. Henry had dropped Kate and was racing toward the fire with his knife and tomahawk. Willie had stopped and produced a pistol with which he disabled another adversary by sending a lead ball into his thigh breaking the bone.

The fact about arrows that are wound with cloth and then dipped in pitch is that they lose any fine accuracy. Sure, such an arrow could find the side of a barn or its roof but hitting a running dodging man was next to impossible. Willie however was hit a glancing blow which did little more than leave a slight welt on his flesh. The Saint was nearly on them now with his companions, a few steps behind him. One warrior came on and the other turned and fled. The warrior swung with his knife and to the Saint's horror he recognized Little Tree. Side stepping as he had when he ran the Muncee gauntlet, Henry brought down the blunt end of his tomahawk on the back of Little Tree's skull. The Muncee brave collapsed in a heap, unconscious. Lying by the fire was a Delaware and a Mohawk and The Saint was sure he saw Senecas and Onondagas among the ranks charging the barn.

There had been other fires and none of the trio was surprised to see the barn begin to blaze.

"The heat and smoke will force them out. We need to do all we can for them."

Suddenly a line of musketry fire exploded to their right followed by a second volley. The aim was sharp and more raiders fell from the onslaught. The lines that were obscured by brush and trees suddenly appeared. The psychological effect it had on the attackers was palpable. Convinced they had been drawn into an ambush of staggering proportions they made quickly for the safety of the north.

"Who are these men?" Van Campen asked the question everyone else was thinking. A short while later as the fire was finally extinguished, the wounded tended to, and a tally of the casualties was taken, a colonel in full colonial uniform presented himself to Covenhoven and the other defenders.

Everyone recognized the colonel. It was the militia leader, Colonel Antes.

"How in the name of Aunt Hilda's garters did you come to be here?" Covenhoven wanted to know.

"Colonel Long briefed me of your somewhat foolhardy expedition and I determined that if it was to have a tinker's dam's chance of success that I would have to supply my reinforcement support to help with the plan. The German lad who had bravely served as the messenger the day before guided us here. On the way we met the women and children from the settlement and came on the rest of the way at double time when we heard the battle."

The hostile casualties were hard to gauge because native custom was to carry off any of their wounded or dead, but it was agreed that this was a force at least fifty or sixty strong and that as much as a third of them were killed or wounded in the fight. The settlers had only two wounded and the militia had one dead and five wounded. In retrospect it was a rousing victory at a period of time when such victories were rare for the revolutionaries.

Chapter 66

When Little Tree came to his senses a short time after the battle ended; his former friends interrogated him.

"So, Queen Esther has finally sided with the British?" Henry's tone showed his enmity.

"My queen has always been on the side of her people," Little Tree said with contempt. "Why would her son choose to go against her?"

The Saint smiled, "I was her son only when she could brag about me. So long as I did what she wanted, I was her son. When I did what my heart and my head told me to do then she cast me off like so much dirt."

Little Tree didn't understand the metaphor of "heart." Natives felt with their stomachs or loins.

Henry changed directions, "How is my brother Tall Oak?"

Little Tree bowed his head and murmured to the ground, "Our brother now hunts with his fathers."

Henry felt like he had been pole-axed, "What happened, Little Tree?"

The Muncee stared straight ahead and a tear ran down his cheek, "When he returned, our queen was very mad at him. She said that Tall Oak had made himself out to be her equal and he would pay the price for such treachery. All his possessions were taken and his family was sent away north."

Willie and Henry shuttered imagining Tall Oak's family as slaves to Senecas or Mohawks. Henry thought of Snow Goose, "And what of the tall maiden, the one called Snow Goose?"

"She was sent to tend the fires of Red Jacket in Salamanca."

Henry struck his hand with his fist at the news, "How did our brother die?"

More tears from the Muncee and he put his face in his hands at the thought. In a moment he raised his head and in a monotone voice he rasped, "He was made to walk his life away."

Few types of executions were as barbaric or as horrific as was this one. The victim had his bowels cut open and a rope tied to his innards. The other end of the rope was tied to a tree or in this case the stake in the center of Queen Esther's town. Tall Oak would have been either beaten or whipped into walking around the stake until the rope slowly, painfully pulled out his life.

"How can you follow such a demon?"

Little Tree buried his face in his hands again.

Back at Fort Horn the Saint began to question Little Tree again, "I saw Muncee, Delaware, Shawnee, and at least three different nations of Iroquois take part in the raid. Has Two Sticks returned?"

"No, Old Smoke and a white man named Butler have gotten all the tribes together. Old Smoke promises that the land will be returned to the people and Butler says the Great White Father from across the big water will help make it so." Then the warrior got that vacant stare again and said, "What is coming is death and destruction for the whites. No town will be safe. No high walled place will withstand what is to come." Little Tree took in a deep breath, stared at Henry, and with an air of resignation spoke. "It is coming soon."

Chapter 67

Henry reported what he had been told by Little Tree to the Fort's commander and the other officers.

"We must get the people to prepare to move into secure areas at a moment's notice."

Colonel Long turned to Lieutenant Van Campen, "Moses, you must move out in the morning and make haste to the Loyalsock. Take with you the two most experienced classes of militia. I don't need to tell you how very important your mission is or the dire consequences your failure might allow. Henry will be your scout."

Cookson Long's worried expression betrayed his feelings, "I'm sorry I can't send more men with you."

Then he turned to Sergeant's Scout, Miles, "Willie, you will accompany Colonel Antes back to his stockade and then proceed on with my dispatches to Colonel Hunter at Fort Augusta."

Now Covenhoven got his orders, "Robert, you will organize patrols to both warn any settlers that are still here of the danger and scout the land for any signs of hostile activity."

With that the commanding colonel left the gathering and entered his headquarters to write his dispatches for Colonel Hunter.

Later that night, before they turned in, Willie and Henry had time to reflex on the day.

"Don't tell me that God didn't have a hand in our victory today," Henry told his friend.

"God or devil, I just don't know." replied his companion.

"Why do you say that, Willie?"

"Fire and the smell of gunpowder could only mean your devil. It must remind him of his home."

Unfortunately for the militia, Colonel Long's campaign got off to a disastrous start because of a singular act of brash incompetence known as Captain Berry's Expedition.

Robert Covenhoven's two brothers, James and Thomas, played a role in this tragic affair. Robert's father, Albert and sister, Isabella along with his brothers managed a small farm between Mill Creek and the Loyalsock. They located there along with other relatives named Wyckoff and Van Nest to farm. Both of Robert's brothers served in the local militia under Colonel Hepburn, in Captain Berry's company.

Dire dispatches from all the outposts found their way to Colonel Hunter's desk at Fort Augusta. Hunter in turn used his talent with the pen to paint a bleak outcome for the settlers in the Wyoming and Susquehanna valleys. The Executive Council, acting in concert with the Board of War, declared that the frontier raiders were acting under orders of the British and that they posed as grave a threat as the enemy's activities in the east.

Captain Berry was a young impetuous officer previously dispatched from Fort Augusta. He was to eventually join Colonel Butler's two hundred and fifty man regiment at Wilkes-Barre, but for now he was serving under Colonel Hepburn in what he saw as a collection of poorly trained bumpkins. With his indomitable talent he would win the day and rise in the ranks. This unit was in the field when word reached them that raiders were in their area, Berry was excited to finally be able to show his prowess and true to his self-absorbed personality, acted on his own authority.

News of raiding and the stealing of livestock including some prized horse flesh further prompted Berry to hurriedly begin his pursuit of the raiding party to overtake them. He was already hearing the praises in his head that he would get returning the prized animals. Captain Berry was two hours out of Hepburn's encampment when the colonel found out about his plan.

"That damned fool with get himself and everyone with him killed," the colonel was seething fire at the young officer's half-cocked notion.

By coincidence, Robert Covenhoven was with Colonel Hepburn when the Berry's plan came to light. He immediately volunteered to catch up to the small force and give them the colonel's orders to return. He caught up with Berry's group about two miles south of the Loyalsock Narrows.

"I have express orders for your return given to me by Colonel Hepburn."

The captain smugly replied to the scout, "He is a militia commander and as I am regular army I must refuse his order. We shall march on."

What an anxious little fool. Covenhoven thought. *He's so eager to fight that he'll lead his entire command to their deaths.*

"I don't claim to know about the rules of chain of command, but as you have my two brothers and two of my cousins with you, I'll offer my services as scout."

"Yes, fine then. Let's be on our way," with a wave of his hand the captain started the squad off again.

Robert went on ahead and led the group cautiously through the narrows. At a point several miles further north Captain Berry finally saw the folly in his efforts. Calling a halt he addressed the men, "As we are no closer to capturing these savages than we were this morning, I say we return to our camp so I can make my reports."

Covenhoven spoke up, "We may not have seen any raiders, but I assure you, captain that they are watching us. It would be reasonable to take a different route east toward Picture Rocks to bypass any ambush planned for our return trip."

"That is another day's march and I don't think it is necessary."

"Please, Captain ---"

Berry cut the scout off by raising his hand, "I should think you a coward if not for the tales of your bravery told to me by your relatives. No, we shall return the same way we came."

Robert held his anger then gathered together his brothers and cousins, "Watch my lead and get behind cover at the first gunshot."

As the band of men entered the narrows they were fired upon from all sides. Captain Berry and five others were cut down in the first volley. Robert Covenhoven, his brother James, and a half- breed nicknamed Sharpshins escaped by diving into the Loyalsock and letting the swift current in the narrows carry them a safe distance below the ambush. Thomas Covenhoven, Peter Wyckoff and his son Charlie, and a black freeman named Pike were taken prisoner. Pike was burned at the stake two days later in Queen Esther's Town. The Wyckoffs and Thomas were sent on to Fort Niagara and would be ransomed back two years later.

Colonel Hepburn left the Wallis encampment the following morning with a contingent of twenty men to search the area after the return of the three survivors. The bodies of the dead were found and buried. One additional item of interest was also discovered. Among the scalped bodies of the slain, in the moist soil, was the distinct footprint of a hobnailed boot such as those worn by those in the British ranks.

There was no doubt now as to British involvement. A country that held honor in such high regard was orchestrating the vilest type of slaughter among the frontier settlements and farms.

Berry's tragic expedition took place on June 10th. June 10th was also the date of the ambush at Thomson's farm where John Thomson and a man named Shufelt were killed and young William Wyckoff was carried off.

Captain Reynolds and a force of about fourteen men were journeying from Wallis' encampment to Fort Horn with supplies for the militia there. The Saint was assigned as scout accompanying this detail. They had just crossed the Loyalsock at a point called the Sand Island when they heard the sounds of an attack and surmised it was coming from the Thomson place. The rangers practically ran the two miles to Thomson's farm. There they saw the unthreshed grain in the wagon and the barn both ablaze. The house hadn't been torched and Reynolds figured that they had gotten too close to the scene for the raiders to have taken the time to torch the home before they fled.

Henry's frustration at what was becoming nothing short of a futile effort to protect the settlers was turning into a fuming rage. He thought of the Silverthorne's and the rage turned into a fear. Not for himself, but for those he cared about.

A quick inspection of the cabin turned up no one so the pursuit began. Thomson's powder horn with a round through it was found a short distance from the house. A distance into the woods the bodies of Thomson and Shufelt were found. They had both been killed with the blow of a tomahawk to the back of the neck, but the Indians hadn't taken the time to scalp the victims. More than one man could read the tracks going southwest away from the scene of the murders. It was clear that one of the sets of tracks were of boots common to the settlers. "It's probably young Wyckoff," someone said. Half the men present knew that young William had offered to help harvest the wheat that was now burning back near the barn.

The Saint offered, "I might be able to catch up with them alone without being discovered, but if we continue in our present strength, I'm afraid the Wyckoff lad will meet the same fate as his companions. From the tracks, the war party looks to be about thirty in number so one or two of us couldn't hope to rescue him."

Captain Reynolds agreed with his scout's assessment of the situation, "We must make French Margaret's Town before nightfall." Motioning to his scout he ordered, "Lead the way."

Chapter 68

June 10th, this day of cruel destruction and the shedding of blood was not yet finished. Two wagons of settlers; six men, two women, and eight children; were journeying on the public road between the Susquehanna and the Lycoming fortification.

Both women, Mrs. Smith and Mrs. King, were traveling with their children in an effort to join their husbands on the deeded tracts of land by the Loyalsock and Lycoming creeks. Leaving the safer area in Northumberland was risky, but as their men were working their homesteads, both women were determined to join them.

Four of the men in the small convoy were farmers and relatives of the women. Traveling together for mutual protection had been done by everyone since the troubles began. The remaining two men were militia members from Captain Reynolds' company accompanying the group to provide for additional protection.

A raiding party wanted no part of such a traveling group, but these were full blown war parties roaming the area now. The wagons were trying to reach the safety of the Lycoming encampment before nightfall.

The ambuscade happened at dusk near where West Fourth Street and Cemetery Street converge in present day Williamsport, in a growth of wild plum trees. The assailants fired at the wagons from both flanks. Most of those exposed were either killed or wounded in the first barrage.

Meanwhile Peter Smith and John Harris, Jr. had joined Captain Reynolds' party. Both Smith and Harris were on horseback coming down from Smith's place to meet the wagons at the Fort. All heard the sounds of ambush and immediately started for the site. Smith met his two oldest children running on the road away from the massacre. They told their father that their mother was dead and that, "Indians were tomahawking any still left alive." It was a miracle that the boy and girl had managed the getaway. Now insane with grief and blood lust Smith raced on to the horrific scene. All the men had been killed and scalped. His wife had suffered the same fate and to his grief and suffering so had his two middle children. Missing were Mrs. King, her two offspring, and the two youngest Smith children. Reynolds' unit had reached Smith and Harris as Peter Smith screamed to the heavens like a wild animal.

Captain Reynolds assessed the situation, "This work is too dangerous to be done by torchlight. We must return to Colonel Hepburn now and return at first light to tend to our dead and plot our course."

"Smith won't leave his wife and children here," the Saint reminded Reynolds.

"Put them over the two horses and bring them with us, but be quick about it. There are at least thirty sets of eyes on us," Reynolds ordered.

Reynolds was wrong in this last assessment. The Tory butchers that led this campaign of terror thought that a larger detachment of militia would be chasing them so after the carnage they split into two groups. One group would head north back to Tioga with the four captive children. The other group would head west over Bald Eagle Mountain and make for the Alleghenies. Mrs. King and four of the youngsters couldn't be found so it was deduced they were carried off for ransom or into slavery.

William King was with Colonel Hepburn when the rescue party returned. He fell to his knees as Captain Reynolds reported the details of the day. His wife and children were missing so his grief was mixed with a small degree of hope that his beloved and their issue had somehow escaped into the thickets.

In the morning a detail returned to bury the dead and figure out what to do next. King and Smith were present to search for family. It was soon clear that the raiders had split into two groups and the directions they were heading. It also showed smaller tracks so some of the children were now known to be carried off. The smaller tracks were all with the group heading north so all of the detail went after them except for two. Covenhoven had joined this mission along with the Saint. They headed west figuring that the raiders that were traveling the lightest were still up to mischief and doing mischief took time and that time would allow them a chance at the fiends.

"If they headed toward the Grand Island we'll pick up Willie and the three of us will find them and stop them," the Saint said as they hurried on their way.

"And if Moses is about, I'm sure he'll want to come too."

Covenhoven picked up his pace to keep up with his determined friend.

The number of the attacks and the fierceness of the outcomes had those trying to protect the settlers disheartened and discouraged. Henry was of a mind to show the Tories and their native allies that while wanton attacks exacted a price, they also came with a price.

William King continued to search the area and had ended up following signs of a person who had walked and then crawled down to a small stream nearby. There he found his wife lying by the water. She had been shot and then stabbed, but miraculously had been spared a scalping. She had bled profusely from her wounds but was still hanging on to her life. King turned and raised her to him. She recognized her husband, smiled and then died. He buried her there along with the men of the ill-fated party. He abandoned his farm along the Lycoming Creek and returned downriver to Northumberland.

Legend has it that the plums from that grove of trees where the massacre took place were the largest and sweetest around for some fifty years after the attack. This incident would go down in history's annals as The Plum Tree Massacre and stands today among the most vicious acts of barbarism committed along the frontier during the American Revolution.

It is with some amount of incredulity that it is noted that Peter Smith took what remained of his family and returned to his farm. No one can claim to know the workings of this man's mind. It would be nice to think it was his pioneer spirit or stubborn determination. Perhaps a simpler reason was because his wife and babies were buried there and he didn't want to leave them.

Chapter 69

The Saint and the Dutchman met up with Willie and Van Campen near Fort Antes. The latter two had just finished a job for Colonel Long and were returning to report.

"We're onto a party of raiders and mean to catch them. Forgo your report and join us," they were told.

The foursome headed to the Grand Island and picked up the raiders trail just northwest of the present town of Lock Haven.

"What settlements are still occupied north of here, northwest of Fort Reed?" wondered Covenhoven out loud.

"We'll make for Renovo," said Van Campen, "I have a hunch."

Now that tracking was replaced with a destination the pace was nearly doubled. Renovo was a small settlement on Kettle Creek with a mixed population of white and native inhabitants. It hadn't been subjected to any discord up to the present time and the settlers felt secure enough to continue farming the creek basin. It would be the scene of another massacre unless they got there in time. If the war party had a white as its leader they wouldn't move nearly as quickly as if a brave was in charge. All four quietly prayed this was the case as they raced for the hamlet.

At a point two miles south of Renovo the scouts caught up with the raiders. A group of ten warriors and two loyalists were gathered apparently to plot the attack on the settlement. It looked like only the whites and one or two of the natives had rifles. The rest were equipped with bows, war clubs, tomahawks, and knives. All the scouts had rifles and all except Henry had pistols; Henry having discovered that while he was without peer with a long rifle, he was a poor shot with a handgun. Van Campen, a deadly shot with a pistol, had a leather brace of three handguns strapped across his chest.

Swiftly and quietly the four scouts worked their way around so that the attack would push the raiders toward the creek. When they got to a spot about seventy yards from the preoccupied bunch they would launch their charge. The loyalists were so cock sure of themselves they didn't even bother to post a sentry.

The scout's rifles erupted in unison knocking down four of the ambushers. The whites and some of the remaining warriors panicked, but three braves remained calm and prepared to repulse the charge. And the four did oblige them by immediately charging, covering ground at a remarkable rate with their long rifles on their backs and hand weapons drawn. At about thirty yards the three armed with pistols discharged them. Another brave was gone and a second shot in the shoulder writhing on the ground in pain.

Henry evaded the last one standing and continued running toward Kettle Creek. He wanted to take a white man alive so more could be learned about the British plans for the war in these parts.

The three remaining Indians had already begun to ford the stream but the two whites, outfitted in their hobnailed boots, hadn't yet made the bank of the creek. The Saint caught them as they entered the water. Both had thrown away their long rifles as soon as they started their run so neither would put up much of a fight. The Saint was certain that they were cowards at heart and bullies to boot. Striking the bigger of the two with the blunt end of his tomahawk, Henry shoved the other down into the stream. The larger man started to regain consciousness as his face hit the water, but he remained disoriented until Willie collected him a few moments later. Henry stood over the man he had pushed into the water as the wet man spun to face him. The loyalist was indeed a sniveling coward who was crying and begging for his life.

"I'm not going to kill you; much as I have cause to do so. You'll be tried fairly in a court by free men and then you will be hanged," the Saint matter-of-factly told him as he was bound tightly for the trip back to Fort Augusta.

Willie came over with the other bound Tory, "The dutchies are finishing up with the others. Do you want to continue after the rest?"

Before the Saint could answer a war cry split the sky coming from a ridge above the far side of the stream. It was Spotted Wolf! He punched his right fist in the air and then was gone.

"Willie, I want with all my heart to follow them, especially now, but my head tells me to get these miserable curs back to Fort Horn so they can be questioned."

Chapter 70

"It's a pity that none of the others survived," said Covenhoven sarcastically when the two returned with their prisoners. "Some are just too tightly strung."

"I don't hold with murder, Robert," Henry told them all. Sinking to that level of barbarism didn't set with the Saint and he meant to do something about it. Covenhoven had suffered great personal loses at the hands of raiders just such as these, but acting like them wasn't the answer.

Covenhoven's face visibly darkened and a menacing expression crossed it, "And we don't hold with the murder of innocents." Covenhoven's words were slowly and evenly spoken as he faced the Saint eye to eye.

"Let's head back to Fort Horn to sort this out," Van Campen's suggestion broke the tension between the two men for the moment.

Neither Henry nor Covenhoven ever brought up this matter again to anyone. Maybe it was the accounting of the Dutchman's loss or maybe it was the realization that terrible things often happen during battle and its aftermath. It probably was the practical knowledge that such matters would not see the light of day if they were pursued.

It was shortly after dark when the relief party returned to the relative security of Fort Horn. The group was ushered before Colonel Long for questioning.

"Before we begin, I want to tell the prisoners that any information you might give us and proven to be true could help in mitigating your fate."

The smaller of the two men looked as if he was going to speak, but a scowl from the bigger prisoner stopped him.

"Lead the large man out into the hall," Long ordered a guard. "Now, tell me your name," Long instructed the remaining captive.

"He'll kill me if I utter a word," moaned the wretch.

"We'll kill you if you don't. He has no power over you here. His life is already forfeit."

The little man considered what the colonel told him, "John out there was the head of the raid," the prisoner began. "He's a subaltern in Major Butler's Rangers and can tell you much more than you can ever learn from me. My crime is that I am a loyalist who can speak a couple of the savage's tongues."

"You were there when your band of cutthroats killed women and children back on the Lycoming yesterday," accused Covenhoven, "and you nearly killed me back on the Loyalsock that same morning."

The prisoner swayed, as the weight of what he had been part of suddenly was placed on his shoulders, "I know that I shall burn in the fires of hell for all eternity for what I have done, but if you want any information about what is planned for the future then you must break Standholm."

"Place this man in the holding cell, and then bring me in Stand-holm," Colonel Long barked.

Long couldn't operate under the normal protocols and conventions of questioning. If any of what this provisional ranger knew could help in keeping the settlers safe then he needed it now. The large man once again stood before the American colonel.

"We have learned that you are an officer in King George's Provisional Rangers. As you are dressed in civilian garb, I can have you taken out and summarily shot as a spy."

The big man didn't even flinch.

"But before I do though, I'd like to introduce you to Willie Miles. Willie is half Shawnee and is well versed in several methods of extracting information from those that are, well shall we say, reluctant to speak."

Willie shot a look at the colonel in surprise.

"Now Mr. Standholm, Willie doesn't really care if you talk or not. All he really cares about is that he will be able to question you in his way. You have been around the red man long enough to know how refined and exquisitely terrible their methods and devices can be."

Large beads of sweat appeared on the prisoner's brow.

"Have you thought of the method you will use this time, Willie?"

Miles had caught on, "I think that I will use the one thousand deaths method."

"How marvelously cruel, yet effective," Colonel Long nodded his approval.

"You are all savages!" cried the Tory.

"Still, we mean to know what you know and Willie here does love his work."

Now the big man began shaking all over, "Alright, I'll tell what I know."

The subaltern's knowledge about the British's future plans for the revolution's frontier was sketchy and general at best. He knew that a large force of loyalists and their native allies was to strike and strike soon. He did not know exactly where, but he thought it would be further northeast. He did not know exactly when, but soon. All forts, especially from Muncy to the Wyoming Valley needed to be alerted. Long immediately thought of what a prize Augusta would be for the British, but knew that if the strike force didn't have a dozen artillery pieces, minimum, an attack there would be futile. An enemy trying to move that many cannon would invariably be discovered well in advance of the goal and would be thwarted with all the surrounding forts mounting a counter-attack.

After the questioning was finished and Standholm removed, Colonel Long asked Willie to explain, "one thousand deaths."

"I have no idea," the scout replied. "Now let me ask you a question, colonel. How did you know your tactic would work?"

The colonel reflected a moment and then said, "The worst torture for an evil man concerning his unknown fate is his own imagination."

Chapter 71

The danger was apparent everywhere and word spread almost daily of new attacks and attempts. By now, most of the settlers were massed in the network of forts and strong houses spread along the lengths of both the west branch and north branch of the Susquehanna River. The wheat and rye crops were left to ripen in the fields without much thought for harvest because the enemy was watching and waiting.

Colonel Zebulon Butler and Colonel Nathan Denison, local men who had commanded the 4th Connecticut Continentals and the 24th Connecticut Militia respectively in Washington's Army, were given marching orders to take command of the defenses at Wilkes-Barre and Forty-Fort. The monument to the fight in Wyoming, PA describes the defenders under Denison and Butler as "the undisciplined, the youthful, and the aged."

After Augusta, these poor defenses were the best the Continentals had on the frontier in spite of having a large civilian population to protect.

The claim on Wyoming Valley by Pennsylvania and Connecticut is often given as a reason for Pennsylvania's slow response in sending a trained relief force to help in the valley's defense. The real truth was that General Franklin, in Huntington, had his own threats to face and Colonel Hartley's new command was undermanned and poorly equipped.

Like Denison and Butler, Hartley was sent from Washington's command to head up this mission. The indecisiveness by Colonel Hunter at Augusta frustrated Hartley and led him to plead with General John Potter to issue his own orders to supersede Hunter's and allow him to try to reach the area of conflict in time. Potter was at Augusta by coincidence from the west so he was reluctant to step into the disagreement. Potter would refuse Hartley's plea citing political reasons. Hunter wanted his own scouts to join Hartley's force feeling that with Willie Miles and the Saint doing their part; Hartley would stand a better than even chance of reaching his destination.

By the time Hunter's orders reached them at Fort Antes and they joined Hartley's force it would be too late. Major John Butler, who was no relation to Zebulon Butler, was leading a force of six hundred Indians and one hundred Tories south from Tioga down the Susquehanna's North Branch. A series of forts served this fertile valley. South of Wilkes-Barre was Fort Durkee and to the north was Forty-Fort, Wintermoot's Fort (Tory), and Fort Jenkins on the west side of the river and Fort Pittston located across the river from Jenkins and on the same side as Wilkes-Barre.

On July 2nd The British force captured Fort Jenkins and took command of Wintermoot's small stockade. They were within several miles of Forty-Fort and should they take it the entire valley would be in peril. Lieutenant Daniel Ingersoll who was captured by the British earlier that day was sent to Forty-Fort with a native and a Tory under a flag of truce. The British had the young man deliver their terms for surrender, part of which promised safe conduct for the defenders. Ingersoll wasn't allowed to say anything regarding the enemy's strength. After a short discussion, the terms for surrender were rejected. The farmers, which was what the defense forces truly were, wanted to fight. They had livestock and fields of crops at stake.

Lazarus Stewart had arrived at Forty-Fort with twenty additional irregulars bolstering the defenders numbers. The colonial force now numbered around four hundred. Denison and Butler cautioned that they should wait, defending the stronger fortifications until other relief units arrived. Captain Spaulding and Captain Ross were expected as Stewart had been. With these men their ranks would expand to over five hundred men and an advance might then have a better outcome. Stewart whipped the men into a state declaring that there would be nothing left of value to defend if they did not attack the invaders and attack at first light. He labeled Colonel Butler a coward who had received his commission due to his marriage to Revered Jacob Johnson's daughter, Lydia. Johnson was a prominent leader in the Wyoming Valley at the time.

As his honor was now at stake, Zebulon Butler agreed to lead a force of three hundred seventy-four men out of Forty-Fort at dawn with the purpose of locating and engaging the enemy.

John Butler knew the rebels would fight. They hadn't been exposed to the ravages of war so they would foolishly hold material goods above their safety. He had been counting on it. That evening Butler held a council of war with his subordinates along with the Cornplanter, Old Smoke, and Joseph Brant who had recently returned to Tioga.

Queen Esther's beloved son, Andrew had been killed in a raid on a farm on the Towanda Flats the week before so her blood lust had her nearly out of her mind. She was excluded from the plans, but was assured she would have her revenge.

As the colonists marched north the raiders were ready to put their plan into action. At a point where Abrams Creek flowed into the Susquehanna scouts reported to Butler and Denison that the British seemed to be retreating. Some saw the tactic for what it was. Thomas Bennett boldly stated that it was a trap and that he would not become a victim. He and his party of five men returned to Fort Durkee. The rest of the defense force moved onto Swetland's Hill and again began to debate what should be done next.

Denison and Butler again wanted to wait for more men to arrive. In the late afternoon, scouts reported that Wintermoot's Fort had been put to the torch. The common thought now was that the raiders were retreating and the co-leaders, Butler and Denison, led the entire command from Swetland's Hill onto the Exeter plains.

The British Butler had been setting up an ambush that would rank on a grand scale compared to what was seen on the frontier up to that time. He ordered Jenkins' Fort be burned to reinforce the idea of a loyalist retreat, and then placed the Mohawks and Muncees, numbering around one hundred and seventy braves, on the colonials' right flank in a wooded grove. A ravine on the colonial's left position hid the Seneca and Delaware braves that were some three hundred strong. At the far end of Exeter plains one hundred of Major Butler's Loyalist Rangers laid in wait.

At three hundred yards the colonists formed battle ranks and unleashed their first volley. Butler's men were well trained and waited until the order was given to return fire, which was at approximately one hundred yards. The British fusillade was the signal for the warriors on the right flank to attack. Iroquois came streaming out of the woods and was met by Captain Hewitt's company, which managed to push their attackers back to the wood line with savage close quarters fighting. But there were too many. The remainder of the native force now attacked from the left and the provisional rangers, formed in their battle square, advanced from the front. The fight itself took barely twenty minutes. Butler and Denison along with one hundred sixty men escaped and retreated to Forty-Fort. Few men were killed during the actual battle. Nearly one hundred seventy would be tortured and perish in the ten hours of rampant bloodletting by the natives afterward.

Chapter 72

This grotesque carnival of death took place in plain earshot, if not plain sight of the men at Forty-Fort, carried on into the early hours of July 4th. Major Butler's men were too few in number to prevent most of the carnage. In reality, they cared very little.

One account, which stands out for its particular ghastliness, involved Queen Esther. On a very large flat rock she personally bashed in the heads of thirty prisoners; one man's life taken for each year of her son Andrew's life.

Later it was said she remarked, "I grew quite tired from killing all those damn Yankees."

Some historians claim that it was Esther's half-sister or a cousin who wielded the war club that night, but neither of them would have had the burning reason for revenge or the appetite for blood to rival the Muncee Queen.

The next day the British terms of surrender were delivered to Butler and Denison at Forty-Fort. They were given two hours to vacate the fort and could not take with them any weapons. The fort and crops were prizes of war. Personal items that could be transported were permitted to be retained. The native fighters almost immediately violated this condition of surrender. They roamed the settlement taking what they wanted and tolerated no interference. Butler and Denison fled across the river to Wilkes-Barre to avoid being taken prisoners of war. Both knew if caught by the Loyalists, they would be taken to Niagara and ransomed back to their families. From there Zebulon Butler made his way back to Connecticut with his family. Denison saw his family to safety at Fort Augusta and then returned to active duty in Washington's army. Many of the displaced settlers to the north in the valley, including the Lackawanna, headed east toward the Poconos and the settlements along the Delaware. Those in the southern part of the valley made their way down the Susquehanna to Northumberland and Fort Augusta.

The Wyoming Massacre was the first event in what would become known as "The Big Runaway." Most of the settlers on the north branch of the Susquehanna River had fled to safer climes. It would be only a few weeks until the people living along the great river's western branch would be doing the same thing. They would reluctantly leave their homes abandoned and their crops in the field. August third found Colonel Hartley's arrival at Wallis' house. Still four days march from Wilkes-Barre, and by now known by common knowledge, too late to avert the disaster that had happened there.

Chapter 73

A meeting at Wallis' fort of Colonel Hartley, Captain Brady, and Captain Walker was quickly called. It's primary purpose to plot a strategy of protection for those settlers remaining along the Loyalsock and Lycoming creeks. Walker had been an engineer under Colonel Kutzuscko in the Continental Army. Brady had been previously been released from active service by Washington to return and defend his home.

"It is too late now for me to press on to the northeast, but I feel that there are some things we can do to discourage this wanton pillaging of our people here. What do you gentlemen recommend?" inquired the Colonel.

"I wish that my Samuel was here to help with the planning," replied Captain Brady. "He was at his best in plotting how to keep this type of vermin at bay."

Unfortunately, Samuel and Haverford had been brevetted as scouts from the eligibility lists and told to report to Fort Pitt before the Wyoming Massacre. Captain Brady had a long held animosity toward the red man that went back to his childhood when a young friend was carried off in a raid. It was learned years later that the child had died in captivity.

"We don't have a fortification large enough here to hold a substantial number of refugees if they seek sanctuary," Captain Walker stated.

"Then you shall have plans for such a structure to present to me by this fortnight," Colonel Hartley instructed him. "By that time we shall have a working plan to stem the raiders' damage. Captain Brady and my scouts, come walk with me"

Hartley released Captain Walker to return to his own quarters for the purpose of working on the structural defense that would be named Fort Muncy.

"Colonel, the populace is nearly equally divided about staying and defending what they worked so hard to build and fleeing to Augusta and safety. I frankly stand with the former," Captain Brady was not one to give in. The four men had stopped at the edge of the front yard of the Wallis' home. The fields spread and fell away to show a vista of land that spread from the nearby creek to the expanse that was the river nearly a mile away.

"Only well provisioned structures providing sound defenses can hope to survive what this enemy will throw at them. A cold winter will provide a respite. The British and their loyalist lackeys don't like to campaign in snow."

Colonel Hartley's words came from a man who had been formally educated back in his home of York, Pa. He was in fact a lawyer by trade, but had spent a sufficient amount of time in the wilderness to become a proficient commander of rangers. Rising through the ranks, at the age of thirty he had been promoted to colonel and was an officer Washington knew he could depend upon. His analytical mind was as sharp as a gossip's tongue and it was now calculating at full speed all the facts that had been given to it. A stoic expression appeared to transform the colonel's features. He turned to face his companions, "Here is what we are going to do."

Chapter 74

On August 11th a band of harvesters volunteered to help Peter Smith with gathering grain from his fields. This was the same Peter Smith who had lost his wife and four of his six children at the Plum Tree Massacre a couple of months before. Three militiamen were to stand lookout and guard the harvesters while they loaded the wagons with the wheat and corn. Among the guards was Captain Brady's son, James. James at some point turned his attention to helping with the gathering, leaving his rifle propped against a tree some distance away. This is what those in hiding had been waiting for. The ambush killed two men outright and wounded the young Brady.

As Chief Bald Eagle stood over his helpless prey, he was heard to shout; "Now I will have red hair on my brag belt to rival Spotted Wolf's!"

What followed was a sickening scream from the young victim. The survivors made tracks back to the encampment where Captain Brady was training a class of recruits. The news brought him off his horse and nearly buckled his knees. While Samuel was the oldest and most capable James was the red haired favorite of his mother.

Mary and John Brady had a total of seven children. The news would be a great blow to her, but with James' younger brothers and sisters needing her, she would have to buck up for their sakes. Summoning every ounce of composure Brady addressed those present, "The worst that could happen here is now happening. I need two volunteers to ride to the farthest reaches of souls to sound the warning of the extreme danger."

No man spoke.

"Is there no one here that will ride to save their neighbors?"

A small voice from the back said, "I know the way north of here as well as anyone. I shall warn the Gott's, the Chamberlains, David Aspen, the Shaner's, and the Robb's."

With that Rachel Silverthorne jumped onto Captain Brady's mount and was off before she could be stopped.

Covenhoven spoke up, "I'm your man to take the news west."

Colonel Hartley loaned his stallion to the Dutchman for his ride.

Once the riders were gone, Captain John Brady gathered some men and went to retrieve the body of his son. Upon the return to the scene of this day's ambush, the rescue party found young Brady shot, speared, and scalped. Remarkably he was still alive. He was bandaged and then taken to the Brady homestead where his mother cared for him until he died five days later.

The heroic acts of Covenhoven and Silverthorne are credited with saving the lives of scores of men, women, and children. Rafts were hastily floated filled with women and children with men walking the banks on either side of the streams driving livestock ahead of them and watching for ambush. More than once Rachel believed the intruders were chasing her, but she spurred her ride on and completed the circuit back to the encampment as the sun was setting.

During that evening more than one family looked back in the direction of what had been their home to see its blaze outline both the forest and the river behind them.

With the influx of more than twenty-five families Captain Walker now had the manpower and beast power needed to complete Fort Muncy with haste. The structure's ten-foot palisade was completed in a week. Additional dwellings and a large pen would be finished shortly after.

After Hartley saw that the people would have a formidable defense, he put his plan into motion. Hartley had reasoned that a small force of rangers could penetrate deep into the villages of their tormentors and that the natives would never dream such an offensive could be mounted against them.

"Hurt them the same way they are hurting us," was the way Colonel Hartley put it. It was up to Henry and his fellow scout, Willie Miles to lead this expedition of fifty-seven men north, avoiding the large war parties of the Iroquois, until they were well into their territory. Now no longer acting as defenders, these rangers would strike the enemy on their home soil.

Chapter 75

Henry and Willie had the men follow the Loyalsock until its waters culminated in thick, boggy swamp. There they began scouting ahead while the main body cleared a roadway on which their pack animals could travel. About two miles southwest of the native village of Wyalusing, the two scouts came upon a small war party returning with plunder and two captives. Kate and Miles' long rifles took their toll and the remaining braves panicked and ran off leaving both the loot and the prisoners behind. The main body caught up with the scouts about two hours later and a small party was detached to return the captives to safety. The rest would continue on to the Indian village and put it to the torch.

They now proceeded to Wysox and Towanda and set those towns ablaze along with the surrounding fields of crops. Finally, Queen Esther's Town stretched before them. Hartley was amazed at its appearance. It had nearly a hundred cabins that were of the English style rather than the typical long houses built by the Iroquois. All were neatly arranged with streets and yards. Additionally fields of crops spread out in all directions toward the horizon.

Only a few older men and some boys tried to put up a defense. They were quickly swept aside and everything was set on fire. A small party went on to Wilawanna and did the same thing there. Finally, the unit reached Tioga. The inhabitants had already fled so the central jumping off point for all the British mischief on the frontier up until now was burned to the ground. Many of his men wanted to continue on to Salamanca, the Seneca stronghold, but Hartley knew that his small band would find themselves outnumbered if they attacked there.

"No, we must be satisfied with what we accomplished. There will be empty stomachs among these people this winter. That will be the message."

Willie and Henry watched the two great native towns engulfed in flames.

"It is too bad Queen Esther isn't here to see how beautifully her town burns," Willie remarked.

"The death of her town will cause her more grief than the death of her son," the Saint replied. *The terrible outcome, even more terrible than the fighting and killing, will be the empty bellies of the children on both sides this winter,* he thought.

Hartley's men were led back by their scouts taking a slightly different route so they were less likely to cross paths with the enraged warriors returning to their burned out villages. As it was, they still had an encounter with a returning band of raiders. Henry had detected them before they became aware of the Rangers. He managed by gesture, to position Hartley's men for their best fighting advantage. After a brief skirmish near Indian Hill, the braves soon saw the outcome was in doubt, and having no real stomach for a fight, broke off the battle and again pressed on to their homes.

The campaign was an astounding success. More than half-dozen native villages were destroyed and with it a significant amount of food and food stores. Its psychological effect on the Iroquois was even more profound. While the British with their native allies had smashed at the colonists with a hammer, Hartley had taken a leather-sharpened razor and had exacted a heavy price with the accuracy of a surgeon. Queen Esther had become a broken woman who, some said, was prone to fits of madness. She spoke of taking a white demon to her bosom and how he had caused her to lose everything because she couldn't see his true spirit. Esther traveled north to Cayuga Lake with a remnant of her people. There the fallen queen married a Tuscarora chief named Steel Trap. She was allegedly killed the following year by one of General Sullivan's fighters, but that has never been confirmed.

Colonel Hartley was declared a hero upon his return to his hometown of York, PA. The Continental Congress and General Washington publicly praised the soldier statesman. Hartley was subsequently selected one of Pennsylvania's delegates to the Constitutional Convention and played a role in the creation of the foundational document of the United States. He also served in Congress for six terms dying there in 1800 at the age of fifty-two.

Chapter 76

On November eleventh, a British force of three hundred Iroquois and two hundred of Butler's Rangers attacked the village of Cherry Valley in upstate New York. The officers of nearby Fort Alden were quartered in the homes of the civilian residents of the town, as was the custom of the time. The remainder of Colonel Alden's 7th Massachusetts was in the fort. The attack was made before dawn with the raiders overrunning the town in a matter of minutes. Colonel Alden was seen by those in the fort running and then stopping to fire his pistol at his pursuers. The pistol misfired several times probably due to wet powder. Some believed he would have made the safety of the fort if he hadn't paused in the useless attempts to use his sidearm. As it was, he was struck square in the forehead by a thrown tomahawk upon making his last effort. He died before he hit the ground.

Lieutenant Colonel Stacey was captured and subsequently taken to Niagara. In all eight officers and sixteen enlisted men perished in the attack on the town and subsequent attack on Fort Alden. Fort Alden held off the raider's attacks and when a number of the raiders were killed or wounded in the assault on the fort, the Loyalists broke off the raid and retreated west. They knew that Colonel Herkimer with his Hudson Valley militia would be after them. The real tragedy was the loss of thirty civilians, mostly women and children, during the massacre. News of Cherry Valley traveled south into Pennsylvania. Some said that this raid was in retaliation for the burning of Tioga, but the Tories needed no provocation to commit their atrocities. It was a very bloody and tragic autumn along the Mohawk.

Another hero for the Americans made his appearance at Fort Muncy in mid-summer 1778. Colonel Daniel Brodhead had suffered with Washington's troops at Valley Forge. He had more recently led a successful campaign against Tory-led Lenape's and Mingos in the Ohio Country in April 1778. Now Colonel Brodhead would briefly garrison Fort Muncy with regular troops having been specifically ordered there by Washington following the American victory at Monmouth, N.J. This leader's future included taking part in the doomed attack on Fort Detroit in March of 1779 under General Lachlan McIntosh. He then would be promoted to General of the Western command after McIntosh's debacle.

Having received marching orders for Fort Pitt in late January, Brodhead requested from Colonel Hunter, the use of his two scouts until his unit reached its new post. Henry and Willie now found themselves temporarily attached to the eighth Pennsylvania. The eighth's path of travel took it first to Augusta and a meeting with Colonel Hunter. Hunter had secured some better muskets for his troops and gave Colonel Brodhead two dozen Brown Bess' to replace some of the more inaccurate French made muskets.

Back in the familiar barracks that night, Henry quipped about an irony he had just thought about, "Willie, do you know that if my father hadn't been financially ruined I might be a subaltern or lieutenant fighting for the other side right now?"

Willie looked over at his friend and smiled, "Even your God would never have made that big of a mistake."

Chapter 77

Brodhead's force arrived at Fort Bedford three days later without incident. Aside from sporadic raids, this outpost had seen little real fighting. From Bedford the regiment made its way to Fort Ligonier, traveling on the road British General Braddock had constructed during The French and Indian War. Now the scouts were beginning to see some activity by the local tribes.

"I make them to be Mingo or Wyandotte," Willie whispered to his friend as they spread out to investigate. "Nothing unfriendly, but stay alert just in case."

Both men came to a small draw and saw the smoke of cooking fires on the other side of the tree line. Suddenly an arrow landed at each man's feet. Both scouts slowly strapped their rifles to their backs. Only a fool didn't know that each arrow shaft could have just as easily been protruding from their chests.

Three braves stepped out from cover. "Do you speak the tongue of the Mountain Shawnee?" asked the leader. He had seen Willie's necklace and thought correctly that he might be a Shawnee.

"No, my people are from the great water from where the morning light comes. Still the words are enough alike that I can speak and sign when they are not."

"Why have you come here?" the Mingo wanted to know.

"Did your father raise a dolt?" Willie's question was playing with fire, but certain courtesies should be shown out of respect. "What are you called?" Miles wanted to know.

"Forgive me, I am called North Wind and these are my brothers, Two Stones, and Long Trail."

"I am called Strong Arm." Said Willie puffing his chest out "And my companion is known by several names. He is the Sure Shot, but some know him as Foxtail. Now because of his just deeds he is known as the Shaman."

"I have heard of a white man called Sure Shot who was the adopted son of the Blood Queen. Are you this man?"

"Yes, for a while the Muncee Queen known as Esther called me her son."

"Did she cast you out?" asked the Mingo leader.

"No, I came to know that her spirit was one of blood lust and death so I followed the right path and left her to her ruin."

"That is wise," the leader of the trio acknowledged. "Still, I must know why you are an arrow's distance from our village."

The Saint answered, "We are guiding nearly two hundred soldiers to the large fort at the three rivers west of here."

"You must go now and go quickly before the Snake-eaters find you and our land runs red with blood."

Snake-eaters were the less than complimentary name that some tribes gave the Senecas.

"Where are the Iroquois?" the Saint demanded.

"They are less than a day's journey from here."

"Which direction did they go?"

The Mingo pointed north.

"How many were there?"

"They have a hundred warriors and half as many whites with red coats."

This band of invaders might have been sent out to sever the routes of travel from Harrisburg and Carlisle west to Fort Ligonier and Fort Pitt. But why try this during the winter? It didn't make sense.

"We will travel on toward the setting sun without delay. Thank you for your warning."

Henry and Willie reported back to Colonel Brodhead with the intelligence. The commander scuffed the ground with his feet.

"The British don't campaign during the middle of the winter. They think it's uncivilized. What could a force that size be doing out in the wilderness in late January?" Brodhead was stumped.

"My guess is that it isn't any type of formal military expedition. The crown has been paying a handsome scalp bounty and some captives might prove to be quite attractive to ransom," Henry concluded.

"Bandits, savages, and bounty hunters," Brodhead roared. "I mean to drive them back to the shores of Erie and beyond!"

"Not at the expense of your orders, Colonel. Willie and I have some friends at Fort Pitt we mean to see and chasing all over tarnation after such rabble would only get you court-martialed."

Henry had caught himself admonishing a colonel. Brodhead seethed. His face and neck became beet red. Suddenly his demeanor changed completely.

"Perhaps you're right, chief scout. I swear though I'll get my chance at them someday," then the colonel leaned closer to Henry and whispered, "If you ever speak to me that way again, I'll have you strung up."

Chapter 78

Brodhead arrived at Fort Pitt on the first of February. Henry and Willie found out that their friends were on a mission into the Ohio country, but were expected back at any time. Sam Brady and James Haverford checked in the very next morning. Their reunion was happily celebrated over fresh Johnnie cakes and hot coffee. As the meal went on, Henry couldn't help but notice that when there was a pause in the conversation; Sam seemed to get a preoccupied look in his eyes.

A little later Brady got around to the subject of his lost brother, "I've got some news that might keep the two of you out here a little bit longer, Henry," Samuel began. "Word has it that there are two Lenni-Lenape (Delaware) running around out here with the Seneca sporting bright red scalps on their brag belts."

"What do you want me to say, Samuel?" Henry asked. "We can't abandon everything we've been fighting for these past few years to chase down and settle our personal scores. We are obligated to see this through to its end, then I intend to do everything I can to finish my nightmare."

Henry heard those words come out of his mouth and the wisdom in them shocked him. There was a time when he would have dropped everything to go after Spotted Wolf, but with Willie's persuasion, and his own experiences he came to see that a greater work needed to be done first. Personal scores to settle had to wait. *I'm fortunate that I took Willie's advice in the beginning,* Henry thought. *I wonder how many times it saved my life.* He remembered Spotted Wolf standing defiantly back in Renovo and how much he wanted to put everything else aside and go after him. *That's when I truly grew up,* he decided.

Brady sipped his coffee staring into his cup for a second before looking up again at his three friends, "I have sworn two oaths before God and I will break neither. First, I will fight for my country until the British are gone and then I will avenge my brother's death."

The others glanced at the troubled Brady and Henry said, "We would expect nothing else."

After the reunion, Henry took Haverford aside and asked him to watch out for Samuel.

"In many ways he treats me like a brother, so I look out for him like he is my own blood," the ex-renegade remarked. He smiled and grasped his friend's elbow in the native way.

The Saint returned the gesture and then joked, "Your hair has just come back to a decent length. It would be a shame for you to lose it now."

The trip back to Augusta and then Fort Horn would be by a more northerly route using the Forbes road and then a portion of the Warrior's Path that stretched from Kittanning eastward to the Grand Island. In the five-day journey back they saw sign of men constantly, but no one wanted to make contact. It seemed to the scouts that others using the trail were giving them a wide berth.

"Well Henry, your legend as the Shaman has made you into a fearsome being normal men apparently don't want to face," Willie laughed then continued, "I wonder how much awe you would create if they could hear you snore or break wind while you slept."

Henry scooped up some snow and threw it at the back of Willie's head.

Chapter 79

As the winter of 1778 passed on into 1779, the activity on the part of the raiders was all but halted as everyone predicted it would be. But as the winter turned into spring, a second wave of raids on those who chose not to flee or who had returned began. Most notable that spring was the second fierce blow dealt to the Brady household. Captain Brady had gained a reputation among the Indians as a fierce opponent. Following the death of his son James, he prosecuted a campaign against them nearly as notable as Tom Quick's, but his was a crafty and measured effort that thwarted the few attacks tried by the raiders around Fort Muncy that winter.

It was on April 11th, 1779 when Brady was returning with Peter Smith; yes, the same man James was guarding when he lost his life; when Brady was shot off his horse a mile to the east of the fort. Smith, seeing that the wound was fatal for Brady, lay upon Brady's mount and spurred it on toward the fort. The Saint and Miles returned with Smith to the spot of the ambush to find the dead man with his scalp intact.

"Why wouldn't they take his hair?" asked Smith.

"The only thing that I can think of is that they feared him and his vengeful spirit even in death, and figured we'd be on them before they could work up the nerve to scalp him," Willie's assessment was right. They feared the Saint as much, if not more than Captain Brady.

Later that week, Henry, Covenhoven, and Willie made a wide circuit to the west perhaps fifteen miles north of Muncy ending about a week later at Fort Horn. In that week, they surprised no fewer than four raiding parties driving each one off and inflicting stinging casualties. Each party they encountered was small, no more than three or four warriors in number. This told of the effect Hartley's raid had on the psyche of the natives. They now overwhelmingly chose smaller numbered raiding parties rather than pouring back into Pennsylvania en masse on the attack.

Henry's practical observations were also having an effect, "Shoot to wound the leg; that will rid the woods of three raiders. The one wounded and the two that will be needed to carry him off."

The Saint's reasoning made good sense so the three men put that strategy to use quickly sending the raiders they found packing.

At Fort Horn, Colonel Long was waiting with news and orders: "Butler and his minions are up to their old tricks again," Long began. "But your action with Hartley has impressed Washington enough that he is contemplating another such action against the six nations. This time the fight will be taken even deeper into the very heart of their homeland."

"If you want to kill the snake then cut off its head and that's Niagara," observed Covenhoven.

"That would take cannon and siege guns to go against a French-built stone fortification and we have precious few cannon as it is. But let's not dwell on strategies best left to the general staff."

Long paced behind his desk then sat down on the desk's edge. Crossing his arms he looked over his three scouts and issued their orders, "Captain Brady's death has emboldened some of the invaders. It will be up to the three of you to keep them off balance by being everywhere at once. All three of you are known and considered powerful foes by the Iroquois. I'm creating four two man skirmishing teams. Each man will choose a partner to train from the young men currently available. No married men are to be selected. You will range north until you locate your adversaries then you will use every means at your disposal to thwart their plans and punish them for their ill-conceived efforts."

"Who's the fourth senior man?" asked the Saint.

"Lt. Van Campen will make you into a nice even number."

The four veteran scouts picked young men who had wilderness experience. Covenhoven picked his nephew, Zachary Trech, who was eighteen, and had spent most of his life hunting, trapping, and exploring. Willie picked an orphan named Gifford Hough who had learned to fend for himself at age ten when a raiding party captured his parents and a sister. The lad hid in a tree for nearly a day and a half and hadn't been found by the attackers. Van Campen selected his brother, Levi who was actually older than the twenty-four year old Moses. Fred Baskins was Henry's choice. Young Baskins had impressed The Saint by his cool demeanor when escaping the raiding party at Pine Creek the year before. His speed afoot impressed him too.

Covenhoven with his charge patrolled the area around Pine Creek, sometimes venturing as far west as Potter's Fort near present day Centre Hall. Miles and Hough made the circuits between Fort Augusta and Northumberland. The Saint and the Baskins lad traveled east to the Lycoming and the Loyalsock making Ft. Muncy their base of operations. The Van Campen brothers headed north through the Pine Bottoms directly into disputed territory and trouble. Less than a week into their patrol, Moses and Levi came upon a raiding party of ten Senecas. The braves had four men they were holding as captives no doubt taking them to Tioga for reward. The Van Campens brazenly attacked the Indians and nearly succeeded in freeing the prisoners, but fate in the form of a rifle ball struck down Levi killing him outright. Seeing his brother fall, Moses knew his own capture would be imminent so he hid a knife down his boot. When the scout was overpowered no one bothered to look in his boot. That night as everyone bedded down near the mouth of Tunkhannock Creek Moses cut himself free then freed the other captives. The newly freed men surprised the sleeping natives and killed all but one with their own weapons. That lone warrior would rouse others, possibly nearby, to attempt to retake the former prisoners. The freed men rearmed themselves quickly taking back the rifles the raiders had taken from them when they were captured. They all made tracks to the south and safety except for Van Campen. He would finish his mission without the help of his brother. Meanwhile, the Saint and the Baskins lad were moving around providing cover duty for the remaining settlers to plant and cultivate their crops. There wasn't half the number of families in the valleys as there had been the previous year. And there wasn't the number of men available to keep everyone safe.

Chapter 80

By late spring 1779, after Captain Brady's death, the deadly incursion of Tory-guided raids were starting up again and worrying those on the frontier. Captain Brady's widow, Mary Quigley Brady had recovered enough from her husband's death to determine that she would take her family to the relative safety of the tract of land outside present day Lewisburg deeded to her late husband following his service in Bouquet's Campaign during Pontiac's War. Henry and young Fred accompanied her and her brood on their journey then continued on to Fort Augusta.

Colonel Hunter had orders for Henry and for Willie and their wards, "The Dutchmen will continue to do what they were instructed to do, but I have new orders for you four."

Colonel Hunter held up an official document from Pennsylvania's Council of War: "Colonel Hartley mentioned to the council the valuable service done by his locally acquired scouts. Hartley credited the accurate information provided by these local scouts as essential to the success of his campaign last fall. I have been instructed to provide similar support to a larger expedition under the command of General John Sullivan. You are to report to General Hand at Wilkes-Barre and await further orders from the Continental Command."

This action was to be many times larger than Hartley's foray in terms of personnel and included eight pieces of artillery. Twelve hundred packhorses would transport the supplies. Eight hundred head of cattle were to provide provision for this large force of men and no fewer than one hundred twenty barges were readied for ferrying the soldiers and their supplies up the north branch of the Susquehanna River into the heart of the six nations lands. Washington's orders to Sullivan were short and clear. Sullivan was ordered to enter into the lands of the six nations for the purpose of prosecuting the war by the destruction of the towns and villages therein and the eradication of crops and stores so that the British at Fort Niagara would be forced to provide food and shelter for the resulting refugees.

Nearly thirty percent of Washington's regular Continental Army would be committed to the cause. General James Clinton was to lead five regiments down from Lake Otsego, NY and join Sullivan at Tioga. Colonel Daniel Brodhead was to lead his regiment out of Fort Pitt up the Allegheny River to cut any retreat to the west from Fort Niagara.

Brodhead relished his orders and Samuel Brady was ecstatic at the notion that he might finally get his chance at the murderer of his brother. His father's murder had stoked the fires of his vengeful passion until it was white-hot. "Grey" Haverford worried that his friend would enter the conflict ahead much as the Norwegian "berserkers" did centuries before.

Sullivan completed the first leg of his march at Easton on May 7th. Delays in completing the supplying of eleven regiments to travel that distance through the wilderness had a domino effect in creating still further delays. This slowed the construction of a road through the Poconos and prevented Sullivan from leaving there until June 23rd. The four scouts sent by Colonel Hunter had been at Wilkes-Barre for almost three weeks working with Colonel Proctor getting the barges with the mules and oxen needed to pull them rounded up and readied. This duty was unpleasant, noisy, and had a certain stench about it that Henry and Willie disliked.

It was in June that General Brodhead began moving his regiment up the Allegheny. Word had gotten to Brodhead that a raiding party of Delaware and Senecas had massacred the people of Perry's Mill. A skirmishing troop was sent on ahead of the main body to try and catch this war party that was rumored to have taken several victims with them.

Grey approached his friend and fellow scout, Brady with an idea, "Samuel, I want to try a trick that just might get us close enough to free the kidnapped before they are put to the knife." Grey then explained his idea in detail to his friend.

"I like it Grey, especially if it gets us in close," Samuel's cold smile was unsettling to his friend.

Before dawn the next morning twenty rangers, dressed as Senecas, made their way upland following the tracks left by the raiding party. It was in those morning hours that Brodhead's advance team caught up with the perpetrators of the Perry's Mill massacre.

The Indians were wary of this band of warriors coming on toward their fires, but they moved like Senecas and looked like Senecas so they awaited their arrival into their camp with no real apprehension. At a spot between forty and fifty yards from the edge of the campsite the "Senecas" formed a line and then fired a volley at the Indians. A second line then fired into the confusion. Brady had attached his bayonet and was in the camp a few seconds later. Amid the smoke and acrid air of battle he located the body of Chief Bald Eagle. Haverford watched as Brady lifted the dead chief's head and removed the skinning knife from its leather sheath. Expecting Samuel to exact his revenge on the body of the Delaware, he was surprised when he saw his friend let the head drop and instead cut free the brag belt from the corpse's side. Because eight captives were freed from their bondage by the morning action, no pursuit of the remnant of the raiding group was made. It was more important getting the women and children to safety. Samuel took the red patch of his brother's hair and buried it in a hole he had dug at the base of an oak tree.

"Now brother, rest," these were the only words Samuel said over the spot.

Later as they made their way back to General Brodhead's encampment the two friends recounted the day.

"I thought you were starting your own brag belt, Samuel," James told his friend.

"No Grey, I won't say that I wasn't going to but I stopped because I saw myself as not being any better or more civilized if I had. Henry's speech back at Fort Pitt made me come to grips with who I want to be. I can't figure out whom I am to go after for my father's murder. Do I continue on a path of blind vengeance?"

Henry had been concerned that Samuel might go down the same path that the madman, Quick had taken and told him about the hermit.

"For how long, and who do I set my sights on next? Suddenly no further reckoning makes sense. I'll see this fight through to the end and then I'll return to my family and try to find some peace."

Chapter 81

It took over a month before Sullivan's men were ready to start the second leg of the march. On the last day of July General Hand's brigade headed out to provide an advance guard for the army. General Maxwell's brigade traveled on the eastern flank and General Enoch Poor's brigade covered the western flank. Captain Gifford's company was the spear of General Hand's troops. Henry and Willie with Hough and Baskins was the tip of Hand's spear.

On August 3rd the division arrived at the mouth of Tunkhannock Creek. On the fourth they arrived at the abandoned Vanderslip and Williamson farms at place called the Black Walnut Flats. The scouts had seen some sign of being watched, but no opposing force could be determined. The next day, General Sullivan arrived at Wyalusing. The town had nearly been reconstructed after Hartley's burning it almost a year before. Crops were in the field and grain stores were located. No resistance from the enemy however. Wyalusing burned again.

"This ought to make 'em plenty sore," Hough told Willie.

"Mad as hornets, Giffs me boy," Miles replied.

A bad rainstorm held up further progress for several days. But on August 11th Sullivan reached Tioga. This planning center for the British and a stopping off point for the raiders going south and then returning north would now have Fort Sullivan constructed on it and would be used, ironically, as the American base of operations. While Sullivan awaited General Clinton's arrival, several operations were carried out. Colonel Procter took his artillery pieces across the river at Sheshequin and bombarded the settlements of Standing Stone and Newrychaddwick reducing both to a pile of burning splinters. Later Captain Gifford ventured west to the town of Chemung where the first stiff resistance was met.

"The Senecas won't simply roll over, especially when they're fighting for their own land," Henry and Willie both warned Captain Gifford.

"Nonsense, we'll give them a volley or two which they never will forget," Gifford haughtily replied.

"This city boy is going to get more of his men killed and hurt than he has to." Henry told the other three scouts. "Get to a safe vantage point and rain lead on the village, but don't venture in with the first wave."

Gifford's men blasted the town with two thunderous volleys of shot then broke for the town with bayonets fixed. The scouts picked targets of opportunity and probably saved several American lives in the process. Just as the first of Gifford's men reached Chemung, a rain of musketry met them. The American advance hesitated for a second then overran the defenders. Chemung was burning in less than half an hour.

Gifford's company had suffered twenty casualties including seven dead. It was a high price for the Americans to pay for a village of twenty wooden huts.

Chapter 82

Finally on August 22nd, General Clinton arrived with his force. Now an army of nearly four thousand, Sullivan began his push up the Chemung River four days later. At the Indian village of Newtown loyalists numbering twelve hundred natives and six hundred provincials manned a breastworks they had built awaiting Sullivan's arrival. Major John Butler with Captain Joseph Brant led this defense.

Sullivan's battle plan was to have General Hand's infantry prepare for a frontal assault on the breastworks while General Poor's and General Clinton's forces would lead a coordinated attack on the flanks. Before the assault, Colonel Proctor's cannons were brought up to soften the breastworks. Two three pounders, four six pounders, and two howitzers sent ball after ball smashing into the wood and earthen defense opening several breaches in it. Clinton and Poor were delayed by swampy terrain, but Hand's frontal assault was all that was necessary to scatter the remaining defenders before them. Actually, the bombardment had induced most of the Indians to quit the fight before the infantry assault. They had seen themselves in the role of a superior attacking force too many times to stick around and play any part in such a reversal of fortunes. Henry and Willie had passed through one of the breaches in time to see the tail feathers of the enemy pass over the next hill.

"I don't think we can catch 'em," said Willie seriously.

Before them lay the Indian/tory village of Newtown and beyond that settlement, the Six Nations heartland. No concerted effort would be mounted against Sullivan main force by the British and their Indian allies for the remainder of his time in western New York. Ambushes as a means of counter-attack was now the Loyalist's only option and that option would soon be played out. Now Washington's orders could be followed with maximum results. Villages would be burned; crops and food stores would be taken with any excess destroyed. General Sullivan sent back his cannon to Fort Sullivan following his victory at Newtown. He put his men on half rations and began making his way up the western side of Seneca Lake. Henry and the other scouts sent by Colonel Hunter did their part in keeping the main body of the army safe from ambush. Several times they came upon the skulking enemy only to turn things around and ambush them instead. After one such experience, Henry and the others were back at a campfire getting some rest and food. The next day they would push into the Genesee Valley.

"We are outstaying our welcome boys," said Henry to the little group, "it's nearly the middle of September and by now Butler will have gathered enough men to stage a counter-attack."

"I don't care much for destroying crops. I'd rather raise 'em," observed Fred Baskins.

"Aye, this is dirty work," agreed Hough.

"But necessary work," added Willie.

Henry agreed with Willie, but his heart was with Baskin's words, *I would rather be raising crops than burning them too.* He thought.

Chapter 83

On September 11th General Sullivan chose Lieutenant Thomas Boyd to lead four scouts out to determine the exact location of Genesee Castle, a stronghold of the Seneca.

Instead, Boyd took a platoon of twenty-three men including First Sergeant William Parker and left camp during the evening to complete the task. Willie and Giffs were on point with Henry and Fred covering the rear. Boyd's band came across an abandoned Indian village and the Lieutenant decided to wait for the main elements of Sullivan's force to catch up with them. At dawn, Henry and Fred were fired on by some Loyalist scouts. This brought up the rest of the platoon and Boyd put the attackers on the run in short order. Wanting to possibly gain a prisoner, Boyd pushed forward against the advice of both Henry and Willie.

"This will end badly," Willie's words were soon fulfilled.

Coming around a slight draw, the American platoon was met by six hundred provisional and native allies. The exchange was fierce and brief. Eleven colonials lay dead including Gifford Hough. Willie had an arrow through his shoulder and was bleeding badly. Fred Baskins was nowhere to be seen and Henry was momentarily dazed by the fierceness of the onslaught.

As the smoke from the musketry drifted over the scene, Henry found his friend with his back resting against a sugar maple.

"They've hit me a good one this time," Willie coughed. "There's blood in my mouth. I can taste it."

"I need to get you to cover before they hit us again."

Henry supported Willie as they stumbled their way from the field of battle to a small stream that flowed into Lake Conesus. Willie now collapsed, as it seemed he could go no farther; Henry gave him a drink of water.

"I didn't listen to the Manitou," the wounded man began. "He gave me a dream before we left Wyoming, but I wouldn't listen. In it I saw the river of my life spreading out wide before me," a fit of coughing briefly interrupted his account. Continuing on he told his friend, "All this I saw and I saw more. You were paddling a canoe to the far shore. Sure Shot, you pulled the canoe onto the bank and waving to me you turned and walked into the forest. When I awoke from the dream I knew that our path together would soon be at an end. I didn't tell you because of all that was happening. I would not leave you so The Creator has taken me, instead."

Willie had become Henry's closest, most trusted friend and the reality of his end came as a crushing blow to him.

"Be quiet and save your strength. We'll both get out of this yet."

Half an hour later Willie seemed to rally. He tried to get to his feet looking all the while at the distant lake.

"Sure Shot, I see my mother. She is calling for me to join her," reaching out to his vision with both hands, Willie Miles joined his mother at the fire of his ancestors.

Henry caught Willie as he collapsed and sang his death song for him with his voice breaking all the while. Then he covered his slain companion with rocks and returned to the site of the skirmish.

The one thing Lieutenant Boyd's blundering did for the main force of Americans was to warn them about the ambush that was planned for them along the ravines leading to the Genesee Castle. Butler mistook Boyd's rush as being much larger than it was thinking it was, in fact, Sullivan's main body. When he discovered his mistake, he knew that any element of surprise concerning Sullivan was lost. The only thing left to do was to take the prisoners gotten from the skirmish and find out as much as he could about Sullivan and his plans. Six prisoners were taken to the village of the Seneca chief, Little Beard. There both Major Butler and Joseph Brant questioned them. Three of the captives, including Fred Baskins, had been wounded and one died before the examination began. Butler wanted nothing to do with torture, but once he had all the information he thought could be gotten, he and Brant left the prisoners to Little Beard and his tribe of vengeful sadists.

The five remaining prisoners were taken to a large oak tree at the edge of the village. Two of the men had their throats cut as an appetizer for the main course. Boyd, Parker, and Baskins were tied to the oak. Their fingernails and toenails were pulled off. Next Little Beard cut off their right ears, their noses and their tongues. Their right eyes were gouged from their sockets. All the wounding was designed to exact excruciating pain, but not death.

From an outcropping of rock about three hundred yards in distance Henry arrived to witness the horror in full flower. The Saint could not stand to witness the suffering. He had Kate and Willie's rifle with him and knew he had those two shots, but no more if he was to escape a similar fate. Wiping his face, and blinking back tears Henry made his first shot. Baskins slumped forward, shot through the forehead. The Senecas looked desperately for the source of the musket ball. As Henry exchanged Kate for the other long rifle, he noticed a Delaware warrior among the Senecas. It was Spotted Wolf. He would not be distracted; he must not be distracted now from his goal. A second round found Sergeant Parker ending his misery. A brave pointed in the direction of the rocks where Henry was hidden and the chase was on. Meanwhile, Boyd had his abdomen opened and was made to take his own life by walking out his insides much as Queen Esther made Tall Oak do. Little Beard had the dead men beheaded and their hearts cut out and feed to dogs.

Only Sullivan's approach cut the desecration short. It also saved Henry's life as his pursuers cut off their chase to avoid their own demise. Little Beard's village was destroyed. Today it is the site of Cuylerville, NY. A commemorative marker for the oak tree, known now as the Torture Tree, stands in its place today.

Chapter 84

Sullivan forces next marched on to Genesee Castle, which would be his high water mark of the campaign. He dispatched all of its defenders and annihilated the place. An Indian who witnessed the aftermath of the destruction commented that, "You could not feed a child for one day" from what was left. Butler hastily returned to Fort Niagara and Sullivan decided not follow him.

In all, Sullivan destroyed forty Indian villages and burned hundreds of tons of crops and food stores. He would be second-guessed by critics down through the years for not attacking Fort Niagara. Other historians agreed with Sullivan's return, noting that he had accomplished his orders. Further, they speculate that Sullivan saw the winter coming. If he had not been delayed in getting started, he might have headed west. As it was, he had a limited number of heavy guns to attack a stone and earthen stronghold so he did the only thing he could do and that was to be satisfied with the victories up to this point and return his army intact for Washington's use.

There was another reason for Sullivan's decision. He saw the four thousand-man force he led turn into huge, vengeful entity intent on retribution. The general had seen the nearly rapt joy with which they decimated the Genesee Castle. He didn't know how discriminate they could be now. He feared they would destroy everything in front of them becoming no better than their heinous enemy. Only in the toil of his men working to get back to the more familiar confines of the eastern theater would the discipline return and the men's sanity with it.

Henry decided he would not be returning with the army. His own morality had been tested and he feared for his soul and sanity. Besides it was time. Henry spoke with Captain Gifford and then with General Hand.

"We need your skills to help us get back south. I know Captain Gifford told you the same thing. Won't you please reconsider?"

"You can order me to take you back, but I ask you to release me to finish a sworn oath I made years ago," Henry then explained the terrible circumstances that led to the oath.

"I'll sign your release, but I have grave concern that you will meet your fate before you can satisfy your oath," Hand sighed and his face betrayed his trepidation.

Henry did return with Sullivan's men as far as Tioga and watched with the rest of them the burning of Fort Sullivan four days later. The Americans would leave nothing that could provide aid or comfort to the enemy. After a brief encampment at Wysox, the army traveled downriver arriving at Wyoming on October 7th.

A pleasant surprise awaited Henry when he got to Tioga. Moses Van Campen had been using Fort Sullivan as his base of operation. That evening Henry and Moses planned what they would do next now that the major threat to their home had been eliminated.

"There's a gal I've been sweet on since I can remember," Henry started. "My life would be made the best if I could make her my wife." Henry was calling to mind Rachel Silverthorne, of course, "but I need to do one more thing before I can think of such happiness."

Van Campen knew Henry's story. He also had some news from Fort Pitt that might be encouraging to his friend, "Bald Eagle died at Samuel Brady's hand."

Technically, no one really knew which rifle ball claimed the marauder, but if the tale helped the young scout then he would perpetuate the legend.

"Samuel recovered his brother's last measure still on this earth and was able to lay him to rest."

The Saint was happy to hear of Brady's accomplishment. It gave him hope that the blood feud he was locked in might soon be put behind him too.

Moses went on, "Brodhead's effort successfully cut off the Ohio country to the Iroquois, not that the Seneca would be driven out of their home to begin with. They would have put up a terrible fight for each foot of soil lost."

Both Brodhead and Sullivan choose wisely when their mission was accomplished, thought Henry.

"Besides, the Iroquois that wished to leave went north into Canada anyway," Van Campen added. He washed a big bite of beef down with some cider, and then continued: "Not every, Seneca is fighting on the British side, Henry. I've been doing some good with the help of Walking Bird and his eagle clan."

Walking Bird was a war chief and a distant cousin of Red Jacket.

Moses went on, "It seems that Brant and the British took sides in a disagreement Walking Bird had with Little Beard. Walking Bird had had it with Little Beard and his clan and not only stopped supporting the English; they actively fight 'em. Here's the real kicker, my friend," Van Campen smiled broadly when he thought of it, "the Delaware Nation signed a peace treaty with us a year ago. Most of Spotted Wolf's own people now consider him a renegade."

Henry sipped at his drink and pondered the news, "Spotted Wolf will be conspicuous out here with Bald Eagle dead and no help from the Seneca so he'll be easier to track. I mean to find him and end this. Spotted Wolf is a coward at heart who prefers to kill only by ambush or if his foe is a helpless captive. He won't get much support from any Iroquois now so he'll high tail it, my guess is the Ohio Country. I'll chase him till I catch him."

The Dutchman smiled again and replied, "We'll get started tomorrow."

Could this really be the beginning of the end of my quest? Thought Henry as they prepared for what awaited them tomorrow.

Chapter 85

The next morning the chase started. At Salamanca they met with Walking Bird.

The chief of the eagle clan began, "Red Jacket cowers with the rest at the "Peace Fort". No doubt he will return here soon covering his manhood with his hands. With his serpent's tongue he will wheedle back into the good graces of his clan." With that, Walking Bird turned and spit on the ground.

Henry now spoke of his mission, "We seek a Lenni-Lenape who is a killer of the helpless and has no honor among his fellow man. His name is Spotted Wolf. He fought with Little Beard at the English's big defeat." The last part was added to inflame the Seneca against their foe.

"I will help you find this miserable weasel. If he tarries at the "Western Gate," we will trap him for you."

Runners were sent out toward the Niagara country to find out the Delaware's location. Later, at a meal for the scout's benefit, Henry noticed a familiar face among the women serving the men. It was Snow Goose. As she gave him a piece of venison, she tried to cover an ugly scar on he left cheek.

"Who did this to you, sister?" Henry wanted to know. The tall maiden seemed bent and her spirit seemed broken.

"What do you care about that female slave?" asked Walking Bird.

Henry stood touching the hilt of his knife, "Because she tended my fires and was promised to me."

Walking Bird motioned for Henry to be seated, "She came as you see her from the Blood Queen. No man will have her because of her mark so take her if you wish."

"I'll be back for her after my promise is kept. Let it be known that she is under my protection. If she is mistreated in any way, the guilty will answer to me."

The vow carried weight among the natives. They knew of the reputation that accompanied the man. That night Snow Goose again tended the Sure Shot's fire.

"What about your gal? I'm not so sure she'll understand this," observed Van Campen.

"This is the sister of Tall Oak who thought of me as his brother-in-law even though if what Walking Bird says is true, she remains a maiden," Henry informed Moses.

Van Campen noted that in spite of the flaw on her cheek she was still a handsome woman.

"The mark denotes a fallen woman. Any brave that took her would have to concede that his wife was a whore."

"You mean even if the wedding night would prove it to be otherwise?"

Henry softly touched the girl's arm as she took back a drinking skin. She smiled at him.

"Indians feel the need to keep up appearances too," he said.

Three days later a runner returned to Salamanca with news of Spotted Wolf. "With his chief and many of his fellow warriors dead, he had little standing at the council fires of the English," the runner explained to his chief. "A week ago he left to seek his kind in the Ohio Country."

"So he's gotten past me," Henry exclaimed. Turning to Moses he said, "I'll not expect you to venture with me out there though I know you would offer."

Moses blushed. He wanted to return to Fort Horn to check on his mother and sisters.

Henry put up his hand to stop his friend's protest, "I intend to travel first to Fort Pitt and look up Samuel and Grey. They have experience in the Ohio and I can use their smarts. Who knows, maybe they'll go on the mission."

"I know they will," Van Campen affirmed.

After making arrangements to provide for Snow Goose at Salamanca, Henry started down the Allegheny toward Tionesta. Moses headed back east overland then used the west branch of the Susquehanna making Fort Horn a little over a week later.

Just north of the lake at Tionesta Henry came across a hunting party of Shawnee. Henry had on Willie's necklace, which he would forever wear as a remembrance of his friend. The braves saw the token and greeted Henry cautiously. The scout told him his name and the ice was broken.

"The whites have taken to shooting all the people friend or foe," one of the hunters said. "We would be far to the west but war has come there too."

"I have heard that many Shawnee are now fighting for the British," Henry said.

"Not everyone believes the English. Some elders still remind us of the death blankets," this was the Shawnee leader's measured answer.

The British at Fort Pitt had attempted to give Indians blankets infected with smallpox during Pontiac's War in 1763. General Amherst, the commander of Fort Pitt at the time, even wrote about the plan. "Giving blankets to the Indians" became a metaphor for giving a gift with terrible results. It would be replaced later with "Giving firewater to the Indians."

Chapter 86

The next morning Henry parted company with the Shawnee hunting party. He now was using sections of the Forbes' Road so that he was able to quicken his pace arriving at Fort Pitt the evening of the second day. Samuel had made plans to return to see his mother, brothers, and sisters, but Grey jumped at the chance to go on the quest.

"I have asked the Manitou to ease your mind, Henry. Then I prayed to God for the same thing."

"They're the same, Grey. But, thank you."

"I know they are the same, but I needed the practice."

Two days later the two headed into the Ohio Country. Henry found out that the Delaware were actually split on whom they supported. Many had sided with the British. These tribes settled at Scioto and along the Sandusky. White Eyes, the leader who signed the peace treaty with the Americans, had lived at Coshocton. This town would be the first stop for Henry and Grey in their hunt for Spotted Wolf. White Eyes had been murdered several months after signing the treaty under what was said to be mysterious circumstances. Pro-English warriors tried to convince the rest of the village that the local colonials had assassinated him. Pale Elk, the current chief of the village, wasn't sure who had committed the deed. He welcomed Grey as a known friend and accepted Henry with the universal sign of peace. Haverford quickly let Pale Elk know why they were there.

"We seek a Delaware called Spotted Wolf. He has declared a blood feud with my friend and we mean to see it to its end."

"Why do you take part in this? Isn't the nature of things such that it is between two warriors?" asked Pale Elk.

Henry now spoke up, "That is how it should be, but Spotted Wolf has seen fit to use the murder of innocents and the employ of kidnappers and assassins to achieve his ends."

"I know this because I was one of those Spotted Wolf used," added Grey with a note of shame in his voice.

The look of astonishment on Pale Elk's face was clear, "You have always spoken the truth to me and my people. I see no reason to doubt you now. The brave you seek was here, but left three days ago for the Sandusky. He tried to persuade the men here to join him and raid the whites around the big fort to the east. When no one jumped to follow him, he called us women and said he would find his true brothers at Sandusky."

The feelings of the men of Coshocton were raw concerning the death of White Eyes and both scouts thanked Pale Elk and left Coshocton quickly behind. Staying might have provoked one of the Delaware into trying to avenge the death of his chief at their expense. The trail was leading them into hostile territory. The Miami would strike out at any white because, as the Shawnee hunting party had told Henry, the whites were now killing Indians indiscriminately. Any Lenni-Lenape they came across now would be pro-English; the same for any Shawnee.

Haverford's days as a smoke warrior came into play. Henry wouldn't part with Willie's necklace so he was instructed to put it inside his buckskin blouse to keep it from making noise. When Haverford was satisfied they would move silently they started off.

"No fires. We eat the jerky we have and any roots or fruit we find."

Henry was receiving an advanced course in wilderness tactics from a master.

"We want no contact with anyone. Strive to locate and skirt all. If you are detected, it may be necessary to kill because if by allowing life you would be assuring capture and failure."

Henry thought that Grey might be reverting to his old ways and it troubled him. Grey saw the look of concern on his friend's face. He slapped him on the back and said, "Don't worry, Henry. Remember we are smoke, but we are also just."

In three days they had traveled a zigzag route past Killbuck, Mochican, and Tiro. As they skirted the Miami village of Ashtonazi in the early morning of the fourth day, a dog began to bark. A youth, no more than fourteen, threw back the covering on his lodge and grabbing a spear dashed into the woods. He was coming right at Henry and closed to within thirty yards.

"I'll teach you raccoons to raid our larder!" then he saw the white man.

"Kill him, Henry!" Haverford hissed through his teeth, but it was too late. The lad sounded a war cry that had the men of the camp scrambling.

"Let's get out of here!"

The pursuers knew the lay of the land while the pursued did not. The scouts were quickly surrounded and captured. They were taken to the Miami leader who questioned them.

"I am called The Stalker and now you will tell me your names."

"I will tell you their names, mighty chief," said the Delaware stepping from behind the questioner into full view. The black haired one is called Grey Feather and the other is known as Foxtail." Spotted Wolf strode up to Henry and murmured, "Your hair will adorn my belt this very night."

Turning back to the Miami chief Spotted Wolf went on, "You have caught two famous American spies; the English will pay you well for their scalps."

"You speak only half truths, Spotted Whelp," Henry replied. "We have come to settle a blood feud between us that started with the killing of my master whose red hair is on your brag belt. I mean to have your life and so end this evil."

Spotted Wolf smiled malevolently, "Brave words for one who is bound hand and foot and who is my prisoner."

"Brave words, indeed," repeated the Miami leader. "Cut him free and give him back his knife."

Spotted Wolf couldn't believe what was happening, "Chief Stalker, you will be judged a traitor by the English. They will send their Red Coats to punish you!"

Henry worked the feeling back into his hands and accepted the antler-handled knife. The gathering formed into circle about thirty feet in diameter. Spotted Wolf got his first up close look at Henry in five years. The youth had grown into a hard, sinewy figure of a man that looked to have fire running in his veins. The Delaware knew he would have to rely on treachery if he wanted to win. As the two opponents began to circle one another, Spotted Wolf scooped up a handful of dirt and threw it in St. Albans' face. Treachery and cunning were two traits Indians admired in a fight. There were no Marquees of Queensbury rules in a knife fight. The tactic had the desired result and Spotted Wolf was on Henry on an instant. The assailant came straight on trying to bring his blade level on into his belly. Henry instinctively covered the vital areas and received a nasty gash on his left forearm for the effort. With his sight restored, he fought on. As the two feigned and circled, the scout noticed a brief opening left by his opponent each time he came in at him. As Spotted Wolf made his next move, Henry swung low striking the brave down though the foot as he rolled to the side out of harm's way. The wound crippled Spotted Wolf. The pain sent him to the ground, but he quickly stood again. Spotted Wolf knew it would soon be over and he was at the heights of desperation. He couldn't maneuver with only one good leg. He looked around for relief from any quarter and saw none.

"Finish him, Henry," shouted Haverford.

"I curse you, Foxtail," Spotted Wolf's oath was spit out between his clenched teeth.

"You won't have your throat cut as you did to Constance and you won't be wounded and then scalped alive like you did to Thomas, but you will die!" With that, Henry grabbed the knife hand of his foe and shouted, "I give your knife back to you!"

The blade entered the left side of the Delaware between the third and fourth rib and found the heart. Spotted Wolf looked at Henry with shock in his eyes. He tried to spit on him, but a spasm shot through his body instead. The surprise in his eyes turned into the glazed look the eyes take on as the spirit leaves the flesh. Spotted Wolf slumped into a macabre sitting position stone dead.

"Release the other white," ordered the Miami leader.

"Don't remove the knife from his body," Henry requested.

"Then how will you take his hair?" one of the Miami warriors asked.

"I don't want his hair. Let the blade remain as a sign of an oath fulfilled. I only want the patch of bright red hair that hung from his side. With that I will be able to let a good man finally rest."

Chapter 87

That evening, after a meal of rabbit and venison, Henry St. Albans, bondservant of Thomas McAdoo, buried the last remnant of his master. He found an oak, like Brady did for his brother, and buried the remnant at its base.

Standing there by the small patch of disturbed soil after his last task was completed for McAdoo, Henry spoke, "You taught me so much, Thomas. There isn't a day that goes by that I don't think of you and wish I still worked the soil back on your farm with you. I will send word back to New Jersey that the feud is over and you are now at peace."

The Miami treated Henry and James with the honor of visiting chieftains. A healer treated Henry's wound and in a couple of days he felt able to start back. This time a cadre of Miami braves would accompany them as far back as the Allegheny.

At Tionesta Henry learned of some horrible news. A fever had struck Salamanca killing nearly half of the inhabitants.

"I must go see about Snow Goose," Henry told Haverford. "With sickness in Salamanca I'll understand if you choose not to come along with me."

"I have no desire to face the plague, but I'm going just the same because you are my friend," with that Grey lifted his pack into a canoe and climbed aboard.

The journey to Salamanca was a solemn one. Henry and Grey stopped about three miles from their destination and deliberately bedded down. The scene would be bad enough during the light of day. Neither man wanted to face spending a night in a fever-ridden village.

Henry's sleep that night was fitful. He was troubled by a dream. In it he was following a great bear and a dog through the forest. All came to a clearing where a tall Indian maiden stood. As he watched in his dream, Henry saw the maiden transform into a beautiful white goose and fly away. The bear and the dog ran after her. He felt in the dream like he couldn't go on due to a sadness that suddenly welled up in him. Then he awoke.

Early the next morning they entered Salamanca. Walking Bird had survived the sickness, but it had claimed the life of one of his daughters. The horrible sickness had all but run its course there. What remained to be done was to burn and mourn the last of the dead.

"What of Snow Goose?" Henry asked the chief.

"She cared for the ill when the sickness came," Walking Bird began, "But then she too felt the fires rage within her body and alas, she went on her great journey two days ago."

Henry knew then that his dream from last night was to show him what he intuitively knew. The sister of Tall Oak, betrothed to him and then taken from him by the Muncee queen, was gone.

Henry looked at Haverford and said, "Let's go home."

Chapter 88

He had to find Rachel. She was his last chance at salvaging some normalcy in his life.

"What do you want to do when all of this is over, James?"

The former renegade scratched his head at the Saint's question, "I'd like to try my hand at farming. It was only a short time I had to help the Brady's, but it felt natural to me. If the government gives out tracts of land in exchange for service, I mean to have a place in the Ohio. Maybe I'll find a gal to warm my bed at night and fed me breakfast in the morning."

Henry laughed out loud at the preposterous thing he had just heard. Slapping James on the back he told him, "We have the same dream, you and I. Only I know who I want to cook breakfast for me."

At Fort Augusta both men received their final discharge papers. These documents attested to exemplary service to the country and could be used later to acquire land and material. Then it was on to Muncy and then the farm on the Loyalsock. Henry was to be knocked off his feet again. Oliver had pulled up roots again for parts unknown. Some people thought that he was headed to Western Virginia while others thought it was farther west into a place called Illinois. Evan Silverthorne had been wounded and then captured. Arrangements were underway to have him paroled. Margaret had been placed into voluntary service prior to Oliver's departure. Her whereabouts was also unknown. News about Rachel was a little more definite. She had married John Hollingsworth settling on land not far from John Brady's widow.

"Bad luck, Henry," Haverford said placing a hand on his shoulder.

"We had no "understanding." The way times were, it would have been unfair. I always thought that she and I were meant for each other, though."

Henry thought about it a moment and then said, "I want to say goodbye to her."

Two days later Henry and Grey stood at the threshold of the Hollingsworth homestead. Rachel greeted both men by hugging them around the neck.

"John is out in the barn. I'll fetch 'em," with that the young newly-wed dashed off to retrieve her husband.

"She's grown even more comely," said Henry. "Marriage seems to agree with her."

Soon Rachel and John were running back to the house hand in hand. John had always been a steady sort of fellow by Henry's recollection, and the joy he saw in Rachel's face warmed his heart.

Dinner that evening was rabbit stew with fresh baked bread and sweet cream butter. Milk was the beverage. Fresh picked apples from the "Liberty" orchard sliced and eaten just so made a fine dessert to end the meal. After visiting around the hearth for several hours, Henry asked if they could bed down in the barn.

"Of course, silly," replied Rachel, "I only wish our cabin was big enough for you to stay here. You'll join us in the morning for eggs and biscuits."

"You'd have us spoiled," joked Haverford.

Later in the barn as the two scouts bedded down. Henry remarked, "I am at peace with Rachel's decision. She'll have a good life with Hollingsworth" As the Saint rolled into his blanket he continued, "I want to get an early start in the morning."

His companion knew what he meant.

Early the next morning, well before any light shown in the little cabin, the frontiersmen started out.

"Where to now, Henry?" Grey Haverford asked glancing over at his friend.

The Buckskin Saint was looking to the west.

About the Author

Joseph Berube is an avid life-long student of American history, especially the late 18th and early 19th centuries, so it seemed only natural to combine these two passions in *The Buckskin Saint,* his first novel. Born and raised in the mountains and valleys of rural Central Pennsylvania, he still lives among the forests and streams of Pennsylvania, not far from his childhood home along with his wife Jan and a large grey tabby named Tobey. He is currently working on his next novel.

www.ingramcontent.com/pod-product-compliance
Lightning Source LLC
Chambersburg PA
CBHW021953010726
47494CB00003B/719